The Lies of Lena

KYLIE SNOW

FOREVER

NEW YORK BOSTON

Forever
Hachette Book Group
1290 Avenue of the Americas, New York, NY 10104
read-forever.com
@readforeverpub

Originally published in 2024 by Kylie Snow. First Forever ebook edition: August 2025

First Forever trade paperback edition: January 2026

Forever is an imprint of Grand Central Publishing. The Forever name and logo are registered trademarks of Hachette Book Group, Inc.

The publisher is not responsible for websites (or their content) that are not owned by the publisher.

The Hachette Speakers Bureau provides a wide range of authors for speaking events. To find out more, go to hachettespeakersbureau.com or email HachetteSpeakers@hbgusa.com.

Forever books may be purchased in bulk for business, educational, or promotional use. For information, please contact your local bookseller or the Hachette Book Group Special Markets Department at special.markets@hbgusa.com.

Library of Congress Control Number: 2025946615

ISBNs: 9781538781074 (trade paperback), 9781538781081 (ebook)

Printed in the United States of America

LSC-C

Printing 1, 2025

TOVAGOTH
ERETESIA
KALRAEL
OTACIA
FORT MAURA
FORT LAITH
TEMPLE VALOR
DARANOIS
MOUNT ROZAVAR
AMES
HALSTED
BALIFOR
FORSMONT
RENRELL
TEMPLE AZRAE
FALTRUN
TEMPLE RAVAIANA
TEMPLE CELLUNA
WRENDIER
VALLEY OF AWAKENING
NEREIDA
TEMPLE TITHARA

PLAYLIST

THE DEATH OF
PEACE OF MIND-BAD OMENS

ODONATA-YAIMA

FOREVERMORE-BROKEN IRIS

LUMINARY-JOEL SUNNY

KYO-YAIMA

MAY YOU OPEN-YAIMA

BAD DREAM-CANNONS

WHERE'S MY LOVE-
ALTERNATE VERSION-
SYML

PRONUNCIATION GUIDE

LOCATIONS:

Otacia- **Oh-tay-shuh**

Faltrun- **Falt-rune**

Forsmont- **Fours-mont**

Wrendier- **Ren-dye-er**

Ames- **Aims**

Rozavar- **Row-za-var**

Oquerene- **Oh-kur-een**

Nereida- **Nur-ay-duh**

CHARACTERS:

Lena Daelyra- **Lee-nah Day-lie-ruh**

Torrin Brighthell- **Tour-in Bry-thell**

ryia- **Rye-uh**

Hendry Bonnevau- **Hen-dree Bon-uh-vow**

Roland Aubeze- **Row-lind Awe-bez**

Edmund Estielot- **Ed-mund Es-ta-lot**

Igon Natarion- **Eye-gone Nah-tar-e-on**

Viola Sonnet- **Veye-uh-la Sewn-it**

To the three mother figures in my life.

My late mother, for raising me and always having my back no matter what. My grandmother, for loving me and supporting me always. And my late aunt Ani, for always believing in any dream I had, and whose birthday I am publishing this book on.

I wouldn't be who I am without them.

CONTENT WARNING

Please read with care. This book contains explicit sexual scenes, explicit language, violence, gore, torture, dismemberment, sexual assault, rape, loss, and grief.

Your mental health matters.

PROLOGUE

My first memory is from age four. While faint, I remember running barefoot in the frigid snow, with nothing but my mother's pull guiding us to our unknown destination; the words she constantly repeated echoed in my head.

Mages are hated, Lena. We must never show who we really are.

For a child to hold in their magical abilities, it required significant strength and discipline. At four, I had neither, so it was no surprise that while passing through a small village, I tripped and used a protective barrier to keep myself from hitting the ground. I immediately knew my mistake, but with no time to lose, my mother grabbed my hand, and we ran. We were so poor, and my only shoes were so large they couldn't stay on my feet as we bolted away.

A group of men from the village chased after us, and after what seemed like ages of sprinting through a frozen forest, we finally lost them. My mother grabbed me close, and I remember thinking I would get scolded, just like the other times I couldn't hold back my powers.

But instead, she cried. She dropped to the ground and pulled me to her chest. My mother had always been strong, and I had never seen her so vulnerable. "I'm sorry! I didn't mean to…I didn't mean to," I whimpered as I tried to comfort her.

She sobbed so hard she struggled to find air, but eventually, she collected herself and wiped her face. "I know, sweet pea. I'm sorry for getting upset." She stood up and brushed the snow off her pants. "I just want us to be somewhere safe and warm. Not on the run." Tears began to fill her eyes once more. "You don't deserve this…none of us do."

Her embrace was offering the slightest bit of warmth. "Why do they want to hurt us?" I had asked with pure childhood innocence.

She smiled with a look in her eyes that I couldn't comprehend until I was older. "People fear what they do not understand," she answered.

Mages are hated, Lena.

And nothing rang truer. Being a Mage meant immediate banishment. Being a Mage meant any protective law did not apply. Being a Mage meant being seen and treated like a monster, even if you were only four years old.

I never forgot that day. I knew I had to be strong. I had to be disciplined. And so, I suppressed my magic as much as physically and mentally possible. Typically, magic doesn't present until much older, but unfortunately for us, I was an exception. Although I didn't have another slip-up after that day, I always feared that eventually, something would happen, and we would have to run, never finding a place to call *home.*

It wasn't until I was twelve years old that we found a more permanent residence. Like most territories in Tovagoth, the mighty kingdom of Otacia had an intense hatred for Mages, but its population of about ten thousand meant we could blend in. It was a place where we had no track record, and two copper-haired sorceresses would be hard to forget.

The kingdom was separated into three areas. The higher class lived elevated and tucked safely in the middle of the kingdom, called the Center. The folks in the middle class lived in the Inner Ring, also slightly elevated, while the lower class lived in the Outer Ring, which is where my mother was able to find a small cottage for us to stay in.

It was ruled by King Ulric La'Rune, a powerful, vicious man feared by most. He owed his popularity to the loyalty he had to his people and kingdom, and to his precise skills on the battleground. On the other hand, his wife, Queen Ryia, was adored by all. She was seen as a compassionate, loving woman. Even now, she sometimes graces the Outer Ring with her presence, stimulating the economy of many small businesses. Ulric never did bother to visit. Some would say their balance of brutality and kindness was what made the kingdom so successful.

As for their children, it was known they had a son, Prince Silas La'Rune, who they kept hidden away in their castle. As new villagers in Otacia, and lower class at that, we didn't know the whole story of what happened to their only other child, their younger daughter, all those years ago. All we know is she was stolen from the castle as an infant and later found deceased in the Northern Woods.

Since that tragedy, the King and Queen swore to keep their elder son safe. They would not allow him to leave the castle walls until he turned eighteen, adequately trained and prepared to face any threat. No one besides castle staff or perhaps soldiers in training knew what he looked like. Mother wondered if the kingdom was genuinely defended if something so terrible could happen to the Princess, of all people. But the kingdom has had no incidents since, and everyone was seemingly safe.

And I didn't practice my magic. I shoved every instinct as deep in my core as I could.

Mages are hated, Lena.

And as long as that part of me was kept hidden, I would never feel at home, not in any kingdom, and certainly not in my body.

PART ONE:
THEN

CHAPTER ONE

"Chamomile, milk thistle, sage, and a little bit of Epsom salt," Mother said as she sprinkled the salt into the pot of water. "Lastly, some honey. It helps with the flavor and is known to help heal wounds."

She slowly stirred the mixture in a small steel pot being heated on our wood-burning stove.

"So, *this* really helps heal people?" I asked skeptically.

She smiled, swirling her hand as she enchanted her creation. "Well, with a little magic, it does." The golden mist that sparkled and extended from her fingertips had me letting out a small gasp. Before I knew it, the mist faded. I looked away.

Of course, she enchants her elixirs.

I assumed as much, but Mother knew how badly the use of magic affected me. She never used it in front of me anymore.

"Lena," she started. "I know you haven't used magic in a very long time, but—"

"I know, Mother. But as I've told you countless times, I have no interest in learning," I said with crossed arms. Since moving here, this was the first time I allowed her to show me how she makes anything besides bread or scones. She knew I didn't wish to learn anything regarding magic, even something this small. In recent weeks, she has been not so subtly trying to get me to learn something, anything. I always declined until today.

"Lena, you are sixteen years old. You are more than capable of learning basic magic."

I felt my hands trembling.

Mages are hated, Lena.

Those words would forever haunt me. I turned back to her, her coffee-brown eyes sparkling with hope. "I know you want this for me," I said softly. "I just…I can't. It isn't necessary. We'd only be asking for trouble."

"Isn't necessary?" She frowned. "Yes, you were small, Lena, when your powers surfaced. It wasn't necessary back then. Frankly, teaching you anything other than self-restraint wasn't safe. I haven't even heard of a four-year-old discovering their powers…" —she shook her head and looked at me with determination— "…but that is only proof of how special you are. How strong you could be. Yes, here in Otacia, you may never need to know how to defend yourself. But if for some reason we had to leave—"

"Why would we have to leave?" I challenged. "The only thing putting us at risk is you enchanting your items! Don't you think one of these days word will get to the castle about your miracle elixirs—how somehow some herbs, salt, and fucking honey can cure disease?!"

"Watch your tongue!" she snapped. I knew I had crossed a line. "Innocent people are dying here! I don't care that they're just humans. I have the ability to help." Her fists were clenched at her sides. "I don't do the full potency of my power. Just enough to slowly heal over time."

"And what if someone discovers what makes that happen? What if someone bursts in while you're enchanting and discovers who we are?"

"It's been four years—"

"Yes! Four years!" I cried as I threw my arms up. "We have managed to stay somewhere for a whole whopping four years. Four years of having a *home*. And I am terrified of having to leave it."

Sadness swept over Mother's face, and my throat burned as I held back tears. I shook my head and slumped into the kitchen chair, propping up my elbows and burying my face in my hands.

Mother set down her wooden spoon on our dining table and placed a gentle hand on my shoulder. One tear escaped, and it took all my willpower to keep the rest at bay. "I never want to be on the run again. I want to have a *life*. I want to have friends. I want to be close to people. Not live with this constant debilitating fear." I shook my head again. "I just…I just want to be normal."

Mother crouched beside me, pulling my hands away from my face and into hers. I hesitated but met her stare.

"How awfully boring that would be," she said with a soft smile. I couldn't help but return it. "You can have friends, Lena. Be close to people."

"But I always have to hide who I really am…" I sighed. "So, I can build relationships, wearing a mask."

"As much as being a Mage is part of who we are, it doesn't define us. Even if I couldn't use my magic, I would still be myself." She tucked a copper coil hanging in front of my face behind my ear. "I know you are scared. But you deserve to live, Lena. I won't push you anymore. But know that I am always here to teach you when you are ready," she said with another gentle smile that sent more tears rolling down my face. I wiped them away.

"I'm sorry…for the foul language," I said abashedly, looking down at our worn wooden floors.

Mother let out a chuckle. "You get that from your father."

That made me smile. I had never met him. Mother always spoke fondly of the brown-haired, green-eyed man she fell in love with over seventeen years ago. He was a flirty, foul-mouthed fisherman, quite opposite to my soft-spoken mother. She always said that he enthralled everyone who met him, and all would say he was far too handsome to be a fisherman.

After almost a year of their romance, Mother fell pregnant with me. Even though there was a 50 percent chance I would be a regular human, there was also a 50 percent chance I would be a Mage.

The small village of Renrell hated Mages almost as much as King Ulric. Mother didn't believe my father would shun her. But she couldn't be sure. At best, he would be forced to leave the village he loved, that his family had lived in for generations. To live a life secluded until it was known whether or not I was a Mage and if I had any abilities that needed honing. At worst, he would turn on her and let the most anti-Mage villagers have their way with her. While she didn't believe he would do the latter, there was too much of a risk. So, she left one day in the middle of the night. Never to see him again.

"Oh—it's almost 7:00!" Mother exclaimed. I stood from my chair as she rushed over the leather crossbody filled with the items I was to deliver to the Inner Ring. Mother and I traded off duties. Sometimes, I handled deliveries while she operated our stand at the weekly market. Venturing up to the Inner Ring was intimidating, but I kept to myself and only had to socialize with the people whose orders I was fulfilling. Overseeing the stand was a much more challenging task, and honestly, Mother knew more about her items than I did, given my lack of interest.

I slung the bag over my body and let out a huff. "Wow, there's a decent amount in here." I could already feel the weight pulling at my shoulder. This would undoubtedly be uncomfortable. I let out a breathy laugh.

I'm so proud of her.

Word of how excellent the goods at Waylon's Bakery & Apothecary were had reached the Inner Ring. The middle class wouldn't set foot in the Outer Ring, but some were okay with items being delivered to them. Customers always asked my mother why it wasn't named "Minerva's Bakery & Apothecary." She always smiled and said she named it after a good friend. She never mentioned it was my father's name.

Mother slipped me the order list and the map I used nearly every week to decipher which homes each order was going to.

"Good luck at the market today," I said, giving her a big hug.

"Today is going to be a good day, Lena." She pulled away, beaming. "I can just feel it."

CHAPTER TWO

I stepped outside, and the spring breeze was pleasant as it blew past. It was a relatively warm day for early April. Our small cottage was nestled in a quiet area of the Outer Ring. The sun shone brightly, casting a warm glow over our cozy abode.

The Outer Ring wasn't glamorous, but it certainly wasn't as atrocious as the more privileged viewed it. The pathways were made up of broken stone, and because most homes were tiny, they were packed somewhat close to one another. Thankfully, there was enough room for me to tend to a garden.

Gardening had become a peaceful hobby of mine. All around our home burst with colorful flowers—roses, daffodils, lilies, peonies, and more—all that I had planted, making the drab exterior of the cottage seem not so bland, at least in the spring and summertime. The ivy growing up on the sides of our home was not my doing, but I loved it all the same. I also helped grow some of the herbs we utilized for Mother's elixirs, though we still had to do plenty of scavenging outside the kingdom walls.

Behind our home was a river that twisted throughout the Outer Ring, adding to the peaceful atmosphere. Those from the Inner Ring and Center typically looked with disgust at the Outer Ring, but I think their ill feelings stem from the work of Serpents Cove, a section of the Outer Ring that was dark and notorious for illegal activity. I was never to get close to it and never spoke to anyone who lived there. Other areas really weren't so bad.

Our weekly market, for example, was a significant event with vendors selling anything from fresh fruits and vegetables to jewelry or sewn goods. If those above gave it a chance, perhaps the people here wouldn't be so poor.

It was a miracle we had started having customers from the Inner Ring, and the extra copper my mother had allowed me was used to purchase an obsidian dagger I kept hidden under my cloak and sheathed at my side. Mother didn't know about it, simply because I didn't want another lecture regarding defending myself. Truthfully, I never thought I'd need to use it, but the small comfort it gave me was worth the loss of copper.

I sighed and strolled toward the large stairway entrance to the Inner Ring, about a ten-minute walk from our cottage. Though I kept to myself, many neighbors waved at me as I passed.

I ventured up the giant steps, observing the guard stationed at the top. Outer Ring citizens were allowed to visit the Inner Ring between 6:00 a.m. and 10:00 a.m. Not a minute before and not a minute later. It had been about a year since we started making deliveries, and the guards paid me no mind as they knew I never stayed past curfew.

I made it through the first couple of orders rather quickly: an elixir for one home and an order of pastries for another. As I continued my venture, I strolled past a luxury dress shop, one I couldn't help but gaze at every time I encountered it.

What it must be like to own pieces like this.

I was still taking steps forward, admiring the fine gowns displayed in the window, when suddenly someone rammed into me so hard that I fell to the ground.

"Oops," a snobby voice said sarcastically. I glared up from my position on the ground to a girl wearing a gorgeous ivory and bronze dress, dainty silver jewelry resting along her neck. Her two friends next to her wore equally stunning attire and equally repulsive sneers. Their clothing wasn't fancy enough for royalty but most definitely enough to live close to the castle, unlike my deep blue cloak, cream chemise, and brown overdress. The dress fit me decently, and, as always, I felt pretty enough in it until I stepped up here. It was hard not to feel inferior.

I grasped my crossbody and gathered the wrapped pastries that had fallen out after I fell.

"What is a dirty peasant girl doing in the Inner Ring?" she asked as her two friends laughed. They didn't look much older than me.

I shifted back onto my feet. "I—I'm just making deliveries, ma'am." I hated that my voice shook. This wasn't the first time I had been harassed coming up to the Inner Ring, but usually, it was just dirty looks. Gods, I felt small.

"I-I'm just m-making d-deliveries, ma'am," she mocked as they all continued to laugh.

I lowered my voice, attempting to keep it steady as I said, "I don't want any trouble." The looks on their faces made me want to ram my dagger in their throats.

Calm down. Keep it under control.

I took a deep breath through my nose. The last thing I needed was to lose control.

She closed the gap between us, flipping her brunette hair over her shoulder. "Then don't get your *filth* anywhere near me," she spat. She eyed my bag, which had been adjusted to lie on one shoulder instead of across my body, and ripped it off me.

"Hey! Give me that back!" I protested.

She pulled away as I reached forward in an attempt to grab it. "Aww, what are you going to do about it?" She flipped open the bag, and her friends started reaching in. I felt the tears pool in my eyes.

We can't miss these orders. It will mess up everything Mother has worked for.

"Please," I begged. "I need those!"

I hated how pathetic I sounded. Hated that I couldn't hold in my emotions.

She pulled one of the scones out, unwrapped it, and took a bite.

Fire flowed through my veins. Anger consumed me. That was all it took for me to whip out my dagger and aim for her neck. All rational thought went out with the pure rage and humiliation I felt. I stopped at her neck, holding the blade sideways, pressing it into her hard enough for it to hurt, but not hard enough to cause real damage. The girl shrieked, and her friends stilled, their faces paling.

"Hey!" I heard a voice growl behind me. I whirled around, dagger still kept at the girl's neck, to see a male charging up at us.

Fuck.

Based on his toned build, I assumed he was in his late teens. He towered over me as he approached, jet black hair flowing loosely with the springtime wind. He wore a white tunic, which seemed luminescent against his golden tan skin. A sword hung across his back, and his dark brown leather pants were form-fitting against his defined legs. The look was finished with black leather boots.

Inner Ring.

His jaw was clenched, and he focused on me with striking gold eyes. I swallowed.

He's going to turn me over to the guards. He must know these girls.

Fear began to sweep over me, but to my surprise, he shot his eyes at the girl under my blade.

"See what happens when you take what isn't yours?" he said matter-of-factly.

The girl gaped at him. "You're going to defend the charlatan holding a knife to my neck?"

He slowly looked back at me and gazed into my eyes. I tried to calm my shaking and not look like a complete weakling.

"Lower your weapon," he said softly.

I hesitated momentarily but ended up conceding, lowering my weapon while still keeping it where I could use it. He glanced back to the brunette. "That doesn't belong to you." He nodded to my bag. "Give it back, or I will get the guards."

The girl's friends just stood there, frozen.

She let out a dry laugh, then softly touched her chest. "Get the guards if you wish. She just tried to kill me. I did nothing wrong."

He smirked. "We both know that isn't true, darling." He purred as he got close to her. She drew in a breath, and despite her resentment toward him, I could tell she was attracted to him. I couldn't blame her. She glanced over his shoulder, made eye contact with me, and then looked back at him.

She paused and then let out yet another dry laugh, her brown eyes trailing back to me.

"Pfft. Here are your pastries back. They're stale anyway." She tossed the bag on the ground before I could catch it, and I heard the shattering of the remaining elixir inside as it hit the ground. The boy's eyes widened.

"Oops," she said dryly. She didn't bother to look at him again as she and her friends strolled off, chucking the pastries they had in their hands on the ground. Thankfully, only the main bitch unwrapped hers.

The stranger kneeled to the ground and picked up my now dripping bag.

"Thank you for your help," I muttered, wiping my eyes. I didn't even realize the tears had actually fallen.

Pathetic.

He looked up and smiled softly.

"Of course." He stood up and handed me my belongings. "It's a shame about what was in your bag. What a repulsive girl that was," he said with a curled lip, looking in the direction they had left. "I've never seen anything like that before."

"Really? You must be new up here then," I said with a slight laugh, slinging the bag back around me. "Although to be fair, it's never been that bad before." I paused, examining my bag and what was inside. Thankfully, the elixir was kept in a separate compartment of the bag, so the baked goods wrapped inside were unharmed. "I don't know what we are going to do," I mumbled. "That was an elixir, and the man purchasing it really needs it."

Not only that, but the business's reputation was on the line too. One unpleasant experience could ruin everything.

"You don't have any more?" he questioned.

"No, my mother makes the elixirs as they're ordered. She will have to remake it…and I still have all this to deliver too…" I glanced up at the colossal clock tower in the distance.

Almost 8:00 a.m.

Under no circumstances were those from the Outer Ring allowed in the Inner Ring past 10:00 a.m. Any business would need to be conducted beforehand. The kingdom ruled it this way, so we lower peasants weren't a bother to those of more importance.

How am I going to do this?

"Well, why don't I help you?" he offered as if reading my mind.

I frowned at him. "What?"

"If you have directions, I can deliver the rest for you while you let your mother know what needs to be remade." He slid his hands into his pockets and gave a charming smile.

I studied him as I considered the proposal. I didn't want his help, but I was running out of time. He seemed trustworthy enough, I supposed.

"Why would you do that?" I asked skeptically.

"I don't have anything else better to do." He shrugged. "My mornings are pretty dull. This is the perfect way to switch things up. You can't be up here past 10:00, correct?"

He looked me up and down, and I felt my face flush.

I guess it's obvious I'm from the Outer Ring.

"Correct," I muttered, looking down at my feet. Being seen as a second-class citizen never got easier. Even though it's all I've ever known.

"Well, then we best hurry." He reached for my bag. "Don't forget about the thing she bit into."

"Right." I handed him the slip with the orders, the names of each customer, the price of their purchase, and the map with directions.

"They should only take about forty minutes. Which is about the same time it will take me to run home and back after my mother makes another one." I took a long breath. "Can we meet back up here? We will, of course, pay you."

He waved a hand in dismissal. "That isn't necessary. I *want* to help," he murmured while looking at the map. I wanted to plaster him with more questions. I was still surprised anyone from up here would even want to speak to me, let alone help, but I didn't have the time.

I shook my head. "I'm sorry, I didn't even ask your name. I'm Lena Daelyra." I extended my hand toward him. "And you?"

He examined my hand, then met my eyes. "Quill. Quill Callon," he replied, beaming while taking my hand in his. I thought he would give me a handshake, but he instead brought my hand to his mouth and gave it a light kiss. He met my widened eyes with a grin. My knees nearly buckled at the gesture.

Someone from the Inner Ring…kissing the hand of a lower-class peasant? Is he ill?

"I—I will see you in forty minutes," I stuttered as he let go of my hand.

He adjusted my bag on his shoulder and gave me a lazy smile. "See you soon."

I held my breath and turned away, my anxiety a pestering pit in my chest.

I hoped trusting this stranger wasn't a mistake.

CHAPTER THREE

"You did WHAT?" Mother screeched. I had told her what happened at our market stand, and upon only hearing the minute details, she decided to close for the rest of the day. When we returned to the cottage and I told her the whole story, she was furious.

"He wanted to help, so I—"

"So, you gave a boy, who you've never met, the rest of our orders? He probably just left with everything, Lena!"

"He saved it from being stolen in the first place, plus he looked like he had at least some money. I doubt he needs to steal food." He didn't look poor like us, but he didn't necessarily look rich either.

"Or maybe, since you gave him directions with the amount of money we should be making, he's fulfilling the orders and keeping the money for himself!"

My heart sank.

My Gods, I'm a fool.

Mother just looked away, shaking her head, beginning to make the elixir once more.

"I'm…I'm so sorry." The kindness, the kiss on the hand, he knew what he was doing. He completely fooled me. I hung my head low and went to my bedroom, shutting the door behind me as I pressed my back against it, and slid onto the floor. I sat there in silence for a moment.

Another thing I messed up. I was an idiot to think he wanted to help.

I buried my face in my hands and sobbed quietly.

Nearly thirty minutes went by. I could hear clanking dishes and hurried footsteps coming from the kitchen while Mother attempted to remake the lost items. I knew I should be in there helping, but my shame kept me paralyzed to my wooden bedroom floor. Plus, I would probably find a way to mess that up too.

I stared ahead at my small bed, the ivory sheets and peach-colored quilt calling my name. It was thin but just enough to keep me warm at night. Across from my bed was my pine dresser, and a brass-framed mirror was sitting on top of it. I didn't have many cosmetics, but near it lay a soft pink blush, mascara, and red lipstick. The blush and mascara were worn frequently, but I never felt there was an occasion for such a bold color on my lips.

I stood up and walked over, realizing I probably had black streaks staining my face. I glanced in the mirror, and staring back were my red, puffy eyes and, sure enough, black droplets running down my cheeks.

I hated myself. I hated feeling this way too.

I wasn't ugly. In fact, I didn't mind my bright green eyes and the flecks of gold that warped through them. Mother said they were just like my father's. I fetched a cloth and began wiping the tear streaks away, feeling sick to my stomach.

My red-copper hair was tied in a half-up style, which I opted for most days, with a bun tied in the back and a few loose pieces pulled out in the front. I could see my own pointed ears, even if no one else could. Mages know now that their ears must be glamoured to appear like the rounded ears humans had.

No, I wasn't ugly. But my insides sure as hell were.

I was nothing but a shell containing so…so much rage. I couldn't think of the last time I felt happy. I couldn't think of one thing I had truly done right in my life.

Just as I was going to go on another downward spiral of self-loathing, I heard knocking at the front door. I froze, and as Mother opened the door, I heard a familiar voice.

I quickly exited the room, and standing at the door was Quill, holding my crossbody and handing Mother the bag of money that we had earned.

His eyes met mine.

"You came back…" I whispered as I retrieved my bag from him. I was so grateful I cleaned up the smudged mascara.

He frowned. "Of course I did," he stated, handing it over. "I was waiting where you told me to, but you didn't show. Thankfully, your home is marked on your map."

My cheeks flushed.

Mother was peering through the sack of copper when she spoke. "Oh, that was my fault." She looked at him. "I couldn't believe someone from the Inner Ring would help us, truthfully. I convinced Lena here of that. But I was wrong." She pulled out a generous amount of the copper pieces and held out her hand to Quill. "Thank you so much for your help."

He glanced at her extended hand and gave a soft smile.

"Payment is not necessary. You earned that money, not me," he said kindly.

Mother looked at him in confusion and then back at me. I gave an uncertain shrug in reply.

Then her eyes shot open as she glanced at the simmering pot on the stove.

"Oh shoot!" She ran over and then glanced at the wall of dried herbs that hung above the counters. "I didn't add sage, and there's none left." She ran her fingers through her hair, not caring if it fumbled up her bangs, and shook her head. "I need to run outside the wall and get some."

"No, let me do it," I insisted. "Finish up the rest of what you're doing. I'll go."

"I don't want you outside the wall alone, Lena."

Before I could respond, Quill stepped in. "I'll go with her."

I whirled at him. "I can take care of myself." It came out colder than I intended, but I couldn't stand appearing like a helpless little girl. My mother gave me a disapproving look.

Quill, to my surprise, chuckled. "Oh, believe me, I know that. You almost gutted that girl after all."

My eyes widened, and after a second of silence, Mother quietly asked, "What does he mean, Lena?"

"Alright." I ignored her. "Let's go then." I retrieved my cloak from the hall tree and rushed out of the house, Quill following close behind.

We headed to the entrance to the kingdom, or in our case, the exit. Large steps went from the gates that were kept open, all the way to the castle, the Rings being the only thing breaking them up.

"What was that about?" he asked.

"She doesn't know about the dagger," I muttered.

"You're not allowed weapons?"

"That's not it…" I trailed off. "If she knew I purchased this dagger, it would be me admitting that I should learn to defend myself. Which…I just don't wish to have that conversation with her." I couldn't tell him Mother would be even more insistent that I start practicing my magic. No, I could never tell him anything relating to that.

"It's not bad to know how to protect yourself, should the opportunity arise."

"You say that as if you have experience," I replied.

He let out a soft laugh. "No, thankfully, no real-world experience. But I have had a lot of training," he said, eyeing the weapon resting on his back. "Better to be prepared."

I gave a slow nod and looked away. We marched on, the silence between us eventually becoming awkward until he spoke again.

"How old are you?"

"You ask a lot of questions," I murmured. "Sixteen, and you?"

"Sixteen."

I gaped at him, and he chuckled. "You seem surprised by that."

"You appeared older to me…" I mumbled as I glanced away.

We made it down the entrance steps, then to the bridge that separated Otacia from the outside, and I could feel Quill tense up beside me. I glimpsed at him and saw that his carefree expression had vanished, and his jaw was tightly clenched.

"You alright?" I inquired softly.

His chest rose, then fell. "Yes," he gritted out.

I looked up and waved to the guard I saw anytime Mother and I scavenged. He was too far up to have a discussion, so I didn't know his name, but he always gave us a big smile and an enthusiastic wave. He had to be around Mother's age.

"Don't tell me you're scared, Quill," I teased. "You're supposed to be here to protect me."

I felt him relax as he let out a breathy laugh. "Don't worry, I'm more scared of getting on *your* bad side than whatever's out here," he teased back.

I gave him my middle finger while trying to contain my grin, his surprised yet amused look satisfying me. I glanced back up at the guard, who looked at me with a puzzled expression.

I know, seeing a little thing like me being vulgar is surprising.

I chuckled. I wasn't short, maybe 5'5", but my reddish hair and big eyes made me appear a lot more innocent than I was. Someone like Quill, nearly a foot taller than me and built like no sixteen-year-old I'd ever seen, seemed much more mature. However, I suppose it would've been a brow-raising action from him as well, being from the Inner Ring and all.

So many of them acted like they had sticks up their asses. But I hadn't scared off Quill thus far. Yet.

We crossed the bridge, and Quill took another deep breath. I studied him as he took in the surroundings with broadened eyes.

"It's so…vast," he whispered.

The sun had cast a golden light on the trees of the Western Forest, and the air was filled with the fresh scent of pine. I could see wonder flickering in Quill's eyes as if he were utterly captivated by the view of the forest.

This wasn't even close to the most beautiful part either.

"Yes," I said tenderly. "Have you…never seen it?"

He ran his hand through his raven-black hair. "Uh…not in a very long time." He scanned the forest again, then met my eyes with a dreamy smile. "It's breathtaking."

I studied him more, trying not to fall in love with that look. Then I glanced back at the trees, at the various shades of green, and smiled as I listened to the calming sounds of birds calling to one another.

Perhaps I do not appreciate the scenery as much as I should.

I gave Quill a grin. "If you think this is breathtaking, you should see Amethyst Pond."

Curiosity sparkled in Quill's eyes. "Where's that?" he asked.

"About a half hour into the forest. It'd be best for you to see it without expectations and on a warm day," I replied. "Perhaps another time; come this way. The sage should be over here."

We wove through the trees, branches cracking under our feet.

Abruptly, I got this feeling of…being watched. I slowed simultaneously with Quill, who must've sensed the same thing.

"You feel that?" he asked quietly.

"Yes," I whispered. I held my breath.

The feeling was dark and cold—strange. Chills spread across my body, and the hairs on the back of my neck raised. But just as I began to panic, the feeling was…gone.

I let out a shaky exhale.

"Does…does that normally happen?" Quill questioned, eyes darting around the forest. "What was that?"

"I'm not sure…and no." I wrapped my arms around myself, looking up into the trees surrounding us.

"Have you encountered any witches in this forest?" he whispered.

I shot my gaze back to him, acknowledging the worried look on his face. Witch was a common slur for my kind. I hated it.

"No. No, I haven't," I said coldly. My eyes traveled away, and I resumed walking toward our destination.

He would never treat me with kindness if he knew who I was. I can't forget that.

I thought back to the conversation Mother and I had earlier. I could create friendships…so long as my mask was on. But I had no interest in that. I didn't see a point.

We continued quietly to a familiar area where I knew sage was planted.

"Here," I said while pointing at the plants. Bluish-purple flowers appeared in clusters, and I knew I had found what I was looking for.

I crouched down and began to snip off the leaves of the plants with the small clippers in my bag.

"That smells…earthy," he said with a scrunched-up face as he watched me.

"Baby," I teased. "Be happy we aren't out here picking valerian."

I could feel him pause, so I looked up at him again, his expression pleasantly surprised.

"What?" I asked plainly.

"You're just…not like anyone I've met before."

"How's that?"

"Well, normally, the girls I meet are—"

"Polite? Soft-spoken? Enthralled by you?" I retorted.

He blinked. "Well, yes, something like that."

I let out a fake laugh. "Welcome to the Outer Ring," I muttered as I resumed my snipping.

"I didn't mean it as a bad thing…" he said quietly.

I paused. "Pfft" was the only response I could think of. I finished gathering enough sage to last us for a while, hopefully, and stood back up.

"That should be enough. We should hurry back." I breezed past him, heading back to the kingdom. We walked the rest of the way in silence.

CHAPTER FOUR

When we returned to the cottage, I quickly handed Mother the sage before she insisted Quill and I wait outside. The last thing we needed was for him to see her enchant the elixir. I thought he'd finally leave, but he said since he was heading back up to the Inner Ring anyway, he'd stick with me until my task was complete.

How annoying.

Though, if I was being honest, it was nice being in the company of someone other than Mother.

Quill had his hands in his pockets and didn't bother to hide himself staring at me.

"I..." I started. "I planted most of the flowers around the cottage." I internally cringed. I was not too fond of small talk, but the awkward silence was a tad worse.

"Really?" he asked, now scanning around our home. "You didn't strike me as a flower girl."

My cheeks heated.

Why would *a dirty peasant girl with anger issues strike anyone as a flower girl?*

His smile finally returned as he met my eyes. I twiddled my thumbs, turning to view my work.

"It helps…taking the time to tend and grow something."

"Helps what?"

I stared at the vines trailing up the side of my home.

It helps deal with all the rage inside me…deal with the pent-up magic that wants out more than anything.

I never expressed to Mother the difficulties I had…how awful it felt to just exist on a day-to-day basis. She had enough to worry about.

Before I could respond, Mother threw open the door and handed me back my crossbody with the new elixir and scone, the fabric still damp from the broken brew from earlier.

"It's 9:30. You're going to have to hurry." She glanced at Quill and gave a warm smile. "Thank you, again, for all of your help."

He nodded, giving her a dazzling smile. "My pleasure."

"Let's go," I mumbled.

We quickly made it to the first home, where a lady had purchased a single scone, the one that bitch took a bite of.

I knocked on the door and smiled as a woman answered the door.

"Delivery from Waylon's, ma'am," I chirped as I handed over the wrapped scone.

"I thought it would never get here," the woman whined. She shoved the copper into my hand and then shut the door, not even giving as much as a thank-you.

"My Gods," Quill breathed. "I did not receive reactions like that."

"That's because you are one of them," I muttered. I looked again at the giant clock tower built in the Center; its time was visible throughout the entire kingdom.

9:43 a.m.

"Come on, let's get this finished."

We quickly strolled past an area that gave an excellent view of the castle. I stopped in my tracks every time I passed it, glaring upward. Today, the sun beamed down on its intricate obsidian exterior, casting an imposing shadow over the Inner Ring. Its gothic style was both chilling and stunning. I couldn't help but marvel at it every time.

Quill stopped beside me, studying me as I looked up in awe.

"I always wonder what it's like up there in the Center. Never having to struggle or starve or use cold water," I said with quiet resentment. I met eyes with Quill, who looked at me like I was a kicked puppy.

"I don't need pity…I was just thinking out loud," I said quietly while averting my eyes.

We continued walking and came up to the last house. I had grown to know Gerald and his daughter Guinevere, who was around my mother's age. Gerald was sick with some disease, making it hard for him to get out of bed these days. My mother's elixirs had shown significant improvement in him, allowing him to enjoy his daily walks again these past weeks.

I took another deep breath.

"Do you want me to do it?" Quill offered softly.

"No," I sighed. "They are nice."

I knocked on the door, and Guinevere answered, her usually beaming face nowhere to be found.

"Oh, Lena," she cried. "I'm sorry. My father passed away a few days ago…"

I froze, my eyes finding their way down to the elixir in my hand. Mother's words came back to me. *I don't do the full potency of my power. Just enough to slowly heal over time."*

The amount she was using must not have been enough…

"I will still pay for this, of course," she reassured me as she touched my shoulder. "This has been a great help to us. Seeing him go to his favorite coffee shop, walk around while enjoying the weather…it has been a blessing."

My shoulders sagged. "I'm so sorry for your loss," I said solemnly. "Don't worry about purchasing this. It's—"

"No, I want to." She carefully retrieved the elixir from my grasp. "You never know when something like this will come in handy again," she said with a smile that didn't quite reach her eyes.

I nodded, attempting to keep my lip from quivering. She handed me the copper.

"Tell Minerva I said thank you."

I nodded, and she shut the door.

Quill and I stood in silence, and I wiped away the one tear that rolled down my face. I stiffened as he ran his hand up and down my back in a comforting motion, goosebumps spreading across my body in response to his touch.

"You've offered them a wonderful gift," he whispered. "You can't always save everyone…"

"We can't save anyone," I corrected softly. "Can only help ease their suffering. At least we were able to do that."

I turned to him, unable to look him in the eyes. Seeing another look of pity would send me over the edge. I extended my hand, holding the little bag of bronze I had just received. "I already spoke with my mother. She agreed we would give you this for your help."

"I appreciate that, but—"

"Just take it!" I shouted as my eyes shot up to his. His golden eyes widened, and he stepped back. "Please, don't look at me like you're too good for our money. Take. It."

His lips went into a tight line as he eyed the coin pouch. He reluctantly took it, and I sighed in relief, my shoulders drooping as I looked at the ground.

I stiffened as he gently grasped my chin and tilted my face upward. My stomach flipped as my eyes met his, the morning sun illuminating the striking honey hue of them.

"I do not think any less of you for living in the Outer Ring, I hope you know," he said confidently. "Not even a little bit. In fact, you are the most fascinating person I have ever met." He gave me a lazy smile.

I felt my face flush. "You don't need to lie to me," I breathed, trying not to focus on the butterflies in my stomach. The corner of my lip turned upward. "You damn brown-noser. Most fascinating person? Please."

He snorted. "I'm not lying." His eyes danced as he brushed my hair behind my ear, utterly unaware of the pointed cartilage that was hidden with magic. "Your attitude excites me, actually."

Chills once again went down my body at the smokiness of his voice.

No, no. I will not fall for an Inner Ring boy.

"You've only seen a fraction of my attitude." I crossed my arms. "I don't think it would be as exciting at its full capacity."

He chuckled. "Is that a challenge, Lena?" he purred. The sun beamed down on us, his golden skin looking even more beautiful against the light. It was certainly a contrast to my pale skin, which could blind someone if they looked at me too long.

He must be playing with me. I swallowed, and after a moment, I broke our gaze when I glanced at the clock.

9:58 a.m.

"Oh my Gods!" He recoiled at my reaction. "I have to get back to the Outer Ring!"

He whirled toward the clock and, with no words, grasped my hand and started pulling me toward my home. "They'll arrest me if I'm still up here!" I cried.

"That won't happen. We'll make it," he assured me.

And we did, with just seconds to spare. He ran down the steps with me as I caught disapproving gazes from the guards now stationed at the entrance.

We stopped to catch our breath after a few steps into the Outer Ring. Just in time.

After a moment, I couldn't help but start laughing at how close we were. Quill, still catching his breath, looked at me with happy surprise.

Once my laughing died down, I just smiled at him. "Thank you again. You really saved my ass today."

"It was my pleasure," he replied, once again with that lazy smile that was beginning to affect me.

"How can I repay you?"

"Didn't you already?" he asked as he waved the coin bag.

"Oh, right," I said, rubbing the back of my neck.

"Although," he continued, "you could repay me by showing me Amethyst Pond, the place you told me about."

"I knew the copper wasn't enough." I smirked.

"As I told you, the money is unnecessary." He stepped closer. "It is just an excuse to see you again."

My heartbeat quickened, and then my smile faded.

I couldn't get close to anyone. Certainly not in any romantic sense. I didn't want that anyway. Getting close to him would put us at more risk, and I would not have it.

I glanced at the sword on his back.

Still, there was one way he could be useful to me—one way he could actually help in giving me back some of the power that I always denied myself.

"I'll show you Amethyst Pond on one condition."

"Alright," he said with an intrigued look.

"Teach me how to fight."

He blinked.

I told myself I was not interested in him or his friendship. But learning to fight in a way that had nothing to do with magic could be just what I needed. Gardening could only help so much with all the pent-up trauma I had.

"I don't know anything about fighting nor how to use my dagger properly. You said it yourself—it doesn't hurt to know how to protect myself. I want to know everything you do." I stepped closer to him. "Teach me."

He considered, pulling his lips to the side.

"Very well," he said after a beat, then turned to walk away.

"W-when will I see you again?" I exclaimed.

He half turned to me, giving me his signature lazy smile. "Soon, my Flower." And he strode away.

I just stood there, comprehending all that had happened.

Flower? That's my nickname?

I slowly turned toward the cottage and tried to hold in my smile.

Flower. That bastard.

I wore a grin the whole way home.

CHAPTER FIVE

"That guy was a total flirt," I told Mother while washing the dishes. I had just strolled in moments before, struggling not to show amusement.

"Why do you sound annoyed by that?" Mother questioned as she wiped down our kitchen countertop with a damp rag. "I thought he was handsome—and my, was he sweet!"

I paused, soap dripping down my hands.

Yes. Yes, he was.

I'd be lying if I said I wasn't mildly fascinated by him. No one from the Inner Ring had ever shown us kindness, save for Gerald and Guinevere, and that was because we were of use to them. Everyone else looked at us like we were a total other species.

They wouldn't be entirely incorrect about that.

"Well," I said as I resumed my dish cleaning. "I guess he's just not my type," I lied.

Mother chuckled. "Please, I think he is everyone's type."

I gave her a raised brow. "Oh, really?"

She swatted me with the rag, and I chuckled softly. I then mentioned how we planned to hang out again, and through Mother's excitement, I could tell she believed it was a date, despite me denying it. I purposely left out the training part.

The day went by quickly. After helping clean the disaster left in the kitchen after Mother's frantic cooking, I went to tend the garden, the sun providing precious heat.

The rest of the afternoon was for my studies. Mother was willing to let me go to the public school in the Outer Ring, but we determined that it was less of a risk for me to be homeschooled…less of a chance to get close to anyone.

If I were different, I would want that. I saw kids my age walking from school most afternoons, hearing their chatter as if they had not a care in the world. I couldn't imagine what that was like.

After dinner, my body was weary. I crawled into bed, trying my hardest not to think about Quill. His lazy smile was the last thing I thought of before I drifted to sleep.

I felt a cold presence over me, but I couldn't move my body. I couldn't even open my eyes. I just lay there, paralyzed.

Something was whispering, but it was so faint I couldn't decipher it.

I wanted to scream, ask it what it wanted, but I just lay there, hearing its soft murmur, unable to move a muscle.

My eyes flung open, and sunlight had begun to shine through the gossamer curtains in my bedroom. I was covered in sweat.

What the hell was that last night? Surely a dream?

I wiped the sweat from my forehead and flung my quilt off me; the coinciding breeze felt terrific. Sitting on the edge of the stiff bed, I kept attempting to recall what that voice was trying to say. It must have been a dream, but I always believed dreams had a deeper meaning. That presence was similar to what I felt in the forest yesterday.

I wonder if Quill had the same dream.

I ran my hand through my hair. My copper coils were more defined since I had washed my hair last night.

I heard a knock on my door, and Mother scurried in, excitedly clenching her teeth.

"Well, don't keep me in suspense! What is it?"

She proceeded to tell me, while lightly bouncing up and down, that the Queen was visiting today. Had the news been about the King, that bouncing would be trembling. But Queen Ryia was as kind as they come. She came down last year and seeing her dazzling attire and hairstyle had left me both star-struck and annoyed.

Quickly, we got ourselves ready to avoid missing her appearance. Yet again, I did my signature half-up hairstyle and opted for my prettiest dress, if you could call it pretty. It was a deep navy blue, and its length almost reached the ground. My favorite part was the petal sleeves, but though the dress was lovely, it was a tad too large for me. I wore a black bustier over it, which gave a slightly more flattering look.

I met Mother in her room, where she was fussing over a piece of hair that was not cooperating. She huffed, slumped her arms down, and blew up on a stray piece of hair in front of her face. She turned to face me after noticing my presence and looked me up and down.

"You look beautiful, Lena." She smiled with tears in her eyes. "You look so much…older than last time we saw the Queen. Like a woman."

"Thank you," I replied sheepishly, scratching the back of my head. It was true, the looking-more-womanly part. Compared to last year, my hips had widened, and my chest had grown.

We headed out, strolling toward Linora Park, arguably one of the prettier areas of the Outer Ring. It was a large, open field of grass, save for the decent-sized pond on the outer edge that had a wooden bridge crossing over it. It was forbidden to fish, but I knew plenty of fish swam beneath. Most days, the park was filled with residents having picnics, children running through the field playing games, or local musicians trying to earn some copper for their talent.

Now, the park was packed like sardines, chattering voices filling the air. The number of people crammed here made me feel uneasy, but it was incontestably the happiest the people down here got. My lips couldn't help but turn upward at that fact.

"Shh, she's coming!"

Various voices began whispering and gushing at each other as trumpets and drums began playing in the distance in a beautiful and powerful melody.

It was too mobbed for me to push to the front. Mother, on the other hand, had gotten a pretty decent spot. I pulled myself up on a lamppost, and the added height its stone base gave me provided a perfect view of the incoming Queen over the crowd.

The music began to crescendo as Queen Ryia's guard marched down, her float behind them glistening in the morning sun. Gems dazzled along the outsides, a rainbow of color. I fought the urge to roll my eyes but couldn't help but slightly gawk.

I could never imagine having wealth, even a fraction of that.

The Queen was now around forty feet away from me, give or take. Her obsidian, satin gown, a perfect match to the kingdom's gothic castle, hugged her body in all the right places before spilling delicately on the floor beneath her. Her shoulders were bare, showcasing her sand-colored skin, and her hair was pulled into a sleek updo, its color almost the same shade as her dress.

In short, she was stunning.

She waved at the crowd, giving a genuine smile. She never threw gold; it would quickly turn into a fight. So, after her greeting, she would shop at local businesses, spending a generous amount at each one. We were to head back to our stand after this, the market commencing again on any day royalty appeared.

She continued to wave when her gaze landed on me. She stopped in her tracks, her hand frozen in mid-air.

I gulped, my smile disappearing.

Was she looking at…me?

A moment later, she resumed her waving, yet her eye contact remained on me, *me* without a doubt.

And then she continued looking at everyone else once more.

Perhaps she found it improper, a person just holding on to a lamp-post while royalty was present. I nervously lowered myself and decided to head to our stand early.

When Mother met me back at our stand, after plenty of citizens had streamed into the market, she gushed over the Queen, just like she had in the past. After that, she gave me a raised brow.

"Why did you leave early?"

"I…I just wanted to get a head start on setting up." Indeed, my early arrival allowed me to get our stand looking extra clean and welcoming. I wasn't about to tell her of my strange interaction with the Queen.

The market was soon bursting with energy, and local musicians played their tunes in all different areas. People sold a wide variety of goods, from food to clothing to jewelry, perfume, and so much more.

Before we knew it, the Queen was gracefully walking through the market, guards surrounding her in a square. She made her way around, both Mother and I trembling with nerves. In previous years, she hadn't made it to our stand, as there was a total of ninety vendors. She probably went to half during her time here, which took up nearly the entire day. But then, once again, the Queen's gaze turned to me, her electric blue eyes meeting mine, and I realized I had never seen her this close before. She spoke something to her guards and walked up to us, the guards trailing behind her.

I could hear Mother suck in a breath, and I stiffened.

"Welcome, Your Majesty," Mother breathed while bowing. I matched her a beat later. "We are known for our baked goods and our elixirs," she stated as she raised her head.

"So I've heard," Ryia mused. "Word has spread in the Inner Ring of your business."

Mother and I exchanged wide eyes, somehow surprised that the Queen knew such insignificant matters regarding the Inner Ring.

"I'll take everything you have in stock," she continued. "I would love to try some, along with my staff."

I thought Mother would faint as she processed the information.

"Oh, that is so kind, Your Majesty!"

We counted the price of everything as quickly as possible.

Twenty-three, thirty-one, thirty—shoot.

I could feel the Queen staring at me, making me lose count, and my cheeks heated. I dared to look at her, and to my surprise, she was beaming at me.

I returned a nervous smile and continued counting.

"The total for everything…is three-hundred-twenty coppers," Mother hesitantly stated.

The Queen raised her arm and signaled for one of the guards, who walked up and handed her a black velvet pouch. Without opening it, she gave it to me.

"I do not carry copper," she said. "But I do carry silver. There are one hundred pieces in there. I don't wish to count it out, so keep it all," she said with a wink.

Mother and I gaped before Mother finally spoke. "Th-thank you, Your Majesty." One thousand coppers equaled one hundred silvers, which was also ten gold. She had given over triple the amount.

We both bowed, and the Queen smiled softly before walking to the next place.

"Oh…oh my gosh!" Mother squealed, grabbing my hands. We both couldn't help but jump for joy. She gave us enough to buy food for at least two months!

We closed our stand after the Queen's guards collected our items, and we moved swiftly on our way back home.

"Let's get pizza tonight! We deserve it," Mother said as she nudged me with a smile. I smiled back, but when I looked away, my lips began to turn downward despite the blessing that had just occurred.

Why was she staring at me?

CHAPTER SIX

"So, what do you know about combat?" Quill inquired.

He showed up at our cottage precisely one week after we met, on market day once again. We heard a knock on the door just past six in the morning, and Mother answered it, saying Quill looked happy as could be. I groggily rolled out of bed, then once what she said registered, my eyes flung open, and I rushed to put myself together. Quill just waited at the dining table, smirking as he watched me run back and forth from the bathroom to my bedroom.

Mother wanted me to run the stand today but instead happily allowed me to do the deliveries so I could spend time with Quill, thinking it was a date and entirely unaware of the deal we had made. After we delivered the orders together, we headed to the Western Forest to train.

I picked at a speck on my shirt, feeling a little awkward. I opted for a gray tank top paired with black leather pants and boots, the closest thing to training attire I owned. I threw my hair into a messy bun; loose copper waves had already fallen and framed my face. "Nothing, truthfully. I probably couldn't hold my own if it came down to it," I answered honestly.

He tensed. "Then why did you pull your dagger on that girl?"

I crossed my arms. "At the moment, I didn't care. I just wanted to hurt her," I stated bluntly. He clenched his jaw in response, and I put my hands on my hips at his reaction. "Do you think I'm bad for that?"

Quill had chosen to wear an emerald-green tunic. It was embroidered with silver decals that swirled along the neckline and the cuffs of his sleeves that he had rolled up to his elbows, exposing a matching silver watch. On the bottom, he wore sand-colored pants that hugged his legs beautifully and the same black boots as before. His sword was wrapped around him like last time.

He looked me up and down. "No," he answered softly. "But you can't let your emotions cause you to make poor decisions. It is not wise to go into a battle you are not positive you will win, or at least are not sure you'll have a fighting chance in." He bit back a grin. "I did enjoy seeing you making that girl shudder, though. I bet she's never felt terror like that before. I hope she never forgets it."

I blinked. Perhaps this middle-class lad wasn't as uptight as I thought.

"Well, since you know nothing about fighting," he continued, "and your body…isn't exactly toned, we will need to work on your strength before we learn how to use different weapons."

I flushed. "Wow—'isn't exactly toned.' How kind of you." I looked away, dusting my shoulder.

He smirked. "It's not a problem in the looks department, Flower." His smile faltered. "But it can be detrimental when it comes to fighting."

I rolled my eyes, ignoring my silly nickname. "Well, let's get on with it then."

"Alright. How is your stamina?" he asked.

I thought about the different ways I exert my energy. Until four years ago, my stamina was great since we traveled on foot the whole time. Now? I hardly went anywhere, save for the times we scavenged the forest.

"Probably not the best," I muttered.

He then instructed me to attempt four laps around the grove of trees near us, the circumference having to be close to a quarter mile.

By lap two, I was completely winded. I stopped and put my hands on my knees, gasping for air when I couldn't go any longer.

"Yikes," he laughed, running up to me. "This may take longer than I thought."

I shot him an evil glare, and he just chuckled in response.

"You think this is funny, don't you? Watching me suffer," I staggered out.

He grinned. "I can't deny that watching you all hot and sweaty is rather enjoyable."

I curled my lip, and without a second thought, I punched him in the arm.

He looked at his arm, then back at me, wicked amusement in his eyes.

"Yeah, we definitely need to build your strength. That was pitiful."

I huffed, then continued my run, having to constantly stop to catch my breath until the fourth lap was complete.

After completing my run, he led me through various core exercises, all of which I failed miserably. After a beat, he ceased his mocking after most likely noticing my evident frustration with myself. Instead, he was direct and short, as if he knew that coddling would have bothered me even more than mocking.

"So…" I huffed while doing sit-ups, Quill kneeling in front of me and holding my feet to the ground. "Did you see the Queen a few days ago?"

"Hm?"

"When she came to the Outer Ring," I breathed, attempting to ignore the curling of my toes at his pine and citrus scent. Was it a fragrance, or did he naturally smell that fucking good? "Did you happen to get a glance?"

"Oh. No. My home isn't close to the stairs. But I did hear about it," he said plainly. I groaned as I continued the sit-ups. "Did you?" he asked.

I paused at the top. "Yes. She bought out our entire stock. She's very generous," I said after a moment of contemplating. "I think the kingdom would be better if she had the final say on things, not Ulric. I don't care much for him."

"Don't stop," Quill snapped.

I quickly resumed. "Yes, sir," I muttered while rolling my eyes. That made his lip curve upward. "So…what's your story? You've been to my home, know where we work, and have seen me in a ridiculous bun." I jokingly gestured at my horrendous hairdo, struggling with my breathing as I hurled my body up and back down. "I don't know anything about you."

"I like to be a mystery," he purred.

I let out a breathy laugh. "Of course you do." I wanted to keep talking, but my workout demanded I stop.

By the end, sweat dripped down my body, and the curled baby hairs surrounding my hairline were stuck to my face. I pressed my fingertips to my cheek, and my skin felt hot to the touch.

I probably look like a mess.

I struggled to raise my body for the final time after completing a hundred sit-ups.

"Excellent, Lena," he praised.

"Don't lie," I panted, my forearms now resting on my knees. "This was all pathetic."

"No, all this showed me was how determined you are." He held out a hand and lifted me to my feet, then checked his watch. "Time's up. I'll walk you home."

I was regaining my breath when he smirked at me again. "You know, if your mother doesn't know we're training together, she's going to think other activities took place when she sees you like this."

I could feel my face heating further.

"You're insufferable. You know that?" I said in defeat.

He laughed, then started walking toward the kingdom.

Cocky bastard.

We made it back to my home, and I hoped my deep breathing, along with the cool breeze during the walk, corrected my flushed face.

When I reached the doorway, I turned to Quill.

"Thank you for today, even though you're a bit of an ass," I simpered.

He put his hands in his pockets and gave me a cocky smile. "When I see you next, I expect to see some improvement." Quill had given me a list of daily exercises to do after he mentioned he could commit to training me every Thursday morning. "If you struggle to complete four laps by next week, I will punish you with an extra one."

I crossed my arms. "If I keel over from overexertion, you'll be the one who gets punished."

He replied with a dazzling smile that revealed his bright, white teeth. If someone from the Inner Ring could be this beautiful, I could only imagine how a member of the Center looked.

He stepped forward, and I stiffened as he leaned in, his lips mere inches from my ear. "I think I would enjoy you punishing me," he whispered.

My eyes fluttered at the meaning behind his words, or rather, where my thoughts went. My mind was aflutter as he pulled away, and I thought I might hit him when he gave me a wink.

"See you soon, Flower," he said smoothly, then strolled away.

I exhaled, not realizing I had been holding my breath.

Why do I let him affect me this way? It's exactly what he wants.

I released my hair from the bun and strolled inside, the silence letting me know Mother was still at the market. I quickly scarfed down a bowl of yogurt and one of the muffins she had baked yesterday. Who knew exercise could make one so hungry?

Quill was on my mind the entire time. When I was done eating, I rested my head against the back of my chair.

He's such a damn tease.

I couldn't get him out of my head. I couldn't stop thinking about his remark. About how I might look had we engaged in the "activity" he had implied—how *he* might look.

I shook my head and grasped my neck, not wanting to acknowledge the obvious. But I couldn't help it. I kept thinking of his body and the green tunic he wore. The sleeves rolled up to expose his beautiful, golden forearms. Thinking about the muscles that were visible through his light-colored pants. Thinking about his eyes that were always looking at me like I was, just as he said, the most fascinating person he'd met. Thinking about his scent.

I bit my lip, and then I thought of that lazy smile of his, and it was all I needed to head to my bedroom and pleasure myself.

I could only think of the shit he would give me if he knew what I was about to do. The dark amusement that would fill his eyes. And that only aroused me further.

And I wondered if he'd do the same, thinking of me.

CHAPTER SEVEN

Thursdays had quickly become my favorite day of the week. My life had gone from painfully mundane to somewhat exciting. It was both a physical and mental challenge to complete all the exercises he planned for me, even with my daily practice. To keep my mind clear of dirty thoughts anytime he smirked or laughed or just looked at me was a whole other challenge.

By the third week, I was already noticing changes in my body and my stamina. Even though I wasn't feeling relief from the pain of holding in magic like I always did, it certainly was a good distraction.

"You've improved a lot," Quill commented as I finished my laps in record time. "Now, if you want to really start packing on muscle, you'll need to focus on what you eat. And how much."

I groaned. "I'm not ready to learn with a weapon yet?"

"Patience, Flower," he said as he tousled my hair. I swatted him away, and he chuckled. "What do you eat on a daily basis?"

I thought about it. We didn't always have a ton of food in the house. We had been able to eat more these past few weeks, however, thanks to the Queen's generous purchase.

"It changes, but usually baked goods—bread, pasta—and soups. Pizza sometimes. You know…affordable things," I said sheepishly, kicking at the dirt on the ground.

"Oh, right." He rubbed the back of his neck and then paused, slightly blushing. "Do you need help with that, Lena?" he asked gently.

I glared at him. "We don't need handouts. We're getting by just fine," I replied coldly. I knew it was a sweet gesture, but I couldn't take him looking at me as helpless, as poor. It pissed me off.

"There's nothing wrong with asking for help if y—"

"Just stop!" I yelled, the quiet of the forest even more apparent after my outburst. He clenched his jaw.

His jaw.

Gods, my mind was a scrambled, pathetic mess.

I shook my head. "Just stop," I repeated calmly.

He approached me and gripped my shoulders. "You feel out of control. Believe me, I know the feeling."

I gazed up at him, and his solemn expression made me believe him.

I lowered my brows. "Perhaps, but I doubt you know what it's like to be poor," I said quietly. "To be looked down on like you're something different, just because you're less fortunate."

Just because you're a Mage. How could he know the feeling of being hated for simply existing?

"I don't…but I know how it feels to be dealt a series of cards you didn't ask for. That you don't want."

"And what cards are those, Quill?" I questioned.

He just gave me a blank stare in response.

I shook my head again. "Don't expect us to relate on anything when you tell me nothing meaningful about yourself."

His lips formed a tight line, his hands sliding down my arms and back to his sides in defeat.

After a moment of awkwardness, he spoke again.

"What is pizza?"

I turned to him and narrowed my eyes.

"What?" he asked.

"You've got to be kidding me."

He frowned, and I couldn't help but laugh. Even though the Inner Ring was so close, it was like a whole other world.

"You've never had pizza before?" I asked incredulously.

He gave a half smile. "Am I missing out?"

I laughed through my nose. "I think it is pretty good. Though it probably pales in comparison to Inner Ring delicacies," I said, unable to hold the slight bitterness in my tone.

"You'll have to show me sometime," he said sincerely.

I looked at him with a raised brow, then smiled softly.

"Perhaps I shall."

Quill proceeded to tell me how I should eat: higher calories and more protein. Instead of going through my normal exercises, Quill began to show me evasive maneuvers. No weapons were used, but he showed me some of his favorite ways to block hits. We did that for our remaining hours before I was thoroughly spent, and we wrapped up for the day.

We didn't speak much on our way back. But before we reached the bridge leading back to the kingdom, I said, "Listen."

His golden eyes met mine, and he wore an expression I couldn't decipher.

"I am grateful for your help. I don't mean to…" I sighed as my eyes fell to the ground, attempting to find the right words. "I don't mean to get angry. I don't really have an outlet for…for all I feel. I don't mean to take it out on you."

I was slightly startled when his hand took mine. I met his gaze once more, and it was as intense as ever. He studied me, his thumb dragging along the back of my hand, and I decided to keep going. "I just wish to know about you, too." I frowned. "I suppose I don't understand why you are so secretive with me."

His jaw clicked. "It is not that I wish to be. It…it is complicated."

I looked away. "Right," I mumbled. His other hand found my chin, tilting me to meet his eyes again. The gesture set my heart racing.

"Ask me one thing, and I will tell you."

I raised my brow. "Anything?"

He nodded. I tried to think of all the questions that I had and which were the most important. I settled with the first that came to mind.

"How did you learn to fight?"

He took a breath, and the hand that held my chin fell back to his side. "I am training to be an Otacian soldier."

My eyes widened. "A soldier?"

I didn't know why I hadn't considered it. He certainly had the build of someone who would be a soldier. Boys were recruited starting at age twelve but could start training later if they chose. It always surprised me that some parents would willingly enlist their children to fight, though being a soldier, a protector of Otacia, was one of the greatest honors one could have.

"When did you begin training?"

He grinned. "That's two questions, Flower."

My shoulders dropped, and he squeezed my hand. "I was twelve when my official training started. However, my parents would give me pointers before then. They wanted me to have every advantage when it came time to train with my peers."

"You live with both parents?" I asked.

"I do," he said with a frown. "I couldn't help but notice I have not seen your father," he hesitated. "If you wish not to speak on it, I understand."

"No, it's alright." He traced his thumb along mine. I couldn't tell him the truth, so I told him what my mother told those who asked. "My father passed away before I was born. I never knew him. Waylon was his name, which Mother's business is named after."

"I am sorry for your loss," he said with apologetic eyes, and I felt guilt wash over me.

Another one of my fucking lies.

I gave him a small smile, and we continued to walk, his hand sliding free of mine. "I suppose I don't know what I am missing."

"Well, my father is alive, but our relationship is not one to envy."

"How so?"

He tensed. "He…he is not the loving sort—quite a cold man. I cannot recall ever even being hugged by him."

I looked at him in sad surprise, and he gave me a pitiful smile before looking forward as we made it over the bridge.

"Do you train with the Prince?"

He stopped and frowned at me.

"It's just," I continued, "I've heard whisperings about the Prince here and there. They say he is a great fighter."

Quill smiled slightly. "I don't train with him per se, but he is training amongst us Inner Ring initiates."

I gasped. "So, you've seen him?"

Quill quirked a brow and followed it with a smirk. "I didn't take you for one of the many girls that gawk over the idea of the Prince."

I rolled my eyes and nudged him with my elbow. "I do not gawk. I am simply curious." I looked up at the obsidian castle as we entered the kingdom. "I just can't imagine how lonely it must be for him."

In a way, yes, I could.

As we continued our path to my cottage, I stopped and spoke again, lightly touching Quill's arm. "Thank you, Quill. For letting me in a little."

He smiled at me, and his face slightly flushed. His lips parted, but before he could give me a reply, a scream came from down the road.

Our heads quickly turned to see Otacian soldiers lined up, a couple of them dragging a woman and man from their home. I recognized them. Iliera and Xaro were their names. They were friendly neighbors, and Mother sometimes played cards with the brown-haired woman on Sunday afternoons.

"Please! Otacia is my home!" she cried.

"Otacia is no home to witches," the soldier replied harshly.

No way.

People began to gather around, yelling slurs at the couple and spitting at their feet. When a Mage was banished from Otacia, they were thrown out with nothing but the clothes on their backs. The kingdom confiscated all belongings, whether personal or for survival. It was then up to the Mages to survive in the forests and find another place to live, though it wasn't a surprise if hateful citizens decided to hunt them down.

The only positive was it was spring, so at least they need not worry about the elements.

The guards pushed them forward, the crowd's words making me want to vomit. They were people, just like them. Good people. Iliera's tears were overflowing, and then her frightened eyes met mine.

I didn't show fear, anguish, or disgust like those around me. Instead, I gave her a grave nod.

My heart hurt for her, and she saw it in my eyes before I forced the expression away and turned to walk back toward my home.

I hoped she felt seen. I hoped she knew that in this kingdom—this *world* full of hateful humans— she was not alone.

I am not alone.

Quill followed me, remaining silent until I stopped at my cottage door.

"Lena?" He grasped my arm, and I slowly turned to him. "Witnessing that affected you," he stated softly.

"Yes. It did," I muttered.

"Is it because you don't feel safe?"

Yes, but not in the way that you think.

"It is a scary thought," he continued quietly. "Their kind being able to blend in so easily . . . that they're able to hide their ears."

I squeezed my hands tightly, my nails digging crescents into my palms in an attempt to hide my shaking. "They were kind," I whispered. "I knew them. And they were kind. I don't enjoy the thought of them being thrown to the woods with not a single belonging."

He looked at me with raised brows, and after a moment of silence, Quill replied, "What a beautiful heart you have."

My brow furrowed as I looked up at him in surprise, and he gave me a warm smile in response. "I must go now, though I so badly wish to stay," he murmured. To my surprise, he kissed me on the forehead. "I will see you next week. Practice those maneuvers."

I nodded and watched as he strolled away.

I was left flushed and confused. My sorrow for the couple remained, but the thought of Quill's words brought a small smile to my face.

I was used to the sadness that came with the hatred of my people. No, it wasn't an everyday occurrence that Mages were discovered and thrown out of the kingdom.

As I entered my home, I wondered just how many of my neighbors held the same secrets that we did.

CHAPTER EIGHT

Mother hurriedly entered our home about half an hour later, and I knew word had spread about what happened to our neighbors.

"Are you okay?" I asked as I ran up and hugged her.

She let out a soft cry. "She was my friend. Gods, I didn't even know she was one of us." She pulled away and wiped her eyes. "It surely is a wake-up call."

Seeing Mother cry always broke me. So much suffering she had been through...

"We should lay low for a while," I said calmly. "Maybe make less potent elixirs...I don't know." I sighed. "How were they found out? Did you hear anything?"

"Someone said something about ice coming from Iliera." She

shook her head. "She must have just acquired it. I wonder what could have caused her heartbreak."

"What do you mean?" I asked.

"Elemental magic is heavily tied to our emotions. Only tragic devastation unlocks ice."

There was so much I didn't know regarding our powers.

"I know she and Xaro were trying for a baby," she continued. "I wonder…" She shook her head again at the thought and exhaled sharply. "You're looking…different," Mother mumbled, changing the subject.

My eyebrows scrunched together. "How so?"

"I don't know…stronger? More fit?" She smiled. "You look good."

"Oh…thank you." I suppose Quill's regimen was starting to have its effects. I would do my routine in my room, save for my cardio. If she ever heard me working out, she made no mention of it.

"How are things with Quill?"

To that, I walked over to the kitchen and grabbed a blueberry scone to munch on. "Fine."

"Just fine?" Mother followed me and sat at our dining table, giving me a raised brow. "You two have been spending time together for the last three weeks, and it's just fine? What do you two do together, anyway?"

I willed my face not to show any signs of emotion. "We just… hang out. Talk." It was not entirely a lie. "I don't know much about him still. But he told me he's training to be an Otacian soldier."

Her eyes broadened. "Oh my, that explains his build."

I stuffed the rest of the pastry in my mouth, hoping this conversation would end.

"You'll have to be careful dating a soldier."

I choked on my scone. "We are not dating!" I exclaimed as bits of the pastry flew out my mouth.

Mother just laughed.

The following week, I was already prepared when Quill showed up at the cottage, wearing the same outfit I wore every week. I felt ashamed at first, but I didn't have many clothes. At least I cleaned them. Plus, Quill never mentioned anything about it either.

Except for today.

"Dress in something nice today, darling," Quill said with a grin.

Today, he wore all black—a button-up shirt and trousers, still paired with black boots. He wore a navy cloak and, as always, sported his sword. He looked infuriatingly sexy, like always.

I crossed my arms at his comment, suddenly feeling insecure. "Excuse me?"

"We're going to take a break from training today," he continued, walking closer to me. "I want you to show me around the Outer Ring."

I blinked. "You want me to give you a tour of the Outer Ring?" I asked skeptically.

He smiled softly and shrugged with one shoulder. "I want to be more familiar with your home. Show me some of your favorite places—where you like to spend your time."

Other than me doing my studies, I mostly spent my days at home tending the garden, and, if not doing that, sitting by the creek reading a novel. But I supposed there were a few places I liked to visit.

"Very well, then," I replied, the corners of my lips turning upward. I had never known anyone from the Inner Ring entering the Outer Ring for fun, let alone wanting a tour of it. Save for the Queen, I supposed, though she was from the Center.

While Quill waited in the living room, I entered my room and released my hair, loose waves falling against my back. I hadn't worn my hair entirely down in...I didn't know how long. Since it was May, I put on my cream chemise again, this time pairing it with a deep blue overdress similar to the shade of Quill's cloak, and slipped on a pair of slippers. It was not fancy, but I hoped I looked decent enough.

Quill was waiting at my dining room table, and his eyes rose from the ground to meet my gaze as I exited my room.

"Is this better?" I asked sheepishly, brushing the wrinkles out of my dress.

He looked me up and down with a grin. "You look beautiful."

I couldn't help but smile at the compliment.

"So, where to?" he asked. "Pizza?"

I laughed. "Pizza for breakfast? Um, no."

I decided to first take him to Sen's Bakery. We walked into the small establishment, the smell of cinnamon and coffee filling the air.

We stopped at the end of the line formed, a handful of people ahead of us waiting to make their purchase. "They have wonderful cinnamon rolls here," I said with an embarrassed smile. "I can't always afford them, but with the Queen's donation, we can get one each."

"I will be treating you today." He tapped the small pouch secured along his belt.

I frowned at him. "You know I don't like that."

"Yes, well, I am the one who wanted to do this today. It is only fair."

My lips formed a tight line, but I didn't argue. Quill looked at the other things available in the bakery box, but we ended up settling on three cinnamon rolls, Quill being kind enough to get one for my mother as well.

We walked toward Linora Park, and since it was still early, the only people outside were artists painting in the grass.

"I enjoy coming here. Most of the Outer Ring is…unkempt. At least in comparison to the Inner Ring." I beamed at him. "But not here. It's like its own little island here."

"It's relaxing." Quill grinned back as we sat in the grass, enjoying the blissful morning breeze. The sky was light blue, and the fluffy clouds mesmerized me as they slowly moved across the sky.

He brought his cinnamon roll to his lips and took a bite, and I started to feel nervous as I watched him chew. "I've never had food in the Inner Ring…so I'm not sure how it compares," I said with a wince.

His eyes rolled back, and he smiled. "This is amazing," he said, licking his lips after swallowing. That shouldn't have turned me on as much as it did. "You know, I actually really like it down here."

I gave him a skeptical look, which earned me a laugh. "Truly," he continued. "I very much like the people here, the energy. People are not concerned with image or status or materialistic desires. They just live." He leaned his head toward me, his eyes looking up to where the top of the castle was visible. "Everyone thinks they will reach happiness if they have those things. But it is a constant fight to keep it." I watched him as he took another bite. After he swallowed, he continued, his voice lowering as he said, "Image is a constant act. Status is dependent on that act. And material relies on status." He sighed. "It is all so dreary." He turned to me with his lazy smile. "I suppose I sound like a privileged bastard."

"You took the words right out of my mouth," I teased, and he laughed, lying back in the grass after finishing the rest of the treat.

I lay next to him, and we stared at the sky. "It does make sense, though," I responded. "I think most of humanity is unhappy in some way. Regardless of what they do or do not have."

We lay there in peaceful silence and continued to gaze up at the sky as I ate the last of my cinnamon roll.

After a few moments, he turned his head to me, and a mischievous look crept over his face.

I turned on my side, my elbow propping me up and my hand resting on my cheek. I raised a brow, mirroring his expression. "What?"

He propped himself up too, and his eyes went down to my lips. He leaned forward, and before I could react, he slid his tongue over my bottom lip and pulled away with a grin and half-lidded eyes. My eyes could not have been more expansive, and I knew my face had to be red.

That was the *last* thing I was expecting him to do.

"You had icing on your lip," he said in a smoky voice.

"O-oh," I breathed. His eyes darkened as they trailed to my lips, down my body, and back to my eyes again.

Oh Gods, how am I supposed to react?

Part of me wanted to get up and run far, far away. And the other part, the more dominant part, wanted to jump on top of him and take him right here in this park.

My heart was pounding, and I was thankful that Quill sat up and stood, reaching his hand out so I could stand with him.

"Where to next?" he asked as if nothing happened.

I was tempted to stab the male for making me all high-strung like this. I lifted my shoulders and shook off the thoughts.

"Wait," he said as he gave me a devious smirk. "I recall us making a deal. You said there is a pond we should visit. On a warm day, yes?"

We were nearing the kingdom's exit, heading for Amethyst Pond. Quill was right; I had made a deal with him. I was more than excited to see his reaction to it. Just as we were on our way out, taking a different way than we normally had, Quill's eyes drifted to one of the darker alleys.

"We don't go over there," I whispered, putting my hand in his, surprising myself with how comfortable I felt doing so.

"Why ever not?"

"You haven't heard of Serpent's Cove? It's where the main gang of criminals live. Drugs, violence—you do not want trouble with them."

He frowned toward a group of men perched outside one of the taverns. Their eyes trailed over me, over my body. I shivered in disgust. Even if some might think I was a pretty girl, I was still that, a girl.

He continued his glare, and a man with dark hair and a beard ultimately caught him and leaned off the wall, giving him an equally nasty stare. Quill didn't back down, and neither did the man.

"Quill!" I hissed quietly. He turned his head to me first, dropped the staring contest, and eventually, his eyes met mine.

"Lead on, Flower."

When we finally left the kingdom and passed the bridge, I turned my head toward him.

"What was that about, Quill? Do you want trouble?"

He gave me an exasperated look. "Did you not see how they gazed at you? Like predators to their prey. I did not like that."

I flushed. I did see it, but it was common knowledge most of those men were creeps.

"I am fine. They can't hurt me with their eyes alone, gross as it is." I tugged on his sleeve. "I won't, however, be fine if you go and get yourself pummeled over it."

He tensed and looked forward, us winding through the trees of the Western Forest now.

"You don't think I could take them?"

I clicked my tongue. "It's not that, and you know it. There are a lot of them, and only one of you. Let's forget about them, okay?"

He nodded, but his frown remained.

After a half hour, we made it to Amethyst Pond. Steam emitted from the pond's pure violet water, and an array of flowers were in bloom all around us. I watched Quill as he took it in, complete awe on his face.

"Wow," he whispered. "I see why it is called Amethyst Pond." He glanced around the environment. "Just beautiful." He crouched down and dipped his hand in the water, the corners of his lips turning up as he swirled his fingers. "How pleasant."

I stepped to his side. "I suppose it's warm enough to enjoy on a chilly day, but I prefer it in warmth."

He squinted his eyes. "Are those…?"

"Yes, amethyst crystals are scattered all along the bottom of this pond," I replied as Quill stood. "It's remarkable—"

I did a double take when I caught Quill unbuttoning his shirt.

"W-what are you doing?" I stuttered.

He grinned at me. "What, you bring me to this and don't expect me to swim in it?" he asked while stripping off his shirt.

My mouth fell open.

His body was unlike anything I'd ever seen, certainly nothing like the other boys my age. He was perfectly sculpted, with defined abs and lines pointing downward in a V. His golden skin only made his body appear more toned.

He unbuttoned his pants, his eyes on mine and a mischievous smirk on his face. I quickly turned the other way as he chuckled, and then moments later, I heard a large splash. I whirled over and watched Quill emerge from the water. He brushed his dark hair out of his face, water dripping down him, and his grin was broad.

I glanced at where his clothes were discarded.

He took off *everything*.

"Well, you aren't just going to leave me alone in here, are you?"

I crossed my arms. "I have no interest in getting my clothes wet."

"I'll look away."

I hesitated, and Quill gave me a pout. I couldn't help but grin as I motioned him to turn around.

Am I really going to strip in the middle of the woods?

I studied the muscles in Quill's back, and after debating it for a few more seconds, I slowly began to remove my clothing.

My overdress fell first, then my chemise. My hands trembled as I quickly removed my undergarments and discarded them on the ground.

And there I was. Entirely bare for the world.

I dipped my toes into the water and slowly lowered myself in, just the bottom of my hair getting wet. The last thing I needed was my mascara pouring down my face.

"May I turn around?" he asked.

"I suppose."

Quill spun around, then looked at me with a playful grin.

"Oh, stop your gawking," I giggled as I splashed him.

"It is of great difficulty not to."

I splashed him again, and his eyes widened in excitement as he splashed me back. "It's not wise to start a battle you cannot win, remember?"

"You don't think I can take *you*, Quill?"

He smirked, inched closer to me, and dipped his head down, the water line just below his nose. I could feel my heartbeat quickening as he gripped my waist, pulling me on top of one of his thighs, my sex now resting on his bare skin.

My eyes enlarged as he pushed his leg higher, pressing it into me, and I inhaled sharply at the pleasurable feeling. My hands shook as they gripped his shoulders. He then gently spit the water he had collected in his mouth over my lips, not hiding that wicked amusement in his eyes. I felt desperate pressure between my legs.

Fuck.

I squealed as he lifted his leg slightly higher, causing part of my body to emerge from the water.

My eyes quickly shot downward at myself, noting the droplets dripping down my now-exposed breasts, and then drifted back to Quill's face. My chest was rising and falling, my body trembling as he took my appearance in.

What if he doesn't like what he sees? What if I repulse him?

My breathing became labored. I believed my body to be decent enough, but I had never let anyone see me like this before.

"Lena," he whispered in a sultry voice, his eyes now trailing up from my breasts to meet mine with an intensity I'd never seen before. "You're even more beautiful than I imagined."

I exhaled as he slid his left hand down to my ass and wrapped his right arm around my waist, pulling me close.

What I had been dreaming of for weeks came true as he tugged me close and pressed his lips against mine.

CHAPTER NINE

He gently began to pull away, but I wouldn't have that. I grabbed the sides of his face and pressed my lips onto his again, parting my mouth and then sucking on his bottom lip. He moaned softly, a noise that sent heat throughout my body.

He slid his tongue into my mouth. His sweet taste had me running my hands through his hair as our tongues did delicate circles around one another. Over and over and over again.

It felt like electricity was pooling at my fingertips—like my entire being was buzzing with every stroke of his tongue, every brush of his fingers against my body.

I couldn't contain my urge to grind up against him, so I rubbed myself against his thigh that had me propped up and groaned with pleasure.

Fuck. This felt so good.

Taking things slowly was probably wise, but I couldn't think straight. I just wanted him. I wanted to see and feel and kiss every single part of him.

I pulled my left hand out of his hair, trailed it down his chest and perfectly defined abs, and then gripped his hard length, causing him to inhale sharply.

"Lena—" he breathed, then devoured my mouth hungrily.

He was perfect, and the skin on him was so smooth.

I had never been so aroused. I hoped I knew what I was doing. I had never touched a man before, but I did what I thought would feel good for him. I began rotating my hand along his shaft, barely able to grip his size. His moans kept me sliding my pussy against his thigh harder and faster, the friction becoming unbearably pleasant.

He cupped my right breast with a firm grip and circled his thumb against the hardened peak as his lips trailed to my neck, kissing it desperately.

"Fuck, Quill—" I panted. I stroked him faster, and his deep growls against my neck were about to send me over the edge.

I want him in my mouth, inside of me. I never want this to end.

He slowed and began to pull away, and before I could protest, he lifted his hand to my cheek.

We breathed heavily as we stared into each other's eyes. His pupils were dilated, his eyes half-lidded.

He is perfect. Beautiful. Kind. And he sees me…maybe not that I'm a Mage, but everything else about me. All the good. All the bad.

I ran my thumb against his lips.

And he still wants me despite it.

As he went in to kiss me again, a cracking sound came from

beyond the grove of trees surrounding us. Quill quickly turned, immediately on alert. I knew better than not to trust his instincts, and the simple fact became clear.

We weren't alone.

"What was that?" I whispered.

Quill released me and focused on scanning the forest.

"I'm going to get out. You stay in here for now, understand?" His voice was low, his words spoken in an icy tone I'd never heard from him before.

I nodded as he lifted himself out of the pond. I admired the view of him, just as beautiful as I imagined, but I couldn't focus on it entirely as fear began to settle over me.

Who is here?

Quill quickly put on his undergarments and pants, not bothering with his shirt, as he unsheathed his sword.

We stayed frozen, scanning the forest, when we heard another crunch, absolutely confirming something was around us. A person? An animal?

Or, as Quill might be thinking, a witch?

"Lena, get out and get dressed. If someone appears, I want you to run."

"But Quill, I can fight—"

"No," he snapped. "If I tell you to run, you run."

I hesitated, then moved to leave the pond when the crunching continued and got louder, freezing me in place.

Footsteps. Multiple of whatever was approaching.

I held my breath as he shifted his body in the direction of the sounds, and three males appeared just beyond some trees. Males we knew.

Those bastards from Serpent's Cove.

Damnit! This is why you don't fuck with them!

"Oh, please don't stop on our account," the male whom Quill had stared down chimed, his oily, dark hair rustling in the wind. "It seemed like you two were rather enjoying yourselves."

I felt sick.

How long were they watching us?

"We don't want any trouble," Quill gritted out, clenching the handle of his sword.

"Really?" The man looked to both of his comrades. "'Cause when you stared us down earlier, it sure seemed like you wanted trouble." They inched in closer to Quill, and I made to move out of the pond to stand by him.

"Stay, Lena," Quill barked.

I froze, and the men laughed. "You know," the dark-haired one continued, "you pompous asses from the Inner Ring think you're so much better than us." He chuckled. "Well, not above fucking one of us." His eyes gleamed with desire as he shifted his gaze toward me. "She is rather fuckable, isn't she?" He grinned, exposing yellow, crooked teeth.

I tensed. These men were pigs.

"If you know what's best for you, you will leave here immediately." Quill's tone was nothing but calm fury.

"Ooh, that sounds like a threat, doesn't it, boys?"

The men smirked and drew their weapons. The dark-haired one

and the one with a long beard drew swords, and the more petite man wielded a dagger.

"You know what we should do? Drag that bitch from the pond, plow her, and force him to watch."

Quill's face paled, his eyes glowing with intense rage. He bared his teeth, and he swung at their leader.

The man fumbled back, angling his sword to a fighting position. "You've made a big mistake."

Quill gave a sinister grin. "We'll see about that."

Quill attacked in the blink of an eye, his movements smooth and precise, like a true warrior. All three men dived for him at once, Quill dodging their movements until the one with the dagger dragged it across Quill's chest. I gasped as blood began to flow from the wound.

"Quill!" I cried and went to exit the pond to help.

"Stay put!" he snarled. It took everything in me not to jump out. How could he expect me to sit back and do nothing?

He performed a series of movements, sword clashing against sword until Quill found an opening and impaled the one with a beard in his chest. Blood spurted out of his mouth.

Holy shit.

My breathing staggered, watching Quill withdraw his sword from the man's chest. The man slumped to the ground, a pool of blood forming underneath him.

"You bastard!" The one with the dagger bellowed and charged once again at Quill, simultaneously as their leader. Quill held up his sword and blocked both of their blows at once, then kicked the legs of the man with the sword out from underneath him. He then twirled his own sword and stabbed the man with the dagger right in his neck, a sickening amount of blood spilling out.

The leader glanced at Quill in fear, which quickly turned to anguish as he raised his sword again.

"When I'm through with you, I'll make sure she suffers," he spat, ticking his head toward me.

Quill growled as their swords clashed once more. His chest was still bleeding, but he fought as if nothing were hurt. It was clear just how much Otacian soldier training he had. He moved gracefully, like someone who would quickly ascend the ranks.

The man knocked into Quill, causing him to fumble back, leaving a perfect opening for the man to strike him.

Panicked, I instantly searched around me and found a decent-sized rock. I hurled it for the man's head, and it made a cracking noise on impact. He gripped his head and cried out in distress, and Quill saw his opportunity and plunged his sword into the man's back.

He cried out and tumbled to the ground just before the pond, his eyes unfocused as his head fell to the grass.

Blood. There was so much blood.

I panted, my eyes averting to Quill as he stared at the bodies in horror.

As quickly as they had arrived, they were all gone.

CHAPTER TEN

Quill just stood there, breathing heavily and trembling as he gaped down at the bodies of the men he just killed. The blood on his sword was dripping atop the blades of grass he stood on.

He shifted to me, his look filled with nothing but shame. He stared back down at the bodies, and I knew immediately I needed to comfort him. I exited the pond, quickly squeezed out my hair, and dressed while Quill still fixated on the deceased men.

I softly touched the back of his shoulder. "I'm so sorry you had to do that, Quill…" My voice cracked. He turned toward me, and my eyes flashed down to his chest, which was still bleeding.

"Fuck," I said under my breath. I grabbed my dagger and used it to cut off the bottom of my dress.

"What are you doing?"

"This will soak through quickly, but it's better than nothing." I wrapped the fabric over his wound and around his shoulder, tying it together. He winced.

Gods, my palms, they were burning. Why were they burning?

"I'm sorry you had to see me do that…" His voice was hoarse and laced with shame.

I touched his cheek and met his eyes, ignoring the ache in my hands.

"You have *nothing* to be sorry for." My eyes trailed back to the bodies before us. They weren't the first dead bodies I had seen, not the first people to be slain to save my life. I suppressed a shudder.

"We need to get to my house and get you stitched up," I said as I examined the gash across his chest.

"No." He shook his head. "I-I need to get home—"

"Absolutely not, Quill!"

I'm sure his parents would want that, but Mother and I knew how to do stitches well, and we also had healing elixirs that were better than anything anyone could give him in the kingdom.

I wish Mother could just heal him. I wish I knew how to heal him.

I sighed. But stitches and an elixir would do.

Quill bent down and wiped his sword on one of the men's shirts, clenching his jaw as he did it.

"Let me carry your sword for you."

"Lena—" he began, and I gave him an annoyed look. He sighed. "Very well."

I slung his sword carrier over my body, and he sheathed it for me. It was heavier than I expected. He slipped on his shirt and cloak, wincing in pain, and we gave one last look at the men and all the blood before we left.

Between Quill's black shirt and dark cloak, it was fairly simple making it back without alerting anyone he was injured. We strode as hastily as we could without arousing suspicion, Quill keeping his face a mask of calm.

Mother greeted us with a big grin as we entered the house, which turned into a frown when she observed my torn dress. I instructed Quill to sit on the couch in our living area and to take off his shirt, and Mother's expression then went from confusion to shock as she saw Quill's bloodied makeshift bandage.

"My Gods, what happened?" she breathed as she placed a hand on her chest.

I went into one of our cabinets that contained our first-aid supplies.

Towels, a bucket, rags, a healing elixir, needle and thread, and bandages.

"Assholes from Serpent's Cove, that's what happened," I muttered as I grabbed all of the necessary items and stood up to face her. Mother walked up to Quill and took his bloodied shirt from his hands, a shameful expression on his face. Thank the Gods he wore a black shirt today because even after cleaning a lighter shirt, it would've been impossible to sneak back into the kingdom without alerting authorities.

"They were going to hurt me, but Quill stopped them," I added softly, washing my hands under the cold stream from our sink. It did nothing to calm the burning in my hands. I sighed and added water to the bucket.

"Then, once again, you have my thanks, Quill." Mother smiled, but it quickly faded. "How…how exactly did you stop them?"

He looked at me. Those men might have been monsters, but we could still get in trouble if anyone found out he had killed them. I clenched my jaw.

"Quill fought well and disarmed them all," I quickly said. Mother turned to me, and I tried to keep my face neutral. "They got scared and left," I lied.

Quill gave me a thankful look, but I could sense how terrible he felt about it.

"Well…I hope they don't change their mind and come back," Mother said, eyes worried as she glanced at our front door.

"They won't," I mumbled softly as I approached Quill. I had him scoot over onto a towel and sat next to him. I untied my torn bit of dress to expose his horrid gash.

Mother gasped. "Do you want me to stitch it?"

"No. I can do it," I said. Quill gazed into my eyes and smiled gently. It meant a lot knowing he trusted me. I had given Mother stitches many times on the road. Even though she could heal herself, she insisted it was a skill I needed to know. She would always remove them and heal herself afterward.

I dampened one of the rags in the bucket and brought both up to his chest. I let the water drip down, cleaning away the excess blood. He winced at the cold, his stomach flexing in response. "I'm sorry." I cringed.

Mother began scrubbing the blood from Quill's shirt in the sink.

"This is going to sting a little," I said apologetically after placing the rag and bucket down and reaching for the healing elixir. He just nodded, and I placed a dry rag on his stomach, pulled off the cork to the bottle, and then poured it on his gash. The elixir bubbled as it hit the swollen cut, causing him to hiss. "I know it hurts, but I promise it will help."

He let out a breathy laugh. "It's already starting to feel better."

"There are numbing properties to this one, so hopefully, the stitches won't be too unbearable. It might even prevent it from scarring."

I readied my needle and began stitching, neatly weaving the thread through his wound.

"That's amazing," he whispered. "I don't feel a thing."

I smiled but didn't meet his eyes. Word getting out to the Inner Ring had been a blessing financially, but the elixirs in our home were more potent than those we sold. Those for sale eased pain, but couldn't erase it as this one had.

"It's probably the adrenaline. Surely you feel something?" I asked dishonestly.

"No, I feel nothing."

Quill just continued to study me as I sewed his wound.

"What would I do without you?" he teased, and I glanced up to see his lazy smile.

"Certainly perish," I teased back, continuing to stitch his wound. "I think I should be the one saying that to you," I said quietly enough that Mother couldn't hear over the running water. I paused and looked at him intently. "Thank you. For doing what you had to. I know it couldn't have been easy."

His brows knitted. "Actually, it was one of the easiest things I've ever done." I blinked at the remark, and then he lowered his voice. "The thought of them doing anything to you, especially…what they were suggesting…It would've taken a great effort *not* to kill them."

I flushed and resumed my work.

"Do you think I'm a monster?" he whispered, and I glimpsed up at him, noting his worried expression.

"The furthest thing from it."

As I finished the stitches, Mother walked over, holding his clean shirt.

"It's damp, but the stains are less noticeable, and the smell is gone. Thankfully, you wore a dark shade." She examined the shirt. "Your cloak should conceal it well enough. But do you wish to stay until it's dry?"

"No, that's alright. I really need to get going." He stood up and retrieved the shirt, putting it on. "Thank you both so much for your help."

"Thank you for protecting Lena again." Mother went to hug Quill, and he winced. "Oh, sorry!" Mother cringed.

Quill just laughed softly. "I shall give you my hug of thanks next time," he bowed, then turned to me. "And I'd do it again in a heartbeat," he said quietly before strolling outside, the door clicking shut behind him.

"That boy…he is so special," Mother whispered, looking out our window.

"He is…" And I knew I couldn't deny him for long. What would have happened in the pond had those guys not appeared…we would have gone all the way. I needed to make sure pregnancy was not a possibility.

More importantly, with the danger that had begun to appear as of late, it was time for me to learn something new. If not for my own sake, then to protect Quill if it came down to it.

"Mother?" I said with my eyes on my palms.

"Yes?" she replied, turning her gaze from the window to me.

I exhaled and met her stare. "I want to learn enchantment."

CHAPTER ELEVEN

"So, let's start with the basics."

I had never seen such happiness on Mother's face until I finally agreed to start learning magic. However, my desire had nothing to do with caring about magic and everything to do with getting laid. I bit my lip to prevent my smile from creeping over.

Okay, that wasn't entirely true. Being able to make healing elixirs would be beneficial. Even though Quill's wound wasn't fatal, what if it had been? What if one of those men had managed to strike him? There would have been nothing I could have done to save him. Perhaps I could even learn healing magic on its own.

Wow.

Somehow, Quill had managed to enthrall me so profoundly that it overpowered this fear I had felt my entire life. Well, not completely. The thought of using any other sort of magic still made me break out in a sweat. But throwing some herbs in a pot and using a small amount of magic couldn't be that hard. And how could learning healing be dangerous?

"Lena, are you listening?"

I snapped out of my daydream. "Yes, sorry."

Mother plopped a thick, ancient-looking tome on the table, and my eyes widened.

"You've kept a spell book with you?" I hissed in disbelief.

"Yes," she said quietly. "I know many by memory, but there's plenty I do not. You never know when one might come in handy."

I figured I would have to ask Mother about a contraceptive elixir in as nonobvious a way as possible, but knowing that it was most likely in this spell book helped a lot.

She flipped open the book to one of the first pages.

"Healing elixirs, infused with healing magic," she said as she pointed at one recipe. "Depending on what type of elixir you wish to enchant, you must tap into that power source. Healing is one of the more novice-style magic types."

I furrowed my brows. "Well, what are the harder types?"

"Healing magic can be learned by any Mage, as you know. Elixirs infused by elemental magic can obviously only be made by those who have unlocked that power," she mumbled as she flipped through the book. I wondered how old this tome must be as the pages were yellowed and crinkled. "Not only can the difficulty vary based on the type of magic, but also its efficacy. Expert healing Mages can make elixirs that heal gaping wounds, whereas the novice ones can maybe heal a paper cut." She stopped flipping and looked at me. "That will be our first goal."

Mother decided on the most basic healing elixirs to start, and though she had memorized it, she let me look in the book at the recipe listed. I trailed my fingers along the aged, darkened pages.

I wonder where she got this from…

Mother gathered some dried herbs along with other ingredients that I was familiar with.

Chamomile, milk thistle, sage, Epsom salt.

Life had changed so much in the month since I had met Quill… since I held my dagger to that girl's neck. My hands and body had ached with the desire to let out my abilities my whole life, but never as much as in the past few weeks.

I mixed the ingredients over the wood-burning stove, just as I had seen Mother do many times. That wasn't the hard part.

"Okay," Mother said cautiously, removing the mixture from the heat. She looked at me with nothing but seriousness. "Healing magic resonates here—" she said as she touched her fingers to each of her palms.

I frowned and stared down at my own palms.

"Oh, I'm foolish," Mother muttered, then pulled a knife from a drawer and dragged it across the skin on her forearm, blood beading along the fresh cut.

I gasped. "What are you doing?"

"It'll be easier for you to tap into the power this way." She pushed her bleeding arm forward. "Look and identify what you feel."

With wide eyes, I focused on the bleeding cut.

Heal it. I want to heal it.

I began to feel burning in my palms, and my eyes shot down to them again.

"Did you feel anything when Quill needed those stitches?"

I blinked. "Y-yes…my palms started to burn, just as they are now."

"Excellent!" Mother exclaimed. "Now, hold your hand above my cut. And concentrate. Will yourself to heal me."

I began to shake, worried I might do something wrong. Slowly, I brought my hand above her sliced skin and closed my eyes.

Heal her. Heal her.

I repeated it in my head over and over until I gradually felt the burning subside. My eyes shot open to my mother's wound, and I could only stare in disbelief.

"By the Gods," she whispered.

A warm glow emitted from my palms before slowly dissipating. I withdrew my hand, and she carefully wiped away the blood, revealing perfectly smooth skin.

"You grasped that much faster than I expected." She grinned. "I believe you to be gifted, Lena. I always have."

I didn't reply—I just gave a nervous smile at the small relief that release gave me.

We spent the rest of the day making multiple healing elixirs, and it began to feel like second nature. Mother warned me not to expect the rest of my powers to come so quickly, but I took the win anyway.

The paralyzing feeling took over again, and I felt a…presence over me. Try as I might, I could not move my arms or open my eyes.

"Lena…Lena…can you hear me?"

I jolted up from my bed in a cold sweat, panting and with a dull headache. My room was still dark, the small clock on my nightstand displaying 2:14 a.m.

Another nightmare, one just like before. Only this time, it was a voice. Familiar, yet not. I sighed as I pulled the cover off, letting the air cool off my body.

I was going crazy. It had been weeks since this last happened. I had almost forgotten all about it. Was I losing it? Or was that perhaps someone trying to talk to me—someone who knew my name?

I needed to tell Mother, but that could wait until morning. After cooling down, I snuggled back into my quilt and, after a long while, drifted back to sleep.

When I mentioned my nightmares to Mother, she just shrugged them off, and I felt silly for even mentioning it. She said it could just be sleep paralysis, which wasn't as comforting as she thought it would be.

Another week had passed, and I couldn't wait to see Quill, but I was also nervous. We had been so…close, intimate, the last time we saw one another. I wasn't sure how we would talk about what happened.

And then there were his injuries. Mother's healing elixir would have helped, but it wouldn't have been as powerful as possible since we couldn't risk arousing suspicion. I knew it would be healed, though the stitches would need removal if he hadn't already removed them himself.

I just wanted to see him. So, I waited.

And I waited some more.

And he never showed.

It was now 7:00 a.m., and Quill was still nowhere to be seen. He had been consistently on time for the last five weeks. This was the first time he hadn't shown.

What if he regretted what happened between us? What if he got in trouble? What if he was hurt?

My mind instantly went to the worst-case scenario, and I was brought back to reality by Mother's hand on my shoulder, her deep green cloak on as she was about to head over to our stand.

"I'm sure everything's okay. He may be busy today."

I frowned and looked at my feet. "I'll just wait in case he shows up," I said quietly.

Mother nodded, then left.

I finally went to deliver orders just before 9:00 a.m. The entire time I was delivering, my mind kept wandering. I kept glancing around, hoping to see him, but I never did. Once the last order was complete at 9:38 a.m., I decided to walk through the Inner Ring in the hopes of catching him. Like always, I passed well-dressed folk who gave me dirty looks like I was some rat. Normally, it would bother me, but I only cared about seeing Quill.

I should know where he lives.

It was almost 10:00 a.m., and I sighed in defeat, making my way down the steps and back to the Outer Ring. As I made my way home, I glanced back at the darkened area that was Serpent's Cove, and my stomach dropped.

What if they took him?

I froze.

What if he never made it home? Or what if he did, and they stole him from his home?

Fuck… what if he'd been there this entire time?

What if he was being tortured?

Anger took over as my thoughts continued to spiral, and I found myself charging toward Serpent's Cove.

If I knew one thing for certain, it was that Quill would do whatever it took to protect me. He'd proven that on multiple occasions. So, if the Serpents had him and were trying to find me too, Quill would remain silent.

They better hope to the Gods he is okay.

Under my cloak, I gripped my dagger, staring at the men smoking outside, backs resting against the brick building of the tavern from before. Despite it being morning, there were many outside, probably all drunk.

I made eye contact with a man I had seen last week; his smug look turned to disdain as I charged toward him.

"Where is he?" I demanded.

He cackled. "Who do you think you're talking to, little girl?"

I whipped out my dagger and, without thinking, swung it at the man. He cursed as he dodged it.

"You bitch," he huffed, then wielded the sword on his back.

Panic overwhelmed me as he prowled toward me. My head craned up to meet his sneer, and I feared I was in over my head.

No. Quill needs me.

I smothered the panic down until all that was left was vengeance.

The man began swinging his sword, and, using the maneuvers Quill had taught me, I dodged every one of them.

"Tell me where he is, you bastard! What did you do to him?" I shouted.

The man let out a cruel laugh, and I bit back my tears. I spun my dagger when I saw an opening and slashed his leg.

He yelped, then went to swing once more. I barely dodged, and the tip of his sword slashed my cheek, blood now coursing down my face.

The man saw an opening and took it, slamming his body into me. The power of it had me on the ground in seconds, my tailbone throbbing in pain from the blunt force. He stepped forward and kicked me in my side, and I choked as the wind was knocked out of me.

"You know," he hissed, "a few of my men are missing. I wonder if you had anything to do with that, considering your boyfriend glared them down last week." He delivered another kick to my side, and I cried out, his comrades cheering beside us. "But, seeing as though you're a weak bitch, I don't see that as a possibility."

I clenched my fists, holding on to my dagger as tears flooded my eyes. He kicked me over and over again.

He wasn't wrong. Quill was the one who had taken out those men, and I had just stood there and watched. If they took Quill, how could I stand a chance?

My head was spinning as another kick turned me to my front, and I took that opportunity to shove my dagger into his lower leg. He cried out, and just as the other men came charging at me, I heard a voice yelling my name.

"LENA!"

CHAPTER TWELVE

My eyes shot to my right, and I saw Quill rushing to me. Not imprisoned. Not being tortured.

Fuck, he wasn't even here!

The man with my dagger in his shin ripped it from his leg, and blood spurted out. He gave me a savage smile as Quill came closer.

"Quill, watch out!" I screamed.

His eyes widened, and he moved out of the way just in time as the man launched my dagger toward him, barely missing.

"Let her go!" Quill raged. The darkness in his eyes was unlike any time I'd seen him, even during what happened at Amethyst Pond.

One of the other men let out a dry laugh. "Let her go? She's the one who charged in here and attacked!"

His eyes shot down to me in disbelief.

"Why would you do that?!" Quill demanded.

"You…you didn't show up. I-I was worried they took you…" I slapped my hand to my forehead, feeling like a complete idiot.

A second later, the man I had stabbed seized me by the neck, raising me to his eye level. I reached for his grasp and began to choke.

Quill unsheathed his sword and walked closer.

"Put. Her. Down."

The man laughed. "You think I'm scared of you, boy?"

Quill gave a dark smile, his voice low as he said, "Your friends sure as hell were."

I couldn't breathe.

"Q-Quill—" I barely choked out as the man bared his teeth and tightened his grip on my throat. I wanted to tell him to run, but I couldn't get out any more words as the man squeezed harder.

In the blink of an eye, Quill charged forward, moving savagely as he pierced his sword through the man's side.

His eyes enlarged as they slowly traveled to his fatal wound. Even the men around him stilled in fright, gaping at what they witnessed.

Quill's expression remained dark as he withdrew his sword, causing the man to collapse, me with him. My body hit the stony ground once more, and I gasped for air. Quill took a stance as he eyed all the men readying their weapons, but Otacian soldiers infiltrated the area before they could strike.

"Drop to your knees!" they ordered. The men of Serpent's Cove snarled but obeyed.

"Are you alright, miss?" one of them asked as they raised me from the ground and surveyed my wounds.

"Yes." My voice was hoarse from being strangled.

"That bitch is the one who started this, walking in with a dagger and attacking us like it was nothin'." The man speaking then pointed at Quill. "And that one killed Fang. Just stabbed his sword through 'em."

The soldiers glanced in Quill's direction, then looked back with raised eyebrows. I met Quill's eyes, the rising and falling of his chest, and the sweat beading along his hairline portraying just how terrified he was. But instead of them asking Quill questions, they asked the man, "How much have you had to drink today, sir?"

"You've gotta be kidding me," he snapped. "You all turn a blind eye to injustice just 'cause he's one of you!"

"Do you need medical attention?" the soldier asked me, his blue eyes laced with concern.

"No," I said softly, touching the cut on my face and wincing. "Just a scratch." I let out a nervous laugh and looked back over to Quill, whose brows were tightly knit.

He was pissed at me, and I couldn't blame him. I stood as the men involved were arrested and the body of the man named Fang was being dealt with. The soldiers asked if I needed to be escorted home, but I insisted I could make it myself. Then I rushed away, Quill following.

We walked together silently for a couple of minutes, Quill just slightly behind me. Then he grabbed my wrist, whirling me around to face him.

"How could you do something so stupid, Lena?" Quill fumed.

I bit back tears. "I was worried you—"

"Yes, you already said that." He ran his hand through his raven-black hair. "The first thing I told you when I started to train you was you cannot let your emotions lead you to make poor decisions." He put his hands on my shoulders, his face just inches away, his honey-colored eyes looking deeply into mine. "I don't care if you thought I was in there or not. I would have never wanted you to do what you just did—risk yourself for me."

I crossed my arms, tilting my head as I assessed him. "Would you have done it for me?"

He tightened his jaw. "That is not the point," he gritted out. "I am well-trained and actually would have stood a chance."

"So, you're saying I'm not well-trained?" I challenged.

He sighed, eyes trailing over the fresh cut on my face. His thumb brushed just next to it.

I hated him being angry with me. I just wanted us back to how we were before. His eyes trailed down to my lips, and when they met mine again, they softened.

"I have been training for many years, so even though I am training you well, Flower, it is not enough. Not yet."

"Are you saying you will train me for years then?"

A slight smirk appeared. It was an effort not to plant my lips on his, but before I lost control, he lowered his hand and wrapped it around mine.

"Let's get you home and cleaned up," he said quietly.

We continued the rest of the way in silence. His hand in mine was a source of comfort, yet the feeling gave me so many flutters I feared I'd fly away. I was grateful for it, though. Otherwise, the hum of pain radiating from my ribs might cause me to keel over.

The creaking floorboards welcomed us as we entered my home.

Thankfully, Mother hadn't returned from the market yet. The stinging in my cheek was bothersome but not too painful.

"Where do you keep your first aid? This cabinet, yes?"

"I-I'll grab it."

I trembled as I walked over to fetch the supplies. I knew Mother kept the spell book in the same place, and we didn't need him finding that. If he wasn't here, I knew I could just heal my cut myself.

I gathered the items and began to take them to the bathroom to clean my face when Quill stopped me.

"Allow me?" he asked softly.

I nodded as he motioned for me to sit on the couch. I gently sat and watched as he went to retrieve water from the sink, mirroring what I had just done for him the week prior. His brows came together as he began to fill the small bucket, the water grazing his fingertips.

"Does it not get warm?"

"We're in the Outer Ring, Quill. The only time we have warm water is if we heat it ourselves," I commented as I motioned toward the stove.

"Oh, right," he said, flushing.

He stepped over and set the bucket down, dipping the rag in as he sat beside me. He tilted my face toward him with his hand on my chin and began to clean my wound gently.

I stared into his amber eyes as they studied my cut. His full lips were just barely parted, his muscular forearms…

I squeezed my thighs together, attempting to ignore the friction I so desperately desired.

"Where were you?" I asked quietly.

His beautiful eyes flickered to mine.

"I got caught up in some…family drama. I couldn't get out of the house when I wanted," he mumbled, placing the rag down and getting another ready. He lifted the healing elixir and raised an eyebrow at me. I nodded, and he poured some on the dry rag in his hand. He hesitated as he brought it to my face.

"It's okay," I said softly, and he placed it on the cut, causing me to wince.

"I'm sorry," he whispered, dabbing the area. His mouth was so close to mine.

"How is your injury?" I asked.

"Good. I took the stitches out myself. I have a scar, but that is to be expected, being a member of the army. I will have many more scars in the future, I'm sure."

I frowned. If I could have healed him, he wouldn't have scarred.

He would never *scar if I could use my magic freely.*

"Do your parents know about me?" He stilled as my words came out. "Surely they ask where you're off to at such early hours every week."

He clenched his jaw. "My mother does. Not my father." He placed the rag down and ran his thumb along my cheek. "Good thing you don't need stitches. That man better not have scarred your beautiful face," he mumbled, then dragged his hands down my sides, causing me to wince once more. "Let me see," he murmured.

I hesitated but lifted my shirt enough for him to see my side. Horror overcame his features, and he cursed under his breath. A small gasp left my lips when I glanced down.

My ribs were covered in dark red bruises that I knew would be purple in a few hours. Not surprising as that man had kicked the shit out of me. It was still surreal to look at, though. I imagined my neck was bruised too.

He tensed. "I am so sorry I wasn't here," he whispered as he studied the bruises.

"I'm sorry I panicked…" I whispered back. "…And I'm sorry you had to take another life to save me."

He looked back up, held my face in his hands, then pulled my mouth to his, kissing me deeply. My heart began to race as I scooted closer, wrapping my hand around his neck, gripping the hair at his neckline.

He pulled away gently and rested his forehead on mine. "I would gladly do it again if it came to it, Lena. Do not be sorry." He kissed my forehead. "But please, don't put yourself in danger. Especially for me."

I pulled away and laced my hands behind his neck. "There are few things I would put myself in danger for, and you are one of them." I smiled. "But I will try to think things through next time, should there be a next time."

He gave me his lazy smile, and I wanted to rip his clothes off at the sight of it. I wondered if he saw that in my eyes as he pulled me closer and began devouring me. A small moan escaped my lips, and I felt his smile as he continued to trace his tongue over mine.

His hand trailed down to my hips, and he pulled me on his lap, my legs now resting on either side of him.

"Quill, my mother—"

"Shh," he hushed as he kissed me again, his hands now gripping my ass.

I moaned again and couldn't stop as I began to grind myself against him. He growled against my lips, then receded, a playful smile on his face.

"Do you know how badly I wish to remove these off you, Lena?" he asked as he tugged on the loops of the pants I wore today.

"Then fucking do it," I responded with my own lazy grin.

His eyes flashed, and his mouth captured mine once more, our tongues exploring each other as my hands ran through his hair. The smell of pine and citrus overwhelmed my senses. Why did he smell so damn good? Everything about him was addicting.

He began trailing light kisses down my cheek and along my jaw until he reached the side of my neck. Then, carefully avoiding the sore areas, he drew my skin into his mouth and sucked hard, causing me to hiss. He chuckled against me, then trailed his tongue over the small hurt and transitioned into kissing my neck passionately.

"I desperately wish to taste every part of you," he whispered between kisses.

I rolled my hips against him, and his answering groan was pure ecstasy. His hands began to follow up underneath the back of my shirt, cautious not to hurt me with my wounded sides. His calloused fingers ignited goosebumps all over my body. Just as my shirt started to lift, I heard Mother's voice outside, and our eyes shot open.

"Shit," I muttered as I flew off and plopped down next to him; both our breathing staggered. Quill gave me a grin, and I bit down on my lip to try and prevent mine.

Mother opened the door, saying goodbye to one of our neighbors, when her eyes caught on Quill and me. I could feel my face heating. She had an *"I know what's going on"* look as she pranced over to stand before us.

"Hello, Minerva," Quill greeted with his usual smoothness as he lolled on the couch. His black hair was tousled messily from my fingers running through it.

"Hello, Quill. So, you showed up after all," she said, crossing her arms and giving a smile. "Hope I wasn't interrupting anything." Her eyes trailed to me, and then her brows raised as she examined my face.

"What happened?!" she exclaimed.

"I'm fine," I interjected. "Quill, once again, saved my ass." I rubbed the back of my head.

I gave her the rundown of what happened, once again leaving out the details that a man died.

"Wait, people were talking about that at the market as I was leaving."

Quill and I glanced at each other.

Fuck.

"They said one of the men was stabbed and *died*," Mother persisted, the crease between her brows deepening.

My eyes nervously went from Quill to my mother.

"That was me, I-I killed him," I blurted out.

Mother's eyes widened, and Quill put his hand on my shoulder. I glimpsed at him, and he smiled softly.

"I killed him," Quill said calmly. "Lena had hurt him, and I could tell his ego would not have let that slide. He was choking her." He inhaled. "I had no other choice."

"You went in there wielding your fists and managed to hurt a guy?" Mother questioned in disbelief.

"I gave her a dagger!" Quill exclaimed, Mother's eyes flying to him.

"No." I shook my head quickly. "I bought a dagger before I ever even met him!"

"Whoa, whoa, whoa." Mother held up her palms. "There is a lot of lying in this room right now." She faced Quill. "Thank you for saving my daughter again, but I'm going to have to ask you to leave."

"Mother—"

"We need to talk in private."

"I understand," Quill replied before I could protest. He grabbed my hand and kissed it, smiling at me through his dark lashes. "I will see you next week. At the *correct* time," he insisted. He stood up and nodded to Mother before heading out the door.

She stared at me for a moment, her arms crossed against her chest.

"Tell me what's going on."

CHAPTER THIRTEEN

Iknew lying wasn't a good idea at this point. So, I told her everything. Why I decided to get a dagger, how Quill had agreed to train me, and how he had killed those men in the forest that day.

She just sat next to me in silence for a while. She ordered me to heal my neck bruises and the cut on my face but said it would be too suspicious to heal everything completely, especially those bruises on my ribs. Those I was to deal with.

"I don't understand why you would hide getting a weapon from me. I've *always* wanted you to be able to protect yourself," she said quietly.

"I just…" I sighed. "I knew how much you wanted me to learn magic for that same reason. If I admitted I wanted to be able to protect myself—"

"You didn't want to argue about magic."

I nodded, and she exhaled loudly.

"I know how hesitant you have felt about magic, but if you still feel that way, why learn enchantment…to make elixirs?"

I flushed, and she sat straighter, surprise on her face.

"You wanted to learn the contraceptive elixir, didn't you?"

My eyes were going to pop out of my head. "N-no." I started shaking my head.

"Don't lie to me, Lena—no more lies." Then, to my stupefaction, she began to laugh.

I glowered at her. "What is so funny?"

She held her hand to her mouth, attempting to contain any future chuckles. "It's just, after how many *years* of trying to convince you to learn any magic, liking a boy is what it took."

I groaned, stood from the couch, and began heading to my room. "It wasn't just for that. Obviously, I have been getting in danger lately. I may need to know other things in a dire situation."

"That is what I have been saying this whole time." I was almost in my room when she spoke again. "How did he not get in trouble for killing that man?" Her tone had changed, and I halted where I stood.

I pivoted to her. "I'm…I'm not sure. It was almost like the guards didn't notice him." I pinched the bridge of my nose. "And as for those in the woods, I'm not sure if they've been found or not."

"By the Gods, Lena," she muttered. "I can't believe you kept this from me. Why?"

"Quill felt shame and fear from it, even if he wouldn't admit it. And it felt like the least I could do for him saving me was keep that a secret for him."

"It seems like ever since you met him, there's been trouble."

"You're blaming him?" I asked, crossing my arms.

"No. It's just an observation. We know what has happened in the past when you've been afraid for your life," she said cautiously. She didn't need to say what she meant, as I knew my magic had been uncontrollable in the past when my life had been in jeopardy.

I shifted, my hand now on my doorknob.

"He's in love with you."

I hesitated, then looked at her. "I'm in love with him."

"Love can make you do foolish things, Lena. You need to be careful."

I nodded and opened my door.

"Lena?"

"Yes?"

"I will allow you to still train with him. But you will continue learning enchantment, and not just for birth control."

I huffed and rolled my eyes, my face blushing yet again, and I closed my door behind me, Mother's soft chuckle barely audible.

The rest of the week went by in a blur. Mother made sure to use knowing about my training as a weapon and forced me to study enchantment daily. Thankfully, there had been no other discussion about the contraceptive elixir, though when she wasn't around, I had glossed through the spell book and found the recipe. The issue wasn't gathering the herbs so much as it was wielding and executing the magic itself.

Magic had been dormant in my body for so long that I didn't

even know where to start. Luckily for me, the contraceptive elixir utilized a form of healing magic, and since I had been doing decently with that, I felt optimistic. However, I didn't know when I would feel confident enough that my concoction would do what it was supposed to. Other elixirs Mother began teaching me about were illusion and speed.

"I wonder if there are any Warlocks in Otacia," I thought out loud as I read the recipe for an invisibility elixir, a form of illusion magic.

"It's possible, even though their numbers are less than the Mages," Mother replied.

Humans also considered Warlocks to be witches, but they were different from us. While we both had pointed ears, a Warlock's differentiating feature was their pupil-less eyes. Like us, they could glamour their appearance to appear human. Their abilities, however, differed. Their magic could only work using spoken spells. Most impressively, every one of them could shape-shift, which only a small number of Mages with that as a special ability could do.

"What about Vampires?" I asked, my mouth drying at just the mention of them.

"I try not to imagine them in the city. Typically, they are caught quickly in environments like this."

Though I had never encountered a Vampire, I sometimes lost sleep over the idea. They could only lurk at night, as the sun would turn them to dust. I wondered if I was being prejudiced just like those who feared Mages, but Vampires survived off blood, after all.

"Why do you have two swords, Quill?" I asked, eyeing the second sword and sheath against his back. The week had passed, and Quill was pleased to see my face had healed completely. There might have been a scar, but I healed it myself once I had the chance.

"It's a gift for you, Flower," Quill smirked as he removed the dark purple sheath and pulled out the sword, whose handle was obsidian with silver decals. A blue gemstone lay in its center.

"You got this for me?" I gaped.

"Seeing as though your dagger didn't hold up well in your fight," he said as he placed the sword back in the sheath and handed it to me, "I figured it was time to teach you a more advanced weapon."

"Thank you…" I mumbled, unsheathing the sword myself and staring with awe. "To be fair, you never trained me with the dagger. Only evasive maneuvers."

He smirked. "Yes, I know. We will be going over both today, but don't beat yourself up if you don't grasp it immediately. It will take months before you're truly proficient in either."

He approached me as I continued to gawk at my new sword.

"This is a greatsword," he murmured.

"Well, I figured it would be if you got it."

"No," he chuckled. "It's a greatsword. It's meant to be used with both hands, and its long blade allows for superior cutting capabilities."

"Oh." I flushed.

Dumbass. I should've known that.

"The best advantage of using a two-handed sword is its increased power," he continued. "It's longer and heavier than a one-handed sword, so if we can get this down, learning the latter should be a piece of cake."

I bounced it in my hands, surprised by the weight. I unsheathed it fully, admiring the craftsmanship up close. I didn't even want to think of what it had cost.

"Your arms will be sore after today, but you will grow used to it over time." He quirked a brow. "Are you feeling up to this? If not, we can wait until next week."

"I got this."

He grinned and led me through a few different stances, all of them feeling slightly awkward.

"Will you ever fight against me? Give me some real experience?"

He laughed. "Once you get this down, I shall consider it. Don't want to kill your confidence just yet." He gave me a wink, and I nudged him with my hip.

"I think I'll give you a run for your money," I breathed, the switching of movements beginning to hitch my breathing.

"I don't doubt that for a second."

That made me smile.

"I had a question," I asked as we packed our stuff an hour later. It felt foreign yet exactly right having this sword along my back.

"Anything, Flower."

"Why haven't you told your father about me?"

He was quiet for a while.

I bit my lip. "Are you ashamed of me?" I asked quietly.

He spun toward me. "No. Why would I be ashamed of you, Lena?"

I gave him a knowing look, and he stopped before me. "My father has expectations of me," he continued. "My mother does too, but my father is not as…understanding as her."

"So, it's because *he* would be ashamed of *you*."

"It's because his opinion doesn't mean shit when it comes to you," he stated bluntly. "No one's does."

I blinked. "I think that's the first time I've heard you swear."

He gave me his lazy smile and leaned down so his face was next to mine. "I guess you're rubbing off on me, Flower," he murmured into my ear, his hot breath sending chills down my body, causing me to inhale sharply. He clicked his tongue. "Such a bad influence."

He drew away from me, his eyes lustful as he studied me. He inhaled and glanced toward the kingdom.

"I should be heading home now."

"Really?" I pouted. "You tease me and then say you're leaving?"

He smirked, his eyes darting down at me. "Unless you want our first time to be on the forest floor, I think it is best I go."

My mouth dropped open, and I was left speechless. He continued smirking and laced his hand in mine as we wandered home.

When we had just about reached my house, I got the courage to ask him something I had been thinking about over the past few weeks.

"Hey."

He turned, eyebrow lifted.

"There is this festival next month for the Summer Solstice. It happens every summer in the Outer Ring. I-I understand if you aren't interested, but—"

He pulled me into an embrace and kissed me softly. Gods, I could melt in his arms.

"I would love to go with you," he responded, seeing where I was going with my question. "When is it?"

"Three Saturdays from now. It starts around 7:00 p.m. Well, it starts sooner, but it's more fun at night."

He contemplated. "I don't know if I can be there at 7:00," he said. "But I could probably meet you around 9:00 or so. Would that work?"

I felt my face light up. "Yes, yes, that would be great. It goes all night." I beamed.

He grinned and kissed me once more. "I will let you know for certain next time I see you." He tilted his head to the side. "What does one wear to an occasion like this?"

"Oh," I blushed. "Anything you'd wear would be good. Normally, the women wear their best gowns, the men dressing in the finest clothes they have."

After cutting the dress I wore when Quill was attacked, I realized I didn't have anything for it. Maybe the dress I wore when Queen Ryia visited. Either way, I would figure it out.

"Understood. See you then, Lena." He pressed his lips to my forehead before walking off.

CHAPTER FOURTEEN

"Ugh!" I cried out in frustration, holding my hand over the concoction on our stove. It was a simple stamina elixir, yet I couldn't get anything out.

Three weeks had passed, and the Summer Solstice Festival was tomorrow. While I had healing down pat, stamina was driving me mad. I couldn't seem to grasp it.

It had also been three agonizing weeks of being alone with Quill and not being on top of him. He kept his composure most of the time, insisting on training me like I wanted. But toward the end of our sessions, he would cave, and we would make out in the grass for as long as we could. I would grind on him, and he would grasp my breasts, but it never went further than that.

I did appreciate that he had started being more open with me. He told me about his best friends Hendry and Edmund, two guys around our age who were also soldiers in training. I wondered when I would meet them.

"Don't try to force it," Mother commented. "Stamina comes from the lungs. Focus on pulling the power from there."

"What does that even mean?" I groaned.

"Just try."

I huffed, then closed my eyes. Another few moments went by, and still nothing. My hand slumped down.

"Maybe I'm just not cut out for this," I complained. "What power do I have? Suppressing it all this time has probably ruined any potential."

Sure, healing was easy for me, but that was essentially effortless for every Mage.

"Come, sit down." Mother grabbed my hand as we moved to sit on the sofa in our living room. "You said you are in love with Quill, yes?"

I frowned. "I don't understand what that—"

"Just yes, right?"

Still scowling, I nodded.

"Think of him and feel where that comes from in your body. The warm fuzzy feelings—before you get the wrong idea."

I grimaced and then decided to think of everything about him that made me love him.

"Now, hold out your hand and concentrate."

I did as she said and closed my eyes.

I thought of my first encounter with him, my silly nickname, and his lazy smile. I thought of our first kiss and our banter.

I thought of his kindness and how he teased me. How his hair curled against his forehead, how he smelled.

Suddenly, I felt a familiar tingling in my fingertips. My eyes flew open, and I gaped at the sight. Tiny bolts of electricity were emitting from them.

"I knew it," Mother said with a smug smile.

"H-how do I make it stop?" I panicked.

"Those feelings, imagine putting them away into a box. Imagine closing your chest. That is where that power resides."

I did just that, visualizing a box, smothering my feelings until they were a distant thought. I inhaled, and the electricity faded after a few moments of concentration.

"I…I can wield electricity," I whispered, my whole body shaking with a mixture of relief and fear.

"It seems so. I could wield it after a few months of knowing your father." She held my hand, and I met her warm, brown eyes. "It can only be unlocked after being truly in love. Some people think they are in love with someone, but you know it is real when electricity is your new power. You're very young to have it. To have something so real."

My brows creased, and I looked at my hands.

"To wield it in battle, or in general, you must be in tune with that part of your body. It is how you can turn it off and on."

"I'm supposed to access lovey-dovey feelings when my life is potentially endangered?"

She laughed through her nose. "Not after you get used to the sensation. Once you know what part of you is connected to it, it will be second nature."

We were startled by a knock on our door. Even after all these years, the idea of somehow being caught was always a fear.

Mother opened the door to find a rotund gentleman with a handlebar mustache holding a large package.

"Delivery for Lena Daelyra," he stated.

Mother gave me a perplexed look, then signed for the package. When she finished, the man waltzed away with a smile.

"For…me? From whom?"

"It's anonymous," Mother said, turning the package all around.

We both shrugged, and Mother placed the package on our kitchen table as I closed our door. I just glared at it.

"Well, are you going to open it or me?" Mother asked, barely holding in her excitement.

Hesitantly, I grabbed a knife, slowly opening the package. When I flipped open the lids, Mother gasped, and my mouth popped open. I held the fabric and pulled up, revealing a stunning navy-blue gown. My mouth was still open as I placed the dress on the bare table and picked up the small note that lay inside the box.

I cannot wait to see you dancing in this.

All my love,

- Quill

My face flushed, and I pulled the note close.

"From Quill?" Mother asked.

I nodded, placed the note in my pocket, and grasped the dress once more.

"It's beautiful," I breathed.

It was a halter-style gown made of tulle and pongee. It plunged down the front, and the back was open. Navy and silver flowers spilled down one side of the front, delicately spreading out as they traveled down the dress.

"That had to have cost a fortune, the detail…" She shook her head. "That boy is head over heels."

I smiled, hugging the dress.

"Well, are you going to try it on?" she added.

"Yes!" I squealed.

I ran to my room, stripped off my clothes, stepped into the gown, and hoisted it up, tying the tulle top around my neck. I called Mother in after that to zip what little fabric was on my back.

When she finished, I turned to my mirror and reddened when I saw myself.

"Completely stunning," Mother said with silver in her eyes. She quickly went to wipe at them.

I had never felt beautiful before, but in this dress, I certainly felt special. The plunging neckline ended just below my sternum, and my breasts lay nicely.

I twirled, the skirt flowing around me.

"You'll have to help me with my hair and makeup on Saturday," I beamed.

"Like you'll need it!" she giggled. "But, yes, of course, I will!"

After taking my time and enjoying being in the gown, I hung it up carefully in my closet. I grimaced when I slipped my cream sweater and leggings back on, but as drab as they were, they were comfortable.

After dinner and washing up, Mother turned in early, and I decided to give it a go at the contraceptive elixir.

Wild carrot seed, pennyroyal, wormwood.

I knew these were ones I grew in the garden after I learned that Mother made herself this brew every month. While I didn't think she was in relations with anyone, it's said that this concoction also eliminates the monthly cycle.

I wish I had known about this sooner!

I snuck outside, the summer sun still providing enough light despite it nearly being set. I clipped away at what I needed, then quietly returned.

I got to work, mashing the herbs in a mortar and pestle and adding them to a small pot of boiling water, allowing it to infuse. Once I removed it from the heat, I poured it into a bowl and stared.

Slowly, I reached my hands over and focused on the burning that had begun in my palms.

I can do this.

My palms began to glow, and I concentrated on what the text said: to visualize the magic stemming from your lower palms.

Suddenly, the glow went out, and I cursed under my breath. I tried repeatedly. Eventually, I thought it might have worked, but like hell I'd risk it.

I sighed and tossed my mixture out in the back. So much for that.

I felt tense…and that now familiar sensation began to take hold. I was paralyzed once more. I wanted to thrash out, to fumble out of bed, hell, even scream. But any effort proved futile.

"Do not be scared, child." The woman's voice was clear and soft… almost gentle.

Whose voice is that?

"You will know in time. I am just testing our connection for when destiny takes hold."

What…? Can she read my thoughts?

I could swear I heard a chuckle. "I can in this state, yes."

Why can't I move?

"Our connection is too faint; I can only reach you when you are in deep sleep. Eventually, I should be able to speak to you when you are wide awake."

I wanted so badly to move my body. The woman's tone was kind. But could I trust her?

Who are you?

She hesitated. "My name is Kayin."

What do you want from me?

"Even I don't know that yet. Just that our connection must be stronger. Drift back to sleep, Lena."

And for once, I didn't wake up in a cold sweat. Instead, I peacefully slumbered once more.

I never mentioned my dream to Mother. It was too strange and probably not real. Those with sleep paralysis see hallucinations. Perhaps I was just hearing them. Though Kayin…I am surprised I remembered her name.

Mother was dusting blush on my cheeks after finishing my eye makeup and hair on the evening of the Summer Solstice Festival. It was twisted up in a high ponytail, pieces in the front pulled loose to curl around my face.

"I wish I had jewelry," I murmured as Mother put on my lip gloss. Though both of my ears were adorned with two steel hoops, I wished for something more glamorous to pair with the stunning gown Quill had gifted me.

"This dress would steal the attention off it, anyway." She grinned, then pulled the makeup brush away from my face. "There!"

After, she helped me into my dress. The stunning floral decals still caught my breath, and when I glanced into my mirror again, now fully dolled up, I felt my eyes burning.

"Don't ruin my masterpiece!" Mother squealed, then lightly dabbed around her eyes to avoid smudging her makeup. "Or this one," she laughed.

I wished she had a fancy gown, too, but she wore a green satin dress she had worn the past few years, and it fit her beautifully. Her hair was pulled into a low pony, her bangs lying softly on her forehead.

It was close to 9:00 p.m., and the sun was nearly set.

"What plans do you have?" I asked.

"I am hanging with a couple of my girlfriends," she responded. I was always jealous that Mother had friends. I so desperately wanted that, too. But the joy I felt for her always overpowered any feelings of sadness for myself.

"And then"—she smirked—"we are playing cards and having a sleepover."

I blinked.

CHAPTER FIFTEEN

"At Wendi's house, not here," she assured.

So…that means…

"I'll head out, leave you to…yourselves." She coughed, then handed me a bottle. I examined the container with skepticism, and then my eyes shot wide, my face heating as I realized what was in my hands.

Contraceptive elixir.

"I'm not saying I want anything to happen, but I know how it is."

I wanted to argue, but I was grateful, even though the awkwardness made me want to jump off Castle La'Rune.

"Thank you," I whispered, avoiding eye contact as I took the bottle.

She touched my shoulder for a moment, then headed out.

I stared at the elixir for a moment before removing the cork. I sniffed it, winced, then chugged it—the flavor slightly bitter but not unbearable. I quickly chomped on a mint leaf so no taste would linger.

Would we actually have sex tonight? I wasn't sure. I knew I wanted it—badly—but I was also nervous. I still couldn't understand how a beautiful boy from the Inner Ring could desire someone like me.

I smiled softly while caressing the decals on my dress. In the few months since meeting Quill, my life had never been better…happier. I never thought I could love living this much.

I bit down on my lip.

I love him.

And I was nervous about telling him. I wondered what our future would be. Maybe Mother and I would make enough one day to be part of the Inner Ring, and maybe Quill's family would grow to accept me.

Then, a sadness swept over me.

We could never have children. It would risk everything. What if he wants that? Not that I was ready now, but I would love children one day. But if our child was anything like me, I would be put in the same predicament my mother was. And I knew that while my mother loved me, I also ripped her away from the love of her life.

A knock on the door kicked me out of my thoughts, and I scrambled off the couch, dusted myself off, and reached for the doorknob.

Quill was beaming as I opened the door. The oil lamp by our entrance cast a warm glow over him. He wore a black button-up shirt, his forearms and chest just slightly exposed, showing off his golden skin. His navy pants matched my dress, and a bouquet of white roses rested in a silver vase he held. His smile faded as he looked me up and down.

I tensed.

Does he not like how I look?

He studied me a moment more, and his amber eyes met mine.

"So damn beautiful," he said softly, brushing my hair behind my ear.

I exhaled in relief and smiled as he handed me the roses. I inhaled and lost myself in their wonderful scent.

"Roses, my favorite," I whispered and gave him a warm smile. "This is so kind. Thank you, Quill."

His eyes flickered with an emotion I couldn't decipher. I walked back into the house and placed the vase in the center of our dining table, standing back and admiring the view. "And thank you for this dress…I've never owned something so fancy before."

My cheeks heated again, and my whole body became covered in goosebumps as his fingertips brushed my bare back. I turned, and with his other hand, he embraced me and kissed me softly. Butterflies danced in my stomach even as he pulled away.

"I couldn't resist getting it for you when I saw it." He grinned. "Shall we go then, Flower?" He held out his elbow, and I felt pure bliss as I interlocked my arm with his.

We arrived at the festival in Linora Park. The typically bare lawn was filled with people, twinkly lights, food stands, and tables. Music and

laughter could be heard in the distance, and this place was just…
alive.

People were dancing, twirling their gowns about in a large open spot in front of a band playing upbeat tunes. Quill and I appeared out of place, and it was at that moment I realized the eyes weren't just on Quill as we made our way to the dance area. They were on me as well.

I looked like I belonged in the Inner Ring.

"People are staring," I whispered.

Quill chuckled. "How could they not? You're stunning."

My cheeks heated, and then I saw one of the food stands that was set up. Excitedly, I pulled Quill toward it.

"Where are we going?" He laughed.

We got in line as I pointed to the man behind the stand, handing out steaming pieces of—

"Pizza!" Quill exclaimed with wide eyes. He turned and grinned as he looked down at me.

"Okay, don't get too excited, in case you don't like it." I chuckled as I rubbed the back of my neck.

"If you like it, I'm sure I will."

We moved closer in the line. "It's essentially bread covered with tomato sauce and cheese. But you can get different toppings or eat it plain."

"What do you recommend?" he asked.

"Plain cheese is always good. But you can get it with different meats or vegetables—" I realized I wasn't answering his question. "I'm getting pepperoni."

He bit his lip. "Then I shall get the same thing."

"Copycat," I teased, nudging his side. He nudged me back.

We got to the counter, Quill being as cute as ever as he ordered our two slices. He paid, and I was going to complain but didn't feel the urge to. I was too excited to see his reaction, and seeing the worker's face when he gave a large tip warmed my heart.

We sat at one of the many tables set up by the food vendors. Quill held his piece up to his mouth, then froze, smiling at me with a gaping mouth.

"Don't keep me in suspense!" I giggled.

He took a bite, and I studied him with a curious expression.

He swallowed, twisting his lips to the side as if contemplating how he felt about it.

"Oh no, you hate it."

"No, I'm just thinking of how my parents will feel when I tell them I'm moving down here." He grinned and finished chewing. "This is fantastic."

"You tease." I took a bite of mine. It was fantastic, but I had never had Inner Ring food before to compare it to.

"I cannot believe we don't have anything like this in the—" He hesitated. "In the Inner Ring." He looked to the groups of people dancing while taking another bite. The music was fast and lively, with musicians playing various instruments. Say what you will of the Outer Ring, but we certainly had talent down here.

After we finished our slices, Quill said he wanted to dance with me. We stood and stalked toward the area hand in hand.

"What, you aren't going to lick the sauce off my lips?" I joked. I knew there was no sauce; I was cautious with my eating to avoid getting anything on my dress.

He smirked, then leaned down and dragged his tongue against my lip.

I bit my lip afterward, and he pulled me in the middle of the group of dancing people. He put both hands on my hips while mine laced behind his neck. As we began to sway, I let out an embarrassed laugh.

"To be honest, I have never danced before," I admitted.

He gave me an incredulous smile. "Really? You've been coming to this festival for years and have never danced?" he asked loudly over the music. I shook my head, and he lifted me and spun me around, causing me to let out an embarrassing squeal. He placed me back down, grinning so big his straight teeth were visible. "I guess we'll need to start other lessons then," he teased.

"Oh, ha-ha," I mocked.

After a few songs, I showed Quill around the rest of the festival. We played some of the games set up. I beat him at cornhole with ease, teasing him about it continuously until he beat me at darts, and he enjoyed rubbing that back in my face. We were on our way to dance more when Quill spoke.

"What are people drinking?" he asked, noting the red concoction in most adults' hands.

"It's a popular wine in the Outer Ring, more on the affordable side. But people seem to love it."

"You've never had any?"

I quirked a brow. "I'm sixteen."

He smirked and grabbed my hand as we waltzed toward a stand that was handing out glasses of wine.

"Quill, what are you doing?" I hissed.

When we reached the stand, the woman pouring gave us an *"Are you serious?"* look, and Quill smiled, pulling out *gold*!

My eyes flung open, and so did the woman's.

"Two glasses would be nice. Will this cover it?" he asked smoothly. I thought the woman was about to faint as she nodded quickly and handed over the glasses.

I gaped at Quill as we walked away, drinks in hand, and he eyeballed me from the side.

"What?"

"*Gold?* How rich are you, anyway?"

"You can't think that dress only cost silver pieces, do you?"

"Oh my… I'm going to hit you!"

Quill chuckled and sipped on his wine. He paused, observing his cup.

"This is not all that bad," he commented.

"What are you, a wine expert?"

"I've had my fair share," he replied, the corner of his lip raising as he took another sip.

I raised an eyebrow, then sipped mine. My face puckered at the strange taste, and Quill laughed loudly.

"Don't laugh at me!" I said as I laughed myself. "How do you like this?"

His chuckle eased. "It is an acquired taste. Plus, the feeling you get makes it taste better."

I quirked my brow again. "You're a drunk?"

He grinned. "No, but I have gone overboard a couple of times. Without my parents' knowledge, of course."

"Naughty."

"You've no idea."

I blushed, looking away and biting my lip to hide my smile. Then my face fell as my thoughts drifted.

"What's wrong?" he asked with a concerned frown.

I sighed, taking another sip and grimacing. "I wish you wouldn't spend money on me," I mumbled.

"Not this again," he murmured, kissing the top of my head. "Why?"

"Because…I cannot return the favor."

"You return the favor every minute you spend with me."

I turned to face him, and he smiled into his cup as he drank.

"You are really equating time with me to gold?"

He smiled softly. "I am."

I tried and failed to hold in a smile, looking away to the ongoing festivities. My face eventually fell again. Quill laced his hand in mine, and when I looked at him, he examined me with worry.

"What if you grow to resent me?" I asked.

"Do you know nothing of my feelings for you?" He squeezed my hand. "I buy you things because I *want* to. Because you deserve nice things. Why would I resent you for that?"

I just shrugged and took a large gulp of the wine.

"It's not getting better yet." I grimaced.

It got better.

By the time I finished my first glass, I had asked for another.

Quill got us both one more drink, and the woman was more than excited to see us arrive again.

We walked over to a performance of acrobats on a stage. They had performers the past few years, and I was always enthralled by the ways they could move their bodies. Four of them stood, each on the other's shoulders, and raised their arms in unison.

The crowd cheered, and I couldn't control my giggling.

"Oh dear, what have I done?" Quill shook his head, unable to conceal his amusement.

I sipped down the remainder of my second drink.

"You know, my mother would kill me if"—I hiccupped—"she saw me like this. You too." I pointed a finger at him.

"We'd better keep avoiding her, then." He laughed. I hadn't seen Mother, but it wasn't odd with all the people here. His second glass was barely sipped on, and I frowned, then tapped the bottom of it.

"Are you pressuring me, Lena?" He smirked.

I groaned. "Hey, you're the one who wanted to get this stu—" Another embarrassing hiccup. "S-sorry," I said, flustered.

He chuckled, his laugh sending waves through my body.

"You know, I do not think I have laughed this much in my life," he said.

"Happy I can entertain you," I murmured as I inched closer, kissing him on the cheek, then the mouth. He looked at me with smoky amusement. "Another one?" I asked with my bottom lip protruding.

"Trust me, as much as I'd love to see you wildly drunk, I don't want you feeling terrible tomorrow. That is enough for tonight."

I frowned, and he kissed the top of my head.

The clock was reaching close to midnight. The festival went until two in the morning, though most families had gone home by this point, leaving primarily teens and adults enjoying the fun. The music began to slow, the song playing a raw and sensual beat as Quill and I found our way to the dance floor again. I had ditched my slippers at some point, and my feet trailed on the clipped grass.

We stared into each other's eyes, our smiles fading as we swayed to the music. His golden skin seemed to glow in the night light, always a contrast to my fair skin. His amber eyes began to fill with lust as they trailed down to my lips, his grip on my waist tightening.

"My mother won't be home tonight," I whispered in his ear, the wine giving me liquid courage. I never would've been so bold sober.

He pulled back, wide-eyed. I supposed he, too, was surprised by my fearlessness.

"My, my, Flower," he purred, running his hand along my neck. "And what would you like to do while she is gone?"

I realized my liquid courage wasn't that strong, as I flushed at the thought of all I did want to do with him. He chuckled softly, pulling my mouth to his. For a moment, I felt like I was floating. The music around us blended and hummed, and everyone disappeared until it was just us. Our mouths parted, and our tongues slid on each other's, the warmth between my legs heightening. A small moan escaped me, but thankfully, the music was so loud no one would have heard it.

Quill pulled back, staring at me with that damn lazy smile of his.

Before he could say anything, I took his hand and pulled him toward my home.

We made it there quickly, and Quill closed the door behind us as I turned to face him. My heart was beating so fast I would be surprised if he didn't hear it about to burst from my chest. He slowly looked me up and down, then walked toward me, tilting my chin to look into his eyes. He was so damn tall.

He studied me for a moment. "Can I ask you something?"

Confused, I nodded.

"Why do you think so low of yourself?"

The question took me aback, and I was unsure how to answer. After a moment, I responded, "I have just messed up a lot in my life, for myself and…for others."

"I cannot imagine you messing anything up badly enough to justify your lack of self-worth," he said, and I could tell by the tone of his voice that he wanted me to tell him the specifics.

"Maybe I'll tell you once you tell me all your secrets."

He smirked, then dragged his thumb across my bottom lip. "Cruel, beautiful siren," he whispered. "I love you."

I stilled, my mouth falling open.

He flushed and swallowed. "You don't have to say it back—"

"I love *you*," I said quickly, smiling sheepishly. "I've wanted to tell you for quite some time."

He rested his forehead on mine. "As have I," he whispered, and I pressed my lips to his. We stood there for a while, just kissing slowly until we became more eager—until we were stumbling into my bedroom.

"Are you sure you want this, Lena?" he panted softly against my lips.

"Yes," I breathed, and he motioned for me to turn around.

CHAPTER SIXTEEN

Quill came close, his warm breath on my neck sending chills throughout my entire body. Slowly, he untied the knot that held up the top of my dress and pulled down the small zipper, his hand then tracing my bare back.

"I knew you would look beautiful in this dress," he purred. "But not as beautiful as you'd look without it."

He undid my ponytail, so my hair spilled down in copper waves. He traveled his hands to just below my shoulders and pulled the dress all the way down, the rest of it now pooling on the floor.

I inhaled sharply. All I wore underneath was a pair of black underwear. No bra.

He ran his hands down my arms and began kissing my neck from behind. Chills consumed me once more, my back resting against his chest, my nipples now hardened peaks.

His left hand traveled lower, squeezing my ass as he let out a low growl, his tongue still lightly tracing around my neck.

His right hand gently grasped my breast before it traveled lower as well, toward the front of my underwear.

"May I touch you?" he asked gently.

"Yes," I breathed.

He hummed his approval and slid his hand into my underwear, two fingers delicately slipping through my center with ease. I was soaked.

"Gods," he whispered, circling his fingers on the sensitive bud. I moaned as my eyes rolled back, my head resting against his chest.

He slid his fingers out, and I followed them as they trailed up… to his *lips*.

I gasped as he slipped his two fingers along his tongue, smirking at me as he did it.

"You taste so sweet," he murmured as he pulled them out of his mouth. He grabbed my chin and spun me around, his mouth clashing with mine in a deep, passionate kiss. I loved the feeling of his tongue against mine.

"Can you taste yourself, Lena?" he purred against my lips.

I nodded, and my face flushed further as he grinned and then kissed my neck, his hand cupping my right breast again. I moaned louder as his thumb traced the peak, then squeezed it gently.

He broke away and pulled back, observing my body. Biting his lip, he knelt before me, slipping off my underwear. My breathing staggered, and here I was, completely exposed. He saw everything. He looked up at me through dark lashes.

"Damn perfection." He stood, unbuttoning his shirt, his voice low as he murmured, "You've no idea all the things I wish to do to you."

When he tossed his shirt to the floor, I was left in awe at his muscles. He looked like no teenager. No, he looked like a man—a perfectly sculpted man.

I gave a roguish smile. "Then show me," I whispered. I ran my hand down his chest and his hard stomach as he studied me with lustful eyes. When I pulled away, he began unbuttoning his pants, and I fought the urge to look away.

He slid his pants and undergarments down, the length of him springing free, and I gasped again, the cocky bastard smirking at my reaction.

I had never seen a naked man before and had only felt him in the pond. He gripped himself and stroked, his length reaching his belly button.

That's…supposed to go inside of me?

He lowered his hand, then tilted his head, examining me with playful eyes. I hesitated, then wrapped my hand around him, causing him to inhale sharply, the muscles on his abdomen tensing. Gods, if that wasn't the hottest thing ever.

I wrapped my left arm around his back, and he held me close as I began to work him up and down. He groaned as his lips met mine again, the pressure between my thighs becoming unbearable at the sound of his pleasure.

He hooked his arms under my legs without warning, causing me to squeal as he lifted me and gently laid me on my bed. He stepped back and observed me.

"Can I admit something to you?" I asked quietly, a smirk spreading across my face.

He gave me an amused grin. "Please."

My heartbeat quickened, and I squeezed my legs together, running my fingertips along my breasts. Quill's eyes dilated at that. "That first day you trained me. That was the first time I touched myself to the thought of you."

His eyes flared, and he released a breath at my confession. He wrapped his hand around his length, stroking himself as he stepped forward. My breathing hitched as I watched his eyelids grow heavy, the veins in his arm becoming pronounced while he slowly pleasured himself.

A mischievous smile took over his face. "Show me."

I could thank the alcohol for my lack of embarrassment. Or perhaps it was the way Quill was looking at me. I felt no shame as I trailed my fingers down my stomach and placed them between my legs.

Using three fingers, I began circling my clit, loosening breathy moans as I did so.

"Let me see you," he breathed.

I bit back a smile, pulled my knees up, and spread them apart.

Quill's eyes darkened. "Fucking hell, Lena," he panted as he stroked himself. "You are so beautiful."

And for the first time, I truly felt like I was. I grinned as I quickened my pace, my eyes rolling back and my breathing becoming louder as the ecstasy grew.

I heard Quill step closer, and my eyes found his. He smirked as he knelt on the ground, his strong hands softly gripping my legs, his lips now kissing my thighs.

"Quill, what are y—"

"Shh."

He continued kissing closer and closer until I felt his warm breath against that sensitive area. I stilled, and then he dragged his tongue across my center, and I cried out, gripping his hair in my hand.

Oh my…

He continued with upward licks, and I fought the urge to grind myself against his face until I couldn't help myself anymore. I held him close as his tongue teased my clit, circling the area as pressure built.

"Fuck, Lena, how do you taste so good?" he murmured against me before his tongue continued its assault.

He then gently plunged a finger into me, causing me to cry out in pleasure. He pumped it in and out as he softly sucked on the sensitive bud.

He looked at me through dark lashes, his mouth hovering just over my pussy. "I first touched myself to the thought of you the night we met," he confessed.

I had no time to respond before he sucked on my clit again, his finger moving quickly. The pressure built and built before it overflowed, my body shattering as I throbbed around his fingers, crying out his name. He pulled away and put pressure with his thumb, doing small circles as he rode out my orgasm.

I was panting, and when I looked down to see him, he was grinning, his lips glossy.

Fuck, I will never forget him looking like this.

He removed his finger and leaned over me, and my eyes trailed down to his length again.

"Do you still want to?" he asked softly.

"Yes," I answered instantly.

He bit his lip and pulled my body closer so my ass was almost hanging off the bed, then pushed his cock down, the tip of his length sliding through my slit. I bucked my hips and moaned at the sensation. He was breathing heavily as he lightly pushed himself on the entrance.

"This will probably hurt, Lena."

"I know." I smiled. "It's okay."

He pushed in further, and I winced at the burning sensation.

"I'm sorry," he whispered. "Tell me to stop, and I will."

"Don't ever be sorry," I breathed, and he pushed himself in further. I cried out softly, and he retreated again before going in deeper.

"About halfway, Flower," he murmured.

"Just push it all in," I respired.

"Are you—"

"Yes."

He clenched his jaw, then obeyed as he slid his entire length inside me.

I cried out at the pain, and he searched my face with worry. "Are you okay?"

I winced and gave an embarrassed laugh. "I...I think so."

He smiled sweetly and kissed my forehead before continuing, going back and forth gently. The pain eventually transitioned to deep pleasure as he began to trace his thumb around my clit once more, the burning sensation beginning to cease.

"Better?" he asked.

"Yes, much better," I whispered, my eyes rolling back as he picked up his pace.

His moans were the sexiest thing I'd ever heard. He held my hips as he slid in and out, faster and faster, the sound of skin against skin filling the air. I couldn't help how loud I was moaning; it was so intense.

Quill then pulled out, sliding my body over so I was entirely on the bed, and he crawled on top, resuming where we were. He lowered his body until he was holding me close, then continued his movements, his groans so close to my ear. I wrapped my legs around his hips and held him tight.

"Gods," he panted. "You feel too good."

He slowed his movements and pulled his face back so that we were looking at each other.

His golden eyes bounced between both of my mine. "I love you, Lena," he said softly, and my heart melted just as it had when he had said it earlier.

I reached my hand up and held his cheek. "I love you too, Quill."

His eyes flickered, and he smiled and ran his thumb along my bottom lip. "Your eyes are so stunning. Such a beautiful shade of green."

I laughed softly. "My eyes? Have you seen yours?"

He chuckled and kissed me again, then pulled back and increased his pace.

"Quill—fuck!" I wailed. The bliss I felt was blinding as he scooped me close and moved in me quickly. The pressure again built up until I cried out, another orgasm rippling through my body. I was breathless as I throbbed around him, squeezing his cock tightly just as he found his own release. I held him close as he moaned loudly, pouring himself into me.

We lay there for a moment, our bodies sweaty and staggering for breath, before he pulled himself out and lay beside me, facing me. I turned to meet his gaze, a smile creeping over both of our faces.

I never imagined anyone loving me or ever getting close to anyone in general. I never imagined being intimate with anyone.

Perhaps we could be together. Maybe I could even tell him about who I really am one day.

"Thank you for allowing me to be your first time," he said softly. "And thank you for being mine."

My eyes widened. "I was your first time too?"

He brushed my hair from my face and smiled. "You were."

The idea of him even touching another female made me want to burn down buildings, so knowing I was incorrect in my assumption of him having been with other girls made me kiss him gently.

He pulled me so I was now lying on his chest, his hand tracing lazy circles on my back.

"How come you seem so…experienced, then?"

He chuckled. "Having guy friends teaches you many things— things you don't even want to know."

I looked up at him. "Edmund and Hendry?"

"Hendry. Some of my other friends have lost their virginity too. So, I suppose I knew some from that." He blushed. "But really, I was just guessing."

I dragged my teeth along my bottom lip. "You guessed well, very well."

"I'm glad." He grinned. "I am taking a tonic, just so you know."

I blinked. "Oh, I am as well."

I knew humans created contraceptives of their own, but their success rate wasn't nearly high enough for me to risk it.

I think this may be the first time in my life I am grateful for being a Mage.

He continued running his fingertips along my back.

"Did…did I make you feel good?" I asked quietly.

"Gods, yes," he groaned and kissed the top of my head.

"Even though I…"

Didn't reciprocate what he had done for me…

Sensing what I meant, he tilted my chin up toward him. "Everything was *perfect*. We can try other things the next time if you would like to. But you were perfect." He kissed my forehead, and I snuggled close.

"Thank you for coming today," I said, and I felt him try to hold in a laugh. "That's not what I meant, you goof." I pinched his side, and he pinched me back. "I've never gone to that festival with anyone other than my mother. It was…" I sighed. "So nice. I hope you had fun, too."

"More fun than I have ever had, save for this, of course." His lazy circles ceased as he squeezed me tight.

I was having trouble keeping my eyes open, the warmth from his body lulling me to sleep.

"Can you spend the night?" I whispered.

He kissed my forehead again. "I wish I could…but if I don't want to get caught by my parents, I'll need to be in my bed before morning."

I tilted my head up toward him. "They think you're home?"

"Well, my father does. My mother knows, but I said I'd be home by midnight." He glanced at my clock, which read 1:43 a.m. "So, I don't want to get in trouble with her either."

I clenched my jaw and looked down.

"What's wrong?"

"I don't want to be a secret forever, Quill," I said quietly.

He stilled for a moment. "I don't want you to be either, believe me."

"I know you say you don't care what your father thinks, but if that were so, wouldn't you just bring me over, and that would be that?"

"It's more complicated than that."

"How so?"

He flexed his jaw, and I sat up, holding the sheet over my chest.

"You still won't tell me, will you?" I asked in disbelief.

"Lena, I—"

I shook my head incredulously, then lay on my side of the bed with my back to him.

"Please don't be angry with me," he pleaded, and I could hear the hurt in his voice.

"You say you love me…but you keep me a secret from everyone. I don't even know which house you live in. Do your friends even know about me?"

He hesitated. "Well, it's—"

"Don't lie," I said sternly as I turned over to face him.

He sighed. "No, they don't. Like I said, it's complicated."

"So, tell me."

He was silent.

"Quill—"

"I can't!"

I flinched. He had never raised his voice to me, and it caused my stupid lip to tremble.

Don't you dare cry, Lena.

He covered his eyes. "I…I'm sorry, Lena. You just have to trust me."

I wanted to. I had given him all of me, and I did love him with my whole being. But something was…off. Even though I myself lived a secretive life, he was far more closed off than even *me*. Something was wrong.

And I was going to figure it out.

CHAPTER SEVENTEEN

Quill held me and played with my hair until I drifted to sleep, and when I woke up in the morning, his side of the bed was empty. I was tangled up in my sheets, my quilt tucked around me. A sweet gesture before he left.

Last night had been…outstanding. But I was sick of his secrecy, and when Thursday rolled around, I would follow him home. I didn't care if he would be upset with me.

But how do I avoid being caught?

I stayed lying in bed as I brainstormed, and then the idea came—an invisibility elixir.

I had been working on healing and stamina elixirs, but Mother and I had never tried an invisibility one. Still, I had to give it a shot. I would go out to train, and after he walked me home, I would take the elixir and follow him.

It seemed easy enough. Even if I didn't get answers, I could find out where he lived, at least, since I apparently did not deserve that information either.

It was just past seven in the morning, and as I went to leave my bed, I remembered I was naked. I threw on a nightgown and peeked out my door.

Silence.

Mother must still be at Wendi's house. I sauntered to the bathroom and hopped in the ice-cold shower, wincing like I did every morning.

To have hot water… it must be so lovely.

When I left the bathroom, squeezing my hair and wearing a bath towel, Mother strolled in with a quirked eyebrow.

"Well?" she asked as she hung up her cloak.

I sucked in my lips and turned the other way.

"Oh. My. Gods," she breathed as she walked forward. "It happened, didn't it?"

"I'm not telling you anything," I mumbled as I strode toward my bedroom.

"How was it?"

I paused.

"Amazing. Now, no more questions," I said quickly as I escaped to my room.

After I reentered our living area, dressed in a sweater and pants with my hair pulled back, I went to the kitchen where Mother was making breakfast. She told me about her night with the ladies and how she almost won a hundred coppers playing cards. I told her about mine, save for the sex details. That would be dreadful.

Although I did wish I had a friend I could talk about things like that with.

"I want to learn the invisibility elixir."

Mother gaped at me for a moment before she continued making breakfast. "Why would you want to learn that? You can barely do a stamina one, and that's one of the easiest."

I huffed and crossed my arms as I leaned against the counter beside her. "Well, maybe I could learn it, but you make it." I took a deep breath. "Quill is hiding something from me. He won't let me meet his parents. He won't even tell his friends about me, and you already know I don't know where his house is. He says it's complicated but proceeds to not tell me *why* it's complicated."

"I did always find that strange," Mother said, stirring the porridge she was cooking. "So, what, you plan on following him, then?"

"Yes. After we finish my lessons."

"But that's at 10:00 a.m.—the Inner Ring will be closed off."

"Doesn't matter if I'm invisible."

She sighed. "What if something happens?"

"Like what?"

"I don't know," she huffed while throwing her arms up. "What if they're a family of murderers or involved in gang activity or something?"

I rolled my eyes. "I highly doubt it's that. But regardless, I have to see for myself what he's hiding. I have to know."

I spent the week learning the invisibility elixir and making more healing ones. I actually was having an easier time grasping illusion magic than stamina, though my invisibility potion only lasted fifteen seconds.

"I need more than just seconds," I grumbled after ingesting the mixture and witnessing it fail.

"The longest I can get you is maybe thirty minutes," Mother groaned. "And I'm still nervous about it. I haven't made many of these. If I knew how to conjure up a familiar, I would make a bird to spy on him or something." She rubbed the back of her neck. "I suppose my suppression has kept me from learning a lot too."

By Wednesday, we finally got it to the full thirty minutes. Mother and I had cheered, but to be safe, I stayed in our home the entire duration of it. I wouldn't want to become visible out in the open suddenly.

"I will make three for you, just in case." She sighed. "I'm going to be worried sick."

"I will be fine. Quill wouldn't hurt me." I looked to the ground in introspection. "I just don't know what he's hiding. That's what scares me."

Thursday came around, and everything was normal; Quill helped deliver our orders, and we trained and did our usual flirting. I was beginning to get decent at wielding my greatsword and was skilled with my dagger. At least, I felt like I was. The whole time I had been with him, my chest felt…weird.

I would be betraying his trust, but what did he expect?

"You okay?"

"Yeah, why?" I asked, winded from the set of movements I did.

He frowned, his lips pulling to the side. "You've just been quieter today than usual."

"Really? I don't think so."

It was hard to focus, knowing I was going to be following him, and also because the second I saw him, I started thinking about Saturday night.

Gods, I wanted to go to bed with him right now. But I wouldn't give in to him again. Not until I knew what was going on.

"Are you angry with me?" he asked quietly.

I lowered my sword. "Why would I be?"

His frown deepened, and I froze as he unsheathed his sword.

"Try to hit me," he ordered.

"What?" I stepped back. "Are you crazy?"

"You said weeks ago that you wished to battle one on one." He looked me up and down. "So, try to hit me."

He was right, but still, the thought intimidated me. "What if I hurt you?"

He snorted, and his cockiness had me raising my sword and getting into a fighting stance.

"Very good," he praised.

I swung my weapon without wasting more time, and Quill clashed his with mine. Vibrations went up my arm, and I struggled to keep hold of the blade.

"That isn't even at my full strength," he taunted, but his grin was pleasant. "Again."

I backed away, readied myself, and tried again. I swung, this time lower, and Quill blocked it with ease. Before he could order me, I swung repeatedly, him blocking every move with little effort.

Frustration built up in me, and I yelled as I swung and swung.

"Lena—" Quill started, but I kept going until our swords clashed, our faces inches apart. My head was craned upward to glare at him while he examined me with a mix of worry and concern.

I pushed away with a grunt and sheathed the sword behind my back. I hated that I was angry. I hated that he didn't trust me enough even to know where his fucking house was!

"I know you're upset with me," he said carefully.

I turned to face him and put a hand on my hip.

"Just please know I am…" He considered his following words, then exhaled. "I'll tell you more soon, I promise."

"Right…"

"I mean it."

His tone and the intensity of his expression almost made me believe him. He pulled me in and kissed me, then hugged me tightly. I hesitated, then hugged him back just as hard.

"I love you, Lena. I love you," he murmured into my hair.

"I love you too," I whispered

Please forgive me, Quill.

I stepped inside and closed the door to my home after Quill departed, then waited a few moments before I opened it again, making sure he was a safe distance away. Mother gave me words of encouragement and apprehension before I chugged one of the invisibility elixirs. She confirmed it worked, and then I opened the door to leave.

Pulling the hood of my cloak over my head, I began following discreetly behind. Gods forbid my potion failed; this would hopefully conceal my identity enough.

I kept a tasteful distance as Quill wove his way through the Outer Ring and up the steps into the Inner Ring. I made sure to avoid accidentally running into anyone, thus blowing my cover.

I wondered what his house would look like. Maybe I'd even see his parents. He told me he had no siblings, but that could be a lie.

I held in my sigh.

Why? Why so many secrets?

I expected him to walk up to one of the homes around the clock tower or perhaps one of the more elegant homes nestled near the Center. Instead, he went down an alleyway.

Strange.

He went down farther, and he angled his head in my direction. My heart stopped, but he looked straight through me before continuing.

I might be invisible, but I should play it safe, just in case.

The alleyway was a dead end, nothing but lush, overgrown hedges bordering the white fence that enclosed it. My brows drew together as I watched him go to the right and move through one of the bushes.

What the hell?

I waited a moment, then made my way through the same plants, finding a secret path behind one of the bushes. Quill twisted at the rustling noise I made going through the brush, and I froze. He scanned around, then continued.

Invisibility elixir, you are my best friend.

We strode through for a few minutes, it being nothing but plants surrounding the narrow pathway, and then suddenly he turned, going through yet another bush. I did as well and gasped at what I saw when I reached the other side.

Obsidian walls.

I was about to have a heart attack.

We're in the Center! Just by the castle! What the hell is Quill doing here?

I then realized I had lost him. Panicking, I glanced around. Then, as I was about to follow this new, cleanly cut path, I heard someone yell. I jerked my head upward and saw a royal guard standing atop the wall.

Shit!

"What do you think you're doing?" the guard exclaimed, crossbow aimed at me. "Run, and I will shoot!"

I shakily raised my arms, not knowing what else to do, and another guard descended from the post and grabbed my wrists tightly, cuffing me before lugging me toward the castle.

I was in trouble, so much trouble. Not only for sneaking into the Center…but if they discovered what was in my bag—

Without much thought, I slammed myself and my bag against the castle's stone border, shattering the vials of elixirs.

"Are you crazy! Don't do that, or you'll get a bolt in your head," the man detaining me hissed.

The guard dug his grip into my arms, and I yelped, looking up to meet his gaze. He seemed young—well, older than me. Maybe mid-twenties. His deep brown eyes seemed nervous looking at me, or perhaps concerned. The wind blew his white-blond hair, and I would have been able to acknowledge the guard's handsomeness if I hadn't been scared shitless.

"Do not argue, do not fight. I don't know what you were thinking sneaking around the castle, but if you wish to spare your life, do not cause trouble." His words were clipped.

My lip trembled, but I nodded, looking forward as we hiked up the castle's side stairs. The guard on the tower lowered his crossbow cautiously as he monitored our ascent.

This was the nearest I had ever seen the castle; it felt even taller and more ominous up this close. I tried to steady my breathing as we made our way up the steps, guards exchanging glances and briefly touching on how I was captured. Sweat was dripping down my forehead, and my body was trembling uncontrollably. Another guard stepped in line in front of me, and a door to the castle opened for us. A stairway appeared as I stepped through the entryway, and we began our walk up. Sconces lined the stone walls as we hurried through, leaving it eerie and dimly lit.

I was being led up to the prison.

An older guard was speaking to one of his comrades when his eyes went to mine briefly, then up to the guard next to me.

"Where did you find her, Torrin?" The man almost laughed, but Torrin ignored him as he led me to my cell.

He gently pushed me inside, and I turned to stare at him. My whole body continued to shake.

"You will remain here until morning when the Queen decides on your punishment." I could swear sympathy flickered in his eyes. He took my soaked crossbody from me, its contents only being broken elixirs and copper. I knew I would not be seeing it again. "Good luck," he whispered, then closed the door, leaving me alone in the cold, dark cell. The small, barred windows, one in the back wall and one in the door, were the only sources of light. Both were far too small to escape from.

I was frozen for a moment, standing there in disbelief over what the fuck had just happened.

"Wait!" I exclaimed.

Torrin peered through the opening of my cell door.

"My…my mother will be worried sick if I don't return home. Can I send a note to her? Letting her know that I am okay?"

Torrin didn't respond and walked away.

I stood there for a minute before I began to sob, falling back onto the stone "bed," if you could even call it that. I buried my face in my hands.

What have I done? What will happen to me, to Mother? I had no idea what the punishment for sneaking into the Center would be, but I knew for the Inner Ring, it was a hefty fine. Part of me hoped it would just be monetary, but it would rob us of everything we had. We couldn't afford the Inner Ring trespassing fee, and I could only assume the Center was an even greater sum.

And that was assuming imprisonment wasn't another part. I'd never seen any Outer Ring citizen put to death over being in the Inner Ring past curfew. But I was so close to the castle when I was caught…I didn't even know where I was going!

When my sobbing died down, I curled into a ball. With it being daytime, I had hours more trapped in here. I had to think and come up with some sort of excuse.

At some point, I cried myself to sleep. When Torrin returned to my cell, I jolted awake, and my body began to shake again. I rubbed my eyes and glanced out the little window opening of my cell, and though the sun was still out, it was nearly set, meaning it was probably around eight at night. My stomach was grumbling as no meal had been provided all day.

Maybe the Queen will recognize me…maybe she will be forgiving?

But what would I say? That I was following my mysterious boyfriend and had no intention of entering the Center? Like anyone would believe it. Despite the hours of being held here, I drew up blank when it came to any good excuses.

Torrin handed me a tray of food: a sandwich, an apple, a pastry, and a glass of water. I frowned and looked up at him.

"Seems like a good meal for a prisoner," I muttered.

"Here," he said, handing me a piece of parchment. I took it, and he gave me a quill and a lidded ink pot. "I will obviously read whatever you wish to have sent out."

I hesitated. What should I say? If I told her I was taken prisoner, she would not be any calmer. But if I said nothing and were put to death, she would never forgive me. Still, I couldn't risk her coming here and using her magic to free me.

"What are the odds I am to be put to death?" I whispered.

Torrin raised a brow. "You won't be put to death unless you try something reckless. Like bashing yourself against walls to break free, things of that sort."

My frown deepened. "Imprisonment?"

He crossed his arms. "I don't know what your punishment will be."

I looked down at the paper and began to write.

Mother,

I have met Quill's family. I accidentally stayed past curfew, and they kindly offered to let me stay at their home until tomorrow. Please don't worry. I will see you in the morning.

Love, Lena

I handed the note back to Torrin, who read over my letter. I told him where my home was and watched as he called a guard to deliver my message.

"I will have this sent," he promised. "Rest up, Lena."

I blinked at the use of my name and looked down with tearful eyes as I ate my food.

"Lena?"

My eyes couldn't open, but I was relieved to hear the voice. I felt more awake than I had in the past when we communicated.

Kayin, is that you?

"What have you gotten yourself into?" She was lighthearted in her comment, which annoyed me.

I am in a prison cell, if you must know.

"Sneaking off to see your lover?"

I felt my face frown.

How do you know of him?

"I know many things, and I know you need not worry. You will be fine tomorrow."

Hope bloomed in my chest. But still…

How could you possibly know that?

"Trust me. Try and sleep well, Lena."

Morning came, and Torrin briefly said, "Good morning," as he fetched me from my cell. He didn't speak as I was led up another set of stone steps, these ones leading to the main part of the castle. My eyes felt swollen, just like the many other times in my life when I had cried myself to sleep.

Despite the outside of Castle La'Rune being so dark and gothic, the inside was nearly all white, the floors a beautiful marble.

"Did my note get delivered?" I asked quietly.

"It did."

We stopped in front of an enormous black door, easily four times my height.

Torrin squeezed my arm. "Do not try anything reckless."

"You said that yesterday." My voice trembled as I spoke, and I furrowed my brows as I turned to him. "Why are you helping me?"

His eyes bounced between mine. "He is my friend."

All I could do was blink at that comment, and before I could reply, Torrin opened the doors, and we stepped inside the throne room. The sound of our shoes echoed in the ample, open space.

Ahead of me, Queen Ryia sat on a tall, black throne, her head resting on her hand. The one to her left was empty, the King not present. A handful of guards were stationed throughout the room, and a few moved to block to door from which we entered.

I couldn't acknowledge the blue velvet curtains that rested above the left wall, a wall lined with floor-to-ceiling windows, nor the marble floor that was black now instead of white as we inched forward. No, I had no chance to acknowledge anything in the room once I realized who stood beside the Queen, his hands tucked behind his back.

Quill.

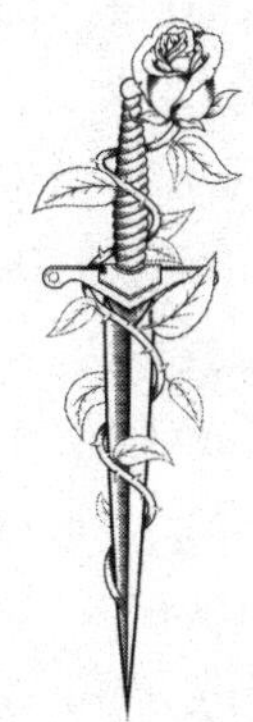

CHAPTER EIGHTEEN

His eyes widened at the sight of me, as did mine.

What the hell is Quill doing next to the Queen? Who was he? A spy? A servant?

No, he wasn't a servant. Quill wore an all-black suit with golden decals. It was even more fine than the clothes he usually wore. His normally tousled black hair was styled back neatly, save for a curl against his forehead. I glanced atop his head and noticed something I couldn't believe didn't catch my attention immediately.

A…crown.

I felt faint. Utterly confused. The Queen's eyes widened, and she glanced at Quill, who clenched his jaw.

"This girl was caught sneaking along the western side of the castle—" Torrin began.

"Torrin, please take the rest of the guard and leave us with the girl."

A guard to our left frowned. "But Your Majesty—"

"I am not afraid of this little girl. Do not question me. Go," she ordered with an icy coldness.

Torrin just lightly squeezed my arm before he stepped away. The sound of footsteps retreating was the only noise until the door loudly clicked shut. Then, it was just the Queen, Quill, and me. I couldn't control my trembling. I still couldn't fathom my punishment, let alone what I was witnessing in front of me.

"Well, Lena, how wonderful to see you again," the Queen said with a smile and in a tone that seemed genuine. "Silas has told me much about you."

I froze, my eyes shooting to Quill. His eyes remained widened, and his breathing staggered. The Queen looked at him and noticed his reaction, her smile fading. "Have…have you not told her yet?"

His eyes darted to hers for a moment, a face of guilt overtaking him before his eyes met mine again.

"I…I don't understand…" I breathed.

But I did. I couldn't understand why, not in the slightest. But I understood the simple fact.

It was not Quill Callon I had fallen in love with. It was Silas La'Rune, the Prince of Otacia.

The room began to spin, and I felt faint. I considered one day telling Quill about who I was—*what* I was. Gods, the mistake I could have made…

The Queen's lips pressed into a thin line. "Take her to your room. Then, after you two talk, sneak her back out the way she came. I'll make sure the guards aren't over there."

He nodded, then went to walk to me. I stepped back, and he halted in place.

"Lena, I—"

"No!" I yelled, tears burning in my eyes. "I'm not going *anywhere* with you."

His lip trembled, color staining his cheeks. "Please, just let me explain—" he pleaded.

It broke my heart to see him like this. But I was too angry, too shocked to react any other way.

"You had your time to explain." I shot my glare to the Queen. "Your Majesty, if there are no charges, I wish to be escorted out of the palace to my home."

"Lena?" Silas begged, walking closer. I stepped back again and gazed into those golden eyes. I knew he was hurt, and I knew he didn't wish to hurt me.

Or did I? I had known nothing about him. He didn't want me to know he was the Prince—who he really was. But why? Even Queen Ryia seemed surprised he hadn't told me.

I didn't want him to explain or to hear him out. Quill wasn't real. The fact that I was so close to telling him the secret about myself made me sick—that secret, to the son of the leader who hated my people more than most—nearly damning my mother and myself.

I'm such a stupid fool.

The Queen looked at me with what appeared like disappointment. The Prince was kept from the kingdom; anyone lucky enough to be in his presence, I'm sure, would be kissing his feet. And then there was me, once again being impolite.

I didn't care. I needed to be anywhere but here.

"Very well." The Queen stood up, and I stiffened. She sauntered over to me, her deep blue, long-sleeved gown gliding against the marble floor. "I will walk you to one of the guards. Silas, you can go get ready for your training."

I glanced over at him.

Training. No wonder he was so skilled. The Prince's regimen was said to be rigorous. It hadn't made sense that a normal teenager training to be a guard would be as polished as he was.

He looked at me sorrowfully and mouthed, "I'm sorry."

My lip trembled as I looked away.

I will not cry.

I followed the Queen out of the large double doors before they slammed shut behind us.

"He's in love with you, I hope you know," the Queen said quietly as we descended the stairs. I looked over at her momentarily before staring at my feet.

"I'm in love with him too," I whispered. "Which is why I can't see him anymore."

"Why ever not?"

"Why? He is the Prince. And I am…me." My tears fell, and I quickly wiped them. I was surprised at how comfortable I felt speaking with her. But Ryia always put out an energy that felt…genuine. "It could never work, and you know that too."

We walked a step further, and guards appeared.

"You would be surprised how people will make things work

for the one they love…despite it all," she said solemnly. I glanced at her again, and the look in her eyes made me wonder if she somehow related to our situation. I opened my mouth to respond, but the Queen walked forward, getting the attention of a nearby guard.

Torrin.

"Please, escort this citizen back to the Outer Ring."

Torrin led me out of the front gates down to the steps that went from the Center to the Outer Ring. It wasn't past curfew yet, but he escorted me anyway. Most of the walk home was a blur, so many thoughts bouncing around my head that I felt like I was in a fever dream of some sort. Nothing made sense, yet everything did.

"I consider Silas my friend," Torrin said quietly as we arrived outside my cottage. My eyes shot to him.

"He told you about me?"

He shook his head. "No, but I caught him sneaking out of the castle once. I was shocked no one else seemed to see him." He ran a hand through his white-blond hair, lying messily across his forehead, the rest of the length just below his jaw. "I decided to follow him, and that's when I saw—"

My eyes bulged. "You didn't see us—"

"Nothing inappropriate!" He blushed and shook his head. "I saw you two in that park of yours. Lying together, eating treats. Then it made sense why the last few months he's seemed so…happy." Torrin crossed his arms. "I never mentioned it to him or anyone. But I recognized you right away. It appears he has told the Queen of you, though."

I didn't know what to say, so I just nodded.

"It's dangerous for him to sneak out like this."

"For him or me?"

"The Queen may be on your side, but the King is another story." He leaned close, gripped my arm, and whispered into my ear, "I know what you are, Lena Daelyra."

My whole body went numb, and his grip on my arm tightened. "Keep your curtains drawn when you are practicing magic. You never know who is peering through." He pulled away, staring intently into my eyes. "I am like you."

I couldn't respond. I couldn't breathe.

He knows. An Otacian guard knows I am a Mage.

"I will be in touch," Torrin said before he departed, and when I opened the door to my home, Mother ran to me crying.

"Lena! Dear Gods, where have you been? I thought something had happened to you! That note—" she cried, pulling me close. That's all it took for me to break down and weep into her arms. She pulled away, concerned.

"What happened to you?" she demanded, holding my face.

And so, I told her everything.

CHAPTER NINETEEN
SILAS

I cannot believe she followed me.

I began to undress in my room, changing into my training attire. I ran my fingers through my hair after my tunic and breeches were on, wanting so badly to run out of my room and explain myself.

She probably hates me now.

I sat on my bed and started to slip on my leather boots when I heard a knock on the door. I knew it wouldn't be her, but I couldn't stop my stomach from flipping at the hope of it.

"Come in," I mumbled.

The door slowly opened, and Mother walked in.

"Well, that could've gone better." She shut the door behind her and crossed her arms. "Why haven't you told her, Silas? I thought you were going to weeks ago."

I sighed, slipping on the other boot. "I was going to, but…" I trailed off. "I just never found the right time." I shook my head and bit down on my lip. "I can't stand that I must wait to see her. She has to be furious with me."

"Yes, she is," Mother said softly, uncrossing her arms. "But she does love you, son."

"How could you know if she loves me?" I muttered.

"I just do." She walked over and sat next to me on my bed. "Giving her time to process and cool off won't be a bad thing."

Mother was always insightful—always seemed to know how and when things would work out. Still, I sighed.

Just under three months ago, Mother had come to me with an offer. To sneak out of the castle for one morning and finally be able to see part of the kingdom. Ever since I was young, when my sister Aria was kidnapped and killed, I had been trapped in this Godsforsaken castle.

I was grateful when my training had started. I learned the way of the sword and other forms of fighting alongside future soldiers, and that's where I met my best friends, Edmund and Hendry, and one of my biggest inspirations, Torrin.

While I was close with them, it never compared to my connection with Lena. Edmund, Hendry, and Torrin still saw me as the Prince. They still saw me as royalty, as someone different from them. But Lena never did. She never held back, bowed down, and certainly never held her tongue. I loved it.

That's why I hadn't wanted to tell her. I didn't want things to change between us. Now that she had caught me in this lie, I didn't know how I would regain her trust. And I had to wait an entire week before I could see her again.

I buried my face in my hands.

"I know you want to go to her, Silas, but trust me, it will be better if you wait."

"I still don't understand why you are okay with any of this," I said quietly, then rested my hands on my thighs. "Royalty must wed royalty. That's what I have been told my whole life. That, when I am of age, princesses from all over Tovagoth will come with their families to offer up alliances to strengthen our kingdom and gain us more riches, more power, more land—you once told me this too."

I had kept Lena a secret for my first few visits to the Outer Ring, and I certainly hadn't told my mother I had been outside the castle walls. I begged her to let me go out again after arriving home that first day, and that was the only time she seemed adamant about it being a one-time thing. She agreed to it the following day. And to my surprise, when I finally came clean about Lena, leaving the castle walls, the training, all of it, she wasn't even upset. It never made sense.

"What changed?" I turned to face her more fully. "That first day out I thought would be my last. Even when I told you about Lena, only speaking about her as a friend, you didn't seem to mind. It just goes against everything I've been told. I am so glad for it, but that doesn't make it any less puzzling."

She gave me a soft smile and placed a hand on my cheek. "It's one of those things I know are meant to be."

I returned her smile and refrained from rolling my eyes. "No one can know if *anything* is meant to be."

She laughed through her nose, then stood and smoothed out her dress. "Head to the courtyard for training. Torrin won't like it if you're late."

She was out the door before I could ask any more questions.

The courtyard was full of soldiers-to-be, ages twelve to seventeen. I had started my one-on-one training far before that. The man who went by my stolen name began to train me when I was four. With play swords, of course. Once he was gone, I was trained by the absolute best in our armies. Considering I had no social life, or any life at all, training took over most of it. I had been far more advanced than any of the boys here when I started at twelve, but still, it felt like the honorable thing to do, to train alongside them.

I walked over to where Hendry Bonnevau was standing, his tawny, bronze arms crossed, listening to what one of our other soldiers in training, Roland Aubeze, was saying to him. Roland was a year under Edmund and me but had a lot of promise.

Roland saw I was walking over and bowed, the corners of his lips pulling upward, before walking away. He was sarcastic and goofy for the most part, but like most people, he felt like he had to put a mask on in front of me.

"Where's Edmund?" I asked, looking around the courtyard for him.

"Knowing him? Probably running here after sleeping in again." I looked at Hendry, who gave me a grin, and his mismatched eyes of deep brown and light blue darted to the side. I followed his gaze, and sure enough, our blond-haired friend was running up the stairs, out of breath. He ran past Torrin on the steps and saluted as he did so. A few more seconds and he would have been late.

"Just made it," he huffed with a smile, bending over to catch his breath. "Slept in by accident."

"Gods, Edmund, you are too predictable." Hendry snorted. "It would have been awkward for me if I would have had to discipline my friend."

Hendry was a couple of years older than us, and since we were not in active war, he was stationed here to train the youngest soldiers. It was weird having him advance to a leadership role, though I suppose he was always teaching us things even before his promotion.

Up the steps walked Torrin, who gave Edmund a disapproving glare.

Torrin Brighthell was one of the best in our army. While he was entrusted with guarding the royal family, he also oversaw the teaching of our soldiers in training. Despite being only twenty-five, he had risen through the ranks with ease. "Edmund Estielot. Almost late again, I see." Edmund shyly rubbed the back of his neck. "You can't expect to be an Otacian soldier if your men cannot rely on you to make it somewhere in time."

Edmund's mouth formed a tight line, and he nodded. "Understood, sir."

"Morning warm-ups begin now. You all know what to do."

We split into our regular groups. Our warm-ups were pretty similar to what I did with Lena. Torrin led my and Edmund's group of boys aged sixteen and older; Rurik, one of the King's generals and the oldest one here at age forty, took the boys thirteen to fifteen. Hendry now taught the new recruits.

Only a few minutes of warm-ups had passed before the sound of a sickening smash suddenly had my head snapping to the side. Leaning over and grasping his face was Roland, blood pouring out of his nose. Stalking above him were three more boys from his group. There were so many soldiers in training I didn't even know their names, but they appeared to be fifteen like Roland was.

"That all you got, pillow-biter?" the blond one spat, his two friends next to him laughing. Roland's hazel eyes burned as he wiped his nose with his forearm and went to stand, only to be kicked by the brown-haired boy standing next to him. Rurik just watched.

"Are you not going to stop them?" Hendry barked to the older soldier, who just shrugged with mild amusement.

"If the lad is a…pillow-biter as they say, perhaps a beating is needed to remind him not to broadcast his deviancy. Can't fight wars effectively if your men fear…" He gave Roland a look of disgust. "Well, you know."

My fists curled at his words, and just as the blond-haired one went to pummel his fist into Roland once more, I charged forward and yanked him by his collar, sending him flying back and crashing onto the concrete. He gaped at me as I glowered at him, his friends giving me the same expression. Edmund ran up and helped Roland to his feet.

"None of you are to put a hand on Roland again, do you understand?" I turned to Rurik, who stared at me with crossed arms and narrowed eyes. "And I will see that you are replaced for your incompetence and unprofessionalism." My fists trembled at my sides, but my voice remained strong. I had never made a command like this, never exercised any power. But seeing my friend being treated so poorly, and after everything that had happened with Lena...

My father always had the final say. But hopefully, he would listen to me when it came to Rurik.

"Roland will train with Torrin," I stated. I felt Roland looking at me with wide eyes, and when I met his stare, he gave me a thankful nod. Rurik stared at me in disbelief, and before he could respond, I was charging back into the castle. I heard the door open behind me, but I was too angry to turn around and see who it was. A hand gripped my shoulder after a few more steps, and I turned to see Torrin.

His dark eyes gave warning, and I shrugged off his touch and continued walking forward, Torrin trailing me. "I do not need a lecture, Torrin. That bastard doesn't belong in the training grounds if he is going to let that occur. You can handle one more boy."

"I am not disagreeing with you, Your Highness."

I halted, then turned with a skeptical expression. Torrin's arms were crossed, but he was beaming at me.

"I saw our future king just now in that altercation. You've come a long way. I am proud."

I blinked. "Thank you."

He patted my shoulder and turned to head out.

I went straight to my father after what went down with Rurik.

"Rurik is one of my most prized generals," my father seethed.

My mother was visibly stressed as she sat next to him. "You think it wise to embarrass me and give orders like you are King?"

Mother shot me a warning look.

Remain respectful, she always said.

I cleared my throat. "I did not wish to embarrass you, my King." From an early age, my father insisted I refer to him as *my King* instead of *my father*. He believed it to be respectful as it was how he addressed his father. "Rurik behaved in an unacceptable manner and—"

"Who are you to say anything about how a general with far more experience than you instructs our soldiers?"

He was testing me. Surely he didn't want me to cower. If I was to be King one day, I needed to be just like him.

The problem was, I was nothing like him.

My heartbeat quickened. "He does not respect one of our prospective soldiers. I made a solution to switch him over to our training group."

"If that was the solution, then why did you threaten his removal from his position?"

My fists shook at my side. "Because I do not believe he deserves it!" I yelled. My mother's hand went over her mouth, and I knew I had messed up.

"Deserve it?" The king snarled, rising from his throne. His black hair and tanned skin were about all we had in common, and the cruelty that radiated from him was nothing I ever wanted for myself. "You have done nothing to deserve *anything* other than pop out of your mother's womb."

I could do nothing but brace myself as he cracked the back of his hand against my face. It stung, but I wouldn't show weakness by grasping it. My father got close to my ear.

"Finish your training and prove yourself on the battlefield, then you can start barking orders. But until then, you are to be the obedient little boy everyone knows you to be."

I stared at the ground, my nails digging into my palms. It took everything to hide the disdain on my face.

"Do I make myself clear?" he shouted.

"Yes, my King," I answered. I didn't make eye contact with him as he stepped out of the throne room, and when I looked at my mother, tears were falling down her face.

The week went by as slowly as ever. Thankfully, Roland was allowed to train with Edmund and me under Torrin's guidance. However, Rurik remained, and it was impossible not to notice his burning gaze upon me every training session. I had made my first enemy, though it sometimes felt like my father was one, too.

It was early morning, Thursday. I had anticipated and dreaded this day. I would go to see Lena and pray to the Gods that she would give me a chance to explain. I had hoped the week had given her time to clear her head.

I made my way down my regular path, my heart beating rapidly. I stopped in front of Lena's cottage, taking a breath before knocking on the door.

After a moment, Minerva hesitantly opened the door, barely peeping her head through, her eyes enlarged.

"You shouldn't be here, Your Highness," she whispered, looking around the neighborhood. It was too early for most people to be outside.

"Please," I begged. "I need to see her. To try to explain."

Minerva studied me for a moment, biting her bottom lip. "This will only lead to heartbreak," she said quietly.

I gave her a sad smile. "Is that not always a risk when it comes to love?"

Her mouth parted slightly, and after a moment, she nodded. "Lena is by the river," she said, her thumb pointing behind her.

"Thank you," I said with a bow and made my way to the river along the backside of their property. Based on what I had seen these past months, this river ran along most of the border of the Outer Ring.

The land behind their property went on for about twenty feet before it descended into a hill, and sitting down there, knees to her chest as she tossed pebbles into the water, was Lena. Her hair, a radiant orange in the morning sunlight, was pulled back into a braid. It was clear that even though she had said she wished not to see me, she could have easily been in bed or already on to her deliveries. Instead, she waited for me.

So, I made my way down to her.

CHAPTER TWENTY

LENA

He lied to me—this entire time.

It had been a week, and I still struggled to fathom it all. I chucked little rocks into the river behind my home and watched as they made their ripples.

Today would be the day he showed. I still didn't know what I would say. I knew I couldn't be with him, but I also craved nothing more than to be at his side.

And then there was everything with Torrin. How did a Mage manage to ascend the ranks of the Royal Guard? He said he was one of the Prince's friends, yet Quill had only mentioned Edmund and Hendry to me.

After tossing a few more stones, thoughts firing off in my brain, I felt someone walk up behind me and glanced back to see Quill. He was watching me, hands in the pockets of his black pants and a somber expression on his face.

Silas. His name is Silas.

I turned to face the river and threw another rock before pulling my legs closer. "Go away."

I heard his footsteps approaching. "I said go away," I repeated. He sat beside me, wrapped his arm around me, and pulled me close. He knew just as I did that the last thing I wanted was for him to leave.

I couldn't stop my lip from trembling and the tears from flowing, and a moment later, I broke into a full sob. He drew me close, and as I cried and cried into his chest, he caressed my head, his fingers gliding through my hair.

"I am so, so sorry, Lena. I didn't want to lie…" he said, his tone so pitiful it made my heart break.

"Then why?" I cried, lifting my head to look at him. "Why did you? Did you not trust me?" I knew I was a hypocrite for saying that, but I couldn't help it.

"No, that's not it at all." He held my face with one hand, then took a deep breath. "My mother allowed me to sneak out for one day. It was just supposed to be for one day." He brushed my tears away with his thumb, then held my face with both hands. "Not only that, but I was also only supposed to go to the Inner Ring, not the Outer, and certainly not exit the kingdom. It was meant for me to experience and see a part of Otacia—to give me a small taste of freedom that I so desperately desired.

"And then I saw you." He smiled softly, then skimmed his thumb against my bottom lip. "You know what I thought? I saw you get pushed to the ground, and yes, my instinct at first was to rush over and protect you. I assumed I knew how you would be—a small, innocent girl incapable of defending herself. Perhaps another girl who would gush over me." The corners of his lips raised. "Then I saw you grab and hold your dagger to that girl's neck." He let out a breathy laugh. "Gods, that look in your eyes. At that moment, you weren't frightened, small, or broken." His smile turned to a grin. "You were a siren. Beautiful, dangerous, and utterly fascinating. So, I asked myself, who is this spitfire, and how can I get close to her? Everyone up there," he said, gesturing toward the Center, "is so superficial. The conversations are bleak. Most of the people are… soulless."

His beautiful eyes met mine again, staring intensely.

"I didn't go over to help you. I came over to have a taste of something *real*. And I couldn't believe how little you thought of yourself. How you had no clue that you were more special than every person in this damn kingdom. I could tell you wore a mask, hiding your true self because you were scared to be her. It was something I related to. But that's why I enjoyed teasing you…enjoyed pushing your buttons. Because I saw her peering through, begging to come out. And I loved every bit of her."

I felt myself choke up more, my eyes stinging and failing at holding back the constant flow of tears.

Still holding my face, he kissed both streams, and his golden gaze burned into mine when he drew back to speak more. "I didn't tell you because I didn't want you to look at me like everyone else does. I didn't want you to treat me any differently. And even though I didn't tell you everything about me, you have gotten the most authentic version of me that anyone has."

I couldn't breathe, mainly because his words struck home. How could I be mad at him when I have kept my secret for the same reasons?

"I know me being the Prince…complicates things," he continued. "But I'm in love with you, Lena Daelyra. Truthfully, I've been in love with you since the moment I saw you."

My hand traveled up to the side of his neck. "I'm in love with *you*, Qu—" I stopped myself. "Silas…"

"You can still call me Quill. Hell, I love hearing you call me that." He grazed his thumb along my jawline.

"But that's not who you are. That…isn't *you*."

"Being Quill, being with you, is the most I've ever felt like myself," he assured me. "The name is the only part that wasn't true, but it represents me almost more than Silas does."

"I understand that…but you're the *Prince*. And I'm nothing more than a common peasant, even if you believe I'm special. There's no real possibility of us being together. Not once you turn eighteen. Once a beautiful princess is brought for you to marry…"

"I will not be marrying anyone but *you*."

"You will *have* to marry a princess, Silas." The name still felt strange coming out of my mouth. "No matter how you feel or what you want…"

"Listen to me," he murmured, tilting my chin upward. "The only person I will marry is *you*," he repeated. "Should that be what you wish?"

I sighed through my nose. "How can a prince be so delusional?" I teased softly.

He bit his lip to prevent a grin from forming, then pulled me in for a kiss. Electricity shot throughout me as our lips touched, and I began to force it down as best I could.

I'm kissing the Prince of Otacia. I'm kissing Silas La'Rune.

My fingertips started to buzz, and a familiar hum in my chest began.

Keep it down, I ordered the magic, closing it inside a box.

He pulled away, still holding my chin. "How is it that I was blessed enough to find you?"

I rolled my eyes and tried and failed to hold in a smile.

"I'm guessing you still can't tell anyone about me, save for your mother. Why is she okay with this? Seems rather odd."

"Not yet. I will still have to be secretive about you until I can find a way for us to marry," he said softly. "As far as my mother goes, I'm really not sure either—maybe because she and my father are so… distant. And she sees how happy you make me." He shook his head. "I'm not sure."

"I love you," I stated, running my hand through his raven-black hair. "But I will never be a princess, Silas. Certainly not a queen." I kissed his cheek. Next year, Silas would be eighteen, and everything would change. He would be introduced to the kingdom. He would be free. "One year. You have me for one year."

"I guess I have a year to convince you otherwise, Flower," he said with his signature lazy smile. I elbowed him playfully, chuckling as I did so, and he flicked my nose. "Gods, I missed you," he breathed. "That was unbearable being trapped, unable to speak with you."

I snuggled into his arm, my voice turning into a whisper as I said, "I'm sorry I left. I'm sorry I didn't hear you out—"

"Do not be sorry. I deserved it." I shook my head, and he kissed the top of it in response. "And I'm sorry you had to spend a day in those wretched cells. Makes me ill just thinking of it."

There. There was my opening.

"It wasn't great," I said carefully. "But thankfully, the guard was kind, made it less scary. Tallon was his name?"

"Torrin," Silas corrected and looked down at me. "He was kind?"

I wasn't sure what to say. I didn't want to seem suspicious.

"I wouldn't say kind, but not cruel. He let me send a message to my mother."

He smiled. "Torrin is a good man. He's actually the one who trains me now."

I straightened. "He is?"

"Yes." Silas raised a brow. "Why, do you like him?" He sat up. "I am not one to share, Lena."

I pinched his side, and he playfully swatted me away with a big grin on his face. I pressed my lips against his again, hard, causing us to collapse into the grass. He laughed against my mouth and wrapped his arms around me tightly as we continued to nip at each other's lips.

The thought of Torrin lay in the back of my mind.

Will he turn out to be a friend? Or an enemy in disguise?

We spent the morning talking, cuddling, and kissing. Thankfully, Mother had already offered to take care of the orders for me today. After she returned to gather some items and left to run our stand shortly afterward, Silas and I quickly snuck to my room and made love far too many times. I was addicted to the feel of his body against mine, every flick of his tongue, every devilish smirk he gave. Everything about him was intoxicating. I would be lying if I said the idea of the Prince bedding me didn't arouse me further.

When Mother finally returned, Silas was already gone. I was washing our dishes as she strolled in, and she demanded I tell her what went down, though if she had taken a peek at all during our encounter, she would have known we had made up. She shook her head after I told her everything he had said, save for the more personal details. She was still high-strung after I told her what had happened with Torrin.

"Lena." Mother paced. "Listen, he is a sweet boy. Attractive. Kind. But…I still can't believe this," she said as her hand went to her forehead. "He is the Prince. And should the King find out about your romance, there would be significant consequences. And don't even get me started if you were to bear his child!"

"Mother," I said, flushing. "I…I know I won't be able to stay with him. But he has one more year before the kingdom will recognize him. I just…" I stopped scrubbing the dish in hand and turned off the water. "I just want this one year with him."

"And you think that leaving will be easier after that?"

I knew Mother had first-hand experience with leaving the one she loved. "If you could've had one more year with my father, you would have, yes?"

Her eyes widened, and then she sighed, her reaction giving me the answer I knew it would be.

"Just…don't get too attached, Lena." She came up and hugged

me. "And please, for the love of the Gods, especially now, do *not* get pregnant."

I groaned and pushed away. That was the last thing I wanted. Thankfully, the contraceptive elixir was nearly 100 percent effective so long as I ingested it every month.

CHAPTER TWENTY-ONE

Nearly three months had passed since I had learned of Silas's identity. His birthday and mine were only days apart, me being born on September 21st and him on September 13th. Since the royal family always threw him a special party on his actual birthday, and obviously, only members of the Center were invited, we decided to celebrate ours together on my birthday. I learned a lot more about him in the past months of our being together, as he was finally able to be completely open with me.

He told me stories from his childhood, how his father had always been distant, so consumed with ruling, while he and his mother had remained close his whole life. Her previous aide, who was like another father to him, was named Quill Callon, the false name he gave me. He said it was rumored it was he who kidnapped his sister, Princess Aria, as he vanished from the village at the same time. I was surprised he would use the name of someone attached to something so horrific, but he said his mother never believed he did it. She still spoke fondly of him after all this time.

"Princess Aria…what do you think happened? And how was that for you as a child?" I asked, my head lying in his lap as he played with my hair. We decided to skip training today and were relaxing in the forest.

"I have a faint memory of only some of it. Being just five years old, it's all a little blurry," he frowned as he began to recall his memories, looking off into the distance. "I remember the panic of those around me, my mother's tears, my father's rage. I remember being put in my room and constantly being surrounded by guards. They would do a twenty-four-hour surveillance. It wasn't until I got older that it finally eased up—once my actual training began.

"As far as what happened, I don't know anything except they found her body in the woods up north. She was only a few months old…" He shook his head. "Just…horrific. Mother was always composed when she talked about her to me, but I know it had to kill her not having her daughter anymore."

I chewed on my lip. "I'm surprised Ulric can rest not having found her killer."

"He still tries to, but it's nearly impossible after how much time has passed," he said solemnly as his thumb grazed my cheek.

We lay quietly. Silence never felt awkward to us anymore.

"How has public schooling been?" he asked.

After I opened up with Silas, I decided to finally do school with other people, no longer feeling the need to be all cooped up by myself. I knew I would always fear being discovered, but damn, did I feel a lot less scared. If I could have a lover, surely I could have friends.

I smiled at how far I had come. "It's been good. It's only been a few weeks, but I think a couple of girls could make good friends."

"No boys coming after my bride, correct?"

I cackled, rolling my eyes. "Oh yeah, they're just lining up for me." I did catch one boy in my class staring at me, but I could've had a booger in my nose or something.

"I wouldn't doubt it. Hopefully, I won't have to duel for your hand, but I will do it gladly if it comes to it."

"You buffoon," I chuckled and pinched his side. He squeezed me back, grinning widely.

"So." I settled into his lap, looking up at him. "How was your extravagant party, Your Highness?"

Silas grimaced, then smirked. "Utterly boring, considering you weren't there."

"Hm," I mumbled, then remembered something. "I wanted to give you a birthday present," I purred, and I lightly touched his length beneath me, causing it to harden under my touch. I did it to tease, as I actually did have a present for him, silly as it was.

"Is that so?" His eyes danced with excitement. I thought he'd lean in to kiss me, but he reached into his jacket pocket instead. "I have a present for you, too," he continued, pulling out a ring box.

I sat up, eyeing the thing in disbelief.

He chuckled. "Don't panic, Flower. It's not an engagement ring—yet." He winked as he opened the box.

I gasped. In it was a dainty silver ring. In its center was a large sapphire with two more petite sapphires next to it. It sparkled, the sun filtering through from the trees above, illuminating the gorgeous gems that had probably cost a fortune.

"Happy Birthday, Lena." He smiled with flushed cheeks.

"Silas…" I breathed as I studied it. "It's beautiful…but I can't accept it." I met his eyes. "I told you I don't like you spending money on me."

"Well, technically, I didn't spend the money." He grinned. "I told Mother about your birthday and how I wanted to get you jewelry, and she showed me this ring of hers."

"It was your mother's?" I asked with wide eyes.

"Yes, do you like it?"

I stared back at the ring in shock, unable to move.

He rubbed the back of his neck. "If you don't, I plan on getting you plenty of jewelry over the years. Just let me know what you like and—"

I hurled myself at him, hugging him tightly and knocking us both flat to the ground. He gave a winded laugh and looked at me with delight.

"As if I would dislike anything you would give me." I nudged him as I smooched his cheek. I sat up, and he placed the ring on my right ring finger.

I beamed at him. "A perfect fit."

"Like it was meant to be," he murmured.

I sighed. "My gift is not as good as what you gave me."

"I told you before, your company is all I could ever desire."

I bit my lip as I reached into my bag and pulled out a feathered pen and ink.

Silas blinked.

"A…quill." I gave Silas an embarrassed smile.

At that, he burst out laughing, and the sight warmed my cheeks. "This is great," he said, chuckling, retrieving the items from my hand.

"It was before I knew why you picked Quill—I thought maybe you were a...pen lover or something," I mumbled.

"Well, I do love anything you get me, so I suppose that does make me a pen lover."

"Pfft." I lay back on his lap, and he placed the items beside him and continued stroking my hair. I purposely rubbed my head against his groin, looking up at him as he inhaled deeply.

He gave me his lazy smile. "What are you up to, Flower?" he asked slowly.

I smirked and flipped over so I was lying between his thighs. I went to unbutton his pants, and his hand gently stopped me.

"What if someone sees?" he whispered.

"Are you scared, Quill?" I teased.

He bit his lip to hold back his smile, then released me from his grip. I grinned as I resumed unbuttoning his pants, pulled down the zipper, and pulled his length out, trying not to flush as I held it and looked at him again.

We had slept together every time we met since I found out who he was, before training when I knew Mother was out, save for today. Mother relieved me of my delivery duties in honor of my birthday, so we went to the forest first thing this morning. No training today, and no sex yet.

I still hadn't put my mouth on him. I wanted to, but the fear of doing a poor job prevented me. But I couldn't hold back any longer. And what better time?

I dragged my bottom lip through my teeth. Silas's eyes darkened, and he stroked my cheek with his thumb. It was rather risky attempting this in the woods.

Gods, Torrin, if you are out there, please leave.

I didn't know if the supposed Mage still followed Silas, and I hadn't heard anything from him since we last spoke.

"Are you sure you want to?" he asked softly, and I stilled.

"Do *you* want me to?"

"Desperately." He grinned. "But only if you're comfortable."

I answered with a smile and dragged my tongue up the length of him. He inhaled sharply, his jaw clenching tightly. I loved seeing how I could make him feel.

I did a few more slow licks, up and down, and his breathing hitched every time I grazed over the tip. I then wrapped my mouth around him and began to move my head up and down.

"Oh…oh my Gods," he breathed, roughly gripping my hair. I glanced up as his eyes rolled, and he let out a deep growl. Pressure built between my legs, but this was for him, not me. I supposed I could give him a decent present after all.

I continued to suck on him, his moans like heaven in my ear. I couldn't fit more than half of him in my mouth without choking, so I began to stroke the rest of him with my hand and continued to focus my mouth on the tip. He throbbed in my mouth with every flick of my tongue.

"Lena—" he growled.

I slowed, batting my lashes as he popped out of my mouth, my hand still holding him. "Yes?" My tongue trailed up him once more, and he groaned. His length was glistening with my saliva, and it was a significant effort not to strip my clothes off and ride him.

"You are intoxicating," he whispered through half-lidded eyes. I responded with a smile, taking my time tracing my tongue up and down. He bit his lip, his cock pulsing with each pass. "You torture me with that tongue of yours," he breathed.

"Torture?"

"Blissful…torture…" He grinned as he tilted his head back, his grip on my hair tightening. I took him in my mouth again, stroking him at the same time. His moans went straight to my core, and my hands began to tingle, my chest beginning to warm.

Damn magic.

I wanted to let it out; I didn't want to focus on keeping the electricity at bay. But before I was forced to will it down, Silas pulled lightly on my hair, his moans increasing.

"I'm going to come, Lena," he panted, and I quickened my pace, slowing only once he began to spill in my mouth, groaning loudly. I swallowed most, but some still dripped from my mouth as I pulled away.

He stared at me in awe as he caught his breath, and I smiled shyly. "What did I do to deserve you?" he respired. "I will never know." He leaned forward, his thumb spreading his remaining arousal across my lips. "Intoxicating…" he repeated. "I am addicted to you, you know that?"

"That sounds unhealthy," I teased, sucking his thumb and the remainder of him into my mouth. When his thumb slipped out, a devilish grin spread across my face. "Though I suffer from the same affliction regarding you, Your Highness."

He smirked. "Then it seems we are both unwell," he whispered, and kissed my lips softly.

# CHAPTER TWENTY-TWO

I had another nightmare…if that's what you could call it. While my body had once tensed and panicked when Kayin's voice filtered through, it now relaxed—even though my body still couldn't move.

"Open your eyes, Lena."

I obeyed and was shocked that I could actually blink—actually see.

"See? We are making progress," she said happily.

I still don't understand any of this.

"All in due time."

She always came in, said a few words, and left. It had been happening more frequently as of late.

"You can trust him, you know."

All I could do was blink.

Who?

"Torrin Brighthell."

My mouth would have fallen open if I could have moved it—but instead, my eyes bulged.

You know Torrin? How?

Another chuckle. *"You will have a note from him waiting on your nightstand. Meet with him."*

I paused for a moment. *How can I trust him when I don't even know if I can trust you?*

She sighed. *"Hear him out."*

Her voice faded, and despite my frustrations, I drifted to sleep.

The second I began to gain consciousness again, my eyes shot open, and I flung myself up. Sure enough, when I awoke just past 5:00 a.m., a note was sitting on my nightstand. I rubbed my eyes as I picked up the small piece of parchment and blinked rapidly—my vision still blurry.

Western Forest. 6:00 a.m.

Do not be late.

-T

I jumped out of bed and quickly got ready, mindful not to wake Mother. While we typically got up early on market days, we tried to sleep in the rest of the week. Torrin must know that.

How long has he been watching me?

Mother would probably not agree with the idea of me meeting a grown man in the forest, let alone a member of the Royal Guard, but I needed to do this.

My mind drifted to the idea of him seeing Silas and me in the woods, and I tensed. That was probably reckless of me to do, but I didn't regret it.

After brushing my teeth, I dressed in a long-sleeved tunic, pants, and knee-high boots. I threw my hair in a braid, slung my sword across my back, and tucked my dagger into my side. There was no way in hell I'd meet him without weapons.

I strolled past the bridge, the sun having just risen, and I waved up at the usual guard stationed there before making my way through the forest. When I worked my way through the first set of trees, I paused.

This forest was enormous. Where could he be in it? I quickly fished out his note that I had stuffed in my pocket, looking at it again.

"You're here."

I shrieked and whirled toward the voice, dagger in hand, and met eyes with Torrin as he put his hands up.

"Whoa! My apologies."

"You scared the hell out of me!" I panted, one hand to my chest, my dagger in the other.

He just stared at me.

"Well?" I pressed, clearly annoyed.

Torrin wasn't wearing his guard uniform today. Instead, he wore a deep maroon tunic, black arm guards, a matching protective girdle, dark pants and boots, and an ebony cloak with the hood pulled down. A sword was strapped around his back, and I could only guess the other weapons concealed at his sides.

He crossed his arms, then smirked. "You seemed to have had fun here a few days ago."

My whole face went red; I knew it did. "You, you did not—"

He raised his hands. "Once I got the hint of what would go down, I left. I had no wish to traumatize myself," he said calmly as his smirk faded.

I groaned in frustration and sheathed my dagger. "Why are you stalking me?"

He frowned. "I 'stalk' to ensure the protection of the Crown Prince. Orders of the Queen."

"Really?" I folded my arms across my chest. "Where were you when those men from Serpent's Cove attacked us? When Q—" I winced. "When Silas was attacked and had no choice but to end them?"

A bewildered frown overtook his features, and his arms slacked to his sides. "When the hell did that happen?" he demanded.

My eyes widened, and I smacked my palm against my forehead.

If he's trying to get information from me, I'm doing a good job just giving it to him.

"What do you want?" I muttered, annoyed with myself for being so foolish.

"The Queen only requested my service in keeping an eye on Silas after your little altercation at the castle." He paused momentarily. "I haven't seen another Mage in quite some time."

I stilled, only my head tilting up to glare at him.

The wind blew his platinum hair, and his umber-colored eyes gazed at me with unsettling intensity. He turned his hand ever so slightly, and the glamour concealing his ears vanished, showing natural, pointed cartilage—the ears of a Mage.

My hand shot over my mouth, and my breathing hitched.

He was telling the truth!

"What are you doing?" I hissed as my eyes darted around us. "Hide them!"

He motioned his hand again as he glamoured himself once more, his ears becoming rounded again.

"I wanted you to know I meant what I said." He glanced around and leaned in close. "I am a spy," Torrin whispered, and my stomach dropped. "Before you panic," he continued, "I wasn't being dishonest when I said Silas was my friend and a good man."

Silas had said the same of Torrin, but what would he say if he knew he was a traitor? A spy?

"For whom?" I barely got out.

His voice was low and smooth. "Our people in Ames."

I frowned, looking into his brown eyes. Specks of orange were present in his irises, nearly glowing in the sunlight. "I haven't heard of such a place," I breathed.

He gave a soft smile. "It's a quaint village, nowhere near the size of Otacia. But everyone there is like you and me."

A place with just Mages? That couldn't be. Mother and I had traveled a great distance around our continent—Tovagoth—and had never encountered anything like it. Then again, there was much to the mainland we hadn't seen, I supposed.

I crossed my arms to try and still the trembling I felt running through them. "If such a place exists," I persisted, "why the hell would you stay here? Silas said he's known you for *years*."

Those brown eyes studied me closely. "A great seer lives in Ames. He is named Igon Natarion. He told me the future of our people depended on me being here." His eyes skimmed the area again, and then he lowered his voice to a whisper. "Something bad is going to happen, Lena. I don't know what specifically, as seers cannot directly tell the future without altering it. But the fate of our people relies on Otacia. On me being here," he repeated.

"So, what, you will be the one saving our people? You alone?" I asked incredulously. I was finding it a challenge to keep my nerves at bay.

He scoffed. "I am just part of the puzzle, as are you." He took my hands in his, and I stilled at the gesture. I angled my head upward to meet his stare. He had to have been a foot taller than me. "When things change…when things go wrong—and you'll know when that moment comes—you find me. Do you understand?"

"You're scaring me." My whole body vibrated with dread, and then my biggest fear crept in. "You…you aren't going to hurt Silas, are you?"

Torrin drew back. "Never," he promised, and the look on his face almost appeared pained. "Silas is my friend. I would *never* hurt him. When things change, it will not be our doing. It won't be in our control."

"What of Silas, then?" I pressed. "What will happen to him?"

Torrin gently squeezed my hands, which were still in his. "It will be Silas who determines the fate of Magekind. It has been seen."

I let out a shaky breath. None of this made sense. I had never known a seer, never known any other Mage, for that matter, but it was known that certain Mages were gifted with unique abilities. I didn't appear to have one, nor did my mother.

"How exactly is that?" I ignored the lump in my throat at the thought of such a weight on Silas's shoulders. "As…as King?"

Torrin's shoulders dropped. "That I am not sure of. I wasn't told any specific timelines."

"So, what, you could still be here as an old man if nothing changed?"

His eyes looked to the ground in contemplation, then rose to mine. "If it is what I must do."

I frowned. Torrin was clearly loyal to his people and to this source, this…seer. "Should I tell him about me?"

"No," he said quickly. "I know Silas loves you. But there are too many forces at play. I don't think it wise, not now. Not yet."

My shoulders sagged. I felt sick keeping all this from him. The voice said I could trust Torrin. But he was committing treason against Otacia, against Silas. If I told them of Torrin, he would be killed. And what would stop Torrin from telling them about me, about Mother?

I had no options. I was damned if I did, damned if I didn't.

"If you so much as think of hurting Silas…" I said with deathly calm, my eyes shooting daggers at Torrin's. I squeezed his hands back, but the gesture showed no kindness. "I will kill you."

Torrin's jaw flexed, and then he smiled at me softly. "We're on the same page then."

I gave him a scowl, and then he began to stride away.

"Wait!" I called, and he halted. "So…what do I do now?"

"Live," he answered, speaking to me over his shoulder. "Be careful, be smart. I just needed you to know to find me when things change."

"Just as I was told to find you."

My body jerked as Torrin's voice filled my head. He let out a laugh.

"If I need to speak to you, you'll hear me like this…in your head." He turned to me, expression blank as he spoke with me telepathically. *"All you need to do is think back your response."*

"You're a telepath?" I asked out loud nervously.

I was blinking rapidly while Torrin smirked and walked away.

Bastard.

"I heard that."

My eyes followed him as he vanished into the trees.

Good!

CHAPTER TWENTY-THREE
ELEVEN MONTHS LATER

It was the sixth of September, the last day I had with Silas before he turned eighteen. Before he was introduced to the Kingdom of Otacia.

I had spent the last few weeks, well, *months* dreading this day—the final day with him.

Over the past year, he had attempted to convince me to stay with him past his eighteenth birthday. He had even resorted to groveling. I wanted to be with him more than anything, but it wasn't reasonable. Not only because of my social status but because of who I was.

I still hadn't told him. I couldn't.

Even if he couldn't see it yet, he would witness the influx of princesses coming to the ball thrown in his honor next Saturday, and it wouldn't be hard for him to get over me. I would be stuck dealing with my nostalgic feelings for...well, forever, I imagined.

I began to feel pain in my throat from the tears I was keeping inside while I sat at my kitchen table, the first time I had ever dreaded his arrival.

Mother walked in from the bathroom, tying her matching copper hair into a low pony. Her chestnut eyes met mine, and my damn lip started to tremble. She gave me a look of commiseration and tugged me into a hug as I rose from the chair.

"This year has gone by too quickly," I cried. "It's going to be so hard to say goodbye."

"I know it has," she said gently while squeezing me tight. Mother herself knew what it was like, leaving the one you loved. Except the love of her life was across the continent, not in the same kingdom. I didn't know which was worse.

She'd been trying to prepare me for this day for the past few weeks, but she knew nothing she could say would soften the blow.

A knocking sound brought me back to the present, and I knew it was him at our front door. Mother squeezed me once more before releasing me, and I wiped my eyes before unlocking the door for Silas, his expression matching mine. The sun started rising behind him, the light spilling from the horizon.

"Hi, Lena," he greeted softly, kissing my cheek. He looked over to Mother. "Good morning, Minerva."

She returned the hello with a warm smile and fetched the bag containing today's deliveries. Mother had grown close to Silas over the last year as well. There had been times when we showed him how to cook, and I found him particularly cute as he assisted with excitement. The Crown Prince had never cooked for himself or fooled around in the kitchen. I treasured how he found delight in the little things.

There were even some mornings when we ate breakfast together, Mother deciding to open the stand later so we could all enjoy each other's company.

She stepped over to him. "It was our pleasure having you in our home and our lives," she spoke with a cheerless smile. I know Mother was biting back tears as well. She then glanced at me. "I have never seen Lena so happy before…not until she met you."

"I didn't know joy until I met Lena," he replied, the corners of his lips turning up as he looked at me. My face crumpled.

"Really," she said as she turned her attention back to him and gently placed a hand on his shoulder, "I care for you like a son. I'm going to miss having you here."

He blushed at her words. "I hope to find a way to stick around," he said with a smile that didn't quite reach his eyes.

She drew him in, hugged him tight, and said her goodbyes before leaving.

A feeling of dread overcame me, and when Silas met my gaze again, I tried and failed to keep my composure. My hand flew over my mouth, and I squeezed my eyes tightly, the tears rushing out without my control.

"Flower," he whispered, rushing to me and pulling me into an embrace. "Please, please don't cry."

"I'm…" I choked out. "I am going to miss you so much, Silas." My fists scrunched the fabric of his cream tunic. "Damn you for being so lovable," I cried and laughed at the same time.

"Lena…" He pulled away and rested his forehead on mine. "I am not going anywhere." He brushed away my tears with his thumb. "I told you I would devise a plan for us, and I have."

My brows knitted together, and I pulled away just enough to see his face entirely. "What are you talking about?" My voice shook. "You'll be recognized. There *is* no way."

"There would've always been a way. I've told you before that nothing can keep me from you." He kissed my lips softly.

"How?" I breathed against his lips. "Do not torment me with false hope."

He retreated slightly and brushed my hair behind my ear. "I already talked to my mother about it. If we still meet at the same time, it will be safe for you to sneak to see me—take the same path as I normally do. She already ensures the guards are elsewhere for me, so the only change would be you going down the path instead."

I thought it over. Not only was the Queen's blessing of the plan comforting, but I also had an invisibility elixir I could use. While it had failed me the last time I used it, the past year has been spent improving my ability to enchant—I was confident in its power now.

I also had Torrin on my side.

This…could work.

"I am not sure why I didn't think of it sooner," he continued. "Probably because I loved getting out of the castle so badly," he said with a shy smile, then kissed my cheek. "I figured I would leave at 9:00 today and show you the path. I know you have seen part of it before, but you'll need to know how to get to my room."

"That gives us less than three hours together…"

His right hand slid into my hair. "It isn't the last time," he whispered. "I promise you."

We spent the remaining time together making love, lying together, and discussing the future. The idea of sneaking into the castle frightened me, and while the Queen might be on our side, the King certainly would not be.

"What if your father discovers our little tryst?" I asked Silas as we made our way up to the Inner Ring.

"My mother would have our back," he assured me, though the look on his face gave a little uncertainty. "So long as our path remains clear on Thursday mornings, I don't see how he will find out. Besides, he has more important things on his mind."

I was silent for a moment as we weaved through the Inner Ring citizens who walked the streets. "What important things are those?"

Silas gave me a side glance, then kept his voice low as we turned down the alleyway from before. "My father wishes to rule the southeast territories: Faltrun, Forsmont, and Wrendier."

It was an effort to keep a neutral expression. The La'Runes had already gained control of Otacia's bordering villages and kingdoms over the past few decades in the name of better defense and economy.

"Why?" The wince Silas gave me was enough to confirm my suspicions. "My Gods, he wishes to be High King of Tovagoth, doesn't he?"

We were entering the alleyway that contained the hidden passage. "I know it sounds bad—"

"Bad? It sounds like he's wishing to go to war. Faltrun alone has a massive army, and I can guarantee their King will not just hand over their territory." I knew enough about Faltrun, considering Renrell, the village my father was from, was one of its territories.

"Everything has a cost." Silas's words were clipped as he spoke.

I grabbed his arm right after we snuck through, making sure no eyes were on us before doing so. "Some things have greater costs than others. Who is to say you won't be there on the front lines if we went to war?"

The thought of Silas fighting in a war, being put in so much danger, all for his father's hunger for power, made me overcome with dread.

"If anything happened to you, I—"

Silas gently grasped my hands in his and sighed through his nose. "Certain things are beyond my control, my father's decisions being one of them. My mother is aware of my disagreement on the matter…but my voice means nothing to the King." I couldn't help but notice the bitterness in his tone.

Silas released my hands, and as we continued walking down the path, my mind went to Torrin.

I had met with him once a month to check in, even though I knew he was always doing his usual spying and probably knew anything I would tell him anyway. I wondered if he was aware of the King's desire to conquer all of those settlements.

I'd grown to like the guy. And it was comforting knowing there was another Mage here I could relate to. He said he'd be willing to teach me how to wield my magic, but the risk for us as individuals and the apparent fate of our people prevented it.

Sometimes, Torrin would speak to me in my mind—our conversations continuing even when we weren't together.

I felt guilty keeping that from Silas, but I knew Torrin would keep our path safe, as he knew Thursdays were our day. He had ensured it all this time.

"I told you he could be trusted," Kayin said in my mind. I could hear the smile in her voice.

My lip tilted upward as Silas and I rustled through the second set of bushes, leading us to the second hidden pathway.

Well, Kayin, it seems you were right. However, he could still turn on me at any time.

She chuckled. *You are such a worrywart. I don't blame you, though.*

Her voice always seemed familiar. Yet still, after a year of speaking to her, the only thing I had come to discover was her name.

Kayin and I had grown closer as the months passed, and now that our connection had strengthened over time, I was able to speak to her while awake and moving, similarly to how I spoke with Torrin in my mind. I could vent to her about girl stuff, and she would tell me how her days had gone, insisting on how uneventful most were. Of course, she never went into crazy detail. She was actually quite funny, too.

She did tell me she was older than me, but her age didn't matter. She was my friend, regardless. She had told me Torrin was her friend and assured me Silas's safety was imperative for Magekind. That gave me some comfort.

When I had brought up the voice in my head to Torrin, he had asked if I was drunk. I punched him in the gut for that one.

I supposed I thought of him as a friend too.

Once he was done being a smart-ass, he told me Kayin had been communicating with him for a few years. Their conversations had been sparse until recently. But, same as me, their communications had increased as of late.

"She somehow has the same gift," Torrin had said one day as he

told me more about his unique ability to read thoughts and communicate telepathically to others. *"It isn't often you meet another Mage with the same gift as you."*

We made it past the area I was caught in the last time I roamed this path a year ago. He guided me where to climb, and we ascended on a ledge in the guard's apparent blind spot.

"My room is up there," he whispered, pointing to a tower on the left side of the castle. "I have a balcony door up there. It isn't too challenging getting up and back down from here…for those with our stamina, anyway." He winked, and I knew he wasn't referring to just exercise.

We still had training nearly every week. I had become well-versed in hand-to-hand combat using a variety of weapons. I had even learned how to use a bow. My skill with the dagger was most promising, but my sword was a close second.

Even Torrin was impressed by my progress. He did, however, try to take credit, saying that since he had trained Silas, he had essentially trained me. I rolled my eyes at that.

"I can meet you here, though, in the pathway." Silas smiled softly. "I would be more comfortable if I was there to help you up the wall."

"Ye of little faith," I teased as I turned to descend. "So," I drawled, Silas dropping down first. "Are you going to dance with princesses at this birthday ball of yours?" I tried to keep my face neutral.

As if Silas would fall for that. He smirked. "Jealous, Lena?"

"Obviously," I muttered as he wrapped his arm around my waist, helping me down the final ledge until we were both on the grass once more.

He chuckled. "Yes. But I will be wishing they were you the entire time." He kissed my forehead.

"As will I," I mumbled before I reached into my bag and lifted out a ring box. "Happy Birthday, Silas."

He gaped, taking the box from me and opening it.

"It isn't a wedding ring—yet," I teased, repeating a line similar to the one he told me last year. The ring he gave me still was on my right hand. "It isn't much, as you know." It was a plain silver band, and even though it wasn't flashy, it took me months to save up for it. "I just figured it matched mine, in a way…"

He slipped the ring on, a perfect fit, and he eyed me with amusement.

"Now, how on Earth did you get this to be a perfect fit?"

I grinned. "I have my ways."

Luckily, he didn't press. I had begged Torrin to sneak into his room to see if he had any rings that could be used to find me the size. He was annoyed, I could tell, but he didn't complain.

Silas studied the band. "You are too sweet." He pulled me close and kissed me, then held me in his arms for a few moments more. I savored the warmth our embrace gave and the lovely smell of him. "Oh, how I cherish you," he whispered before pulling away. "Come to me in a couple of weeks, when we will celebrate *your* birthday, the far more important date."

"Oh?" I asked with amusement. "What do you have in mind?"

He smirked. "All sorts of depraved activity," he teased as he squeezed my ass, and I laughed before kissing him lightly on the mouth.

"My favorite," I purred.

He grinned and pulled my hand to his lips, pecking it softly.

"Until then."

CHAPTER TWENTY-FOUR

Thursday morning came. September 13th. Prince Silas La'Rune's eighteenth birthday. The people of Otacia were bustling with energy, gathered as close to the castle as possible. It was the one day people from the Outer Ring could enter the Center, though we were kept far back, just at the border of the Inner Ring. Lively tunes were being played by a fanciful band just outside the palace, the notes carrying through despite all the commotion going about.

Voices of anticipation chattered around, and my body squished to Mother's as people pressed in to witness. Class for today was canceled in honor of the celebration, so people of all ages were here.

I examined the obsidian walls, amazed yet again by the magnificence of the castle and its gothic architecture. I took my time peering first at the menacing gargoyles and then at the La'Rune family crest that was engraved over the front entrance; the four images displayed on a shield were an owl, a pelican, a raven, and a phoenix. Its artwork was interesting; the pelican seemed to be protecting the raven and phoenix from the owl. As I examined it, I wondered why the phoenix was being shielded. Why would an immortal bird need protection… from a pelican, of all things?

I met eyes with Torrin, who was stationed between the citizens of the Outer and Inner Ring. I knew he was reading my thoughts.

How rude to keep me all the way back here. Couldn't get me the VIP pass?

He snorted.

My gaze moved to the top castle balcony when I heard the music come to a stop—the voices surrounding me quieting down.

Four royal guards walked out, followed by the Queen and King. Ryia was wearing a stunning blue form-fitting gown with long sheer sleeves. Ulric, on the other hand, wore his black, heavy-clad armor, always wishing to look ready for battle. His long black hair and facial hair only added to his intimidating persona. Both their crowns gleamed atop their heads.

Ulric and the Queen paced to the front of the balcony to address the people. "Thank you all for joining us in welcoming our son as your Prince," the King announced, his voice deep and husky. "Nearly thirteen years have passed since our beloved daughter Aria was taken so soon from us. During those years, we have done everything to keep our son safe and craft him into the best warrior he can be."

I scoffed.

If only the kingdom knew just how shitty of a father Ulric really was.

The King turned to Ryia, who smiled softly before facing the crowd.

Her voice was beautiful and clear when she spoke. "We are pleased to introduce our son, Silas La'Rune, your Prince."

The crowd boomed as Silas emerged, his jet-black hair neatly styled, the royal crown on top of his head. He wore a suit of armor, primarily black like his father's, adorned with plate mail and a deep blue cape. The cheering was so loud I thought I might lose my hearing.

"You and me both," Torrin groaned.

Get out of my head!

Torrin rolled his eyes as mine flickered back to Silas.

He was grinning widely. I knew he was looking for me as his eyes scanned the crowd, but with the thousands of people gathered and us so far back, there was no way he would spot me. The smile on his face was so radiant, and in that moment, I realized that while I was dreading this day, he had been dreaming of it—the day he would finally be free.

He stepped forward, and the crowd began to quiet in anticipation of his speech.

"Citizens of Otacia, it is an honor and privilege to be able to serve you." His voice was strong, elegant, and sexy, like always. Around me, girls were gawking at the sight of him, and I had to refrain from glaring at all of them. "The loss of my sister Aria will forever be a scar inflicted upon our kingdom." Voices quieted down further at the mention of the late Princess. "My time in the castle has been used to forge me into the best prince I can be—the best *leader* I can be, and I cannot wait to serve you as my parents have."

There was more cheering, and I couldn't help but join in. I hadn't seen Silas present as a prince since the day I discovered who he was. And what a prince he was. He was everything and more than what I had imagined Silas La'Rune to be. I still couldn't believe he was mine…that he wanted *me*.

For now, anyway.

I sighed and pushed away the thought.

"Now we enter a new era—one where Otacia is stronger than ever before. Where we have obtained more territories to strengthen our defenses, where trade has boosted our economies." He spoke like a true prince—a true leader. He cleared his throat. "I know those in the Outer Ring still have not fully reaped the benefits of our kingdom's success."

At that comment, the King shot a glare at Silas from behind.

"But my promise to you, dear citizens of the Outer Ring," he resumed, "is that conditions will improve, and you will flourish. I see it as one of my most important ambitions." Those surrounding me, fellow Outer Ring citizens, erupted into a cheer, those of higher class merely clapping. The King shifted his glare from Silas to the crowd, and his frown remained. The Queen was grinning and applauding.

I hope Silas won't get in trouble for that statement.

"Oh, I'm sure he will," Torrin spoke in my mind.

I wanted to scream at him to get out of my head again, but his statement caught me off guard.

Will he hurt him?

"I'm not sure what goes down between the King and Prince, but I know their relationship isn't exactly a loving one. I can't imagine him going off script will go over well."

That I did know. Silas had told me he and his father were never close, that just as his father expected him to treat him as the King, he treated Silas as the Prince. Father and son were secondary, if not even considered.

I swallowed and felt my stomach drop as the King stepped forward. Mercifully, his scowl had disappeared, replaced by his usual indifference. Ryia also began to trek along until all three were next to one another, Silas in the middle.

"Citizens of the Center, we look forward to seeing you at the castle's celebration in honor of Silas's coming of age," Ulric spoke, the excitement from the front of the crowd booming. Of course, only the wealthiest and most elite were invited.

"Thank you all for gathering here today. I look forward to serving you." Silas beamed and bowed, and after immense applause, the three of them, followed by their guards, went back inside the castle.

The guards blocking off the Outer Ring began to usher us back, and we all began the descent to our homes.

I already knew about the celebratory ball from Silas, but I couldn't help but feel sad I couldn't go, even if the less attention, the better. It was another reminder that despite everything, this life with him I had dreamed up was not a possibility.

I was outside our cottage, tending the garden in the early afternoon sun later that day, enjoying one of the last days of warmth before the autumn breeze had me snuggled up in much warmer clothes.

I wore a light blue dress Silas had bought me, simple enough not to draw too much attention but beautiful all the same. It stopped just below my knees, was tight around the waist and bust, and was held up by two thin straps. My hair was in a ponytail to avoid having hair blowing in my face as I worked.

As I snipped herbs and placed them in my basket, I began to hear gasping. I wiped my forehead, looked toward the commotion, and my eyes widened when I saw Otacian soldiers headed down our road. I quickly stumbled, running to the front of my home and getting in the same kneeling position as those around me.

Sweat trailed down my forehead. I stared at the ground, the sound of hushed whispering and the clacking of horses' hooves against the cobblestone audible.

Why were soldiers coming down here?

I remained in my kneeling position and tensed when the horses stopped in front of my cottage. "Is this the home of Minerva and Lena Daelyra?" asked a familiar voice. I quickly glanced up to see Silas grinning, sitting atop a shiny black horse.

I gaped at him, then bit back my grin as best I could. "It is," I replied as I stood. A soldier to my left then waltzed over, placing two large packages on our doorstep.

"Gifts from the royal family. You are invited to the celebration tonight in honor of your family's successful business."

My eyes felt like they would bulge out of my head, and I met eyes with Torrin, who was behind Silas on an equally magnificent white horse.

"Looks like you'll be coming to the ball after all."

My eyes darted back to Silas. "Thank you, Your Highness." I breathed, bowing low.

When I raised my head, I was met with his extended arm. My eyes shot to his in confusion, but he just continued smiling.

Hesitantly, I slid my hand into his, and he raised it while leaning down, giving it a soft kiss. I could hear gasps from my neighbors, who were all outside, witnessing something completely unheard of.

It was wild enough that the Queen would sometimes grace us with her presence, but the Prince, let alone on his first day of freedom? And to kiss the hand of a lower-class peasant…

I suppose Silas also did this to show he meant what he said—that the Outer Ring was a priority to him.

I felt my face light up, my cheeks burning simultaneously, and Silas gave me that damn lazy smile as he pulled his lips away. I was used to his lips on my body…but in front of all these people…

I couldn't help but grin wider.

"We shall see you tonight, then," he purred, and he and his men turned and headed back up to the Center.

I gazed ahead until they were out of view, multiple neighbors rushing over and asking me what had happened.

Market day was nearing its end—its start time having been delayed due to the Prince's introduction. Mother wasn't going to believe this when she heard it!

I decided to place the boxes inside on our dining table. I took a peek and was grinning so hard at the sight of two gorgeous gowns that my cheeks hurt. I went to take a shower to get any dirt from gardening off of me. With only hours until the ball, I would need every moment to get ready.

CHAPTER TWENTY-FIVE

"I can't stop shaking," I whispered.

"Neither can I."

Mother and I walked up the steps to the Inner Ring, flashing our invitations to the guards. They gave them a glance, then nodded before letting us in. I had never been in the Inner Ring past curfew. We were met with gasps and glares by the residents, who were in disbelief that Outer Ring women were being escorted to the castle. Outer Ring women over them.

In our package, Silas had gifted Mother and me two glorious gowns. Mother's was a deep burgundy, and while its long sleeves and tight midsection fit her beautifully, the bottom of the gown that puffed out stole the show. It was far fancier than anything we had ever worn, and we both felt slightly silly despite how gorgeous they were. We knew, however, that we would fit in with those at the ball once we arrived.

My dress—Gods. It was a deep emerald, sleeveless piece. Its skirt puffed out like Mother's, but the top was corseted. My breasts thankfully fit perfectly, as Silas had learned my size the past year, considering he'd spoiled me so.

Along the corset and spilling down the skirt were intricate designs made of silver thread. I don't know what caused the whole gown to sparkle, but the entirety of it twinkled even in the dimmest light.

It was a dress fit for…a princess.

Mother wore her hair entirely down for once, and I opted for a half-up style with a crown braid, pieces of my orange hair loosely framing my face. We spent the afternoon perfecting our makeup—shadows, mascara, blush, and lipstick—and we both had never looked so good. The deep brown shade I used around my lids made my green eyes even brighter.

Coming to escort us up to the Center was a guard I had never seen, so Mother and I kept quiet on our way there, with the occasional amused side glances we gave each other as those around us gaped at our appearance.

This entry into the castle was indeed different from my first experience. We were led up the tall black stairsteps that led to the entrance of the towering building. The doors were opened wide, and couples and families dressed in jewels and the finest clothes stepped up and presented their invitations.

It was noticeable how many families had young girls my age. I didn't have time to dwell on it before we were led inside, greeted by a giant marble statue depicting a phoenix, its large wingspan and tail spread and carved with intricate detail.

We were led to the left, and as we entered through another set of double doors, my eyes broadened as they traveled across the enchanting golden ballroom. The ceiling was a mural of cherubs, angels, and, to my surprise, beings with pointed ears. Castle La'Rune was built over one hundred years ago, so I supposed this mural was done before the deep hatred for my kind began. Still, it was surprising it hadn't been painted over. In its center was the family crest again.

The floor was light brown, checkered wood, so shiny you would think it was covered in oil. Golden sconces lined the walls, casting a warm light throughout the entire ballroom. Mother and I continued onward and were met by the gawking eyes of some of the people attending. Those of the Center, gawking at us!

There were tables set up with a variety of fresh fruits and desserts, and I resisted the urge to stuff my face. My eyes drifted to the thrones at the back of the room. Ulric was occupying one of them, and someone from his court was speaking in his ear while he was observing the crowd. He didn't appear amused by the festivities.

I had never seen him this close. His skin was tanned just like his son's, his long hair just as dark. However, his eyes were nearly black, a stark contrast to Silas's golden ones. There were no soft lines on his face, and when our eyes met I quickly averted my gaze.

I continued glancing around the room until my eyes caught a familiar face.

Silas.

He was chatting with a girl and a man, presumably the girl's father. A potential princess, I assume, as there were girls our age *everywhere.* No longer in armor, Silas wore an all-black, fine suit, silver thread like mine swirling in intricate detail.

"I'll grab us a couple of drinks," Mother commented, then strolled off.

Silas's eyes went to look around, and when he saw me, he gave me the most radiant smile, causing the girl and her father to look back at me.

Try not to be so obvious!

I couldn't help but smile back. The father frowned, and the girl just stared, her eyes trailing over me in awe at my gown.

Silas strutted over to me. This was the first time I had seen his crown up close. Sapphires were embedded in a lovely pattern, and the soft lighting in the room made them shimmer.

"Don't you look absolutely gorgeous?"

"You could try and be less obvious," I whispered, looking around at the people quietly talking and eyeballing us.

"I think they are enthralled with how beautiful you are."

I gave a small smile. "Don't be silly. I'm sure it's obvious we are lower class."

"Are you insulting the gown I picked for you?"

"Of course not. I just…" I glanced around the room and took count of all the attractive girls present. My dress was easily my favorite, and I did feel I looked pretty tonight, but still.

"You still cannot see how special you are." He clicked his tongue. "Such a shame."

I blushed. The musicians started playing their instruments—violins, cellos, flutes, and more—and a beautiful, slow song began. Silas grabbed my hand, and my eyes widened as he pulled me to the dance floor. Couples began dancing elegantly, and Silas put his left hand around my waist, pulling me close as we began to sway.

"What are you doing?" I hissed nervously.

"Dancing, as this is a ball, after all. What do you expect?" He smirked at me, and I rolled my eyes. He drew me closer. "Gods, how I wish I could kiss you right now," he murmured.

"Silas," I breathed, and he spun me around, causing me to giggle, and pulled me close again.

His golden eyes sparkled, and he looked so…content.

I watched as his eyes drifted, and I followed his gaze. The Queen and Mother must have been conversing but now both gave us wide eyes that screamed, *Cut it out!*

Silas coughed and put some distance between us as we resumed our dance.

My smile faded as reality set in once more. I could never have this life with him. No matter how badly we both wanted it. I met his eyes, and his expression mirrored mine.

"We will figure this out, Flower," he said in a low voice.

I gave a tight-lipped smile, and he leaned into my ear. "You know what made me choose this dress?" He pulled away, and I shook my head. He grinned. "The color reminded me of those stunning eyes of yours."

I bit my lip. "You're making it quite difficult not to kiss you right now."

To my displeasure, the song ended, and Silas released me. Bowing and pulling my hand to his mouth, he softly kissed it. I saw the ladies around me curtseying to their partners, so I awkwardly did the same.

"Thank you for this dance, Lena," he whispered. There was undeniable energy between us as we studied each other. Love, longing, desire—but it was broken by another father intruding and asking Silas for a dance with his daughter.

I sheepishly bowed, then made my way to Mother, looking back halfway to see Silas's eyes on mine while he danced with the girl. It shouldn't anger me; I knew he didn't want it either. But I hated seeing another in his arms.

I reached Mother, who was still talking to the Queen.

"Lena," Ryia greeted me. "So nice to see you again."

"The pleasure is mine, Your Majesty." Mother handed me champagne, to my surprise. I accepted the glass and took a sip, the beverage light and crisp.

"I see you and Silas were enjoying yourselves." The corner of Mother's lip turned upward at the Queen's words. I gave an awkward smile, gulping down more of my drink, and Ryia chuckled softly. "I know this isn't easy for either of you. But I'm happy you could be here today." She nodded to my mother, then strolled off.

I went to speak with Mother when my friend caught my eye. Torrin Brighthell was standing guard by one of the dessert tables.

I smirked. Indeed, talking to the Prince would be suspicious, but what about a guard? Torrin looked so bored, and without Silas's company, I would be too. Or just jealous. Regardless, a distraction was needed.

I finished my glass and strutted over to Torrin, who was trying and failing at avoiding eye contact. When I made it to his side, he frowned at me.

"What are you doing?" he asked in an unpleasant tone. I put my hands on my hips, but before I could respond, he hissed again. "Ladies of the Center do not make gestures like that."

I scowled as my hands slacked to my sides, and I resisted the urge to give him my middle finger. That would certainly not be Center-like behavior. "My apologies, Sir Torrin," I crooned as I bowed. Torrin's expression was now partially concealed amusement.

"We shouldn't let people know we are connected in any way," he said quietly.

I rolled my eyes. "The only people that matter already know I know you. Well—at least *of* you," I said, then hesitated. "Will you dance with me?"

He blinked with bewilderment. "What?"

I resisted the urge to flush. I suppose my drink was making me bold. "Will a guard from the Queen's royal service please honor me with a dance?"

Torrin's cheeks stained with color, and the Queen walked up next to me. Torrin straightened in response. "Go on, Torrin," she said with a warm smile.

"But, Your Majesty, I—"

"You deserve some fun. Go now. We will be fine with one guard down."

I gave her a nod of thanks as Torrin interlocked his arm with mine, leading me to the dance floor. When we got there, he gripped my waist, his other hand holding mine, and I rested my free hand on his shoulder.

I smiled at his nervous expression.

"Don't dance much?" I asked.

A crease formed between his brows. "I am *positive* I am a better dancer than you."

I didn't doubt it. Still, I grinned. "Let's see if you're all talk."

When the next song started, I was surprised to see that Torrin was actually an excellent dancer. He led me through a series of movements, and I tried not to trip over my feet as he twirled me.

"Trouble keeping up?" he mocked.

I stuck my tongue out at him, and he bit back a smile. He twirled me one last time, and as the lively music ended, his hand was on my hip, his other hand laced with mine once more.

He smirked and followed with a bow, and I curtseyed. To my surprise, he took my hand and kissed the top of it.

It was a formal gesture, but part of me felt like Torrin held that kiss a moment longer.

"Thank you for the dance," he said smoothly, then raised a brow. "Though I think you'll be needing some dance lessons in your future."

I nudged his shoulder. "Rude," I said, then smiled. "But, true."

He coughed, then looked back at his area. "I should get back," he said, his eyes meeting mine.

"Thank you." I smiled, and he just nodded before resuming his duty.

I started back to Mother, who was talking with some handsome gentleman, then decided I didn't want to ruin her moment. I looked around the room and caught Silas staring at me with a confused look on his face.

I held back a wince. Perhaps Torrin and I did seem too comfortable with each other since we technically had only met once, as far as people other than Mother knew.

I almost went to think my response, so used to communicating with Torrin that way, but I just winked at him. His frown dissipated and his eyes flickered to the new girl in his arms.

Ugh.

"Don't be jealous. You know he wants it to be you."

My eyes shifted to Torrin, who was back in position.

Mother is busy. I'm not sure what to do with myself.

Torrin gave a pointed look to the dessert table.

I snorted, then made my way over.

I still find it funny you're on guard duty for the dessert table.

I knew it was for the exit behind him, but I still liked giving him shit. I was steps from him, yet we still spoke in each other's minds. I placed two brownies and a giant sugar cookie on a plate. Oh—and a couple of pieces of toffee and a few mounds of fudge.

"Someone has to protect these poor confections from your gaping mouth."

I whirled my head to see Torrin biting down on his lip to suppress a smile.

You bastard. Are you jealous you can't have any?

Torrin smirked, then grabbed a bonbon off the plate nearest to him and popped it in his mouth.

I watched his jaw as he chewed, his brown eyes squinting as he ate with a taunting smile. I found myself looking at him for a moment too long, at his massive height, broad shoulders, high cheekbones, and sharp jawline. At the column of his neck working as he swallowed the treat.

He is truly handsome.

My whole body stiffened as Torrin's eyes widened, and my own did the same when I realized he had heard my thoughts.

Oh shit!

I quickly averted my eyes and decided interrupting Mother wasn't that big of a deal. I clenched my plate and scurried off.

Torrin being able to read my thoughts was humiliating. What was I doing, thinking such a thing anyway?

"Got enough dessert?" Mother teased as she eyed my plate. Luckily, the man had walked off just as I approached.

I laughed lightly. "Thought we could share." That wasn't the truth; I could've downed all those desserts myself. Now I just felt sick to my stomach.

"It's not a big deal."

My whole body went tense at Torrin's voice. I couldn't even turn to face him.

"You can acknowledge someone is attractive without having feelings for them, Lena."

I felt myself sweating. This conversation was unbearable.

I love Silas. I only want him.

"I know," Torrin said softly in my mind.

"Lena, are you feeling alright?" I was startled by Mother's voice. "You were just staring off into space."

"Oh…yes, yes, I'm okay."

I closed my eyes briefly.

Please stay out of my head unless I say you can be there.

Torrin didn't respond, but I assumed he listened.

The Queen approached me as I was stuffing my face with the sweetest, most decadent fudge imaginable.

"Lena," she smiled widely. "I would like to show you our gallery."

I blinked, then quickly swallowed the treat, sliding my tongue over my teeth and praying to the Gods I didn't have chocolate stuck between them.

As we strolled to wherever this gallery was, I made eye

contact with Silas. He quirked a brow, and I shrugged my shoulders in response.

We went out the other set of double doors that led to the ballroom, and I nearly gasped at the sight of the gallery. Dozens of stunning pieces of artwork were placed neatly along the white stone walls.

"Look around," Ryia commented. "See which one is your favorite."

I nodded, then slowly made my way around the room. Various paintings were hung, portraying royalty, wildlife, or nature. Several marble statues were placed in the center of the room, the work so intricate that the people depicted looked almost life-like.

After several minutes of marveling at the various pieces, I stopped before the art that spoke to me the most. It was a painting the size of the castle doors. Stunning reds, oranges, and yellows depicted flame, with blues and purples delicately placed. The vivid fire swirled around what appeared to be a cloud of black smoke. The description of the piece read: *Death by a lover's fire.*

"This piece was gifted to me by my father," Ryia spoke. "He had it commissioned by a talented painter in Faltrun. He named the piece *Rebirth.*"

I paid attention to the detail, how the canvas showed all the texture of the paint used on it. It was beautiful…despite the eerie words beneath it.

"This one is my favorite," I decided.

The Queen laughed through her nose. "I knew it would be."

I frowned. "How so?"

She smiled softly. "Because it is Silas's, too."

After an evening of eating treats, sipping champagne, and dancing with Mother, the ball ended, and I made my way to Silas as people began to filter out.

"Hey," he said with his lazy smile. "I've missed you," he whispered.

"As have I," I whispered back. My smile faded. "I wish I could hug you goodbye."

He gave a sad smile. "I wish it too." His eyes faltered, then came back to mine. "What was with that dance with Torrin?"

My heart skipped a beat. "What do you mean?"

He frowned. "It's just you seemed awfully comfortable with him."

I kept the nerves at bay and lifted my champagne glass. "Liquid courage always helps."

It wasn't entirely a lie. I wished I could tell him about Torrin… about *me*.

Silas smiled at my comment, then leaned in. "I do rather like you tipsy, you know?"

I bit down on my lip as heat traveled through my body. "It's cruel to tease me, Your Highness."

Silas grinned as he pulled back, taking my hand and kissing it one more time. "Have a wonderful evening, Lena."

Mother and I made it to the front of the castle, where we waited to be escorted. To my dismay, it was Torrin who was our chauffeur this time.

Just great.

He gave us both a nod, then started walking, us following close behind him. Mother and I exchanged words about how much fun we had, how beautiful the Queen looked, and how handsome Silas was. Mother had asked Torrin how he enjoyed the party. It turned out she completely missed our dance together as she was focused on the attractive stranger to whom she spoke. Torrin merely said, *"As good as it could be for a guard."*

Time went by quickly, and when we reached our home, Torrin spoke.

"Lena, may I speak with you?"

I froze, then turned to him, nodding.

"I'll give you two some privacy," Mother said in the awkwardness, then went inside.

We stood in silence for a moment, my pathetic ass unable to make eye contact with him. I noticed his fingertips nervously dancing on his thigh before he spoke.

"I'm sorry for prying into your mind," he said softly. "I…I feel better knowing what people are actually thinking, not merely guessing at it. I suppose I have grown comfortable with us communicating that way." His voice sounded…sad. I met his eyes.

And he did honestly look remorseful, though it wasn't his fault. I enjoyed our way of communicating up until I had a thought I wish I hadn't had. We had been conversing just fine until then.

"Tell me what you're thinking," he pleaded, and my stupid heart fluttered.

"I…I think I have grown *too* close to you," I whispered, and his eyebrows drew together. "I love Silas—"

"I know you do."

"And I realize my feelings for you have become…" I hesitated. "Complicated."

Torrin's eyes widened, and his cheeks flushed. I was in love with Silas. Wanted only Silas. But I couldn't deny the attraction I had for Torrin. I hated that I felt this way.

"I don't need you giving me shit or making fun of me," I said more bitterly than I intended. "I just…I just need some space."

He blinked a few times, a frown now on his face, before looking down and nodding. We were silent for a few more moments.

Finally, he brought those beautiful brown eyes up to meet mine. "I understand. Sleep well, Lena."

I just stared at him as he walked back to the castle, and my heart sank for creating distance between me and my friend.

"Lena."

The voice startled me, and my eyes shot open.

Talk about a rude awakening.

My eyes went to my clock—1:15 a.m. Earlier than usual for her.

Kayin's voice trembled as she spoke. *"Change is coming, Lena— horrible, awful change. Find Torrin in two days. In the night. Go to Ames."*

My stomach dropped, and panic overtook me as I sat up in my bed.

What? Leave Otacia? Why?

Her voice was quieter than usual. *"Torrin will help with what needs to be done. When it is time to leave, find him. He will ensure you make it to Ames safely."*

What the fuck was she talking about?

What needs to be done? What is going to happen?

Silence.

Kayin?

She didn't answer for a long moment.

"It must happen in order to save Magekind. We will speak again in time."

I asked about Silas, but she gave me no response. Torrin told me the Prince would dictate the fate of our people. But what did that mean? I kept begging her for answers, but she ignored my requests.

I struggled to find sleep that night, my tears spilling out over fear of what was to come.

It wasn't until the next morning that the news spread across the kingdom. News that changed everything.

Queen Ryia had been assassinated.

CHAPTER TWENTY-SIX

"How? How could this have happened?" I went into a full-fledged panic as soon as Mother and I heard the news first thing in the morning. My mind automatically went to the worst. Torrin and Kayin—they knew something was going to happen. She warned me last night. She knew!

Torrin seemed to respect and care for the Queen. Was it all an act? Did I make friends with those looking to kill the Queen?

There was no way Torrin would've agreed with such a thing… no possible way.

Then, my stomach dipped.

Silas…

My heart broke for my lover, and then the anxiety that he might be harmed next took over. Immediately, I went to put on my cloak, but Mother grabbed my forearm, tugging me back forcefully. "Where do you think you're going?"

"I have to see him. He needs me."

"Lena, if you think the castle was swarming with guards before, it certainly will be now." I went to break her clutch, and she gripped me harder. "You wouldn't be safe. Even Silas wouldn't be able to stop the King's wrath, especially now that the Queen…" She couldn't even finish the sentence.

"I can use the invisibility elixir—"

"And what if someone barges into his room while you are there?"

"He would protect me," I said sternly.

"But would you want him to?!" Mother yelled.

I blinked rapidly. She was right. I wouldn't want Silas punished for me. But still, how could she expect me to leave him in his grief?

Mother sighed, then slowly released me from her grip. "Wait until the evening."

"But—"

"And please, please be careful. If I lost you…" Tears spilled down her cheeks.

"You won't lose me," I said softly. "I just…I cannot leave him alone in his distress."

I agreed that evening would be best, even though it killed me to have to wait to see him. My thoughts went back to Torrin.

"When things change and go wrong, and you'll know when that moment comes, you find me. Do you understand?"

If he somehow had a part in this…I would kill him myself.

After what felt like an eternity, I finally made my way down our path and crawled up the ledge, taking a beat to catch my breath. I didn't know if Silas was in his room or not. It was almost 9:00 p.m., but given the circumstances, he could be in training, be with the King, or even be forced to sleep elsewhere entirely.

I sighed. After I surveyed the area to make sure no guards were around, despite having ingested an invisibility elixir, I began my way up. I was careful of my footing and was ready to make the final climb to Silas's balcony when a force pulled me down.

"What are you doing here?!" hissed a voice.

My head whirled to see Torrin. There was a fierce rage on his face that turned to bewilderment as I charged at him and pressed my dagger to his throat.

"You…" I growled, shoving him back against the castle wall. "Tell me you didn't have a part in this." Tears began spilling out of my eyes, but otherwise, my face showed no weakness. Silas had said they were friends, but did he betray him? Take away one of the people he loved most? I didn't even have time to register that my damned elixir failed. "Tell me!"

Torrin was taken aback. "Why do you always think the worst of me? Are you crazy?" He went to move, and I pushed my dagger harder against his throat.

"Move, and I will kill you," I seethed. "Who is it? Who is Kayin, Torrin?"

He clenched his jaw, angry brown eyes bouncing between mine.

"WHO?" I yelled.

"Keep it down!" he hissed. "Fuck," he muttered in defeat. "I don't know, and before you slice my neck open, I mean it. Kayin claimed to be a seer like Igon. She was somehow able to utilize *my* gift to speak with you, to speak with me. Turns out it wasn't a shared ability but one that was…borrowed, somehow."

"Damnit, Torrin! And you just trusted this voice?" I had trusted her, too. I was a damn fool.

He tensed. "She knew things only a seer could know. Trust me, I didn't just believe her with nothing to back it up." He sighed and gently touched my arm.

I shook it off. "What information did she give that made you trust her? When did you know?"

He bit his lip, clearly wishing not to tell me, then sighed. "Kayin told me three years ago that Silas La'Rune would find his Soul-Tie at sixteen years of age. That she would be a red-haired girl living in the Outer Ring…and that she would be a Mage."

My body stilled, and I looked at him in disbelief. "Soul-Tie? I don't under—"

"You two were fated for one another, Lena. A Soul-Tie connection is a gift from the Goddess Celluna—" He winced. "Kayin also said you were not well versed in the Gods or Goddesses."

I widened my eyes. It was true I knew little of the Gods the Mages served, though I was aware they shared names with the human ones. I knew little of my culture at all. Mother and I were always so scared of being discovered that we kept most talk of heritage to a minimum.

And a Soul-Tie…that would explain why Silas would be drawn to someone like me. If something like that really existed, anyway.

"I knew to trust her when I saw you, Lena," Torrin continued, my dagger still pressed into his neck. "And Igon had told me before I departed from Ames that I would have someone speak destiny to me. He didn't specifically say who or what. But Kayin spoke just as he said the person would. Gave direction."

"Why?" I pressed. "Why tell you all of this? And if she were truly on the Queen's side, why didn't she see this coming? Why didn't she stop it?"

"I don't know." His eyes bounced between mine in despair. "I was just as shocked by all of this as you. Kayin told me last night that she accomplished what she needed using my gift. And that she will speak to me again when the time is right." He gazed into my eyes with intensity. "I *swear* to you, Lena, I had no idea that the Queen was going to be killed."

I shook. "Kayin told me to go to Ames with you…tomorrow. Did she tell you that?"

"She did."

"So, was it she who killed the Queen? And what of Silas? How do we know he is safe?" My lip trembled. "I won't be going *anywhere* if I think he's—"

"I know," he interrupted gently. "The person responsible for the Queen's death has already been captured. I know not the details, but apparently, the King discovered the scene shortly after the woman took her life."

My stomach sank.

"A…woman?" I loosened the pressure of my weapon against Torrin's neck.

His jaw flexed. "I haven't been told who specifically was caught."

"So, it could be her?"

"I…I don't know," he whispered.

I glanced up at the towering black fortress. Could Kayin be a prisoner in the castle?

"I can't believe this," I breathed as I lowered my dagger.

"Neither can I." Torrin rubbed his neck where my blade was pressed. "I've known Ryia since I was seventeen. She has given me eight years of her kindness." He shook his head. "Kayin clearly knew this would occur. It was fated. Horrible, devastating…and fated."

I frowned at him, and then my expression softened when I noticed the glimmer of unreleased tears in his eyes.

He really was affected by her loss. Or a fantastic actor. I didn't wish to believe the latter.

I felt an urge to hug him. But I desired to embrace Silas more.

"Be careful. I will keep watch until you are finished."

I gave him a grateful nod and made my way up the balcony.

I cautiously peered into Silas's room. He was sitting on the edge of his bed, his face buried in his hands. He was still wearing formal clothes, not bothering to change into something comfortable.

I inhaled sharply, then lightly knocked on his window. He startled, understandably so, and met my gaze. His eyes were glazed over, a light shade of pink, and I could see the tears spilling down his cheeks. He clenched his jaw and looked enraged as he stormed to his balcony door.

I heard the intricate locks clicking before he flung it open, pulling me inside.

"What are you doing here?" he asked coldly as he turned to face me, his gaze intense.

"I-I came to make sure you were okay, I—"

"My mother was just assassinated—we know who did it but have no idea if they're working with anyone. Or their motive." He ran his hand through his raven locks. "It is incredibly dangerous for you to be here. If something happened to you, Lena, I—" His voice cracked.

I placed my hands on his face, turned his head down to me, and quickly pressed my lips against his. We shared a few slow, passionate kisses before I gently pulled away.

"I had to come here and try to comfort you." I caressed his cheek while my other hand rested on his chest. "I am so, so sorry, Silas."

His lip trembled, tears forming in his eyes, but he was trying hard to keep them from coming out, from being vulnerable. I knew that feeling better than anyone, though I had spectacularly failed at it many times.

I continued to caress his face. "You can break down in front of me. Let everything out, whatever you need," I whispered.

A muscle feathered in his jaw, and then he pushed himself into me, our lips clashing once again, only this time it was hungrier— more forceful. I gasped as he lifted me from under my thighs and carried me over to his bed, laying me down gently.

His expression was heartbreaking and lustful at the same time. He looked at me with intense desire, but the tears in his eyes were begging to spill over. Still, he sauntered over to the oil lamps lighting his room and began turning them off as I respired laboriously, desperate for his touch.

Once they were all off, only moonlight lit the room. Silas slowly undid his shirt, pulling it over his head to reveal his perfectly toned body.

I swallowed. He had only gotten stronger and leaner in the last year and a half. Though I supposed I had as well. I had filled out nicely, as Silas always ensured Mother and I were well fed, despite my protests against him spending money on me.

He crawled onto the bed, between my legs, and grasped my chin in his hand, tilting it to the side so he could nip at the space between my neck and shoulder.

He bit down lightly, and I hissed at the small hurt. He then began slowly devouring my neck. My eyes rolled back, and I let out a soft moan. I could feel his lips smile against my skin before he continued. His fingers drifted to the button on my pants, and I quickly helped, biting his bottom lip as I bared my body for him. He shucked my pants off while I flung off my shirt and bra, and then I was completely uncovered.

"You next," I whispered seductively, gaining a wicked smile from him.

He unbuttoned his pants and slid them down just enough for his massive length to reveal itself, where it relaxed just at his belly button.

I let out a hum. "All of it."

He laughed softly and hopped off the bed to completely remove his pants.

He crawled back overtop me and met my gaze, but I craved seeing his face in detail. The moonlight was directly behind him, giving him a splendid view of me. I, unfortunately, didn't get the same.

I inched forward and pushed him onto the bed so I was straddling him. His eyes were now full of mischievous excitement. That look further inspired me to shimmy my way down and slide his length into my mouth. I dragged my tongue all around him, focusing on the tip just how he liked.

"Fuck," he whispered, and I let out a soft chuckle. "What?" he asked with a smirk.

"Such indecent language, Your Highness," I purred against his cock.

He gave me his lazy smile. "Does that displease you, my Flower?"

"Nothing you do displeases me."

I sucked him back into my mouth, and he tilted his head back. The moan he let out had me dripping. I already wanted to climb on top of him and ride him.

I continued my strokes, savoring the feel of the smooth skin of his cock in my mouth. He slid his hand into my hair and began pushing me down on him further. I tried hard not to choke, but, like always, he could barely fit himself halfway before I gagged. He pulled out.

"I'm sorry," I breathed, my apology causing him to grab my cheeks with his right hand, forcing me to look at him.

"You have nothing to be sorry for, Lena. Certainly, never in regard to sex." He released my face and dragged his thumb against my lips. "Ride me."

He didn't have to ask twice. I climbed on top of him, his hands gripping my waist, and I guided him inside me, my arousal soaking the tip of him.

He didn't ease in, not this time. He slammed into me with all his might, and I cried out as I collapsed onto his chest.

"Keep quiet," he murmured in my ear as he began fucking me. "As much as I enjoy hearing you scream, I'll be thoroughly pissed if we have to stop."

I bit down on his neck, sucking in his skin. He groaned with pleasure while continuing to slide himself in and out.

"Gods, Lena, you are so wet."

He slowed his pace, pulling out completely before slowly pushing himself back in. I couldn't hold in my moaning; it just felt too fucking good. But I tried to keep it as quiet as I could. After a few moments, I couldn't take the slow-paced torture. I sat myself up and ground against him before moving my ass up and down. He hissed, and his eyes rolled back.

I appreciated the view while I bounced on him. His Adam's apple protruded with his head lying back, and sweat dripped down his perfectly formed abs. I watched his breaths stagger, his stomach flexing as I drew out his pleasure.

It was of great effort to keep my magic contained; the electricity building inside me from the sight of him, for my love of him, was sending sparks throughout my body.

He was so fucking handsome. More handsome and perfect than anyone imaginable. I began rubbing my clit as I bounced up and down, and Silas admired me with dilated pupils, his eyes half-lidded. Then, a dark grin appeared on his face.

"I need to taste you, Lena."

"Silas—"

He sat up and flipped us around, my back now against the mattress and Silas in between my thighs. I couldn't object; I wanted it just as bad.

My legs were spread entirely as he began kissing down the sides of my thighs. My back couldn't help but arch. Fuck, his teasing was driving me wild. I could feel his hot breath against my clit, and then he licked against the sides of me.

My heart was beating so fast. "Quill," I breathed.

In a flash, he dragged his tongue down my center, and I covered my mouth as a loud moan escaped me. He licked around and around, then brought his focus to the bundle of nerves, flicking his tongue rapidly.

Fucking hell.

It never got old. In fact, it had only gotten better with time as we had both learned how to best please each other. I took my free hand and ran it through his hair, gripping hard. The noises he was making while devouring me were about to send me over the edge.

"Do you know how lovely you taste, Flower?" he mumbled against my sex. A moan deep from my chest came out at those words, and I felt him smile against me before continuing to eat my pussy. My left hand joined the other, both of them now tangled in his jet-black waves. I began grinding myself against his face, and he growled in response.

I never wanted this to end. But my orgasm was building, and I didn't want to deny it.

Silas plunged two fingers into me, his eyes trailing over me with pure lust, and my body melted.

"You are so beautiful, naked in the moonlight, Lena. I could look at this view forever." He curved his fingers upward, hitting a sensitive spot, and electricity internally erupted at the feeling of it. I cried out, and his tongue circled my clit as my body shattered into a million pieces, the release so pleasant I was wailing into my palm.

Huffing, he plunged himself into me, and the feel of his cock inside me after an orgasm was just what I needed. He began pumping his hips, sliding in and out, and I wrapped my arms and legs around his torso.

"Silas, you feel so good," I moaned, my eyes fluttering shut at the delicious pleasure. Silas pressed his thumb against my clit and started making circles, and my moans only got louder. "It's so hard to be quiet."

"I know," he panted. He moved his thumb faster, keeping a perfect pace as his cock stretched me.

"Yes, just like that." The ecstasy was blinding, and before I knew it, another orgasm rippled through me. I was wailing at the same time Silas bellowed, needing only a few more pumps before finding his own release and pouring himself inside of me.

A few moments passed before he collapsed beside me and pulled me so that I was cradled against his chest, both of us sweating and struggling for air.

"That," he breathed, "was fantastic."

It was by far the best sex we had. And with how many times we had fucked over the past year, that was saying a lot. I leaned up and kissed his cheek, and he faced me with eyes twinkling like starlight.

"I am so in love with you, Lena," he whispered, then kissed me gently.

"I'm so in love with *you*," I whispered back. He stroked my hair and rested his chin on the top of my head.

I was so relaxed I could pass out. But while the sex had given

Silas a distraction, I knew there was dark, heavy emotion still within him. I moved over a bit and tilted my head up, causing Silas to look down at me.

For a moment, we just took each other in. And then I could see his tears forming, his jaw clenching once more, and then a single tear traveled down his cheek. The sight broke my heart.

I dragged my thumb softly along his cheek, wiping the tear away. His lip then began to tremble, and as I pulled him in close, he finally let go and sobbed into my chest.

CHAPTER TWENTY-SEVEN
SILAS

I had never truly cried in front of anyone since I was a little boy. It felt pathetic. My father certainly didn't enjoy the sight—he would call me weak for it. But I couldn't hold it in any longer, not after losing the only other person I had a close relationship with. I wept into her chest, and Lena held me, running her hand through my hair and murmuring over and over that she loved me. I was comforted by her soft whispers and her heavenly scent, a mixture of eucalyptus and spearmint.

She was the best thing to ever happen to me.

I didn't much believe in fate. With all those years trapped in this castle, I assumed life would always feel bleak and empty. And then I found her my first day outside the walls. Like destiny was demanding us to be together.

Mother had liked her a lot too. Who couldn't?

Once my breathing began to steady and the tears lessened, I drew back to look up at Lena, whose own face crumpled. I never wanted her to look like that again as long as I lived. I pulled myself together and sat up.

"Do you want to talk about it? Do you know what happened?" she asked gently.

I sniffed, then pulled her back against my chest. "We know who did it. Mother's aide, Amatta." I sighed through my nose. "I've known her since I was a little boy. It just doesn't make sense. Then again, I must not have known her very well…" My mind flashed back to all the signs I potentially missed before snapping back to the present moment. "I should've sensed something was off. Should've done something."

"This is *not* your burden, Silas. This isn't your fault."

"Father claims she is a witch…"

I felt Lena tense against me. She's scared of them. Rightfully so. But I would never let one near her. Ever.

"What makes him think that?" she asked quietly.

"I guess he walked in on it right after it happened. Magic radiated from her palms. He said he was able to contain her before the guards whisked her away to a cell. I guess she put up a decent fight. But thankfully, no one else got hurt." I chewed on the inside of my cheek.

"What do you think her motive was?"

"No idea. Mother was the most honorable person in the entire castle. Even when it came to witches, she was reluctant to throw them out of our kingdom. Her kindness…her ability to see good in people who didn't deserve it…that was her weakness. And now she is gone."

"Your mother was a wonderful person." She stroked my chest, and I resisted the urge to cry at hearing her say "was" when talking about Mother. "You…you aren't in danger, are you?"

"I don't know…"

"There has to be a way to ensure you're safe," she demanded.

"I'm more worried about you sneaking up here." I pinched her cheek playfully with a smile I knew didn't meet my eyes. "Mother should've been the only one who knew about you…but still. If Amatta was working with anyone, perhaps they've been watching the castle, and—"

She was visibly tense but forced a smile for me. "Please, don't worry about me. You have too much to worry about to fret over a peasant girl." She pinched my cheek back. I gazed into her golden-green eyes, and my eyes trailed down to her full lips.

Gods, she is so beautiful.

"You mean everything to me, Lena. One day, you will rule this kingdom with me. I will *always* worry about you."

Her smile faded, and she stroked my cheek. "It's a lovely dream," she murmured. "But not reality, Quill." Her lip quivered, and she buried her face in my chest once more.

I didn't have the energy to convince her, but I knew she would be my queen, my wife, my equal—the latter being true already, even if she or no one else in the kingdom saw it.

I stroked her hair and kissed her forehead, inhaling her scent again. I let out a hum. "Have I ever told you how lovely you smell?"

She let out a soft laugh. "Only a thousand times," she teased. She leaned up and brushed her lips against mine. "I don't ever want to leave," she mumbled, then sat up, her copper curls falling gracefully on her breasts. What a sight it was. "But I have to," she continued, leaning down and planting a soft kiss on my lips. I ran my hand through her silky hair and dragged her down, and she let out a giggle. "No more tonight, I'm afraid, Your Highness."

I groaned with a smirk, and she lifted off the bed and began dressing. The moonlight accentuated her stunning figure. Her wide hips, her perfect ass, her breasts. She was a masterpiece. How could she think she was anything less than spectacular? It had always been beyond me.

"What are you gawking at?" She grinned, but she already knew the answer. I left the bed and walked over to her, and her eyes widened as she looked between my legs.

"You see what you do to me?" I teased, but I sauntered to my dresser instead of claiming her again and slipped on loungewear bottoms.

"Shame." She smiled bashfully as she fastened her pants and threw on her bra and shirt.

I walked over to her and pulled her into an embrace. I knew that the second she left, grief would consume me once more. "Thank you for checking on me, Flower," I murmured. "Thank you for caring."

"No thanks needed." She squeezed me tight. "I love you so much."

"I love you."

We stood silently for a while, lost in each other's arms. When Lena finally pulled away, I began to feel the lump in my throat forming.

"I wanted to give you something…" I began. A crease formed between Lena's eyebrows, and I stepped over to my nightstand. I opened the top drawer and retrieved my mother's favorite necklace. The silver piece had five blue sapphires surrounded by halos of diamonds.

When I held it up to show Lena, she gasped.

"Silas…"

"I want you to have it. Please, Lena." I motioned for her to turn around, and she hesitantly obeyed. I lifted the necklace over her head and clasped it behind her neck, the gems hanging just below her collarbones.

She turned to me, brushing her fingertips over the sapphires. It looked perfect on her. "It's beautiful," she breathed, then met my gaze with teary eyes. "Are you sure?"

"Without a doubt."

Her lip trembled. "Thank you, Silas. I am honored to have it."

I pulled her into an embrace once more. It took great effort not to break down again. "I am honored to have *you*."

We slowly made our way to my balcony door. I held it open for her as she stepped outside.

"Please, please be careful," I begged.

"Always." She went on her tiptoes and gave me one last peck before she went off into the distance. I watched until she was no longer in view and stepped back into my room.

All my emotions crashed into me once more, and I did everything to hold in my sob until I was face-first into my pillow.

My mother, my poor mother. Mercilessly killed like it was nothing. Like *she* was nothing. Like her death wouldn't affect so many people. Affect me.

I hated Amatta. It was the first genuine, deep hatred I had ever felt, next to those brutes that threatened to hurt Lena or the one that I had to put down in front of that tavern. I enjoyed ending them, just like I would enjoy ending Amatta.

She must pay.

CHAPTER TWENTY-EIGHT
LENA

Torrin was by the pathway exit when I made my way down the side of the castle. He fell into pace beside me, looking around us occasionally in case of any threat.

"Silas said Ryia's killer was her aide, Amatta," I muttered. "That she is a Mage."

Torrin whipped his head toward me. "What? There is no way Amatta is a Mage."

"How can you be so sure?"

Torrin went to speak and groaned, realizing he *couldn't* be sure. It was too easy for us to glamour ourselves. "She can't be Kayin if that is where your mind is going. They don't even speak similarly. And I don't mean the sound of her voice. Mannerisms, all that, are completely different."

"She could be working with her, though." I tensed. "Who knows who else Kayin has been speaking to?"

Torrin paled. "I…no." He shook his head. "Kayin said she was working with Igon. And he would never have supported the assassination of the Queen. The King, perhaps. But not the Queen."

"And if she lied?" I pressed.

He studied me, then shrugged in defeat as his eyes went forward. "We will just have to trust."

I stopped in my tracks and then threw my arms in frustration. "I can't go off blind trust! Not when it comes to him."

"Keep it down!" Torrin hissed as he grabbed my arms. "Kayin and Igon insisted that Silas is who will determine the fate of our people," he said calmly. "And while our connection to Kayin is…questionable now, I trust Igon with my whole being."

I bit back tears. "I want to be able to believe that," I whispered.

He squeezed my arms gently before releasing me. "*If you trust in anything, trust me,*" he said to me in my mind as I chugged the extra elixirs in my bag and emerged through the hedges, now in the Inner Ring.

Kayin's words hit me.

You can trust him, you know.

Crowds were gathering the following day, flooding into the Center to witness the trial for Amatta, the supposed Mage who had killed Queen Ryia. It felt surreal that Silas and his family were just here celebrating, only to be mourning in the same spot two days later.

Well, not exactly the same spot. Our focus now was to the left of the castle, at the guillotine.

I shuddered at the King's presence. I noted that no tears were present, though he struck me as a man who had never cried. Next to him was Silas, with the same dark expression, though he was struggling, yet succeeding, at holding back his tears. I wanted to run up to him so badly—be by his side.

The crowd began shouting, hurling slurs as Amatta was brought out by guards. She was gagged, her eyes blown wide with tears and snot pouring down her face.

When they reached the platform, the guards placed her nowhere near the guillotine. Instead, she was being tied to a wooden stake. She was thrashing violently as they secured rope around her body.

She was terrified.

What…what are they going to do to her?

While the King spoke with the guards, citizens began hurling stones at Amatta, one making a sickening crack as it hit her head. People cheered as blood dripped down her skull, and I couldn't help but feel sick.

Mother held my hand firmly, and I looked away. Like before, we were still further back in the crowd but close enough to see and hear *everything*.

The King stepped forward, his height and size daunting, and he held up his hand to silence the crowd before speaking.

"This witch killed your Queen in cold blood. Our loving, sweet Ryia. It was by the blessing of the Gods I was able to stop this monster before she killed any more innocent people."

Amatta thrashed and thrashed, screaming despite her gag, but her attempted words were a mush of gibberish. Silas stared at her with disgust.

Despite the King's claim, Amatta's ears were rounded. Perhaps she refused to remove her glamour in hopes of survival.

"We have set rules in place, so witches know that they have no place here in our kingdom, yet they still plague our lands with their presence. And now, they have killed your Queen."

The crowd roared in contempt, and I squeezed Mother's hand tight.

Wrong…this felt *wrong*.

"That is why, citizens of Otacia, I will be putting a kill order in place for any and all witches."

Silence.

"It is time to put an end to their kind, once and for all."

My whole body went numb. My hearing became muffled. The words that proceeded to fall from the King's lips did not register.

No.

No!

Ulric lit a torch as his speech finished, his eyes intense on Amatta, and handed the flame to Silas.

My Gods…he is going to make Silas do it?

Amatta was still shaking, flailing her body as hard as she could, but as Silas neared, she sagged in defeat. He hesitated for a moment before he lit the wood beneath her, and even with her mouth gagged, her horrific screams filled the entire kingdom.

Flames crept up her legs, up her torso, over her face. Smoke swirled upward, and the nauseating scent of burning flesh permeated the air.

Silas just watched with an apathy in his eyes that sent chills down my spine, a coldness I had never seen on him. The crowd boomed, and my hand shot over my mouth in disbelief at that barbaric act before us. Mother tugged at my wrist and gave me a look that said, *"Don't show emotion."*

I couldn't see Torrin, but I heard his panicked voice.

"Tonight. We must leave tonight."

This. This was what Kayin had warned us about. Mages—we were no longer just to be banished. Our existence was now to end entirely.

I couldn't accept it. Accept that I had to leave. Accept that the home I had grown to love could've changed so much, so fast. Mother clasped my hand, and we tried our best not to appear suspicious as we hurried home, the sound of the brown-haired woman's screams fading to nothing as her body melted away.

"We leave tonight," Mother said frantically, slamming our door and locking us in our cottage.

I couldn't even argue. I was numb.

"You heard the King," she continued, her body shaking as she began packing our things. "There is a kill order on us, Lena. I will not have us be sitting ducks in a kingdom with such a sick leader. This is what that woman Kayin must have been warning you about."

"But…but Silas—" I felt like a shell of a person. This couldn't be real. This couldn't be happening.

"Is the son of that evil bastard," she snarled.

"So, what?" I clenched my fists as reality began to set in. There was now a kill order on all Mages. We get caught, we are dead. "You don't care that we are abandoning him right after he has suffered this loss?" The rational part of me knew we had no choice. "And what…do I…I tell him I'm leaving—about who we are?"

She whirled toward me. "Absolutely not!" She grasped my shoulders. "I know you love him, but we cannot take that risk." She resumed her packing. "We will fake our deaths. Set fire to our house. I will conjure up false bodies so they think we died in here."

"Do you hear yourself?!" I asked incredulously.

"This isn't just a simple banishing and running. This is truly life and death." She wiped a tear that had fallen out of her eye. "I care for Silas greatly, Lena. I said before he's like a son to me. But he is the Prince. He cannot escape his fate any more than we can. It is no longer safe here, and I know that Silas would desire your safety over anything."

I knew that, too. But to leave with no explanation…to make him believe I was dead…

Find Torrin. Go to Ames.

I felt sick that the day had finally fucking come.

"I…I have to see him before we go."

"Lena—"

"No! I will not leave without seeing him!" I cried. "One last time."

CHAPTER TWENTY-NINE

It was past 11:00 p.m. when I finally snuck to see Silas, an invisibility elixir coursing through my body. Torrin was not at his usual post, but I knew he was gathering things for our trip.

Guards were swarming around, but I was confident in this elixir's ability. I executed the recipe perfectly, as my last failing had been unacceptable.

I climbed the ledges carefully, and when I reached his window and peeked inside, he wasn't there.

Shit.

I squeezed my eyes shut.

Torrin? Torrin, can you hear me?

I waited a few moments before I heard a reply.

"Yes, what is going on? Are you all packed?"

Yes, I am packed. I am trying to see Silas, but he isn't in his room.

"You are at the castle?!"

Even in my head, I could hear the anger in Torrin's voice. I clenched my fists. How does no one understand? I felt my eyes burning.

I cannot just leave him without holding him one more time. I can't.

There was a delay in Torrin's response.

"I understand…" he said softly. *"The King and Otacia's favored generals are in a meeting. Silas is there, too."*

I rested my back against the cold stone of the castle, looking out into the starry night sky before my eyes trailed downward. Most people were sleeping now, but the few lights illuminated in the homes below glimmered like stars from this high up. This was my last night here…I still couldn't fathom it.

What are they preparing?

Another pause.

"Nothing good, Lena. Nothing good. It's been hours, so I assume it will be done within the hour."

I buried my face in my hands. *I am so scared, Torrin.*

"I know." His voice was laced with compassion. *"I will keep you and your mother safe as we make our way to Ames. I promise."*

I was startled when I caught movement on my left, and when my eyes darted over, I saw Torrin standing next to me with a bag slung over his shoulder.

He looked around, and I knew he couldn't see me.

"I assume you're here. Your voice sounds louder here."

I am.

I fished into my bag and sipped on the reversal elixir I packed to make myself visible again. When Torrin's eyes met mine, I knew it worked. I glimpsed back at the sky, and he sat down beside me.

You should go. The last thing I want is for you to get caught.

"Come with me," he said out loud softly. "We can go right now."

I turned to him, his expression as strained as mine.

"You know I can't do that," I whispered.

"I know," he whispered back, then, to my surprise, pulled me into a hug. I froze before hugging him back as tightly as I could. The tears couldn't help but pour out, and I was sobbing quietly into his chest.

"Are you going to be able to keep it together when you see him?" Torrin asked just above a whisper.

I don't know…I don't know…

I continued to sob, and Torrin stroked my hair. How could I see him one last time without having a complete meltdown? Without telling him the truth?

"You could leave him a note," Torrin gently suggested. "You could say you came to see him, and he wasn't in his room."

"I need to hug him," I choked out. "I need to touch him, kiss him, hear his voice—one last time."

I pulled away from his hold and sniffled as I wiped my eyes. *I can do this.*

Torrin nodded. "I will stay with you."

I waited half an hour with Torrin, and he did his best to try to keep me calm. I told him talking made it worse, but he insisted that if I held it all in until I saw Silas, I would break.

So, I told him about us. I told him stories he already knew. I told him about the day I showed Silas around the Outer Ring. I told him about my childhood on the run and about the fear that has held me back all my life. He kept eye contact and listened the entire time.

When I noticed the oil lamps being turned on in Silas's room, I wiped my eyes and stood, taking a deep breath.

"You can do this, Lena." He grasped my hands. "He is your Soul-Tie. This is not the end."

I nodded, we squeezed each other's hands, and I made my way to the window. Torrin retreated to where Silas wouldn't see him.

When I peered inside and saw the one I loved, I noted how exhausted he looked—completely drained. He was unbuttoning his shirt when he caught me in the window. Quickly, he trekked to the door, flicking the locks and letting me inside.

"Lena, you shouldn't—"

I flung myself into his arms, and he closed his around me tightly. I repeated Torrin's words in my head.

He is your Soul-Tie. This is not the end.

"I know, I know I shouldn't have come up here. But I—" Had to say goodbye. "I had to see you."

He continued holding me close. "I wish I could hold you like this daily," he breathed. "You're the only thing that grounds me in all this chaos."

He is your Soul-Tie. This is not the end.

"I couldn't live without you," he whispered.

I froze. Why…why, of all times, would he say something like that?

"Don't say that…" I begged quietly.

"It's true. The only good thing in my life is you. I wouldn't have the desire to live if—"

"No," I said sternly, pulling back and staring into his eyes. "You cannot let your will to live be tied to me, Silas. To anyone. Because life is unfair, and tragedy can happen at any time." I touched his face, stroking my thumb along his perfect cheekbones. His amber eyes welled with tears, and mine started too, as well. "No matter what happens…" My lip trembled, but I kept the tears in. "You will *not* give up. You will not break." It took everything in me to keep myself composed. "Promise me."

His jaw clicked, his golden eyes bouncing between mine in contemplation.

"Please, promise me, Silas."

He kissed my forehead. "For you, my Flower, I promise," he whispered.

He is your Soul-Tie. This is not the end.

I pulled away, and my throat burned from holding in my tears.

"I have to leave. I'm not sure when I can come to see you again… with everything happening."

"I understand." He gave me a sad smile. "I will miss you every second."

This is not the end.

"As will I." I pulled him close and hugged him tightly again. It took every fiber in my being not to break. I was going to hurt him so deeply, and all I wanted was for him to know I would be okay. That I would still be alive. To know that I wanted nothing more than to stay here with him.

"I love you more than anything," I whispered. "Always."

"Always, Lena." He rocked me in his arms. "I will love you, always."

I brought my lips to his one last time, the kiss slow yet intense. I savored every second of his tongue around mine, his arms around my body, the feeling of his face against my hands. When we broke our kiss, I studied his face, memorizing every line, every detail.

This is not the end.

I retreated toward the balcony, and Silas opened the door for me.

"Please, be careful," he begged, just as he had the day prior.

"I will be just fine," I said softly, wishing he would remember these words come tomorrow, hoping that somehow, he would know I had lived. Unable to say goodbye without falling apart, I whispered, "Until I see you again."

Silas smiled, and I took a mental picture of him before turning away. I made it around the balcony and down the path before Torrin caught my arms. I stared at him with tears falling out of my eyes.

"You did good, Lena."

I nodded and fished into my bag, pulling out two elixirs and handing Torrin one. We sipped, and we both became invisible.

The walk home was a mental and visual blur as tears kept silently welling and pouring from my eyes.

I'm leaving him. I'm leaving him for who knows how long…

As we entered my house, we sipped a reversal elixir. Mother was packing a bag and froze as she saw us walk in. Torrin ambled forward, and I slowly shut the door behind me before leaning against it, sliding to the ground, and finally releasing my sob.

"Lena…" Mother rushed to me, attempting to comfort me, but

it would never be enough. I supposed she knew the feeling, but she didn't trick my father into thinking she was dead.

I was gasping for air with how hard I was crying. I had never felt this much sorrow. "I…I can't be without him," I cried. "Gods, he is going to be so heartbroken."

"Shh…shh…" Mother pulled me in close.

"I love him…" I wept as she rocked me. "I love him." I felt my body getting cold, colder than I had ever felt before, even when I once ran for my life barefoot in the snow.

Mother held me, continuing to hush me as she swayed me back and forth. My body began to tremble.

Fuck. I am freezing.

"Gods, Lena—" Torrin began, and then Mother shrieked and tumbled back. My head shot up, and when I glanced down at my lap, I choked.

My hands and forearms were covered in ice. The ground beneath me, where my hands were resting, was covered too, freezing my arms and legs to the floor.

Torrin hurried over and knelt beside me.

"Thank the Gods this didn't happen earlier," he mumbled as he held his palms near both of my arms, a light flame emitting out of both.

I gasped. "You wield fire," I breathed, my teeth chattering from the cold.

"Indeed," he murmured. "Just hold still. I won't hurt you." He slowly swayed his palms back and forth, gradually melting the ice that held me in place. Fire magic is the rarest elemental magic to acquire. I didn't want to imagine the pain Torrin must've endured to unlock it.

"You will learn to control it. Don't worry," Mother began.

Then I thought about myself. "I...I have ice magic." It was more of a statement than a question. Mother nodded, and I looked to Torrin, his brown eyes focused on the task at hand. Ice magic is the elemental type that is acquired by immense devastation. Mother also wielded ice, though I had never asked what gave her that power. I would on our journey.

I felt the water dripping down my arms, and after a moment, I was able to break them free from the ice mold.

"I'm sorry," I whispered, then cried more. I didn't have it in me to even feel embarrassed; Torrin had seen me cry more than anyone had, save for Mother.

"Don't be," Torrin said softly. I continued to shiver, and after a few moments, my legs were free. When my sobbing started to quiet down, Torrin spoke to my mother.

"If there is anything I can help with, let me know."

Mother surveyed the bags resting on our dining table. "Everything we're taking is packed. I've stored away as many elixirs as I could comfortably fit." She turned to him. "How far of a travel is it to Ames?"

"About two months."

My heart sank further if that was even possible. Two months on the run. Two months of sleeping on the ground and struggling to find food to eat.

"I will take care of us."

I lifted my head to look at Torrin, and he nodded, helping me to my feet.

A moment later, after changing into dry clothes, I stood at the edge of my room. I was watching Mother conjure a replica of…*me*… lying on my bed. It was quite a disturbing sight. While I had focused on improving basic enchanting over the past year, Mother had concentrated on learning advanced spells, the ability to conjure up illusions being one of them.

"Your jewelry…"

"No. The necklace and ring stay with me." I looked to my closet, where various clothes, dresses, and gowns Silas had all gifted me hung. I held back another sob. All would be turned to ash. Never to be worn again.

I waited in the living area with Torrin as Mother conjured up her own copy, and when she emerged, her eyes teary, Torrin shifted to me.

"I will set fire to both of your rooms, ensuring nobody figures out those bodies aren't real. When I finish, we take these elixirs." He gestured to the glass bottles we all held. "And we run like hell."

Mother stepped next to me and nodded, and Torrin made his way to Mother's room, then my own. Once I heard the fire start crackling, Torrin paced to us.

"It's too risky to talk, so if either of you needs to communicate— think it. And I will relay if necessary."

We nodded, then quickly downed the elixirs before exiting our cottage for the final time. I took in its imperfect stones, the plants I had spent so much time tending to, the ivy I had always adored.

My home. The first real home I ever had.

We raced down the cobblestone road, hearing a shout just before we made it to the exit. Someone had noticed the fire. I turned and felt my stomach flip when I beheld the sight of our house, now engulfed in flames.

"It will be okay."

I hope you are right, Torrin.

We made it down the steps, across the bridge, and into the Southern Forest just in time as the elixir faded. We dashed into the shadows. Each breath was like a shard of glass in my lungs.

I allowed myself one last glance back, the lights from the castle in the distance a beacon in the dark.

This is not the end.

PART TWO:

NOW

CHAPTER THIRTY
FIVE YEARS LATER

Lounging on a wooden bench in the training pit, I watch as Merrick and Elowen battle, thoroughly amused by their repartee. Merrick held up his fingertips, twirling shards of ice in the air before launching them, and Elowen did her best to dodge, quickly evading each spike until one nicked her arm.

"Ugh!" she groaned as blood dripped down her golden-brown forearm. "I am no match for the ice."

She placed her hand over the fresh wound, and a warm glow emitted from her palm, healing it in seconds. She grinned at me.

Elowen Astair was the best healer in Ames. For only being nineteen, she surpassed everyone in that field, old and young alike. What would take me minutes or sometimes hours took her hardly any time at all. Depending on the severity of the wound, of course.

Merrick snorted. "Finally, you admit it," he said smugly. Elowen stuck out her tongue in response. Their banter always amused me, the dynamic of half-siblings being something I could never relate to.

Merrick and Elowen's father, Vicsin Astair, was elected Lord of Ames. When Mother, Torrin, and I had finally arrived here, it was Vicsin who welcomed us with open arms. While I normally resented pity, I was grateful for his kindness. Vicsin was still below Igon, Ames's Supreme, but he was highly respected.

Merrick was also Torrin's cousin. They both shared bright platinum hair, though Merrick's was more silver than Torrin's white-blond. Though Torrin and Elowen didn't share blood, he loved her all the same.

Ames, being a rather small town, had only about one hundred fifty people. But everyone here was a Mage. It was…comforting.

Because the town was so remote, there hadn't even been a home available for us to stay in when we arrived. Vicsin had offered us refuge in his residence with his wife, Heildee, Elowen's mother, thankfully having extra space to harbor Mother, Torrin, and me. Mother and I slept in their basement, and Torrin's room was in the attic.

I remember learning how Torrin's parents had vanished shortly before his departure to Otacia. No one knew what had happened to them, if they willingly left, or if they were captured or killed. Even after all these years, I knew the lack of answers weighed heavy on Torrin. His room was still kept as it was before in Vicsin's home, and his uncle was more than happy to welcome him home.

Merrick and I became close quickly. I had arrived in Ames sick from travel, and he was by my side the entire time. I could tell part of him was closed off, and I felt like we related to each other in that sense. He never wished to go into detail about the strain in his family, but he told me Vicsin cheated on his mother with Heildee, resulting in Elowen. After his father discovered the pregnancy, leaving his mother and breaking her heart, she committed suicide five years later. Merrick hated his father for it and still did to this day.

He had hated Elowen too, even though he knew their father's infidelity wasn't her fault. At that time of our arrival, Merrick was nineteen, Elowen was fourteen, and I was surprised to discover that the two hardly spoke. But despite everything, they worked together to comfort me alongside Torrin while I was unwell. We all had grown rather close these past five years.

Five years…

It had been five years since I had left Otacia…since I went back on the run. Five years since I was in my cottage, relaxing by the river or running our stand at the market.

Five years since I left Silas.

Not a day, minute, or second went by without him on my mind.

It had also been over a year since I last saw Torrin…since he left Ames abruptly without even saying goodbye.

A year since…

I shook my head at the thought. I didn't wish to think of it.

Merrick sauntered over to Elowen and tousled her light pink hair that she kept in a pixie cut. She swatted at him before she brushed her bangs back to where they lay cutely on her forehead. There was a similarity between the looks of them, but Merrick's skin, which was fair like mine, was a stark contrast to Elowen's tawny skin. They both shared blue eyes, yet Elowen's were more pigmented, while Merrick's were nearly gray.

Merrick took a swig out of his waterskin, then wiped his mouth. "What do you say, Lena, you next?"

I grinned as I vacated my seat on the bench. I passed Elowen's petite figure as I made my way down the few steps to the pit. "I don't want to hear you crying like last time."

He laughed, took another sip of water, and then tied back his hair, which, when not in his usual ponytail, rested a few inches past his shoulders. He wore a black long-sleeved shirt, the neckline a dramatic V, showcasing his muscular chest. He paired it with gray pants and black boots; an outfit that lacked color was his usual style. He wasn't adorning his typical bow and quiver. No need for that during our practice today.

It was fascinating because the people of Ames were all Mages, *openly* Mages. I remember my jaw dropping when I first came here, shocked to see so many pointed ears and so many people freely practicing magic.

Many of the townsfolk had no idea how to wield a weapon nor a desire to learn how to. But Merrick and Elowen were intrigued, especially considering their cousin had become quite the warrior over the past eight years. It was another thing we bonded over. Elowen chose to learn using a dagger, and while Merrick could use a sword, he preferred the bow, mostly because he could make ice arrows that had the potential to kill an enemy in one hit.

As for me, it was Torrin who taught me everything there was to know about magic, about wielding and fighting with it. He had trained me for years. Sometimes, he'd poke fun at me while I'd train our friends but would quickly bite back a grin when I'd mention they were his techniques.

I miss you…

Torrin hadn't spoken in my mind since the last time I saw him, though I still would talk to him in my head, hoping somehow, some way, he was listening. His abilities could only go a certain distance; him speaking to me from Castle La'Rune while I was in my cottage was about as far as he could go. Still, I hoped.

Merrick cracked his knuckles and got into a fighting stance. I smirked, flipped my long braid over my shoulder, and thought of my plan of action.

Merrick had acquired ice magic, as had I. A decent handful of Mages in Ames had as well. I suppose it isn't uncommon to go through such sorrow in your lifetime.

Before I could think, he shot a bolt of ice at me. I held out my palm, melting the shard with my fire magic before it could pierce my chest. Merrick grunted and sent five more shards at me, and I whirled my hands to create a circle of fire, melting them all instantly.

Merrick crossed his arms. "And *I* am no match for fire."

Elowen chuckled in her seat. "No one is a match for Lena."

It was true. Now that Torrin was gone, I was the only Mage in Ames who could wield fire, save for Igon. I had unlocked the ability years ago and had excelled with it. Controlling it could be hard at times—same with ice, depending on my emotions. But I could admit I had skill.

Merrick dragged his teeth along his lip ring, then continued his assault. With ease, I melted his shards of ice and elegantly dodged the others. He groaned in frustration and rushed for me. I could have easily used a forcefield and shot him back, but it would've been a cheap shot. I dodged and swept my feet under him, knocking him right on his ass.

Elowen burst out laughing, and Merrick shot her a glare.

I clicked my tongue. "Lunging for me would've never worked."

He sighed and rested back on his palms. The early afternoon sun was shining through the window behind Elowen as a black cat jumped through it. It stretched its limbs before its violet gaze looked to her.

"Would it be weird if I pet you?" Elowen asked in her usual bubbly voice, and the cat shifted into a woman with ebony skin, the same purple eyes sparkling.

"Yes, that would be weird." She smiled, then glanced over at Merrick and me.

"Lena still kicking your ass, Merrick?" she teased.

"Please, I was just about to shoot her in the rib," he said as he tried to pierce me while looking at her. I, of course, caught it in time and melted that one too. Merrick groaned and lay on his back, hands covering his face in shame, and I couldn't help but laugh, the girls joining in with me.

"Yeah, ha-ha," Merrick mumbled while waving his hand in dismissal. "Why are you here, Viola?"

She shot up smoothly and crossed her arms, her deep purple braids swinging just past her chest. "I can't hang with my friends?"

I was introduced to Viola Sonnet as one of Merrick's friends when I first came here. While she didn't have any elemental magic unlocked, her ability to shape-shift like a Warlock made her one of the most powerful Mages in Ames. Her smooth, brown skin and almond eyes weren't the only thing that made her beautiful. She truly radiated confidence. I envied it.

"I thought you didn't want to train today," Merrick grumbled from his position on the floor, the various piercings in his pointed ears reflecting the filtering sunlight.

"I told you—Igon wished to speak with me earlier." She turned her attention to me. "Actually, he wants to speak with you now, which is why I'm here, *Merrick*." She shot him a side-eye.

"Why does he want me?" I asked as I stretched my arms.

Viola just shrugged. "He told me Osrel was taking the day off and wished for help dusting the shelves in his office. Then, we were discussing Warlock folklore for a while. I was just about to leave when he asked me to fetch you."

"Alright," I replied, then grinned. "You can take my place then—kicking Merrick's ass."

Merrick rolled his eyes in response but kept his smile.

"What would you prefer I shape-shift into? A lion? A bear?" Viola taunted as she strode toward him.

"A fish," he muttered as he stood from the ground.

I chuckled and gave Elowen a smile before I headed to Igon's tower. He was the leader of Ames—our Supreme—and a very insightful older man. It was bizarre meeting him for the first time nearly five years ago after hearing about him from Torrin all that time.

I walked up the spiral steps of the tower and into his office at the top. The windows were open, the early May breeze pleasantly blowing throughout the room. The walls were lined with hundreds, if not thousands, of books, and the room had a faint scent of vanilla. There had been a time I snuck in here, peeking at all the various spells and enchantments his tomes contained. Thankfully, when he caught me, he showed mercy and just laughed. If anyone else had done it, I think he would have been displeased. But, for whatever reason, he enjoyed my interest and even began to tutor me afterward.

"Ah, Lena." He was sitting at his desk, stroking his short silver beard. While Igon was in his sixties, he remained in good shape. He was fit, and honestly, I think a lot of the women in town who were Mother's age were attracted to him based on the giggling he'd receive when they'd pass by him. Whether he was aware of it or not, he didn't let on.

He cleared his throat. "Tell me, dear, what do you know of Oquerene?"

I blinked. "Oquerene? The realm we all originated from, yes?" I had read about it in one of the books he let me borrow not too long ago. It was not a spell book, just ancient tales of our people.

He nodded. "It is said that the Mages of today stemmed from that realm—a kingdom above the skies. A place where every creature spoken of in fairy tales resides, the ones said to be extinct…" He paused, then met my eyes with a smile. "Can you imagine such a place?"

"It sounds…lovely," I murmured. "And too fantastical to be real."

He chuckled. "Some believe that Oquerene was also the land of the Gods. That Ravaiana, the Goddess of Life, allowed those who lived there to be immune to the effects of time."

My eyebrows raised. "The people there could live forever? I don't recall reading that."

Igon chuckled. "Well, not forever, no. I imagine that they could still be affected by sickness or violence. But, if the Goddess deemed them worthy, they would not age past a certain point."

I frowned. When Igon learned of my lack of knowledge of our people, he insisted on teaching me as much as he could about our culture. He told me of the Gods—the Gods the Mages believed in, anyway, as they differed from the ones the humans worshipped. One of the biggest differences was the human Gods merely watched over us, while our Gods shared their power with humanity, manifesting in the varied species of magical humans that once roamed the planet. Most had been killed off, but the Mages lived on.

Igon had taken on a special role in my life, almost father-like. There had been so much he'd taught me over the last five years.

My eyes trailed to the large statue of the Goddess Ravaiana at the back of Igon's library. "What could possibly make someone worthy of such a gift?"

Igon smiled. "You'd have to ask the Goddess yourself."

I shifted on my feet. "Being another realm, would it have even been possible to go there?"

There was a twinkle of something in his topaz eyes, something I couldn't place. "If there's one thing I've learned in my sixty-one years of life, is that *anything* is possible." He glanced back down at the map he had sprawled out on his desk. "Come over," he motioned, and I did just that, taking a seat across from him at his desk. His hands were adorned with rings, and he placed one digit on the large parchment in front of him, its material yellowed by time.

"This is one of the main maps used by the other kingdoms in Tovagoth." His finger drifted to an area northwest of Ames, our settlement penned in unofficially. "You see this area here?" he asked, pointing at an area on the map with a unique symbol that had been added, presumably by him—a swirl with a tail trailed downward, an assortment of symbols alongside it that I couldn't decipher. "This is where Mount Rozavar is. I know a man named Immeron. He and his family live at the top of that mountain."

I wanted to touch the map, but I held my hands together in my lap. "I imagine that's cold," I muttered.

He laughed at that, showing bright white teeth. His smile always seemed…familiar. "Quite the opposite. Well, the base of the mountain is. But on the top, it is weather-controlled through magic—the gift of the man's wife. It's actually pleasant up there."

"You've been?"

To that, he smiled almost wearily as he glanced down at the map. "I have. This symbol here," he said as he pointed to the swirl, "only Mages can see it, but it is on the base of the mountain. If approved, you're teleported right up to the top."

"That's incredible," I breathed, then looked at him. "Why are you showing me this?" I asked warily.

"My friends who live up there are expert enchanters, blacksmiths. They have made me many skilled pieces over the years: weapons, jewelry, and armor. Immeron even made a fully functional arm for his wife, who was born without one. Quite miraculous." He grinned, then leaned forward. "Just in case you find yourself in need of his services."

I raised one of my brows at him. Anytime a seer said something like that, there was more to it. This also meant there was a reason he couldn't tell me, as it could alter the future.

When I arrived in Ames and Torrin introduced me to Igon, I felt immense comfort knowing that us listening to Kayin was the right thing to do, though he was surprised that we knew her name.

He didn't offer any ideas as to who she was or where she came from—said, as a seer, that it was information we couldn't know.

He assured us that the Queen's assassination was not anything he or Kayin was a part of, and I could swear his eyes welled with tears when we spoke of it. Even if the Queen was a La'Rune, even if she couldn't stop the prejudice toward our people, she had a good heart, and everyone knew it.

I sighed in defeat and looked back at the map, memorizing the location of Mount Rozavar.

"How has your control of fire been?" he asked after a few moments of silence between us.

"Good. Great, even." I lifted my head from the map, then huffed as I rested my back against my chair, crossing my arms. "Though, still no special ability."

Igon's eyes flickered, and he drummed his fingers on the table. "You are more special than you know," he said quietly.

I frowned, and then my eyes widened. "Wait…have you…have you seen my gift?"

He smiled but didn't respond.

"When will I get it?" I pressed.

"When the time is right. And I won't speak on it anymore!" he responded with a chuckle.

I groaned in frustration, then placed my elbow on the desk to rest my cheek on my fist. "Is it ever torturous? Knowing so much and not being able to say anything?"

Sadness wavered in his amber eyes, and his shoulders slumped as he sighed. "More than you could fathom. It isn't an ability I would wish on anyone."

Igon was a secretive man—no one knew much about him, even I, who had spent so much time in his tower. He came to Ames when he was thirty-six. The people instantly warmed to him, I guess, many saying they felt like they had known him for quite some time. He never married. Never had children. I always wondered why but didn't have it in me to ask.

I gently took my other hand and placed it on his. I couldn't imagine the weight he must carry every day, couldn't imagine all that he really knew.

He gave me a soft smile, then gently squeezed my hand with his other. "Now, don't go pitying me—I know you hate when people do it to you."

I rolled my eyes but smiled, then sat up straight, our hands disconnecting. "Igon?"

His smile faded. "Yes?"

Mine was now gone as well, and I bit my lip before speaking. "Do you…have you seen anything about Torrin?"

There was a gentleness to his features. "He is alive if that is what you are asking."

My shoulders sagged, and I looked to the floor. "I just can't believe he has stayed away for so long. This was his home, after all."

It was quiet, and Igon let out a shaky exhale. "It was me."

To that, my head sprang right up. I had to have heard him wrong. "What did you say?"

He kept his expression neutral, but I could see the guilt in his eyes. "I am the one who sent him away, more or less."

When his words registered, I sprang to my feet, gripping the desk in anguish. When Torrin had left, I immediately went to Igon, who at the time told me he knew nothing of it.

"You lied to me," I gritted out. Any bit of sympathy or warm feeling for Igon was gone at that moment. "Why? What did you say to him?"

Igon clasped his fingers together. He just stared at me.

I could feel the flames burning inside me, and I slammed my fist on his desk, the little trinkets on top of it rattling in response. "Damnit, Igon! You lied to me!" It was taking everything in me not to unleash hell on his library. "Tell me why!"

He looked at me for a few moments, and just before I was going to explode, he spoke. "I told him to leave because of his growing feelings toward you."

I blinked several times, wanting so badly to have heard him wrong. "You forced him to leave because he desired me?" I asked with dark calmness. If my voice didn't portray my anger, I knew my eyes and shaking limbs did.

Igon winced. "Forced isn't the correct word. Strongly suggested," he said cautiously. "It is known who your Soul-Tie is, Lena. It isn't Torrin."

I let out a shaky exhale.

Calm the flames, calm the flames.

My hands were clenched so hard into the wood that I wouldn't be all that surprised if my fingers were indented into it. "Ames was *his* home, not mine. If you cared so much for who I ended up with, then it should've been *me* you suggested to leave." I shook my head in disbelief. "The Prince is married. It doesn't matter who my Soul-Tie is!"

It was true that the news of his marriage a year ago had completely wrecked me. But Silas believed me to be dead. Of course he would move on.

Igon tensed. "I know you are angry—"

"Angry? I'm furious." I seethed. "What, I'm just supposed to be partnerless for the rest of my days? Just because *you* are okay being alone your entire life doesn't mean everyone else is."

Igon flinched, actually flinched at those words, then pointed to the door. "Leave," he said calmly. "Take some time to cool off. You'll see things more clearly later."

I bared my teeth. "Where is he?"

"I can't tell you."

"Where IS HE?" I cried, and my fists erupted in flame, Igon's desk catching fire. I backed away nervously, and Igon cursed as he pushed the contents of his desk onto the ground and frantically ran to the washroom sink, filling a bucket with water. Though he could also wield fire, attempting to calm another Mage's flames was a difficult, if not impossible, task.

I just stood there, my mouth forming a tight line as I studied the flames. I should feel remorse, but I didn't. Even letting out a small bit of fire did nothing to relieve the anger.

Igon poured the bucket over the top of his desk, successfully extinguishing the flames. He looked at me in disappointment.

"I won't forgive you for this," I hissed, and with that, I walked out.

CHAPTER THIRTY-ONE

The rest of the afternoon was spent throwing fireballs in a river just outside of Ames's border. Gods was I pissed.

Poor Torrin…why didn't he speak with me? At least to tell me where he was going…

I sighed. Probably because he knew I wouldn't let him go. Gods-damn bastard. I owed him everything—for Mother's and my safe passage here, for my training, for my new home. He didn't deserve to essentially be kicked out.

And for what? Silas had moved on. Even if he was my apparent Soul-Tie, people love and get married to people who aren't their fated mate all the time.

I shot out blasts repeatedly, crying out in anger. The flames still raged inside of me; the release of my power was futile in extinguishing the pain. Tears poured down my face, and when my vision

275

became too blurred to see straight, I stopped, my arms sagging at my sides.

"Are you alright?" a voice asked softly.

I turned slowly, blinking the fresh tears out of my eyes. There stood Mother, looking at me with concern etched on her face. The spring air blew around us, Mother's bangs and shoulder-length copper hair blowing in the wind.

"No. No, I am not." My lip trembled, and I gazed back at the river. Mother stepped beside me, and we both stared off in silence before she linked her hand with mine.

"What happened?" she asked gently.

I wiped my nose with the back of my free hand. "Igon is a filthy liar. That is what happened."

Mother's head quickly pivoted, and I willed myself not to set every tree in the vicinity on fire.

"He told me *he* was the one who sent Torrin away, after all this time."

Mother gasped, her hand shooting over her mouth. "I don't understand…why? Why the hell would he do that?"

I let out a humorless laugh. "I suppose anyone who makes me happy has to be taken away." And to that comment, my cheeks heated. I had never told anyone what occurred between me and Torrin last year. Thankfully, Mother didn't press. "You know how seers are," I continued. "They can't tell you anything directly. He won't even let me know where he is…" My lip quivered, and sure enough, more tears followed. I shook my head. "Igon didn't appreciate Torrin's affection toward me, considering he isn't my Soul-Tie." I released another dry laugh. "Torrin is so loyal to what everyone else wants of him—never doing anything for himself. I know he didn't wish to leave his home. He was so happy when we finally made it back here. And now he's gone…and it is all my fault."

Mother squeezed my hand. "No, Lena. It is not your fault." I went to shake my head, and then she took my other hand in hers and made me face her. "Torrin is a grown man capable of making his own choices." She paused as if debating on what to say next. "I…"

"Just say it," I muttered as I stared at the ground.

"I was just thinking about Soul-Ties…and how…how I don't think anything would have kept Silas from you," she said quietly.

I froze. I hated that my tears continued to pour. "I've kept away from him," I replied, my voice just above a whisper. "What does that say of me?"

"You know it isn't so simple. It's life or death for you. It wasn't for Torrin."

I wiped my eyes, and even though my heart ached, my internal flames felt contained, or rather ice was now taking over. "It's not like it matters. Silas is taken now. I will never have him."

Mother pulled me into a hug, and I weakly returned the gesture. We stayed by the river for a while longer until I felt composed enough to return to the town.

Ever since our arrival in Ames, we'd had dinner with the Astair family. Merrick had always skipped dinner with them, seeing as he loathed his father, but as he and I grew closer, he decided to join in since I'd be there. Elowen really appreciated it, too, as she loved Merrick's company.

Heildee and Vicsin were nearly done cooking, and Merrick and I were finishing setting the large oak table in their dining room. Mother usually would help Heildee, as they both loved cooking, and sometimes Elowen, Merrick, or I would take over dinner duty. There were a handful of times Torrin and I had together as well.

I knew Mother had begun seeing a man in town named Phillip the past few weeks, and I assumed she was probably with him this evening. I was happy she found someone, as new of a relationship as it was. I gazed out the window, and orange sunlight was spilling into the Astair household, signaling that the sun would begin setting soon.

"Where's Elowen?" I asked Merrick.

"Off healing Fabel's arm. I guess she broke it climbing a tree today," he replied. Fabel was one of the few children in Ames.

I merely nodded, and we were silent for a few more moments.

"What did Igon want?" Merrick asked while placing silverware by each plate. "I was surprised you didn't come back to the pit afterward."

I shrugged, setting down glasses for everyone. "Just didn't feel up to it."

It was silent, and when I looked over to Merrick, his normal icy-blue eyes were swirling—now a deep charcoal. They changed that color any time he was reading the emotions of someone.

"You can't bullshit me, Lena," he said as the corners of his lips tilted downward. I felt my heart speed up. Merrick wouldn't be happy either, finding out our leader essentially banished his cousin. "What happened?"

Before I could reply, the sound of screaming coming from outside made Merrick and me startle. "What the hell?" We glanced back at each other before bolting outside.

"What's going on?" Heildee called from the kitchen, but we were already out the door.

I nearly fell to my knees at the sight. My eyes and Merrick's widened simultaneously as we witnessed an army of soldiers infiltrating the town, raising their weapons on the innocent people who remained outdoors.

Otacian soldiers. They found us.

"I-I need to find Elowen," Merrick trembled.

"Go, I will fight," I assured him, and he ran off in the direction of Fabel's house.

Within moments, Ames was in complete chaos. Soldiers kept pouring in, attempting to capture who they could, or killing who they couldn't. Their numbers were easily double ours, but magic was powerful. We could win. We had to. Blood was already spilling, that of both Otacian soldiers and people of Ames.

I looked around frantically, familiar faces fighting for their homes. When Otacia had put in place its kill order, its other territories had followed suit. They made it their goal to capture as many Mages alive as they could—it seemed the King got a kick out of killing us for all his citizens to see.

But our people were prideful. If we were going to die, it would be protecting our homes and each other, not dying as entertainment.

I raced forward, dodging soldiers as they swung their weapons at me and using force fields as necessary. I had never killed anyone before, but I had a feeling that was going to change. I didn't see Elowen or Merrick, and I didn't see Mother either.

Where are they?

Panicked, I turned to my left, and a soldier was lifting his sword at me. I pushed a force field into him, causing him to stagger back.

His wide eyes focused on me as he kept himself upright, his legs trembling beneath him. Gods, he couldn't have been older than sixteen years old. I was not about to let this boy take me, but I couldn't kill him either.

All I did was blink, and a shard of ice went clear through his throat. His eyes bulged, his blood spilling out as he collapsed on the ground. I whipped my head to Merrick, who made eye contact with me briefly before fighting off two men charging for him and Elowen.

I began to run to them, but I was slammed back—a man pushing me down with all his strength. I fell and landed on my tailbone, the force knocking the air out of me as pain shot up my back. Adrenaline coursed through me, and I raised my arm above my face and produced a force field to block whatever blow was coming my way. I took a chance to meet eyes with the man attempting to kill me, and everything stilled.

Not just any eyes. Golden eyes.

He froze with his sword about to strike, his eyes so wide that the whites were completely visible.

"Lena?" he whispered in disbelief.

My eyes welled with tears. "Silas," I breathed.

I didn't have time to process anything when, out of the corner of my eye, I saw a dark figure—a lion—charging toward us. Silas didn't move, so lost in shock that he didn't sense the threat coming toward him.

But I did.

"No!" I howled as I lunged in front of him, crossing my arms and creating a magical shield so powerful that when Viola crashed into it, she flung backward, shapeshifting back into her regular form. Her braids tumbled in front of her face as she gripped the grass and dirt, coming to a complete stop. Her head whipped up.

She was stunned. Enraged.

I quickly shifted back to Silas, who was staring at me with the same look, shaking as he still held his sword. He wore his crown, black Otacian armor, and a navy cape.

As his gaze burned into mine, the horns atop Igon's tower went off, causing my head to whirl in its direction. It couldn't be…

An order to surrender.

The Mages of Ames looked at each other in disbelief at the blaring noise. We were holding them off well. Why concede now?

I looked back at Silas and got to my knees, hands in the air, as did the rest of my people. Though we did not have a King, we followed our Supreme, especially when ours had the power of foresight.

Without saying a word, Silas sheathed his sword, grasped my wrists, and placed silver handcuffs around them.

I flicked my head up to observe them. They both had a red gem on either cuff that lit up when he locked them. A wave of emptiness washed over me.

My magic…I didn't know how, but…it was *gone.*

Time went slowly as all our people were put in the magic-erasing cuffs. Panic washed over every Mage's expression when they realized what this contraption did.

I had never felt fear like this. Without our ability to protect ourselves, there was virtually no chance of us escaping. What was Igon thinking?

And where was Mother?

I was staring at Fabel's family, thankfully all alive, when Silas knelt before me. I hesitantly lifted my eyes to meet his.

"Where is your leader?" he asked coldly.

I analyzed his face. He looked so…different. His raven-colored waves were shorter than when I last saw him. The hair that once fell at his jawline was now trimmed at his neckline and sides, the top longer and lying loosely. Neatly kept stubble surrounded his lips, and a long scar trailed along the top of his left cheekbone and almost reached his mouth.

And his neck…only a small portion of it was visible due to his armor, but I could tell it was heavily inked.

He was beautiful. But there was no kindness in his eyes.

Before I could answer, a soldier flung Vicsin to the ground beside us.

"Father!" I heard Elowen cry. My eyes shot to her, and another soldier was gripping her arms, keeping her from running to her father's side. I didn't even notice how close by she was. Vicsin coughed up blood.

"Their elected official," the soldier stated. He appeared at least two decades older than Silas, with wrinkles creasing his forehead and gray hair speckled throughout his beard.

Silas held my gaze for one more moment before he stood back

up, stepped over to Vicsin, and studied him with distaste. "Intel claimed their leader was an old man."

"No, I-I am their leader," Vicsin mumbled, blood dripping from his mouth.

He was trying to save Igon.

"What is your name?" Silas demanded.

Vicsin looked at him with hatred in his eyes. "Vicsin Astair."

Silas cocked his head to the side. "I don't enjoy being lied to, Vicsin," he replied with malice in his smooth voice. Part of me couldn't help but feel like that statement was also aimed at me. "Tell me where he is, and I'll consider sparing you."

Elowen was sobbing, that same soldier keeping her from helping him. I couldn't see much of the man's face, but his expression looked almost…sympathetic. "Please, please don't hurt him!" she cried. Silas glanced at her, his dark expression not changing.

"Spare me to be killed with the rest in Otacia?" Viscin spat.

Silas clicked his tongue, returned his glare back to Vicsin, and cocked his head toward Elowen. "Maybe she will make you listen to reason?" He lifted his hand, and the soldier holding her paused before bringing her forward. "Put her on her knees," Silas ordered, and the soldier obeyed. My whole body was trembling, streams of tears pouring down my cheeks.

Not Elowen…not sweet Elowen.

Silas unsheathed his sword and stalked toward her. He glided the blade against her neck as she wept.

"Don't touch her," Vicsin snarled. My attention went to Merrick, who, to no avail, grunted as he strained against the soldier detaining him.

"If you can't tell me what I need, then I'm afraid I'll have no choice." Silas's voice was deeper than when I last saw him, or maybe it was the lack of empathy that made him sound different. That kind man I fell in love with…he wasn't present. Not at all.

Vicsin looked to Elowen in despair. "H-he passed. I was put in charge," he lied.

Silas clicked his tongue again, still looking at Elowen while tightening his grip on the sword.

He's going to kill her.

"He must be in the tower!" I blurted out. Silas paused, then bent his head toward me. "Please, please don't hurt them," my voice cracked.

I could swear I saw a flicker of emotion on his face, but it was gone too quickly before I could tell. He craned his head toward Vicsin.

"See, that wasn't so hard, was it?" He removed the blade from Elowen's neck, and as she slumped in relief, he raised his weapon at Vicsin.

Elowen shrieked, but before Silas could attack, Igon stepped out of the tower. Silas stilled, then slowly lowered his sword.

"Hello, Prince Silas," Igon greeted in a pleasant tone.

Silas gave a smile, though it wasn't a warm one. "You must be Igon."

"The one and only," he stated with a lazy grin, his arms raised at his sides. "Though I don't believe I will be of use much longer."

Igon turned his gaze to me and then began to speak to me in my mind.

Only through fire can the phoenix be reborn from the ashes.

I blinked rapidly, not only at the cryptic message but at the fact that Igon could somehow speak in my mind.

When the hell did he get that power?

Before I could question him, Silas spoke.

"Enough. Where is it?" he pressed. "Where is the Weapon?"

Weapon? What the fuck is he talking about?

Igon studied him for a moment. "You won't find it until it's too late."

"I am not here to play games." Silas bared his teeth. "You have one more chance to reveal its location, or it will be your end."

Igon remained silent, and only a few moments passed before Silas thrust his sword into his chest.

"NO!" I wailed, and instinct took over. I rushed to Igon's side as Silas withdrew his blade, blood spurting out as Igon's knees hit the ground. "No, no…" I wept as I studied his fatal wound. I couldn't heal him; I couldn't even hold him with these damn cuffs.

I looked into Igon's widened gaze, and I thought of our fight earlier as I cried, "I'm sorry…I'm so sorry."

He shook his head and brought his hand to my cheek. "You—" He struggled to speak as his breathing labored. "—will be our savior, Lena Daelyra." He shifted his gaze to Silas…and *smiled*, a real, genuine smile laced with…relief, was it? "I forgive you, son."

Confusion set over Silas's face, and Igon faced me again. His hand slipped from my cheek, and with a shaky hand, he reached into his pocket.

"A…memento," he breathed, handing me a bronze compass. Blood began to pour out of his mouth, and I cried harder as he placed the compass in my dress pocket.

He turned to face our people. Many of their faces crumpled watching the end of a man so beloved…so kind. "Lena Daelyra is your new Supreme."

My eyes broadened, and I heard gasps around me as Igon used the last of his strength to grasp my wrists.

"Find Oquerene," he spoke in my mind. *"Find…Kayin."*

I watched as the life left his topaz eyes, and when he sagged to the ground, I broke.

CHAPTER THIRTY-TWO

Everyone was frozen around us as I wept over Igon's dead body. I was still trying to comprehend what had just happened.

Me, the new Supreme? Why?

I was able to wield fire, an element most Mages didn't unlock in their lifetime, but still, I had no special ability; I wasn't born with any gift. Igon was a seer. Elowen could eliminate pain. Merrick was an empath, for fuck's sake, and Viola was a shapeshifter. They all had abilities that could not be taught or learned. And then there was me. It made no fucking sense.

Igon hinted at an ability earlier today…but what good would it do me anyway, considering these cuffs eliminated all magic?

"You…you bastards. What did you do?" Vicsin growled as he attempted to attack Silas, hurtling toward him. In a blink, Vicsin's eyes were protruding as the soldier who had thrown him to the ground plunged his sword into his throat.

I gasped and staggered to my feet, watching in horror as the soldier withdrew his blade and blood began gushing out of the wound.

Elowen let out a gut-wrenching cry and fell to her knees. When my eyes darted to Merrick, he looked…numb. I was grateful those cuffs were on him; otherwise, he would be feeling everything Elowen was, and it would break him.

The soldier that was holding Elowen bent down, and while I couldn't hear him, I watched his mouth whisper, *"I'm sorry,"* in her ear. She just continued to cry.

"He wouldn't have been able to hurt me, Rurik," Silas muttered.

Rurik shrugged. "Wouldn't want to take any chances, Your Highness." The last of his words had a note of bitterness to it. I realized I recognized the man; he was there when Torrin had led me to my cell in Castle La'Rune all those years ago.

Silas just huffed before ordering his soldiers to round us up by their carriages and to search the village.

"Hendry, take a few men and search this tower. Take anything that seems to have information we need," Silas uttered to a soldier with mismatched eyes and tawny-brown skin. He simply nodded and headed to the tower.

Hendry. His friend he had told me stories about when we were younger.

I had no idea what information Igon had that would be of value to them, no less anything about this "Weapon," but I would hope with being a seer and seeing them coming, he would've hidden or discarded it.

Still, nothing made sense.

Why weren't we warned or prepared?

Silas turned to me and grasped my arm tightly. I winced at the pain as he dragged me to where every other Mage was being gathered.

We stepped over various corpses, some his people, some mine. My heart sank at the different faces I recognized, people who, just hours ago, were laughing or smiling or enjoying the weather. I then realized who I *hadn't* seen.

"Have you seen my mother?" I asked him quietly. He didn't respond; he just continued to pull me. We made it almost to the exit of the village when a voice called out for me, and I turned.

"Mother," I breathed.

She was bleeding at her hairline, but she was okay, alive. She was cuffed and held by a soldier, and on the ground before her was Phillip's dead body. Tears were trailing down her face, and her gaze widened as she beheld Silas. Her eyes then narrowed, a disapproving glare on her face, and when I looked up at him, his eyes quickly flickered away from her before he hauled me away.

The man I had loved would have never wished to hurt my mother or me…but he never knew what we really were. I still couldn't have ever imagined…this.

He dipped his free hand into my dress pocket—my breathing hitching at his closeness. He retrieved Igon's bronze compass.

My nails dug crescents into my palms. "Give me that back," I said calmly.

He gave me a once-over, his face blank as he replied, "No."

Silas, the Slayer of Witches. I knew his reputation; I had heard stories passed around fires over the years. I just couldn't believe them.

Now I could.

All Mages were in one large group now. There had to have been less than a hundred Mages left, considering the amount of bodies that remained on the ground. At the front of the line were multiple horses, Silas now mounted on one of them, and a few carriages.

I glanced around the crowd, and when I saw Elowen, I hurried over to her.

She stood still, her head tilted downward, wrists bound like the rest of us. "Elowen, I…I am so sorry," I whispered.

She sniffed, her blue eyes glued to the ground. I felt someone watching us, and when I glanced to the side, I saw the soldier who had been holding Elowen observing us from a few feet away. His eyes were emerald green, and they looked gentle…almost kind—unlike any look I had seen from any Otacian today, save for perhaps that young boy.

"Mother is dead too…" she muttered, and I whirled toward her. "I walked over her body…she's gone."

"Dear Gods…" I breathed. "I'm so sorry, Elowen. I wish I could give you a hug."

To that she gave me a weak smile. I turned my attention to Silas when Elowen looked back to the ground. He was saying something to his men, but I couldn't make out the words from this distance.

I shifted on my feet when I heard someone walk behind us, and turned to see Merrick, his own blue eyes unreadable. I wished to put my hand on his shoulder—hug him too. But I couldn't do shit in these cuffs.

"How—" I started.

"I'm fine," Merrick said quietly. Elowen looked at him with tearful eyes and decided to walk away at his silence.

"I can't say I'm upset he's dead," Merrick muttered as I turned to face him once again. The cool breeze blew his silver-white strands that were loose in front of his face, and his eyes were glazed over momentarily before he met my stare. "I hated that man. But I hurt for Elowen, even if I can't feel her emotions right now." He let out a shaky exhale. "Thank the Gods I can't. The same goes for all the mourning people here."

I raised my cuffed hands and brushed my thumb against his cheek. "I know what you're thinking, Merrick. And no, you aren't horrible for how you feel about your father."

He clenched his jaw and just stared into my eyes before giving me a soft smile.

"Sometimes I wonder if you have his gift," he said gently.

I returned the smile. I knew he was referring to Torrin and his ability to read minds. We would never mention his name, not in front of Otacian soldiers, anyway. Torrin had a bounty over his head after fleeing Otacia.

I dropped my hand and turned to survey the area, and then I met Silas's burning stare.

Ice-cold rage.

He doesn't think Merrick and me...

I loved Merrick. He was my rock, someone who truly understood me, whether it was because he could feel every emotion I did or because we were kindred spirits. Both of us had endured a lot at a young age. He took care of me, just as Torrin did, and I'll always be in debt to him.

And Merrick was a beautiful man, just like his cousin. He was kind and loving, despite the coldness or sarcasm he masked himself with. I knew masking all too well. Merrick had expressed feelings for me years ago, about a year after arriving in Ames. It was heartbreaking turning him down…

Because perhaps we would have been a good match. But my heart belonged elsewhere. The thought of another man felt like a betrayal at the time. I didn't sleep with anyone after Silas until the day I heard he had gotten married. I just wanted a distraction, to feel anything other than pure devastation. Merrick's friendship meant too much to me for me to consider bedding him, as attractive an idea as it would've been.

And Torrin?

I didn't wish to think of it.

His eyes flickered away as he angled his horse north. The majestic, ebony creature's beauty perfectly matched his.

The soldier who had detained Merrick, a tanned, brown-haired man named Roland, addressed our people. "We will now begin the journey to our kingdom where you are all to be hanged. Consider it a mercy." A smug smile traced his face when his hazel eyes met mine.

Prick.

"Let the march begin!"

CHAPTER THIRTY-THREE

When Mother, Torrin, and I traveled from Otacia to Ames, the journey took us almost two months. How did they expect to travel that long with all these people? To feed us all?

Perhaps they'll just let us die off.

My heart sank at the thought.

We marched and marched for what seemed like ages, through forests and over hills, taking short breaks in between until the sun was fully set and the moon was bright above us. It had to be around midnight when we finally stopped.

As the Otacian soldiers began to set up their own camp, I heard voices behind me asking each other where we would sleep. We were all huddled together in the dark by the time Silas and his men were relaxing with multiple tents set up, roaring fires, and meats being cooked, the fragrance taunting our own rumbling stomachs. They didn't care if we were warm or comfortable. To them, we were disposable, lives that would be ending soon anyway.

I couldn't rest with all the teeth chattering, including my own. I looked at all my people now lying uncomfortably in the moonlight, unable to ignore the silent sobbing coming from many of them.

I had to do something. I was their Supreme, after all.

I struggled to get up on two feet, my legs wobbling from exhaustion. I uneasily started toward the camp, aiming for where Silas was, doing my best to ignore my increasing heart rate.

I slid on mud as I made my way, swaying and thankfully catching myself before I ate shit.

Focus, Lena.

I huffed and staggered up to the camp, and the soldiers rose to their feet, instantly wielding their weapons when I arrived.

I let out a sarcastic chuckle. "You're scared of me with these on?" I asked as I gestured to my cuffs.

Silas remained sitting and studied me with lowered brows, drinking something out of a mug—presumably alcohol—as the campsite reeked of it.

"What do you want, witch?" The one named Roland sneered. His muscular form strode up to me until he was mere inches away. I craned my neck and met his hazel stare.

"My people are freezing. We need a fire," I said plainly. Roland gave me a half smile, looking back at some of his men. I would have considered him attractive if he wasn't such a dick.

"Do you hear that, gentlemen? The witch has demands." He turned back to me, and I tilted my chin up higher. "Not gonna happen. Although," he leaned in and whispered in my ear, "I could keep you warm if you'd like." He moved his head back, and rage over-came me.

"Fuck you," I spat.

The insufferable asshole just grinned before Silas rose, the men around him freezing. Roland stayed relaxed, interestingly. I studied his face, wanting to punch it for the amusement in his eyes.

"Hendry, Edmund, make a couple of fires," Silas ordered. "There will be less of them to make a statement of if they freeze to death."

I stilled and looked over Roland's shoulder. Silas's expression was just…blank, emotionless. My eyes traveled back to Roland, and he spat on the ground next to my feet, grunted, and walked back to where he was sitting.

Charming.

I glared at his back in disgust before turning away. The day I would be able to take my revenge on him would be a good day indeed.

Hendry and Edmund began to walk toward my people, wood in their arms, and I trailed behind them. The blond man who showed Elowen kindness must be Edmund, considering I now knew what Hendry looked like.

They both chucked the wood on the ground by my people, about thirty or so feet apart, and squatted down to start the fires. I resisted the urge to let out another humorless laugh. It would take me all of three seconds to light these fires. But instead, I just watched them do it the hard way.

They carved their notches into the wood, then began rolling the spindles they used for their own fires in between their palms until smoke began to form. My people muttered to each other as they observed them, and after a few moments, the fires eventually started.

As the wood began to crackle and the flames rose, I got a better look at Hendry's illuminated face. His tawny skin was maybe a shade darker than Elowen's, and his hair was shaved on the sides. On the top, his straight, dark brown hair fell just at his eyebrows. His left eye was nearly black in this lighting, his other one blue. The glow from the flames complemented the sharp angles of his face.

Is everyone here just beautiful?

I crossed my arms.

Beautiful men with rotten souls.

Still, I was grateful for the fires. My people slowly moved close, holding out their cuffed hands as best they could to warm themselves.

"I'm going to grab more wood," Hendry mumbled, his voice deep and clear.

"Thank you," I said to him with as much kindness as I could muster, which wasn't much.

He gave me a nod. "Come on, Edmund," he called out to the other man. I looked at Edmund, whose skin was as fair as mine. Now that his helmet had been removed, short, blond curls lay softly around his face. They both stalked off.

I made my way over to Elowen, who was staring at Edmund as he went to fetch more wood with Hendry. Mages were now surrounding the fires.

"He's not like the rest," she said softly as I approached, her eyes glued to him.

I let out a small laugh. "Are you an empath now, too, El?"

She continued to gaze at the soldier. "He didn't have to try and comfort me. He almost looked…like he felt *bad* for what he was doing."

"Well, I imagine it's just like with us Mages," I replied, basking in the warmth of the fire Edmund had started. "There are bad ones out there, of course, but plenty of good ones. I'm sure some of these soldiers are just following orders, just wanting to protect their homes. I'm sure not *all* of them are evil killing machines." My mind went to that teenage boy from earlier.

Poor thing… he was just a kid.

"Well, they're being led by the Slayer of Witches, so if they aren't evil killing machines, they're groomed to be," she said quietly.

I clenched my jaw and glanced over to Silas, who was still sitting at his campsite, drinking and talking with some of his men. All of them were eating and sipping on mugs as well. His eyes caught mine and lingered briefly before averting to the ground.

"Perhaps he's not one either…" I whispered, holding on to the small hope that Quill was still who he was. That the man I loved was still here.

Elowen furrowed her brows, and then a voice behind me began to speak.

"Is that why you protected him?" Viola snarled. She marched over and stood next to Elowen with her arms crossed. Elowen shot her wide eyes before gaping at me.

"What does she mean, you 'protected' him?"

I felt a frisson of dread as my mind tried to conjure an excuse.

"Exactly what I said," Viola continued. "I would've had the Prince's head ripped from his body had Lena not jumped in front of him and used her force field to *protect* him." She inched closer to me. "Why? Why did you do it?"

"Because…" I took a deep breath. "Because there was no chance of any of us making it out alive if you had done that, Viola."

She curled her lip. "We could have stopped them all."

"The sound for surrender went off seconds after that happened," I stated sternly. "And even if we had killed all of them in this battle, King Ulric would have unleashed his wrath on us in retaliation, and we don't have the numbers to have survived that. We would've been slaughtered."

I was amazed I came up with all that, though it wasn't entirely untruthful. Killing Silas wouldn't have saved us.

"That…makes sense," Elowen whispered while looking at her feet.

"As opposed to what?" Viola glared at me with contempt. "At least we would have had a fighting chance. With no magic, we *will* be slaughtered."

Just as I began to respond to her, a voice interrupted. "Excuse me, Supreme?"

I turned to see a couple with a little girl standing beside me. Xaro, Iliera, and Sari were their names. The nice thing about Ames being so small was everyone knew each other, but I actually knew them from Otacia. They were the couple that had been banished that morning I was with Silas. I was so happy when I had discovered they made it to Ames, too, and that they finally were able to have the child they dreamed of.

I focused on Sari and began to feel my anger all over again. Her lip quivered as she clung to her mother's dress, her teeny hands cuffed like everyone else. She was just a little girl…now permanently traumatized. Just like the handful of other children here. It was unacceptable.

"Sari is hungry, and I know plenty of others are, too," Xaro, her father, said awkwardly. "We were wondering if you could see when we were getting food. I assume they don't wish to starve us, right?"

I bit the inside of my cheek. Silas said we wouldn't be able to make a statement if we froze to death. Surely dying of starvation would cause the same problem?

I glanced back over to the Otacian campsite. They all appeared to have plenty of food, considering the decent amounts they were indulging in. But enough to feed nearly a hundred Mages? Doubtful.

Still, I had to ask.

"I will see what I can do." I smiled softly, and Xaro nodded before leading his family closer to the fire.

I sighed internally, and as I went to make my way yet again, Hendry and Edmund walked up with another pile of wood, throwing them into the fires and making them larger. I only made it a few steps before Elowen approached Edmund.

"Excuse me," she asked. He met her eyes as he dusted his hands on his pants. "Are we going to be given any food?"

Elowen's voice was so soft and sweet. I didn't think I'd ever seen anyone mean to her except for Merrick. Though I supposed that was what siblings do.

Speaking of Merrick, he strode over to us just as Edmund responded. "Prisoners don't get food until the third day," he replied gently, empathy washing over his features. He looked down at the little girl and clenched his jaw before looking back at Elowen. "I'm sorry."

Elowen's shoulders sagged in disappointment, and Merrick let out a chuckle, though it was clear he found nothing funny. "You're *sorry*?"

Edmund tensed, then frowned. "Yes. I wish we had enough for everyone."

"What is the point of feeding pigs that are being sent to slaughter?" Merrick spat bitterly. "Unless you plan to eat us, too?"

Edmund didn't respond. He just glared at Merrick with a deepening frown.

"Please…don't fight," Elowen whispered, her eyes now looking downward.

Edmund's anger washed away as he looked back at my friend. Hendry quickly advanced toward Edmund, grabbing his arm and whispering, "Let's go," before they stalked off.

"What the fuck, Elowen?" Merrick exclaimed.

"I-I just—"

"Just what? Think one of those fucks is capable of empathy? He probably just wants to claim your body before he hangs you."

"Shut up!" she cried, whipping her head up, revealing the tears pouring down her face before storming off.

"Real nice, Merrick." Viola shook her head before following behind her.

Merrick and I stood in silence for a moment, his eyes glued to the fire, the flames before us reflecting in his eyes.

"I know you're just looking out for her," I consoled.

"You think he will stop to save her before she's hung?" he strained. "Ask to take her place?"

I blinked.

"No," he continued while clenching his fists. "He will offer her a small bit of kindness so he can sleep somewhat better at night or not feel as awful for aiding in the slaughter of our people. Fuck him," he muttered before walking off.

I stood there alone. All I wanted to do was curl up into a ball and cry. How was I supposed to save our people when I couldn't even manage the conflict between my own friends?

I stepped forward and held my hands above the fire before me. Families were lying all around now in an attempt to get some sleep. Thankfully, the fires had gotten rather large, but there would unfortunately be plenty of people who still felt cold.

I decided it would be best for me to try and get some rest. As I went to sleep at the back of the masses of bodies, my body lying on its side on the cold ground beside Mother, I looked over to see Silas staring in my direction. Even though there was distance between us, I could swear we met eyes.

Are you still in there, Quill?

CHAPTER THIRTY-FOUR

Seven days had passed since we had departed from Ames, which meant we had eaten twice, save for the couple of times Edmund snuck over two pieces of bread, one for Elowen and one for Sari. He had done it while he and Hendry set up fires, and he offered me a genuine apology both times for only being able to sneak that much.

I was surprised by his words, but I was grateful he made the effort. Hendry just gave him a disapproving side-eye but didn't attempt to tattle on him. Merrick still didn't buy his "nice guy" act, as he called it, but part of me believed Edmund was a good man. Maybe even Hendry, too, for letting him try and help.

The path the Otacians had us on trailed through areas with fresh water, so thankfully, we had stayed mildly hydrated. Still, I felt weak and exhausted. And I knew my people did, too.

And filthy. We were covered in dirt from multiple days of

sleeping on the ground, and we reeked. My hair was greasy, still in a braid from the week prior. Taking care of our bathroom needs was the worst of all, though with so many days without food, blessedly, the most I had to do was pee.

We were told that we had one more day until we reached Fort Laith, an Otacian outpost where soldiers could recoup and rest before the long way back home. There, we would stay in cramped prison cells until the march would resume. Supposedly, there were multiple rest stops that they had built over the years.

The fact an Otacian outpost was only eight days from Ames and I never knew it made me nauseous. I wondered how long it took Silas to figure out the best way to ambush us and the best routes to and from. How long had Ames been on his radar?

He had hardly looked at me during the past week. No words had been spoken between us…not like we could really speak about ourselves in front of others, anyway.

I watched ahead, Silas leading the way on his stallion, Roland on his left, and Rurik on his right.

Rurik was a complete prick, even compared to Roland, who at least seemed like he could hold his tongue…despite his moments of levity. Rurik had sworn at, berated, and taunted multiple of our women during this march. Surprisingly, he hadn't attempted that with me yet. Probably because he knew I wouldn't take his shit, as I had advocated for every woman he had harassed.

The final morning arrived, and we were walking yet again. I couldn't believe I was looking forward to reaching our temporary prison. My legs ached terribly, and the exhaustion due to hunger pangs was begging me to collapse.

A decent amount of Silas's men were mounted on horses; I assumed they were higher-ranked soldiers. And then there were a handful on foot, including Edmund and Hendry. Lucky for them, they would be able to relax and drink during this upcoming break while we looked forward to concrete floors.

Better than walking, I suppose.

Suddenly, the snapping of twigs was heard in the forest to our left. Rurik's head turned in response. I so desperately wanted to grab the weapon from his hands and cut his neck open with it.

A gust of wind blew, and the crunching of branches let us know something was approaching. Silas held up a fist, causing everyone to halt. The wind blew again, a lot colder than normal, and chills spread across my body.

Wrong. Something is very wrong.

In the blink of an eye, multiple figures shot out from the forest with hideous screams. From their palms, dark magical orbs shot at the soldiers, and my heart stopped when I realized what we were up against.

The Undead.

I had never seen one before, never thought it possible. It had been centuries since one of their kind had even been spotted. And that meant there was an enemy out there even worse than King Ulric.

A necromancer.

The soldiers wailed out as the orbs struck various parts of their bodies. They were damned now.

Based on lore told over the centuries, the Undead were created by a dark necromancer, who, instead of raising them fully like the necromancers before him, raised them only partially—their souls stuck in an in-between. In other words, they would completely bend to his will. Those touched by this necromancer's power carried the ability to turn the living into creatures just like them, spreading their curse with only one hit of their power, thus adding to their master's numbers.

But that was legend for the Mages that were afflicted by their magic. Humans would die an excruciating death, their soul forever lost as the darkness spread through their body. I didn't know which fate was worse.

After the rise of the Mage who created such a curse, the practice was outlawed, and those with the gift in their blood were put to death.

How had one remained?

Silas quickly acted, ordering his men to attack and angling his steed in the direction of the battle.

The Undead's appearance was chilling. Their skin and lips lacked color…like that of a corpse. What hair they did have was stringy and limp, and their eyes were completely black, even the whites. A black, inky pattern swirled all over their skin, and black fog spread around their feet.

They moved so quickly, some of the soldiers dodging, some unable to move before an orb struck their bodies. They even attacked the horses, Roland's getting blasted before knocking him off the side. He hit the ground hard, then staggered to his feet.

I felt helpless, petrified, but after a beat, I realized the Undead were not attacking the Mages. Only the Otacians.

Why?

In front of me, another orb struck a soldier, and he dropped to the ground and convulsed; the screams of terror were overwhelming my senses.

Roland was just steps from me, his sword impaling an Undead in front of him, only he didn't see the one from behind.

It was going to kill him.

I didn't know why I cared, but I found myself yelling, "Roland!"

He turned sharply, hazel eyes blown wide as he beheld the creature about to attack. He wouldn't have time to deflect.

Without thinking, I quickly retrieved a sword lying on the ground, dropped by that fallen soldier. The grip I had on it was awkward due to the cuffs, but I angled it quickly before plunging it into the creature's back, its black blood splattering all over Roland's front.

Roland was panting as he gaped at me. There wasn't enough time to do anything as an orb shot out from another one of them and hit Edmund in his right leg followed by his left arm. He cried out, and Elowen screamed as he slammed to the ground.

The creature slowly prowled over Edmund, who was now sobbing as he gripped his infected limbs. The pain that came from being marked by an Undead was said to be unbearable.

I saw it grin at him, and I knew it planned to torture him, draw out his suffering. The soldiers around were too preoccupied trying to save their own lives to stop it.

"Hey!" I howled at the creature. It craned its neck to glimpse at me. "Come get me, you ugly bastard!"

It cocked its head to the side, assessing its prey. It was in front of me in what felt like an instant, but before I could attack, Silas's sword was through its neck, black blood gushing out.

It screeched as it fell to the ground, twitching rapidly before going limp. Panting, I met Silas's golden stare, then Edmund's, who looked at Silas and me with broad, tearful eyes. Was he aware of his fate?

I quickly observed our surroundings. The remaining soldiers finally managed to slay what was left of the Undead. A handful of horses had been killed in the attack, Roland's being one of them.

My focus drifted back to Edmund. I was frozen, my heart wrenching despite everything as I watched him cry.

He was going to die.

"Drop the sword, bitch," Rurik snarled.

I forgot the sword was still in my hands. Slowly, I spitefully turned to him, and giving him a dark smile, I replied, "Make me."

I was ready to do something reckless but was stopped by Silas's hand on my shoulder. My eyes darted up to him, his grip firm but not painful. He gave me a warning look before I glared back at Rurik and dropped the weapon.

Our stare-down was interrupted by Edmund's wail. Silas released my shoulder and quickly ran over to him before kneeling at his side.

His face paled as he examined him. "Fuck…" Silas muttered.

"I-I'm going to die…" Edmund sobbed.

"Pussy," Rurik muttered.

Roland shot him a violent glare while Silas kept eye contact with Edmund and took his hand is his. I could swear I saw tears shining in his eyes as he studied his friend.

Elowen ran down and kneeled at Edmund's other side. "Let me help him," she begged.

"Elowen," Merrick scolded, his icy eyes full of warning.

She ignored him and pulled Edmund's right pants leg up above his knee. Black inky swirls, just like that of the Undead, marked only half of his lower leg. "It's below the knee and hasn't spread yet. If we remove his leg, he will live." Edmund bit back a sob as she pulled off his right glove and arm guard, then carefully pushed up the sleeve of his shirt, exposing the same black markings running halfway up his forearm. "Same for his arm."

Before Silas could object, she continued, "Lena can wield fire." She nodded her head toward me. "She can burn the wounds to stop the bleeding. And I'm not only our best healer, but I can take away the pain." She motioned at her cuffed hands. "I just…I need these off."

Rurik scoffed. "Do you take us for fools?"

Elowen clenched her jaw, baring her teeth. "He is going to die otherwise, you asshole!" she spat out. Merrick and Vi looked at me with widened eyes. None of us had *ever* heard Elowen swear.

Silas turned to study me, jaw flexing as he contemplated what to do. Edmund's cries became more devastating, and he shrieked as he clenched his arm, sobbing uncontrollably.

"Please…" Elowen pressed.

Hendry stepped behind and put a hand on Silas's shoulder, and I could see tears forming in his eyes, too.

He wasn't going to let us.

Fuck that.

"You would let one of your men die when there's a way to save him?" I argued.

"What good would a cripple be to us?" Rurik said plainly. "A missing leg and arm…" He shrugged. "He'd be useless,"

My lips curled into a snarling frown. "You are a pathetic piece of shit," I snarled. I turned to Silas. "Let us save him. I promise the second it's done you can put these back on," I pleaded, gesturing to my bound wrists.

"Your Highness, you can't possibly be cons—"

Silas raised his hand as he stood, cutting another soldier off. Keeping his eyes on me, he walked until he and I were face to face. Roland, who stood to my side, studied me with an expression I couldn't place.

"If you so much as—" Silas began.

"I promise," I said calmly.

"There isn't much time!" Elowen cried out.

Silas quickly placed a thumbprint on the reader located on the metal bar that linked the cuffs together. The red gems marking each cuff lost their light as they clicked open.

I could kill him in an instant, and I wondered if he knew that. I ran over to Edmund, kneeling beside him as Silas removed Elowen's restraints.

The black swirling on his skin was spreading, now just below his knee.

"His leg needs to be amputated right above where the markings end," I said quickly. I looked at Silas. "Do you want me to do it, or you?"

"Me," he replied, unsheathing his sword.

Edmund was trembling. I never knew a human could hold so many tears.

"Fuck, fuck, fuck!" he said in panic, shaking violently.

"Shh." Elowen put both of her hands on the sides of his temples.

"Look at me," she whispered. Her hands began to glow a soft, white light, and Edmund's breathing slowly began to stabilize.

He gazed at Elowen with wonder. "T-the pain, it's…it's gone," he breathed. Elowen softly smiled at him.

Silas wielded his sword, a long onyx blade, its handle bejeweled with sapphires, and paused while staring at Edmund's leg.

"Right above where the black stops," I repeated.

"I'm so scared," Edmund uttered to Elowen with an embarrassed laugh.

"You won't feel a thing, I promise." She dragged her thumb along his cheek. "Just keep your eyes on me."

Silas took a deep breath, then swung his sword, a mix of red and black blood spilling out as Edmund's leg was cut clean from the rest of his body.

Moving quickly, I lifted what was remaining of his leg, blood drenching me, and brought my hand just above the wound. I willed fire to emit from my palm and burned the opening until the bleeding ceased.

"Feel anything?" Elowen asked.

He shook his head and gave a soft smile. "No pain, anyway."

Color stained both of their cheeks. It was…sweet. Though I was positive no one else thought so.

I gently placed his leg back down. The metallic scent of his blood alone was going to make me sick, but the putrid stench of the cursed blood was on another level.

"His arm next," I said to Silas as I steadied my breathing and inhaled through my mouth.

Don't get sick.

He turned his attention back to Edmund, who Elowen helped lean down further until his arm was limp against the ground. Silas clenched his jaw, then swung again, the blade going through flesh and bone before his forearm was disconnected. I cauterized the wound quickly, finishing the job at last, but that sickening smell paired with so much gore was all it took for me to place his arm down, turn, and vomit. I felt Silas tense next to me, but he didn't do anything.

When I finished, I wiped my mouth and stood. A chuckle came from Rurik. "Not such a badass if something that small makes you sick."

I glared at him, an evil smirk spreading across my face.

"Funny you say that when I could have you dead on the ground in seconds." My hand began to emit fire once more, and fear swept over Rurik's face. I scoffed as I eyed the soldiers raising their weapons.

My eyes met Silas, who didn't bother raising his sword. Somehow, he knew I wouldn't hurt them. Perhaps because even if I did kill Rurik, I would have to fight off everyone else, and all it would take was a sword to one of my people's necks for me to submit.

Not a good plan.

"I'm a woman of my word." I tilted my chin upward, offering my wrists up.

Edmund spoke softly, Elowen's palms still on the sides of his head as he said, "Thank you, Lena."

I blinked, then gave him a nod and a small smile while Silas once again detained me.

"I didn't know the Undead were real…just a myth. Where did they come from?" Elowen asked me shakily.

I bit the inside of my cheek in contemplation. "The real question is, who is their master?"

Silas wiped the blood off his sword, putting it back in its holder. "We have been dealing with these creatures for months now. You act as though you know nothing of them."

My brows drew together. "Necromancy isn't a type of magic just anyone can learn or wield. It's a power you're born with. To raise a Mage halfway…to create an Undead…you have to have no heart, no soul. Unable to love or feel remorse." I tensed. "You have to be a complete monster. And considering there is a necromancer out there…" I let out a shaky breath. "…that means there is a bigger threat to the world than even your father."

Silas's expression gave no indication of his emotions. Another soldier commented, "Funny how those things only attacked us, don't you think, Your Highness?"

My fists clenched. "I have no idea why they didn't attack us. Mages don't die like humans do." My eyes narrowed on the corpses littering the ground. "We transform into one of them, one of the Undead, adding to their master's numbers." Roland crossed his arms while Rurik glowered at me. "And don't think for a second that a dark necromancer would be on our side either. Someone who is this sick needs to be wiped out before they kill everyone. Practicing necromancy is forbidden by my people."

"Sounds like we're doing the world a service killing you witches, then," Rurik commented.

I was about to kick him in the balls when Elowen began to speak.

"Edmund will still be in a lot of pain, even with the wound cauterized," she said carefully. "If we can make a sleeping elixir, a powerful one that keeps him asleep for a few days, I can heal him well enough that he isn't hurting by the time he wakes."

"You can't just use your magic to put him to sleep?" Roland asked.

Elowen shook her head. "Only Warlocks can do that. Perhaps a Mage could if they had it as a gift. But considering there isn't one here with that power, no."

Silas frowned. "How long will it take for him to heal?"

"A wound this bad?" She took a minute to think. "Probably a week or two before it is healed completely."

I knew instantly that Elowen was lying; it never took her that long to heal someone, even though we'd never been faced with a wound like this. Perhaps it could buy us time to come up with a plan.

"Your Highness, I know we are planning to recoup at Fort Laith, but waiting two weeks? Our families—"

"When we're on the battlefield, these men are your family," Silas said sternly. "We will give Edmund the time he needs to heal, and then we will make it the rest of the way."

Silas shifted, but not to Elowen, to me.

"What do we need for the elixir?"

And it was like history was repeating itself.

CHAPTER THIRTY-FIVE

"Lavender, valerian root, and chamomile."

Silas raised an eyebrow, and I sighed. "And then one of us can enchant it, which gives it power."

"Ah," he commented. "Silly to think those things on their own would do anything," he muttered as I watched him connect the dots and realize Mother was selling enchanted elixirs in Otacia the whole time.

"One of us can look for them in the items you seized," I offered.

"We didn't take any plants," Hendry replied.

"Well…where exactly on the map are we?" I asked.

"You're not actually—" Rurik began before Silas lifted his hand, giving him a warning look and then returning to my gaze.

Gods, that man was fucking annoying.

"Map, Hendry."

Hendry strolled over to one of the carriages, rustling through a bag before retrieving a piece of parchment and unrolling it in his hands. After a moment he brought it over to me.

"We are here," he pointed as I studied our location.

Fort Laith was near, but I nearly gasped when I realized how close to Mount Rozavar the fortress was. Though Igon's penned-in symbol was missing, I remembered its location, as this was the same map.

There was a reason Igon told me about that place, though he couldn't tell me at the time. That had to be where we could seek refuge.

I smiled to myself.

Igon…you were brilliant.

We needed to go there; I knew it in my bones. But getting nearly a hundred Mages there unnoticed was…ambitious to say the least. And that would be after I somehow found a way to free us.

"What are you smiling about?" Roland questioned.

I quickly wiped the expression off my face and focused back to our current location.

I knew Mother and I had traveled in this general area, but finding those herbs would be like finding a needle in a haystack.

Unless…

I sighed and slowly turned to Viola with a cringe on my face.

"Abso-fucking-lutely not," she said, sneering.

"Viola—"

"No!"

I took in a deep breath, then lowered my voice. "I am your Supreme now, Viola. Which means you follow my orders. You will find the herbs I need, and you will not attack any soldiers or the Prince."

Her resentful look sent chills across my body. Fuck, she was terrifying. But I wouldn't let my fear show. I wouldn't cower.

I kept my shoulders high, and my chin tilted up to meet her sneer, as she was a few inches taller than me. We had a stare-off for a few more moments before Viola conceded with a huff.

I nodded to Silas. "Viola can find the herbs I need."

He raised another eyebrow, and my Gods, my attraction to him was still as strong as ever.

Tithara guide me.

After a silent prayer to the Goddess of Wisdom, I cocked my head to Viola. "She's the lion that almost ripped your head off," I explained, and Silas's eyes rounded. "She can shift into anything, so I imagine a wolf with excellent scent shall do the trick."

I took a step toward him and noticed he stiffened slightly. "I know you just put these on, but it may be good to have me there, to be able to stop her if she's foolish enough to defy my orders," I whispered so she wouldn't hear.

Silas sized me up, the gesture unlike the other times his eyes once roamed over me. "Two witches uncuffed is plenty," he said coldly.

Well, that fucking hurt.

I scowled, and Silas stepped toward Viola. The looks they were exchanging were that of pure malice. Like they both wanted each other dead more than anything.

I watched her with a burning gaze.

Please don't do anything reckless, Viola.

Silas released her, and she stared at me for a moment before shifting into a terrifying wolf with jet-black fur. Her amethyst eyes shone with fury.

"The herbs, Viola," I barked.

She snarled at me before dipping her nose, sniffing the ground, and running off. Silas hurriedly named off a handful of soldiers and ordered them to join him in following Viola. I was sure he didn't want her finding more of our people and bringing back an army.

Not that it mattered. There were hardly any Mages left.

It had been hours since Viola and the men left to find the herbs. The soldiers that remained had buried their dead, which took up most of their time, while my people decided to sit on the ground and wait.

They could hardly look at me. And the ones that did, glanced at me in either disappointment or resentment. They were angry I was complying and not taking every opportunity to attack. But my feelings for Silas aside…it just didn't feel *right*. Or smart.

I kept catching Roland's stare. It wasn't his normal sneer, but I supposed his expression could mean anything. Perhaps he was surprised I had saved him—and helped save Edmund.

Elowen continued to hold on to Edmund, making sure he felt no pain. He asked her to stop at one point to see if he could manage it, but the second she pulled away, he nearly wailed in agony. I made sure to explain how wounds from where the Undead's curse had touched weren't like regular wounds, and the pain was far, far worse.

Elowen was so…loving toward him. She eventually pulled his head to rest on her chest, trying to help him fall asleep if he could, and after the first hour, he did doze off.

The view of the two of them had Merrick clenching his jaw and gripping his thighs tightly. I didn't need to be an empath to know he wished Edmund was dead.

"Why did you order Viola not to attack the soldiers?" Merrick asked with a cold tone as he sat next to me. "She could've slaughtered the ones that went with her, came back and ambushed the rest. I just…" He shook his head. "I don't understand, Lena."

I dragged my bottom lip through my teeth.

Because I was once in love with their leader.

It was a pathetic excuse, I knew that. But, while it played a part, it wasn't my only reason for holding off our retaliation.

"Viola is stronger in shape-shifted forms, but she isn't invincible. She could kill a good portion of his men but not all. She wouldn't survive."

Merrick met my eyes.

"Perhaps…" I continued. "Perhaps they will see the good in us, see we aren't monsters." I exhaled. "I know my choices are confusing, Merrick. But I beg you to trust me. I'll do whatever it takes to save us, but I have to do it the right way."

The wind blew his silver-white hair, and his eyes met mine with doubt. "And what way is that?"

The sounds of cracking branches and the rustling of leaves caught our attention, and as the sound got closer, I pivoted toward the grove of trees beside us and saw the herbs in one of the Otacian soldier's hands. Viola had shifted back to her regular form, cuffed, and looking as pissed as ever as they led her forward.

She trudged back to our group, shoving my shoulder as she passed. I would call her a bitch for that, but I knew she wasn't one. She was furious, and I understood.

Silas retrieved the herbs from the soldier's hands before he walked to me and released me from my cuffs again.

I rotated them before I met his amber eyes. "I'll need a boiling pot of water."

Sleeping elixirs utilized a form of stamina magic. While that had once been a difficult form for me to grasp, I now excelled at it.

Over a fire that Hendry had started for me, a pot of water boiled. Only a few ounces of liquid were needed. Otacian soldiers surrounded me as I knelt before it, glaring at me with hands ready to strike should I get any ideas.

I had no mortar and pestle to work with, and it was usually best to use dried herbs when possible. Thankfully, it didn't affect its efficacy; Edmund would just have to swallow larger pieces of the herbs. I did my best to mash and tear up as much as I could before dropping them all in the water.

After a moment, I held my palm out.

Lungs. Stamina magic comes from the lungs.

My eyes slowly closed as I reached within to access the power. When I felt the buzzing in my lungs, my eyes flew open to witness the bright green mist emitting from my hands. It sparkled as it traveled down into the rolling boil, infusing the concoction with everything I could muster. It would be best if he slept for a couple of days. Not too long, as someone else advocating for Elowen would be beneficial.

When I was done infusing the mixture, I slowly closed my hand into a fist, the feeling in my lungs dissipating as the mist faded away.

When I looked up at Silas, his expression of disgust shot a wave of hurt throughout my body.

I always feared that he would be repulsed by me if he discovered what I really was; I just had hoped it wouldn't become true.

"You sure you trust them?" Hendry chewed out as I poured the mixture into one of the mugs a soldier nervously handed me. Without asking permission, I use my ice magic to chill the concoction, so Edmund could consume it sooner. No one complained.

Edmund looked into Elowen's eyes as he said to Hendry, "I do."

I stood up and brought the elixir over, bending down before handing it over to Edmund. "Usually, the herbs are ground up, so they aren't as noticeable. This will be a little more…unenjoyable to consume, I'm afraid."

He nodded gratefully as he eyed the mixture, then shot it down his throat. He grimaced, and then seconds later he passed out in Elowen's arms.

She took a deep breath. It had to have been exhausting using her gift that long, and now she had to resume healing him.

Silas ordered Hendry and Roland to hoist Edmund into one of the carriages, Elowen climbing up with him where she began to repair his wounds. He then motioned at Roland, who stepped toward me with a pair of those evil cuffs. I didn't fight it; I simply held out my wrists while Roland attached them. His expression was unreadable.

"We have one more day until we reach Fort Laith," Silas called out to his men. "Keep your eyes peeled in case any more of those creatures decide to show up again."

CHAPTER THIRTY-SIX

Fort Laith was a monstrous place, a building made of stone with two large watch towers, one on either side. With the number of soldiers that were part of our capture, plus the ones stationed on the outside of the fort and an amount I could only imagine on the inside, escaping here would be nearly impossible.

Despite my fear of what would occur in these walls, my knees nearly buckled at the thought of sleeping somewhere—anywhere— that wasn't the cold ground.

We were led toward the massive iron doors at the entrance, soldiers bowing to Silas as he and his men rode forward. Silas and the handful of soldiers that rode horses began to dismount, and after a few words were exchanged, two soldiers hauled Edmund out of the carriage he was in, Elowen being pulled with him.

I gritted my teeth. I hated how they tugged at her, sweet Elowen, who had never hurt a fly. I hated how I wasn't with her.

Us Mages followed through the doors, revealing a spacious stone hallway lined with more militia. Within a few footsteps, we were led down a stone staircase one by one. Sconces added hardly any light, but enough that we could see.

When we reached the bottom, my people were already being crammed into cells. The doors were made of what appeared to be iron, just like the entrance, and each had a small, barred window at the top. There seemed to be around twenty or so cells, so a handful of Mages were placed in each one.

Except for me. When I was pushed into mine, the door shut immediately. I turned slowly, my cuffed hands held close to my body. The room was plain with nothing but a stone "bed," similar to the one I slept on in Castle La'Rune, and a single toilet.

I decided to lie down, realizing the ground outside was far more comfortable, and quietly cried myself to sleep.

What felt like seconds later, after being startled awake, we were taken one by one to get cleaned up. I guess I could appreciate that. There was a line of showers in the basement where we were to get rinsed. While being watched, of course. The idea of being stripped humiliated me, but the grime that covered me was begging to be washed off.

I was one of the first to shower, and, to my dismay, Roland was the one overlooking.

"You smell like shit," he said plainly.

I gave him a scowl. "What the fuck do you expect?"

He chuckled as I unhooked the Queen's necklace and handed it over; the ring Silas gave me years ago remained on my right ring finger. I went to remove my clothes, which I realized proved difficult while wearing the cuffs.

"You'll need my help," Roland stated. My entire face flushed as he used a knife to tear my dress, pulling the tattered material down until it dropped to the floor. He then unhooked my bra, and when he went to pull down my underwear, I stopped him and said I could do it myself. He backed off, and when I was completely exposed, I refused to meet his eyes.

If I reeked before, I certainly did now. The mix of red and cursed blood and body odor was completely overwhelming.

"There's soap inside the shower, and there is no heat, so the water is going to be cold," he said.

My shoulders sank.

Of course there's no heat.

I had grown accustomed to warm water in Ames. I stepped in and twisted the handle, and ice-cold water sprayed out, causing me to let out an embarrassing squeal. Roland let out a loud laugh in response.

I turned and gave him a death glare.

"What?" he said with a half-smile. "I bet you'd laugh if it were me squealing like a pig."

I gave him my middle finger, his smile broadening, and I winced as I stepped back into the water stream. A mixture of blood and dirt began swirling at my feet, the white tile beneath me disappearing quickly. My teeth started to chatter, but fuck, it felt good getting this muck off me. I reached up and pulled out the hair tie that secured my braid and handed it to Roland.

"I'm surprised these can be in the water," I mumbled, motioning toward the cuffs.

"Wouldn't be a very good contraption if water could break them."

I was surprised by how Roland kept his eyes trained on anything but my body.

Thanks, I guess.

I pulled apart my braid, then dipped my head under the water, gasping at the cold. I turned to where the toiletries were kept—well, where a single bar of soap was.

"No shampoo?"

"This isn't a spa, Ginger Snap," he retorted.

I glared at him as he smirked. Gods, I wanted to smack him. I clutched the bar of soap, and as I tried to reach my head, the soap slipped out of my grasp and fell to the ground.

"Haven't you heard you aren't supposed to drop soap in prison?" he teased as I went to bend down. I sprang my body up before I was able to reach the soap, and when I met him with wide eyes, he busted out laughing.

"You are a piece of shit," I spat.

"I was just teasing. Have a sense of humor." The bastard smirked *again*.

I reached down, making sure to bend my ass away from him, and tried once more to bring it to my head.

I groaned. This was going to be impossible.

"Might need my help with that, too."

"Why would you bother helping?" I muttered.

He crossed his arms. "I can't stand smelling your stench," he replied.

I scowled at him for a few seconds, then sighed as I handed over the bar of soap. Roland was no longer wearing his full armor, just a gray long-sleeved tunic, brown trousers, and boots. It was clear the soldiers were able to shower first, as he looked and smelled clean. With his sleeves pulled up to his elbows, exposing skin as tan as Silas's, he began to lather the soap in his hands before setting the bar down and motioning for me to turn around.

Hesitantly, I obeyed.

Roland wasn't as tall as Silas, who was around 6'3". He was probably a couple of inches shorter, but he still towered over me. He began massaging my scalp with his fingertips, and I tensed as chills spread across my body. I let out a deep exhale.

This feels good.

Roland actually put in a decent effort, making sure to scrub my head nicely. He ordered me to rinse it once before washing my hair again with more fresh soap.

"I can help with your body, too," he said cautiously as he massaged my head. "I'll avoid any areas you wish."

I angled my head toward him, and he pulled his hands back, still covered in soap. He didn't look smug or cruel. He looked sincere. It was confusing.

I turned my head away, and he resumed washing my hair. "Very well," I mumbled.

After I rinsed my hair a second time and Roland rinsed the suds off of his hands, my heart quickened as I prepared for the next part.

He looked at me with a raised eyebrow. "Well?"

I took in a breath. "Not my breasts, crotch, or ass," I said as plainly as I could.

He gave another half-smile and began to lather his hand once more. "I'll start with your back."

He began at my shoulders, and I tensed as he touched me, his grip firm but not painful. No, it felt *good*. He wasn't just lightly running his hands along my shoulders; he was massaging them, and it felt amazing.

"What are you doing?" I breathed, beginning to feel pressure in between my thighs.

What the fuck, Lena?

"I assume your shoulders hurt from sleeping on the ground. I know mine sure as hell do."

He continued kneading my shoulders, and a small moan left my lips, causing me to stiffen. Roland let out a small laugh.

"N-no more massaging. Let's just get this over with." I blushed, and I was grateful I wasn't facing him. Being touch-deprived for so long had apparently messed with my head.

"Whatever you wish, Ginger Snap."

"Don't call me that."

He let out another soft laugh, and when I looked back at him, his hazel eyes sparkled with amusement.

The rest of the shower went by quickly. He took the bar of soap in hand and ran it across the rest of my back, my stomach, and my legs and feet, avoiding all the areas I requested and not even so much as peeking at them. He then handed me the soap and let me wash said areas myself, and then the shower was over. I was handed a scratchy towel and given a brown T-shirt and a pair of pants made of cotton—an outfit they must give all prisoners.

"You have enough of these for everyone?" I questioned.

"We had an estimate for how many were in your village, so there should be enough."

"You must've had this planned for a while," I mumbled.

"Yes," he said quietly.

Roland called for a soldier to take away my clothes. I knew I'd never see them again.

"Can I have my necklace? I blurted out. He turned to me. "Please?"

Once we were to be hanged, any remaining valuables we had would be seized. I hoped Roland would extend his kindness and allow me to stay with mine a little longer.

Thankfully, he listened and fished out Ryia's necklace, hesitating before clasping it back around my neck.

Afterward, Roland led me back to my cell and stopped when we were both inside. "Get dressed, and then you are asked to speak with the Prince."

"Thank you," I said softly. He stiffened at my words and then turned, exited the room, and leaned against the wall beside the cell room door, awaiting me to complete my task while giving me some privacy. He'd seen everything already, but while I didn't see the point in his gesture, I appreciated it.

I sighed as I scrunched my hair with the towel, drying it as best I could, and then slipped on the pants. Once I was ready to put on the top, I frowned.

How am I to get the shirt on?

"Roland?" I asked meekly.

I just stood there topless with those hideous pants on as Roland sauntered back in.

"How am I—"

He walked up to me and placed a thumbprint on the metal link, and the bar split and retracted, the restraints now staying on my wrists like bracelets. The red gems on both wrists still glowed.

"They can be separated and still work?" I asked with wide eyes.

"It's just easier to handle you people that way. Don't want any of you to start swinging."

I clenched my fists and gave him a sneer. "You're saying I could've showered myself?" I gritted out.

He smirked, and I swung my fist to his face. Sadly, he caught my punch with his hand and chuckled.

"Just when I thought you might not be as big of a dick as I thought," I muttered.

"Sorry to disappoint," he teased, his laugh showing his bright teeth. "Though my dick is big," he purred with a wink.

"You're sick," I spat as I pulled my fist back and flung my shirt over my head.

He chuckled, and when my top was on, he reattached the cuffs. "Come on, the Prince awaits."

At that, my stomach dropped, and fear washed over me.

Time to face him.

CHAPTER THIRTY-SEVEN

I was led into a room, rather large in size. The walls were stone, just like the rest of the fortress. Silas had his back to the door and was shuffling some documents on the large wooden table before him.

Roland closed the door behind me, leaving just me and Silas in the room. I was left with my bound wrists, staring at the back of my once lover. He also had clearly showered, as his black hair was styled neatly, and he was wearing new clothes; a short-sleeved black tunic with white edges, a belt around his waist, and trousers and boots. His golden forearms were visible, and just like his neck, they were heavily inked. The moments passed like years, and I wondered when he would turn to face me.

When he finally did, his eyes couldn't hide his emotions: confusion, hurt, disbelief, *anger*…so much anger.

His golden gaze burned into mine. "I…I don't understand," he breathed. "How are you alive!"

I was silent.

How do I even respond?

"I saw your cottage after it was burned down. Your burnt corpse. How…how are you alive?!"

I flinched at his raised voice. How could I explain it to him? No words would suffice. I betrayed him. I knew how badly it would hurt him, not only my leaving but having him believe I was dead.

"We—" I took a shaky breath. "We had to leave. I…I didn't want to." I could feel tears welling up in my eyes. "King Ulric put a kill order on us. We couldn't risk staying there any longer."

I was too fearful to bring up Torrin. I had heard that the people of Otacia believed Torrin Brighthell to be an assassin, believed he played a part in the Queen's death, as he fled the night I "died." That it was all connected. If I told him, he might believe me to be part of it, too. Even though neither Torrin nor I had anything to do with it.

"So your solution was to make me believe you were dead?" He sneered, his rising temper reflective in his honey eyes. "Do you have any idea what that has put me through all these years? To lose you right after I had lost my mother…" His face shifted from rage into disgust. "And you're a *witch*. I cannot believe you lied to me all that time. I cannot believe I was *close* to you."

My heart shattered, but immediately, the pain turned to fury. "You aren't the only one who was lied to, Silas. I did what I had to in order to stay alive."

"Typical, selfish witch," he said, his voice grim.

While his appearance was familiar, I was looking into the eyes of a stranger. There was no holding back anymore.

"Silas, the Slayer of Witches, that's what they call you now? I am *so* thankful I never told you about what I am. Your love was conditional, just as I feared it was. You were raised to hate me—you could never possibly understand." Tension coiled within my knuckles. I wished I could break loose from my restraints. "You are committing genocide for the actions of one," I scoffed. "As if no human has ever committed murder."

Silas studied me, his expression remaining. "Your mother wasn't like that," I continued. "She would be *horrified* to see you like this."

Something flickered in his eyes, and he lunged toward me and seized my throat, squeezing hard. I gasped for air.

"Don't you fucking *dare* speak of her!" he yelled, his pupils blown wide with rage.

I tried to claw his hand off me, but I wasn't strong enough. Tears poured out of my eyes as I struggled to breathe.

"P-please…s-stop!" I choked.

His entire hand was wrapped around my neck as he squeezed harder, and then our gaze stuck.

I only had enough air to get out one word.

"Quill," I cried.

His eyes widened—humanity flickering back into his stare. He released my throat and quickly pulled back. I hunched over, gasping for air.

When I looked up, he was staring at me with widened eyes, frozen. I was still catching my breath when he swallowed and brushed himself off.

"The past doesn't matter," he said blandly, his eyes narrowing. "Why are you their new leader?"

I trembled, now repulsed as I looked at him. "I don't know," I panted.

"Where is he hiding the Weapon?"

"I don't know what you speak of."

"Where are the rest of the Mages?"

I frowned. "What?"

"My intel says Igon knew of a place that kept thousands of your kind. Where?" he pressed.

"Don't you think if he knew something like that, we all would have lived there, too?"

His jaw clicked. "You withholding information will not do you any favors, Lena."

I studied his face. His stubble had been trimmed, and the scar trailing from his cheekbone to the corner of his lip cut into what little facial hair remained.

"Even if I did know, I wouldn't tell you shit." It took everything in me to say those words without my voice shaking.

He stepped forward, and my whole body tensed, my back now pressed against the door. "Whether you like it or not," he said, his voice a deathly calm, "I will get that information out of you, one way or another. And next time"—he leaned close and whispered in my ear—"I won't be as nice."

He pulled back, and his cold eyes locked on mine. The sight sent chills down my spine. I never imagined a day he would frighten me.

He banged on the door, and Hendry emerged, no Roland this

time. "Take her to her cell," he ordered, and I tried my hardest to keep my emotions in as Hendry grabbed my arm.

"Your Highness," Hendry said. "Lady Erabella wishes to see you."

Silas didn't look at me. He just responded, "Very well. Thank you, Hendry."

Silas left the room first, and Hendry tugged me along with him. Just ahead, a woman with blonde hair falling just past her chin walked forward, wearing a gorgeous blue gown, the shade beautiful against her tanned skin.

Erabella.

I had heard the news that the Prince of Otacia had found himself a wife a year ago. I remember it was Viola who told Torrin, Merrick, El, and me the news. I remember casually excusing myself, heading up to the lake just outside Ames, and falling to my knees, sobbing as my fire consumed me. I had already unlocked its power years prior, but at that moment, it was uncontrollable.

The same night Torrin …

I couldn't think of that.

"Keep the prisoner away from her," Silas commanded, as if I were some feral dog.

"Yes, Your Highness."

She grimaced, her brown eyes looking down at me. She gazed back at Silas, her eyes lighting up as she took him in. "Hi, my love."

He pulled her into an embrace, and they kissed.

Funny, out of all the painful events leading up to this, somehow, this hurt the worst. And in that moment, I realized *he* was the one that died that day in the village.

He's gone. He's really fucking gone.

I felt the tears coming, but my anger kept them in.

"I've missed you," he whispered. Silas glanced at Hendry, not making eye contact with me. "Take her away. Now."

Hendry pulled me, but I offered no resistance. I wanted away from this nightmare.

He merely shoved me back into my cell. The door slammed, and in those brief moments of silence, I was finally able to break down.

I didn't know how long I lay on that stone bed, but I felt like my body was full of lead. There was absolutely no desire to move.

I was a fool for letting any part of me believe the Silas I knew was still here. Too much had changed. I needed to get my shit together. I needed to figure out how to get my people out of here.

Just as I sat up, wiping my eyes, my cell door opening caused me to jump. In walked Rurik, and three other men—soldiers—I didn't recognize.

"What's going on?" I asked, and dread overcame me at the sight of Rurik's sickening grin. He prowled forward, the other men having an equal hunger in their gaze, and I shuddered before pushing myself to my feet and backing away.

Rurik clicked his tongue. "You seemed so…fearless when we were marching," he commented, stepping even closer. His silver hair lay long and disheveled, his mustache curling upward with his lips. "But in here, you are completely helpless."

In a blink, he gripped my neck and slammed my head against

the stone wall. Stars clouded my vision, and I fell to the ground when he let me go. He bent down beside me, and his hot breath against my ear made me want to vomit. "I can't wait to break you," he whispered.

My head throbbed as he grabbed my feet, pulling me down against the concrete floor. I screamed, and to that, he punched me in the face. Hard. I heard a crunch, and the pain that shot through my body and the liquid that began pouring from my nostrils told me he had broken my nose.

"We're going to rough you up a bit beforehand."

"P-please, I don—" I began before a different man kicked me in the side so hard the wind was knocked out of me. The kicks kept coming, in my side, my face. Rurik grabbed me by the neck and slammed my head against the ground, the taste of blood following shortly after. With his other hand, he ripped my shirt open and cupped my bare breast.

"Stop!" I pleaded, blood spilling out of my mouth. I flailed my body as hard as I could to no avail, as he held me down and sucked on the skin of my neck. I sobbed as I thrashed.

Silas … he must have sent them …

"Pin her to the ground!" another yelled, and so he did.

I knew what was about to happen, but no matter how hard I struggled, no matter how much I begged, I couldn't break their grip. I kept wailing, and Rurik put his hand over my mouth.

'Shh, it will be much nicer if you don't fight it."

"Come on, it's more exciting that way," another voice chimed in. I was starting to lose consciousness, the pain from my injuries becoming unbearable. Rurik tugged my pants off and began to unhook his belt.

No, no, no!

I lashed out with all the energy I could muster, but two of the men grabbed my legs, spreading them to either side, and there was nothing I could do as Rurik leaned down and plunged himself inside of me.

I cried out, but he wouldn't stop. Repeatedly, he forced himself inside me. Over and over.

For the first time in my life, I wanted to die. I sobbed as my body went limp, accepting that there was no way I could stop their assault on me.

But despite my wishes to be gone…to close my eyes and have all this pain erased, there was a sliver of me that wanted to survive. To overcome all this killing and hate. To save my people.

You will not break.

Those were the words I had told Silas before I left. The words I told myself countless times on my way to Ames when I was sick during travel.

What I told myself the day I got my fire.

"How does my cock feel, you witch slut?" Rurik grunted into my ear, his grip on my hip painful. "Your kind may be a mistake, a complete disgrace," he huffed as he thrust into me harder, tears streaming down my face as I held his horrid gaze. "But your pussy feels amazing."

I didn't know how long I lay there, how long he whispered his filthy words into my ear, how long it was before the door flung open, and I looked to see Silas in the doorway, completely distraught.

"Get the fuck off her!" he bellowed as he raced toward us. "OFF! NOW!"

They quickly began to scramble off me, but that was all I could remember before the world went black.

CHAPTER THIRTY-EIGHT
SILAS

"You look exhausted," Era murmured when we entered our quarters, brushing my hair out of my face. "I was wondering when you'd return."

"Exhausted is an understatement."

Erabella had traveled with me and my men to Fort Laith; otherwise, it would've been months until we'd see each other again.

"You kept me waiting long enough."

"Forgive me," I whispered, kissing her softly. "You wouldn't have enjoyed seeing me as filthy as I was."

She chuckled. "That's true. I am happy to see you're at least cleaned up." Her smile faltered. "How did it all go? Did you lose any-one? And what's this I hear about Edmund?"

I sighed as I grazed my hands along her arms. "We lost just over forty. It would have been less had the Undead not attacked us."

Her eyes widened. "The Undead!" she exclaimed, her hands flying to her cheeks. I nodded and she shook her head. "I don't want you on these missions anymore, Silas. I do not care what your father says. The Undead are too dangerous for you to be putting yourself at risk."

"What kind of leader would I be if I sent my men on a journey that I would not venture on myself?"

She frowned. "A leader that is *alive*."

I groaned, then gave her a soft smile. "You always know what to say, don't you?"

She grinned and kissed me.

Her lips didn't soothe me how they normally did. I was still incredibly tense from everything that happened.

"I need another shower—need to clear my head," I said as I gestured to our master bath.

She nodded, and as I began to walk away, she asked, "Who was that woman you were interrogating?"

I tensed at those words and was grateful my back was to her. "Their leader." I went for our dresser to grab a towel and some clothes to lounge in.

"I thought it was an older man?"

"A lot has happened. I'll tell you more when I'm done."

She gave me another nod, and with that, I entered our bathroom.

After undressing, I stepped into the shower, the hot water relaxing my muscles. As it trickled down, I could feel my nerves starting to settle.

I tried to think of anything other than my altercation with Lena, but it wouldn't give. Especially her eyes when I grabbed her neck. The way she looked at me…the fear in her eyes. She looked at me like I was a monster.

It was not an incorrect assumption. I was certainly nothing like the man she knew. Not even close. Still, I should have never put my hands on her.

I ran my hands through my hair, shampoo bubbles dripping down my body.

She called me Quill…*cried* that name as if reaching for the person I used to be. My whole body went numb at the sound of it leaving her lips. She truly believed that version of me still existed.

I am sure she believes that no longer.

I began to think of those tears in her eyes and how I couldn't even look at her face when Era showed up. I wanted to hurt her, yet I didn't have the balls to even see her reaction.

My thoughts drifted to how she must be feeling sitting in that cold cell, and I felt a tightness in my chest.

I didn't know how I fucking felt. Every good thing about me was destroyed a long, long time ago. But the thought of her crying and scared just shattered what little was left of my heart.

She is a witch. She lied about who she was the entire time.

I sighed, my conflicting thoughts eating me alive.

Yes, but I did, too. Had she not followed me to the castle and found out who I really was after being captured, I'm not sure when I would've told her my secret.

What was I going to do? I needed that information if there was any hope of us finding the large group of Mages and stopping the

Weapon said to destroy our kingdom. But I would never torture it out of Lena like I had with others of her kind. I just couldn't.

I also couldn't let her die. Despite what she was, she was one of the only good things that had ever happened to me. The years with her were the happiest of my life.

Perhaps that made me weak.

I took my time showering, my thoughts a jumbled mess. When I was finally finished, I wrapped a towel around my waist. I made sure to put on a white cotton sweater, something comfortable to sleep in, to hide my back—the place I never let anyone see, not even Era.

When I walked out of the bathroom and into the room, Erabella was lying on the bed naked, giving me a wicked grin.

My cock hardened underneath the towel, and I returned the facial expression. Then, almost instantly, guilt washed over me.

The love of my life was alive. She was alive and alone. It was hard enough moving on when I thought she was dead, but now that I knew she was alive, I just felt sick.

Era noticed the change in my expression. "What's wrong?" she asked softly as she sat up. "The shower didn't help?"

I exhaled through my nose. "Just…a long fucking day."

She patted the spot next to her on the bed, and I sat down beside her. She gently ran her hands across my back over my shirt and began to knead my shoulders. I hissed from the pleasure it brought me.

"I'm happy you're here," I whispered.

She kissed my cheek and skimmed her hand down my chest, then grabbed my length under the towel, causing me to inhale sharply.

"Have you missed me as much as I missed you?" she purred.

Fuck.

I twirled around and cupped her face in my hands, kissing her passionately.

"Let me make you feel good," she offered softly and hopped off the bed to kneel before me. Grinning, she removed the towel, took me into her mouth, and began to suck.

My head rolled back, and I let out a groan while running my hand through her hair, gripping her tight.

I can't think about Lena. Not now. I'm a married man.

But I couldn't stop myself from thinking of her lips, her eyes, her voice. Even those pointed ears of hers.

And I felt guilty for that too.

I couldn't sleep. After Era and I had sex, she passed out next to me, her short blonde hair lying cutely on her face. She looked so sweet when she slept, a contrast to her normal appearance of seductress. Her almond eyes always caught the attention of other men, but I didn't mind. Her eyes never wandered.

I rubbed my temples.

But mine did. Not after other women—I was always loyal to Erabella, even though my sexually depraved years prior to our marriage would sometimes cross my mind. No, the only other woman I had ever thought of was Lena.

I bit my knuckle, resting my elbows on my knees while contemplating my fucked-up life as I sat in bed.

I scared the shit out of Lena. Let her see a sliver of the monster I had become. I put my hand on her throat. I was so damn furious with her and all I wanted in that moment was to make her hurt like she had hurt me.

Honestly, what I did scared the shit out of me, too.

I sighed heavily and hopped out of bed, careful not to disturb Era. I threw on black trousers and a clean pair of boots.

I needed to tell her I was sorry. I didn't care if it made me a pussy. I would still get that information somehow. But I would not hurt her.

I quietly left my room, being mindful while softly shutting the door, and began my descent into the prison.

Sconces scarcely lit up the spiral staircase, and the temperature began to dip the closer to the bottom I got. I made it halfway down before I began to hear screaming.

A woman's voice… what the fuck is going on?

Hurriedly, I ran down the remaining steps and followed the noise as the woman's cries grew louder.

I reached the cell where the screams were coming from and flung open the door.

My eyes felt like they were going to bulge out of my head. Rurik, Jones, Daerin, and Geoff were towering over Lena. Her pants had been ripped off, her top torn in half, exposing her breasts. And Rurik—

He was raping her.

Her eyes met mine, a look of terror and streams of tears pouring out of her swollen eyes. Blood was flowing out of her nose.

I felt an anger in me, darker, more vicious than I ever had before.

"Get the fuck off her!" I shouted as I ran forward. "OFF! NOW!"

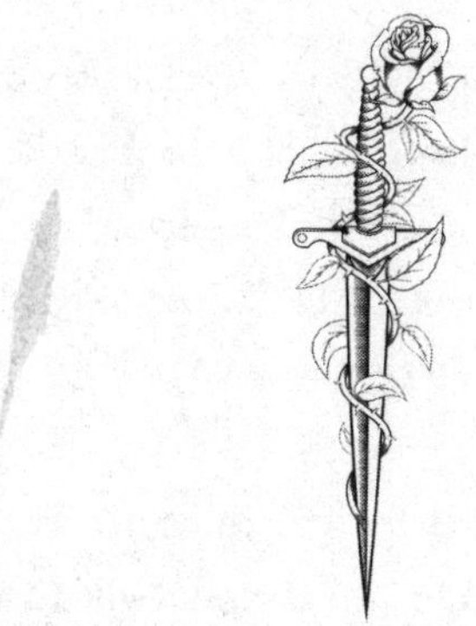

CHAPTER THIRTY-NINE

"S-sire, we—"

Two of the lower-level guards came from behind me, having finally heard the chaos emitting from this cell. They made no effort to stop me when I pulled Rurik off Lena and started beating the absolute living shit out of him. I only got in a few blows before I forced myself to stop.

First, Lena. Then, I will kill all of these fuckers.

"You keep these savages in this cell," I snarled at the guards, my anger unsettling them. I hadn't been this angry in a long fucking time. "I will deal with them shortly."

I quickly turned my attention to Lena, realizing she wasn't awake.

No.

I felt panic wash over me as I put my head on her chest, then sighed in relief.

Still breathing. Good.

"Get Elowen. We need her to heal—have Hendry bring her."

When I was met with silence, I looked back at the guards, eyes wide and eyebrows raised. I knew what I had to say.

"She has information we *need*. Do I need to repeat myself?" I asked coldly.

"N-no, sir."

"Good," I muttered. "Grab me something to cover her with."

One of them rushed to fulfill the task, and when I scooped Lena up in my arms, I examined her face.

Fuck.

Two black eyes formed, and blood continued to drip out of her nose. It was most likely broken. The other guard and I left the cell, shutting in the new prisoners.

"Sire, where are you—"

"I am bringing her to my quarters," I snapped. "Apparently, my damn prisons aren't guarded well enough."

The guard swallowed, realizing his error.

"Stay here. Do not engage. Or you will be in there with them."

He stiffened, then nodded quickly.

After I was given a sheet to cover her with, I rushed away, making it back up those spiral steps and to my quarters. Erabella sprang up from the bed, my less-than-subtle entrance jolting her awake.

"Whoa, what is going on?" Erabella exclaimed as she fumbled out of bed, rubbing her eyes.

"Four of my men beat this prisoner and raped her," I said, my voice shaking. "She's out of it. I-I don't know if she'll be okay."

I gently laid Lena on the bed, fighting the urge to brush her hair out of her face in front of Era. My eyes trailed down to her neck. Because those bastards had ripped off her shirt, her neck was now bare.

And my eyes widened at the sight.

The necklace. My mother's necklace.

All this time, and she still wore it. My eyes trailed to her hand, and a lump formed in my throat when I realized she still wore the ring I gave her on her right ring finger.

Just as I still wore the one she gave me.

"She's going to get blood on the bed!" Era complained. "Why is she in here?"

I was flustered and angry. "Erabella! I do not need to justify my actions to you! You are to stay in the West Hall tonight."

"But—"

"End of discussion!" I snapped.

Annoyed and confused, she rushed out of the room.

Once it was just the two of us, I finally brushed Lena's hair back, examining all the marks and bruises on her face in the room's light. Her eyes were even more swollen and dark than I'd noticed in the dim cell. Hickeys and bite marks covered her neck, and her arms were scattered with bruises.

"Dear Gods…" I breathed, trying to keep my body from shaking any harder from the rage I felt.

How dare they lay a hand on her. Violate her.

I couldn't stop now; my whole body began vibrating, and my need to torture and kill was unavoidable.

She probably thinks I had something to do with this. Fuck!

I pulled back the sheet and tried not to let my eyes linger, but hell, her body was as beautiful as ever. It was stunning when we were younger, but now she looked even more like a woman. I pulled one of Era's nightgowns out of our dresser and carefully slipped it on her. No one should see her naked body unless she wanted them to.

I chewed the inside of my cheek and found myself removing her cuffs. The helplessness she had to have felt…I wanted her to wake up and feel there was a way she could defend herself. A way to fight back. Not that I wished she would try.

After she was clothed and tucked under the comforter, I heard a knock on my door, and Hendry entered with the pink-haired Mage, whose blue-eyed gaze immediately shifted to Lena.

Her eyes widened, and tears began to form. "What did you do to her?!" she cried out.

"Please, it wasn't me. I-I need her healed," I pleaded.

"I need Merrick," she growled, her voice going unusually low. "I will not heal ANYONE until Merrick is brought to me."

I didn't understand. But I didn't care. Lena needed to be healed.

"Hendry, go fetch this Merrick person," I ordered. He nodded and headed off, leaving Elowen and me staring at Lena. We stood there for many moments in utter silence. I didn't know how long. I just kept count of Lena's shallow breaths.

I wiped my forehead, sweat beading at my hairline.

"Gods…" she finally whispered, breaking the silence. I glanced down at her as she shook her head. "After she saved Edmund and probably more of your people…you'd do this to her?" She turned to me. "Why? Are you truly that evil?"

I stiffened at that comment. "I told you. I had nothing to do with this." I looked at her with sincerity. "I swear."

"We'll see," she muttered.

Moments later, Hendry reappeared with a tall, pale man in his grasp. Well, not as tall as Hendry or me, maybe a couple of inches shorter than us. He gave me a malicious glare that only further deepened after he noticed Lena on the bed. He shot his gaze back to me.

"What did you do to her?" he yelled, tugging away from Hendry briefly before he held him again.

"He claims he had nothing to do with it, Merrick. Tell me it's the truth," Elowen whispered.

He nodded, then looked at me. "I'll need these off," he said as he gestured to his wrists. His lip ring glinted off the light coming from the oil lamps as he gave me a dark smile that did not reach his eyes.

I bit the inside of my cheek and nodded to Hendry, who reluctantly removed his cuffs. It was risky. I had no idea what powers this guy had. But I knew that even if he attacked Hendry and me, there was no way he would make it out of this place alive.

He paused as Hendry removed his cuffs, then brought his arms to his sides, rotating his wrists. Focusing his gaze on me, those ice-colored eyes of his began to turn to smoky charcoal, nearly black. It made me retreat a few steps.

That's fucking creepy.

"Now, look at her," he said coldly. "And just *think*."

I raised my brow but did as he said. I examined her once more, again counting her breaths. My mind kept flashing back to her cottage all those years ago…walking through the charred house and seeing a burnt corpse in her room. The love of my life…my best friend…gone.

I exhaled and decided to think of something happy. The first moment I saw her, our flirty banter, the first time we kissed, the first time we made love…and all the times after.

I thought of how her face lit up when she showed me the Outer Ring—her home. How she had the mouth of a sailor and didn't hesitate to give me her middle finger when I would tease her.

How much I had truly loved her.

I flicked my eyes back to his with a tightened jaw, and he looked at me like I had just grown new limbs. He then narrowed his eyes. "Did you have any involvement with what happened to Lena?"

"No," I growled.

"Did you know it was going to happen?"

"No."

"Do you wish to harm her?"

I paused and looked back at her bruised body. The anger I felt toward her was nothing more than a small flicker in the back of my mind. I still felt betrayed, confused, hurt. But no, I never wished to harm her. And I would kill anyone who tried to.

"No."

Merrick blinked, and the dark in his eyes faded away, the icy color returning. He turned to Elowen.

"I…" He went to continue, but his mouth remained open, no words escaping. Then he snapped it shut, sighing. "He's telling the truth. He doesn't desire to harm her. His intentions are pure."

Elowen blinked a few times, then nodded. "I need these off," she said as she lifted her cuffs.

"Of course." I locked Merrick's again first, and he watched me with a glare that said he was envisioning every way he could kill me. Then I unlocked Elowen, and she ran to Lena at once.

"You may leave us," I directed Hendry. I tilted my head toward Merrick. "Bring this one back."

"Silas—"

"No questions," I said sternly. I knew the idea of leaving me alone unnerved him.

Hendry's mismatched eyes narrowed, and then he nodded. As they left, Elowen immediately started using healing magic on Lena, a warm golden glow emitting from her palms.

"What exactly happened to her?" she whispered while she examined her beaten body.

"Four of my men. Not my orders," I said bluntly.

She let out a dry laugh. "But witches are the evil ones."

The remark didn't faze me.

"Will she be alright?" I asked softly.

"If Ravaiana is on our side, yes," she said after a beat. I hoped the Goddess of Life was on our side. If she was even real. "But this will take a while. And Edmund still needs a healer too. I'll have to alternate between them."

I took notice of the dark shadows under her eyes and how drained she appeared. It had been days of constant work for her, with very little sleep.

"I'm sorry you have not had a break," I mumbled and pulled over a chair for her to sit on.

She just nodded, not meeting my eyes as she sat in the chair.

I continued to stare at Lena, soaking up every awful feeling it gave me. I needed fuel for what I was going to do.

I fished through my dresser to get clothes I didn't care to soak in blood, then changed in my bathroom. I didn't worry about

Elowen—I think she cared more about Lena than making an escape. Plus, she wouldn't make it very far.

As I exited the bathroom, Hendry sauntered back in, giving me an up-down. I grabbed my favorite dagger and headed for the door.

"Hendry, stay and make sure no other person is allowed in," I ordered.

"Yes, Your Highness. Are you okay?" he asked cautiously.

"I will be."

CHAPTER FORTY

I was seething at this point—tunnel vision.

Killing had become a therapy to me, a sick therapy. I had told myself I was ridding the world of evil, so that made it okay that I enjoyed ending lives.

Truthfully, I didn't care if they were evil or not. I had grown so numb to everything that the excitement of the kill was the only thing that felt…good.

I slowly crept down the spiral staircase, a predator lurching toward his prey.

It wasn't just Mother's or Lena's deaths that shattered me. No, this was all my father's doing. He sensed my weakness, my hesitancy toward killing. He broke me in a way I still lose sleep over, then rebuilt me into the murderous machine I am now.

Every piece of the man Lena had loved was gone. But I would be damned if I didn't do everything in my power to stomp on those that hurt her. I supposed that part never changed.

I stopped in front of the cell door, the voices quieting as they prepared for their doom. These men had seen me at my most savage, or so they thought.

They had no fucking clue.

I slowly opened the door, making sure to draw out the creaking sound it made to unnerve these sick bastards.

When I entered, the smell of urine overwhelmed my senses, and I chuckled. Big strong men so scared they pissed themselves. Pathetic.

I observed the demons in the bodies of men, trembling as their eyes met mine. A wicked smirk spread across my face.

I'm saving Rurik for last.

"P-please, Your Highness," Rurik cried. "We didn't know th-there would be a problem!"

I bent down, a snarl overcoming my face, flashing my teeth.

"What is the one rule I have when it comes to prisoners?" I said with dark calm.

His eyes widened further, and more tears began to fall. "N-no sexual assault…" I curled my hands into fists. "We were just trying to get information! She didn't let up to your—" I swung my fist toward his face, blood and teeth spewing from his mouth.

I had hated Rurik ever since he defended injustice toward Roland. Even if I couldn't stand to be near Roland now, he never deserved that. My father never punished Rurik for it and even went as far as promoting him. I was sure he did it just to spite me.

I clicked my tongue. "I don't know what pisses me off more, the disobedience or the pathetic lies." I gave a hateful grin, and he looked like he was going to shit himself. "Actually, I do."

I began to beat his face in so much that it started to look like a boulder had deformed it. If he wasn't ugly before, he sure was now.

I gave the other men the same treatment, my knuckles aching from the repeated punches. I knew they would be bruised.

I then turned to Rurik, who was trembling so hard that it looked like he was ready to combust. But he attempted to lift his head high.

Pfft. How honorable.

My smile grew. "Oh, Rurik, if you think this is the only thing you have coming, you're wrong."

He stiffened at my words, eyes broadening.

I turned to ask the question I was afraid of the answer to. "How many of you put yourselves inside of her?"

Jones coughed up blood. "Just Rurik," he gurgled.

I couldn't say I was happy that only one of them managed to rape her, but the less, the better.

I angled my head back toward Rurik. "I want you to watch what I do to them. Watch how they cry and beg me to stop, knowing that you are next…and there's nothing you can do."

I walked over to Jones, twirling my dagger, and then pulled his pants down. He was shaking uncontrollably, snot and tears dripping down his face.

I met Rurik's stare again. "I want you to know what it feels like to be utterly helpless, utterly hopeless." With a swift movement, I stabbed my dagger through his groin in one go, his eyes bulging out of his face as he screamed.

That made me smile. I stabbed again and again, blood rushing to the floor, until he was unconscious or perhaps dead. Then on to the next.

I pulled down the next one's pants. "Please, Yo—" My jab to his groin cut Geoff off, and I glanced back at Rurik, who was wincing and turned away with his eyes shut.

"Rurik, eyes open," I taunted. I waited for him to obey, then turned and continued my stabbing again until Geoff was unconscious or dead.

I repeated one more time, Daerin falling limp just like the rest. To ensure their deaths, I slit each of their throats, blood spraying all over my shirt and the ground. Then, I finally made my way over to Rurik.

"How do you feel?" I asked casually, the sadistic grin on my face unwavering. "Be honest."

"Ready to get this over with," he gritted out.

I nodded, then walked out of the room to fetch a chair. I placed it by Rurik and ordered him to sit in it.

His trembling continued as I cuffed his wrists to the armrests. Then, I pulled out my dagger and began removing his fingers one by one.

His screams were music to my ears. No amount of his suffering would satisfy me after what he did. But nevertheless, it was enjoyable.

I took my time, severing off one finger and then watching his reaction. But by the time they were all removed, he was going in and out of consciousness.

I slapped his cheek. "Stay with me, Rurik. The best is yet to come." I pulled down his pants and twirled my dagger once more. "Watch," I ordered.

Tears were pouring out of him, and he hesitantly turned. I took his length in my hand and sawed it off, sickening cries emitting from his throat, and then he went limp.

I clicked my tongue.

Shame.

I took his cut-off cock and shoved it in his mouth. "A fitting end to you, don't you think?"

CHAPTER FORTY-ONE
LENA

My eyes began to open slowly, and I started to take in my surroundings. I focused on the four posts of the canopy bed I was in, its deep red curtains pulled open.

My body ached...why did my body ache?

I turned my head. Elowen sat beside me, a golden glow emitting from her palms and drifting over my arm. "Lena!" she exclaimed when she caught my eye.

"Elowen? Where am I?" I asked groggily.

Fuck, my head hurts.

"We're in the Prince's headquarters," she softly whispered.

At the mention of Silas, my stomach dropped, and suddenly I remembered everything that happened. I remembered Rurik and those men and—

He did this. Silas did this.

"Elowen, we must get out of here! He is going to kill me!" I trembled as I went to make it out of the bed, not caring that Hendry stood nearby. I hated feeling so helpless, but without my magic—

My eyes darted to my wrists.

No cuffs.

I froze, seated up in the bed, when the door slowly opened, and Silas emerged. His clothes and hands were drenched in blood. His eyes met mine, and fear overcame me.

"I will get that information out of you, one way or another."

I quickly jumped up off the bed at the memory of his words, not realizing my injuries were still present. I suppressed a cry and held my ground.

"Stay away from me!" I shouted, my voice hoarse.

He looked at me…differently, almost in a defeated way.

"I'm taking a shower," he said softly. I blinked, and he walked toward what I assumed was his bathroom. "Keep an eye on them, will you, Hendry?"

"Why is there blood all over you?" I questioned, terrified of the answer. Had he hurt more of my people?

He turned to me, an intense look on his face. "Those that hurt you did not go unpunished, Lena."

I glared at him, and Hendry shifted his feet. "Should I cuff her? What if she throws fireballs at me?"

A small smile washed over Silas as he looked at his dark-haired friend. "Then you'd better watch out." He grabbed the doorknob and went inside the bathroom. A moment later, the water running was audible. Hendry just stood there, ready at a moment's notice to attack if need be.

I didn't know how to feel…or what to believe, but I had my magic. Gods, it felt good with it coursing through my veins again. I don't know if Silas realized just how strong my powers were. How quickly Hendry could be killed.

Or perhaps he simply thought I wouldn't do it.

"Lena, you should sit. You still need healing," Elowen advised me.

I sat down in defeat and pulled the covers over me once more. I had to think. I had to come up with a plan to get us the hell out of here. Elowen could heal me quickly, though if she did, they would realize she was taking her time with Edmund's wounds. Perhaps this time was just what I needed to come up with a plan.

"Are you okay?" she whispered, her palms trailing above my body, the golden glow of healing magic lighting the room.

It took great effort not to curl into a ball and sob. Or light this room on fire. Instead, I nodded. "I don't know what he'll try next to get whatever information he thinks I have…" I muttered, my lip defying me by trembling.

"He had nothing to do with it," Elowen said gently.

I whirled my head toward her. "What are you talking about?"

"When I saw you, I thought the same thing. Thought maybe he was torturing you for whatever information he thinks you have. So, I told him I would only heal you if he brought Merrick to me." She grasped my hand in hers. "Silas didn't lie. He had nothing to do with your attack. He didn't know anything about it. And, some- how, he also has no desire to harm you. Merrick seemed confused by whatever emotions Silas was putting out, but he didn't do this, Lena," she assured me.

I didn't know how to respond, so I nodded, my shoulders slumping. Elowen continued to heal me until the water shut off, and moments later, Silas reemerged. His black hair was tousled and wet, and he wore a white sweater and black trousers paired with leather boots.

"Hendry," he said calmly. "Please escort Elowen back to Edmund. I will let you know when we need her again."

"Sire, she's uncuffed." His mismatched eyes darted to me, then back to Silas. "I can't leave you."

He waved him off. "It will be okay. That is an order. Now go."

I gave a pleading expression to Elowen, not wanting her to leave me alone. She placed a hand on my shoulder.

"It will be okay, Lena," she whispered. She looked at Silas with a fury I had never seen on her face. "If you lay a hand on her, I will let Edmund die."

Silas blinked in surprise, then bowed. "You have my word."

It was strange, almost like little bits of Silas from before were starting to peek through.

It must be an act.

Hendry hesitated, then led Elowen out, leaving Silas and me alone. I stepped off the bed, fire now emitting from my palm.

"Not a step closer," I hissed as he neared me.

He froze in his steps. "I need you to know I would *never* have someone do that to you. Or anyone."

"Right. I suppose burning at the stake is far more compassionate," I said coldly.

He glowered. "We don't do it that way anymore," he gritted out.

We shared a moment of silence. I didn't think he knew what to say.

"Why did you come to my cell?" I questioned. "Did my screams wake you?"

"I was coming to—" He sighed through his nose. "I was coming to apologize for earlier."

"Apologize?"

"For putting my hands on you," he said quietly.

I frowned, the fire surrounding my hand burning brighter. "Seems like something you and your men have in common."

I was surprised to see hurt shine in his golden eyes. "I am angry, Lena. Very fucking angry."

He took a step forward, and my flames flared. He froze in place.

"I desperately need to find the Weapon, Lena. My kingdom depends on it." His eyes trailed over me, his gaze softer than before. "But regardless, even though you are my enemy, I do not wish to hurt you." He gave me a pained expression. "And I certainly would never order anyone to hurt you like…like they did. Would never support that toward anyone."

I blinked and then closed my fist, the fire disappearing. "Your soldiers look up to you and serve you, Silas. What you do to people like me…why would…" I felt bile rise in my throat. "Why would rape be crossing the line?"

A look came across his face like he finally understood me. But he was clearly still conflicted. He just shook his head.

"You will need to give me time…but I'm letting you go," he said softly.

I blinked over and over. Surely I heard him wrong. "What?"

"I'll find a way that we can sneak you out of here. Edmund still needs multiple days of healing, so it should be simple. Your mother can leave with you."

I shook my head. "I'm not leaving my people. Either we are all freed, or I'm staying," I argued.

His brows drew together. "I cannot just let everyone go, Lena."

"Why not? You're the Prince!" I yelled, throwing my arms up.

"Exactly!" he shouted. "I am just the Prince. I, like all my men, follow the King's orders."

"You're telling me none of your men follow *you*?"

He paused, jaw clenching. "Not enough," he said quietly.

"Then you'll have to watch me die with the rest of them," I muttered bitterly, sitting back on the edge of the bed.

His jaw twitched, and we just studied each other. The scar on his cheek was more pronounced when he frowned. I wondered who had given it to him. Was it during training? In battle? Was it from a Mage defending themselves?

And the tattoos covering his skin…seemingly all of it, save for his face, paired with his tanned complexion, made those golden eyes appear even brighter. More beautiful.

My heart leaped in my chest, and I was the first to look away, crossing my arms as I did so.

Out of the corner of my eye, I saw him retreat into the bathroom. Moments later, he came back with a rag and bowl of water. I gave him a frown.

"Let me clean your face."

I scowled at him. "I don't need your help."

He disregarded me and sat beside me anyway. He cocked a brow, and I sighed in defeat, angling my body to face him on the bed.

He dipped the rag in, squeezed it, and gently patted it under my nose.

"I think your nose is broken," he mumbled. "Will that take long to be healed?"

I winced at the pain. "Hopefully not."

He dipped the rag back in the bowl, red now swirling in the water, before squeezing it again and dabbing it around my lips.

"You still have my mother's necklace," he murmured.

I met his amber eyes once more, and he submerged the rag again. "I have worn it every day," I said quietly. "Do you want it back?"

He contemplated my question. "No," he said softly.

His hand grasped my jaw, tilting my head away so he could run the rag along my neck. I tried to ignore how his touch made me feel.

"You have your ring still, too."

I flushed and looked at the sapphire ring still on my right ring finger. "I've never taken it off."

His voice was just above a whisper when he replied, "Neither have I."

My eyes widened as I shot them toward his right hand, where a single silver band wrapped around his ring finger sat. The ring I gave him. I looked into his eyes, and he drifted his gaze away, standing up to dump the water out.

I watched as he carried the empty bowl and rag with him, making his way to the door to exit the room. "Try and get some rest."

"Silas?"

He was just before the door when he turned to me.

I didn't wish to say it. But I did anyway. "Thank you…for saving me."

He tensed. "I could say the same thing to you."

Then he left.

After Silas was gone, I cuddled up in his bed, which happened to be the softest mattress I had ever lain on.

Well, that wasn't true. His one at the castle was softer. But this was a very close second, and after how many days of unsavory sleeping conditions, I savored the feeling. Hated that I savored the scent of him that lingered.

I drifted to sleep, and when I awoke, sunlight was spilling into the room from the large stained-glass window at the back of the room, rainbow colors painting the space beautifully. I sat up, rubbed my eyes, and while taking in my surroundings, I realized Silas was sleeping at the desk beside me, his head lying uncomfortably on the wooden top.

He looked so peaceful when he slept; the hard lines of his face now softened. Despite his now rugged, dangerous look and the tattoos covering his neck and arms, he looked as sweet as ever while in sandland.

He twitched, and then his eyes slowly opened, meeting mine. He winced as he lifted his head and rubbed his neck.

"I'm sorry for taking your bed," I whispered.

"Don't be ridiculous," he mumbled groggily as he sat back in the chair with his arms crossed. He was still wearing the same outfit. "How are you feeling?"

"Sore. But better." I looked away awkwardly. "What…what exactly happened to them?" Considering the blood staining his clothes from before, they must've had an intense beating.

"They're dead," he said plainly.

My head whirled toward him. There was no remorse on his face, no sign of guilt.

I glanced down and nodded, content knowing those monsters were no longer alive, then observed the deep blue nightgown I wore, not noticing it until now. It was made of silk and hugged nicely around my body, though my breasts were barely held in.

"Where did—" I went to ask where it came from when a knock on the door, followed by a figure's immediate entry, startled me.

Strolling in was Erabella, wearing a red nightgown similar to the one I wore, along with a black robe that was trailing on the floor behind her. Her body stilled when she saw me, and she frowned, quickly shooting her eyes to Silas.

He stared at her, waiting for whatever she was going to say.

"Can I talk to you?" she asked him in a pissed-off tone.

He inhaled and stood, glancing at me as he made to leave. "You should shower, Lena. There are towels and an extra toothbrush in my bathroom. I'll bring you a change of clothes."

Before I could respond, he walked out the door, Erabella giving me a glare before following. The door shut behind them, and I decided a shower would help relax my muscles, assuming the Prince at least had hot water.

I shut the bathroom door behind me and stripped off my nightgown. As I went to reach for the lever in the shower, I caught my reflection in the mirror.

Holy Gods.

Two black eyes, though they were fading, I'm sure thanks to Elowen. My neck was adorned with several hickeys and bite marks, and my arms were bruised.

I looked terrible. I glanced away, intent on enjoying this shower, and turned on the water. I put my hand under the trickling stream and sighed in relief.

Hot. Thank you.

I stepped in, let the hot water trail down me, and instantly released my sob as I recalled what those men did to me. What Rurik did to me.

I was happy they were all dead. Men like that didn't deserve to exist. I could only hope they were suffering Valor's wrath in the Underworld.

I scrubbed and scrubbed. I felt dirty and disgusting, and I didn't know if any amount of soap would ever make me feel clean again.

CHAPTER FORTY-TWO
SILAS

"What is going on, Silas?" Era fumed. We moved into a spare room in the Western Hall to talk privately after I placed a new set of clothing on the bed for Lena, the running water letting me know she was still showering. Erabella stomped the entire way. "Why was she wearing my nightgown? Why didn't you come to bed last night? Did you fuck her?"

I pinched the bridge of my nose and let out a long exhale. "No, Era, I did not fuck her." Nor had I ever given her a reason to suspect me of being unfaithful.

I contemplated what excuse I could come up with, but I was falling short. Had it been another prisoner this had happened to, I still would've killed those men. Rape would forever be unacceptable to me. But would I have treated the prisoner with as much care as Lena? No. Would I have dressed them in Era's clothing? Absolutely not.

"We aren't…we aren't fucking savages. Witch or not, that woman saved Edmund, saved Roland." I hesitated. "She saved me, too."

Era raised an eyebrow. "Saved you, how?"

I explained to Era how one of her friends was a shapeshifter and how she nearly ripped my head off before Lena jumped in front of me and blocked her, sending her friend crashing into the ground. Had she not done that, I surely would've been dead.

Era crossed her slim arms, her brown eyes narrowing. "Why would she do that? It makes no sense."

I tensed. It made perfect sense. But I couldn't tell her why.

"I don't know," I lied. "Regardless, I couldn't let her believe I had any part in what happened to her, nor that I supported it. I wanted to make sure she knew I was grateful for what she did."

"And now what? She will be killed once we reach Otacia, anyway. So why does it matter?"

"Because…" I let out a deep sigh. "Because I am letting her go."

Era looked at me like I had sprouted a second head. "What the hell are you talking about?"

"She will fight me on it, but I won't let someone who saved my life be killed. I can't." My fingertips drummed at my sides. "So, I will be letting her go. I just need to figure out how to do it without anyone noticing right away…"

"Silas, have you lost your mind?" she hissed, looking around the room in case someone had snuck in. "If your father finds out—"

"I don't give a fuck what he thinks," I snapped. "I need to go talk with Edmund," I muttered, rushing out of the room before Era could protest.

Halfway to the room Edmund was being kept in, I ran into a pain in my ass.

Roland.

"So. Word has spread." He smirked, stopping me in my tracks. "Jones, Geoff, Daerin, and Rurik. Dead. Killed by you in a rather vicious manner," he simpered.

I glared at him and wondered who the hell he thought he was. "Do you have a problem with that?"

He put his hands up. "Not at all, boss man. I hated Rurik. You knew that."

Rurik was a grade-A asshole. Hardly anyone could tolerate him, even a cocky son of a bitch like Roland. After what had happened when we were boys, what Rurik was willing to let slide when it came to his treatment, I was sure he wouldn't lose sleep over his death.

He placed his arms back down, a frown now taking over. "Is she okay?"

My eyebrows knit together.

Why the hell does he care?

"She will recover," I said flatly. "Now, if you don't mind, I have matters to attend to."

I continued forward, my shoulder bumping into him. He grunted but didn't bother saying anything else.

I entered the room, finding Elowen sleeping next to Edmund. What was left of his left arm and right leg were heavily bandaged, and all he wore were black lounge pants. Like most soldiers, his body was heavily toned, though his skin was free of any ink. He was sitting up against the headboard, rubbing Elowen's back, and was startled when he saw me.

I raised my eyebrow, and he looked back down at her, then continued to rub her back more.

"She can't die, Silas," he said quietly.

Edmund was the closest thing to a best friend I had, save for Era and Hendry. When my intense training began after Mother died, Edmund and Hendry were the only lights that I had. The only ones who, without a doubt, had my back.

I walked closer and pulled up a chair, plopped down, and crossed my ankle over my knee, studying him carefully.

He dragged his thumb over her cheek, and she didn't even stir. The continuous use of her magic must've drained her.

Edmund then looked up at me. "She saw something in me. I'm not sure what, but she did not have to beg to save me. She didn't have any reason to show me kindness, but she did." He sucked in a breath and bit his bottom lip. "Please." His voice cracked.

I studied her petite form nestled beside him, her golden brown skin a stark contrast to Edmund's fair complexion. It reminded me of how Lena's skin compared to mine. I loved how dark my hands had looked pressed against her soft skin when we were together.

I crossed my arms as I assessed my friend. "What do you expect me to do, Edmund?"

"I...I don't know." He shook his head, his blond, wavy hair swaying with the movement. Then he paused, nodding to himself. "I know Ulric would never spare one of them...never let anyone who did go unpunished."

My eyes widened at the ridiculous plan that I could see him getting to. "Absolutely not. I will not let you take the fall for everything."

He gave me a sad smile. "I'm useless with a missing arm and leg anyway, man."

My brows knit together. "Don't say that. I'm not letting anything happen to you."

He looked down at Elowen and ran his hand lightly over her pink hair. "And I'm not letting anything happen to her."

I chuckled as I lowered my crossed leg, causing Edmund to frown at me.

"You know," I said quietly, peering over my shoulder, then looking back to Edmund, "the Mages may have something I need."

Edmund's frown deepened. "Are you suggesting you have a plan?"

"Not yet. But I am attempting to devise one." I ran my hand through my hair. "Lena said she won't leave unless I let go of everyone."

"Wait...you talked to their Supreme about this? Why?"

I leaned forward in the chair, resting my elbows on my knees. "I suppose it didn't feel right leading her to execution when she saved my life as well."

Edmund's green eyes shot wide, and I told him what Lena had done before I nearly lost my head.

"That's crazy, man. I can't understand why one of them would stop your death…even mine is a surprise. But you?" He winced. "No offense."

I nodded. I knew if it had been any other Mage, I would have been dead without a second thought.

Any other Mage would've been dead, too. Because I wouldn't have hesitated.

Edmund continued quietly, "I have a feeling you would say the same thing, though, if you were in her position."

He wasn't wrong. I would never leave without my men, sacrificing them while running away like a coward.

I sighed once more and leaned back in the chair. "It won't be easy sneaking out nearly a hundred people," I muttered.

Edmund's eyebrows raised. "It sounds like you're actually considering it."

"I suppose I am," I said with a half-smile that quickly faded. Elowen stirred but still remained asleep.

"If we had the support of the Mages…if the sources are true, and there are more of them out there, I could perhaps have the numbers to overthrow my father."

Edmund's eyes bulged. "What?" he whispered incredulously.

"I have considered it for a long time. I only trust you and Hendry, and we alone wouldn't stand a chance. But these Mages are powerful, and if we had higher numbers…if we spoke to the independent kingdoms that have resisted Otacia's control—"

"What you're saying is treason," he whispered.

"Would you support me?"

He looked down at Elowen. "You know I would. I'll always be on your side." He resumed caressing her face. "I just don't understand your sudden change of heart. You've hated them as much as your father…you've *never* shown mercy. Not since we were young, anyway." He gave me a wary glance. "Did Lena saving you really affect you this much?"

I contemplated his question. "It just showed me that perhaps I have placed my anguish in the wrong direction. You know I have always hated my father."

"As have I," he muttered. Edmund never enjoyed killing. His older brother was a prime soldier, and he joined our army because he aspired to be just like him. Even though his brother was killed by a Mage that he was attempting to capture, Edmund never felt hatred as I had. As my father had.

I nodded to him and, really, to myself. "I'll need to speak with Hendry. And then with Lena." I stood up and brushed my pants. I paused with my hand on the doorknob when Edmund spoke again.

"Silas?" he said, and I turned my head toward him. "Thank you for hearing me out." He gave me a soft smile. "I've dreamt of the day you become King. It will be a great day for Otacia indeed."

CHAPTER FORTY-THREE

LENA

After my shower, I dressed in the clothes Silas had laid out for me. The same prison attire as before. I clicked my tongue as I examined it. I guess I shouldn't have expected another one of his wife's garments.

I got dressed, wincing at the pain, and sat back on the bed.

What am I supposed to do now?

At least Silas had left my cuffs off. I sighed as my eyes surveyed the room.

I guess it wouldn't hurt to explore.

I stood again and made my way to the walnut dresser that stood across from the bed. The top was pretty vacant, as this fort was only used by the Prince in between battles. I located a brush and a hair tie on the dresser, presumably Erabella's, and brushed out the knots

I had before putting my long, damp hair back in a braid. It fell just below my waist.

I hesitated but opened the first drawer and lifted a lacy red pair of underwear, the matching bra still lying inside.

I guess it would *hurt to explore.*

I jumped as the door opened, dropping Erabella's garments and quickly shutting the drawer, but not in enough time for Roland to miss what I was doing.

He chuckled and leaned against the door frame, then smirked while he crossed his arms. "Damn, Lena, of all things I would expect to see you doing in here, I was not expecting a panty raid."

I rolled my eyes and groaned, plopping myself back on the bed. "What do you want, Roland?" I asked in a tone laced with displeasure.

He sauntered over to me. I expected another smart-ass comment, but when I looked up at him, he just wore a frown. "I came to see how you were doing. And," he said as he held out a pair of cuffs, giving me a guilty smile, "to put these on."

"Pfft. Whatever." I looked down at my lap. I suppose Silas wouldn't trust me like this forever.

Roland gently grasped my chin, tipping my face to him, and my stomach dropped, the gesture taking me by surprise. His hazel eyes studied me, looking over all my wounds. He just shook his head as he dropped mine. "I'm happy that fucker is dead," he said coldly.

"Wasn't he your friend?" I mumbled, holding my wrists out.

He scoffed as he placed one on each wrist, leaving them separate, thankfully. "Friend? Don't insult me. We both are higher-ranking soldiers, but that's about all we have in common. He's been a piece of shit the entire time I've known him."

I remained silent, observing my now bound wrists.

"I'm sorry this happened to you, Lena," he said softly.

"What are you doing?" I challenged, shooting my glare at him. "You're marching me to my death. Don't go acting like you give a shit about my well-being."

He crossed his arms, and I took note of his massive biceps in the navy-blue tunic he wore today. "Last I checked, Ginger Snap, I am not the King. I don't make orders; I follow them."

"I didn't peg you as such a beta," I said with a condescending sneer.

He tilted his head back and laughed, then grinned at me. I didn't smile back.

"Are you hungry?"

"What?" I asked with furrowed brows.

"I'll grab you some food. Something that isn't disgusting prison slop. But—" He smirked. "You have to say please."

"Like hell I'll beg *you* for anything," I retorted.

His eyes lit up with excitement, and I couldn't help but be attracted to his expression. I wanted to slap myself for feeling any-thing but disgust for this man.

"I plan on holding you to that," he purred, then headed for the door.

Cocky bastard.

I decided to lie in bed, as there wasn't much that I could do being locked in this room. I certainly didn't want to see any more of Silas's wife's lingerie. I simply stared at the metal wrapped around my wrist.

Such a terrifying invention.

How did the King even have this invented? *Who* invented it? I couldn't begin to guess. I flinched when the door opened, and I turned, expecting to see Roland with some food.

But instead, Silas walked in. I sat up and crossed my arms as he walked over and sat on the bed, keeping his eyes on me.

"That elixir you used to put Edmund to sleep," he queried. "Do you think it would be possible to make enough for all of my men?"

I raised a brow and thought about it. "How many are there?"

"Two hundred and twenty-seven."

"That would be…a lot," I said. "Why do you ask? Do your killing machines have insomnia or something?"

He glowered at me. "I'm brainstorming ways to get your people out."

I gaped at him. "You…you're actually considering releasing us?" I asked incredulously.

"If that's what it takes to get you to leave." His eyes trailed over me. "Plus, I have my own agenda as well."

"Oh yeah?" I questioned. "And what's that?"

He shook his head. "We'll discuss that later. Would it work?"

I thought on it some more. "Finding the ingredients again, making that amount, and attempting to do it secretly would prove difficult." I paused. "Perhaps I could make a distraction?"

He raised a brow, clearly thinking my idea was stupid.

"I don't know…" I muttered and huffed as I leaned my head against the headboard. "Some Mages are able to conjure up portals," I said softly. "But no one in my village nor I know how to. Save for Igon and…" I left the rest unsaid, a lump forming in my throat at the thought of him. I rubbed my temples and groaned. "I just don't understand why he picked me."

Or why I was telling Silas this. He sat on the edge of the bed. His body now angled toward me.

I continued quietly, "I don't know what I'm doing." I lowered my hands to my lap. "I don't know what I'm supposed to do. I…I wasn't meant to be a leader."

I looked into his golden eyes, and he just studied me, his expression unreadable.

"Most of us don't have a choice when it comes to being a leader," he replied.

"I know," I mumbled. "But you were born into royalty. Igon was a master seer, which proved beneficial in keeping the safety of all of us…up until now, of course." I sighed. "There's nothing special about me. I don't have any gift or people skills or—anything." I shook my head. "I just don't know why."

"I thought you wielding fire was special?"

I scoffed. "Special? It's a tragedy."

He looked at me with a perplexed expression.

"Elemental magic is only developed when you go through certain events. Ice is devastation. Electricity is from being in love. And fire? Fire is rage. Not just regular rage, not just anger—people feel anger all the time. It is from a mixture of rage, devastation, and hopelessness. By having your heart completely broken." I fixed my gaze on him. "I got my ice the moment I left you, knowing I would not see you again for a long time, if ever. Knowing what I would be putting you through." I let out a dry laugh. "And you know when I got my fire?"

His eyes bounced between mine, and I trembled, realizing I wouldn't tell him. I fucking couldn't. Couldn't even think of it.

He clenched his jaw when he realized I wouldn't say, but his face slightly softened.

"Some look at elemental skills as powerful, especially fire," I continued bitterly. "I just see it as being weak—that my body sank to such a low that it allowed this magic to surge through me. Some see it as evidence of things I have overcome. I haven't overcome shit.

"I'm still devastated. I'm still heartbroken. I'm still fucking *angry*." I let out a shaky exhale. "Uncuff me. Let me be to blame for letting everyone escape. You can release everyone, and when I make a scene, they can sneak off. You can keep me here; use me as your example. I can hold the soldiers off while they escape."

He cocked a brow. "You can hold off over two hundred soldiers?"

"Yes."

He frowned. "Absolutely not, Lena." He shook his head. "This whole thing is for getting *you* out. I'm not having you go down for all of them. There would be no chance of your survival."

"I don't care."

He tensed, and my eyes went to his clenched fists.

"I don't care if I die if it saves everyone else. Perhaps…perhaps that's what Igon meant."

You will be our savior, Lena Daelyra.

"No," Silas snapped.

"Silas—"

"No!"

I startled and looked away, pulling my legs close. What if Igon did just mean the savior of our people, as in the people of Ames?

I assumed he meant all Magekind…but how was I supposed to accomplish that? Then again, I wouldn't have had to save the people of Ames had Igon not sounded the alarm of surrender.

Godsdamn seers and their inconspicuousness.

After a moment of silence, Silas looked back at me.

"And electricity?" he asked quietly. I knew what he was really asking.

"I had spent my whole life suppressing my magic until I arrived in Ames. I didn't realize it at the time, but it began to develop when we were in Amethyst Pond," I responded softly, and Silas inhaled sharply. "That's why sometimes…it felt like sparks were flying when we made love." I gave an embarrassed smile. "At least for me, it did." I looked down, studying the sapphire ring he gave me. "Some Mages, I guess, let it release fully. Apparently, the feeling is like no other."

I was surprised my comment caused him to blush. "It wouldn't kill your partner?"

I laughed through my nose. "No. The type that is released during battle is different than the love-making kind. Otherwise, I would've electrocuted you when we were in that pond."

Color stained his cheeks further, and then we were interrupted by the door opening, a smiling Roland entering with a tray of food, his grin disappearing the second he saw Silas.

Silas's expression shifted back to frowning. "What the hell are you doing here?" he demanded. Roland stilled.

Shit.

"I asked him to get me something to eat," I lied. "I…I just was really hungry. I apologize."

Silas turned to me with an eyebrow raised. I looked back to Roland, whose shoulders relaxed a little.

"So, you decided to bring her your meal?" Silas asked him.

I darted my eyes to Roland.

He brought me his meal?

"What can I say? She's very persuasive," he purred and winked at me, causing me to cringe.

Tone it down, for fuck's sake.

Silas's frown deepened.

"I figured the beaten prisoner deserved a decent meal, La'Rune." He plopped the tray on the desk beside the bed.

"I didn't realize that was your call."

Roland tensed, and then Hendry's tall form entered the room. Gods, the man had to be at least three inches taller than Silas. His mismatched eyes just studied us.

"Era wants to see you, Your Highness," he drawled. "I do wish not to be a messenger boy."

Silas nodded. "I'll be back…" He peered at me. "And we will finish our discussion." He shot Roland a glare before exiting with Hendry.

Roland and I just stayed in silence for a moment.

"Thanks, Lena," he said with a half-smile. "Silas would've had my balls for showing kindness, though I may not be out of the woods just yet." He ran a hand through his finger-length brown hair that was kept short at the neckline, looking at the now-closed door.

"Do you show this kindness to all of the prisoners?" I muttered as I stood, eyeing the food on the desk, my stomach rumbling at the smell of it. It had been days since I had last eaten.

He smirked. "No need to get jealous, Ginger Snap. My kindness only applies to you."

I crossed my arms and walked over to him, looking at him in disbelief. When I got in front of him, I realized I didn't even know what to say.

"I am *not* jealous."

He leaned in close, and my breathing stuttered. I felt his breath on my neck, spreading chills and that stupid heat across my body once more.

"I have a feeling I *could* make you jealous if I tried," he whispered in my ear as his hand lightly grazed my arm. I flinched, but I didn't push him away.

"You are delusional," I breathed.

He let out a low laugh, his breath grazing my ear, and my eyes fluttered shut. When he finally pulled away, my lids opened to find him gazing down at me.

What is with this guy?

"Enjoy your food," he said quietly with a soft smile, then headed for the door.

CHAPTER FORTY-FOUR

My meal was amazing. The chicken I was given was surprisingly tender, and the rice and vegetables on the side had been seasoned nicely. Considering everything I had eaten up until this point had been bland and super spaced apart, I was especially grateful for Roland's act of kindness.

As I was finishing up with the last bites, Silas came back, shutting the door quietly behind him.

"We will leave in the night," he said quietly as he approached.

I raised a brow. "We?"

"Yes, we." He exhaled through his nose. "My betrayal would be found out at some point, and if not me, other innocent men would be the ones to suffer for it. It will be myself, Edmund, Hendry, and my wife who will join you."

I blinked. Over and over.

"They're all on board with this?" I asked skeptically.

He nodded.

"And what, you just plan on living with my people and pretending like you aren't the Prince of Otacia?"

"No. I plan on helping you accomplish what you are meant to."

"What, saving all of Magekind?" I replied humorlessly.

Instantly, my stomach dropped when my words registered.

"It will be Silas who determines the fate of Magekind. It has been seen."

Torrin's words from all those years ago…could this be what Igon saw?

Silas didn't respond to my comment. "I will need you to make a distraction. One you have done before," Silas continued, and when I frowned, he said, "A fire."

Silas told me the entire plan. When night fell, I would be the first uncuffed. I would go to the Western Wing and start multiple fires, the last creating a wall to block the soldiers from stopping our escape out of the Eastern Wing. Silas would be with me while Hendry ushered out my people.

I stood up and put a hand on my hip. "Why help? This will be seen as treason."

"I am well aware," he said.

"You won't be able to return home."

"I want to make this very clear. I am not doing this for you." He looked me over, then continued. "I wish to take the throne from my father."

My eyes widened, and my arms slacked at my sides. "What?" I whispered.

He crossed his arms. "I have considered it for a long time. He is still young and in good health. He could reign for decades still."

"Are you saying you wish to kill your father?"

He cocked his head to the side, studying me for a moment before continuing. "More or less, yes."

"How will your people see that?"

I wanted the King dead more than anyone. But if Silas was the one to do it, I worried how his people would take to him afterward. I could not imagine Silas being a more vicious leader than his father, but if he ended his father in such a way… perhaps they'd fear that.

He scoffed. "You're acting as if you don't want him dead yourself."

"No, I just—"

"Can't picture me doing something so violent, Flower?"

I stiffened at the sound of a nickname I hadn't heard in so long. However, instead of it being laced with sweetness and desire, it was laced with bitterness. Still, it affected me the same.

"I don't want you to have to live with something like that," I said quietly.

Darkness flickered in his eyes. "I live with much worse every day, Lena. Regicide would be the least of the horrors."

I wanted to ask what he meant, but I couldn't find it in me.

"No matter," he continued. "Our first job is to gather support. There are territories down east that have resisted Otacia's control. My father has made it clear he wishes to conquer them."

"And you?"

He shook his head. "Otacia doesn't need any more land. We need allies. I suspect these territories will be willing to join our cause if it meant Ulric was no longer King."

I stared down at the ground. It was risky, but Silas had to have considered this plan in advance. I knew the kingdoms of Faltrun, Forsmont, and Wrendier had resisted Otacia's command and remained independent to this day. But still…

"Why now, of all times?"

"Having the Mages on my side would be a big help."

I scoffed incredulously. "You expect the *Mages* to support you?"

He shrugged. "I would lift the kill order. Mages would be welcome in the kingdom. Why wouldn't they support that?"

"You're telling me this grand idea just came out of the blue? Silas, the Slayer of Witches, is suddenly willing to provide refuge after all these years of slaughter? Why not kill your father sooner?"

His jaw clicked, and I just watched him as his eyes bounced between mine, as if debating what to say.

"Because nothing separated me from him before," he said quietly. "And there was never hope of any support. Sure, the territories would be a big help. But…not enough." His golden eyes burned into me. "But your people, if there really are more of you, it could change everything."

I bit my lip, looking at the floor again for a few moments before gazing back at him. "I don't know if the Mages will support you after everything you've done."

He tilted his head to the side. "Would you support me?"

I crossed my arms. "You know that isn't the same."

He laughed through his nose. "Why are you trying to talk me out of this decision?"

"I'm not."

He smirked, his eyes trailing over me again. "I have a feeling you will be persuasive when it comes to your people's support of me."

I stared at him for a moment. "How can I trust your word? That you will follow through with what you say and won't be yet another ruler that criminalizes my people?"

His smile faltered. "You don't have many options other than trusting me."

My heart sank. That much was true. There was so much to consider. For all I knew, he could be warning his men, saying he was pretending and using me to find where the rest of my people were. I couldn't imagine him doing so…but still. I would have to be cautious and keep my eyes on him at all times. Merrick being able to tell if he was lying would come in handy too…

I sighed. "I suppose I don't." I stared at the cuffs on my wrists. "Will you release everyone from these?"

"I will have them separated, but I won't fully have them removed until we are farther away, in case anyone wishes to defy you."

Defy me…not him.

"I have to escort you back now," he continued. "I don't want to raise any more suspicion than I already have."

I nodded and slowly stood, and Silas lightly held my arm as we left the room.

I was led back to a different cell this time, passing the one I was in prior. As we drifted past, I glanced inside to see servants scrubbing what appeared to be a lot of blood from the ground. I felt uneasy, first from picturing what Silas had done to those men and second from what they had done to me. I tensed, tears beginning to build.

"I made sure they suffered," he said quietly, and I looked at him, his vision fixed on the destination ahead.

"I'm sorry you had to do that," I whispered.

He froze, turning to me with darkened eyes and controlled anger.

"I enjoyed doing it. Do not be sorry."

I bit the inside of my cheek, and Silas turned his gaze forward.

My thoughts drifted to when Silas killed those men at Amethyst Pond…how guilt-ridden and ashamed he was. There was no trace of that man here.

But those men of his…I was still not the least bit upset they were dead.

When the new cell door opened, the one I would be staying in, I was surprised to see Merrick and Viola sitting inside.

"Lena?" Merrick asked with wide eyes as he rose to his feet.

I ran in and hugged him. He was unable to return the gesture as his cuffs were still linked together.

"You're looking much better," he said with relief.

I wasn't sure if the two of them knew the extent of what had happened to me. If they did, they did not say.

Silas cleared his throat as he entered and shut the door behind him as I pulled away from Merrick.

"Share the plan with them…quietly," he whispered, nodding toward the open window in the cell door.

"What plan?" Viola questioned in a low voice, eyes like daggers as they beheld the Prince.

I gave them both the rundown of our plan—how Silas would be helping our escape, how I was to create a distraction, and how Silas had ulterior motives in gaining our people's approval.

"This has to be a trap." Viola let out a dry laugh as she paced the room, then paused to glare at Silas. "Why would you be willing to do all this? After years and years of harming Mages, slaughtering us—" She shook her head, then faced me. Her violet eyes offered no warmth. "I hope you know what you're doing. What you're signing us up for." Her gaze shot to Silas. "I don't know how you've managed to make her trust you, but if you so much as try *anything* that makes me believe you a liar, I will kill you."

Silas narrowed his eyes, and Viola looked at me. "I do not care if you order me to stop. I do not care if you get harmed in the process either, Lena. Not when it comes to our people."

I kept my shoulders high. Viola was always more of a leader than I was. She was extroverted and confident and always helped with any conflict that arose in our village, petty as they were. If anything, it would have made more sense if she had been named Supreme.

"I will gladly accept harm to me if I have this wrong—if the Prince betrays us." I turned to him, his eyes flickering with an emotion I couldn't decipher.

"The good thing, Vi, is that I can always tell if he's lying," Merrick remarked, a sinister smirk on his face.

Silas crossed his arms. "Not that it matters, but you have my word," Silas promised.

Viola just huffed and sat back down on the stone bed while Silas turned to me.

"I will be back in a few hours when it is time."

"Okay." I nodded. He stared at me for a moment more before walking up to Merrick, who stiffened.

"Allow me?" Silas asked, gesturing to his cuffs. Merrick hesitated but held out his arms. Silas held his fingerprint and separated the device, allowing Merrick to move his hands freely. He didn't say thank you.

Silas started to leave when Viola spoke. "What about me?"

He turned, slight amusement in his eyes. "Can I trust you not to swing at my face?"

She gave him a mocking smile. "I can never be sure with a face so punchable present."

The corner of his lip went up, and to Viola's surprise, he separated her cuffs, too. She was examining her wrists as he exited the room, giving me a glance before shutting and locking the door behind him.

"Where exactly are we going, Lena?" Merrick whispered.

We sat beside each other on the other stone bed, opposite Viola, who was now lost in thought.

"Mount Rozavar," I said as quietly as possible. "Not many know there is a family of Mages living atop it. Mages with excellent skills." I smiled softly. "Igon made sure to tell me of the place. This must be why. It's no coincidence the mountain is close by."

Merrick gave me a slanted smile. "Seers."

I smiled bigger and rested my head on Merrick's shoulder, his head then resting atop mine.

"How did you know it's near?" he asked.

"When they showed me a map on the road—and before you ask, no, I did not tell him where it was. I didn't even mention where I planned to take all of us."

"A lot of this is wild to me, Lena, but…I trust you."

I reached over and squeezed his hand. "I appreciate it," I

murmured, then hesitated with the next part. I lifted my head up. "Igon also mentioned how the mountain dweller's wife was born without an arm…and how he was able to enchant a prosthetic to work like the real thing."

To that, Viola sprang up. "You're joking."

I shook my head. "I can't help but think that information was for Edmund."

When I turned to Merrick, his icy eyes were wide.

CHAPTER FORTY-FIVE

The hours went by slowly—Merrick and Viola were exhausted, and with their hands now separated, they sprawled out on the concrete, finally getting some rest. I was sitting on the opposite bed, watching as Viola slept on Merrick's chest.

I had always thought they would be a cute couple. I wasn't sure of either's feelings, though I knew Viola usually preferred women. Merrick certainly loved her as he loved me—I knew it wouldn't be weird for me to lie on his chest either.

I began to hear footsteps and sat up straighter as the door creaked open. Merrick and Viola's eyes shot open. I couldn't help the sweat that began to form at my hairline or the quickening of my heartbeat.

You are okay. Those men are gone. They are gone.

Elowen stepped in, escorted by Hendry, who was a whole foot

and a half taller than her. Her cuffs had been removed entirely. I exhaled, and my shoulders sagged in relief.

"El," Merrick murmured, standing and hugging her tightly. She squeezed him back just as hard.

I looked at Hendry, his mismatched eyes catching mine.

"He will be here soon," he said quietly. "He left Elowen uncuffed so she could finish healing you."

To that I nodded, and he left, the lock clanking.

"How are you feeling, Elowen?" Viola asked, rubbing her eyes as she stood, and pulled her into an embrace once Merrick let go. "They've been working you like a dog."

She squeezed and pulled back. "I'm okay," she said in her soft, cute voice. "I have been with Edmund, as you know." She looked to Merrick before her eyes hit the ground. "He's made sure I get as good of treatment as I can."

Merrick tensed, but I quickly spoke. "Have they told you anything?"

"Yes," she whispered. "Edmund tries to insist he shouldn't come—"

"He is coming with us." I placed a hand on her shoulder. "Don't worry."

Merrick just stared at her. "I don't know what's gotten into you, Elowen. Why do you care so much for this stranger?"

She blinked a few times. "I…I don't know," she said. "I just know that I do. That he does, too."

Viola shifted on her feet. "You don't think…" she started.

Merrick whirled his head toward her. "Don't even suggest it."

Elowen was staring at him with confidence when he met her eyes again.

"My Gods," I exhaled. "Elowen, do you think…"

"Yes…" she sighed. "Yes."

It would be the only thing to make sense. Why else would a soldier, trained to kill and view our kind as monsters, be so sympathetic and kind? Why would Elowen, after witnessing what he contributed to, after seeing her parents' bodies, insist so greatly on saving him, on healing him—holding him?

There could only be one answer. Edmund was Elowen's Soul-Tie.

"I don't accept it," Merrick snapped.

"That's not how it works," Elowen growled. My eyes widened at her tone, as did all of ours. I had never seen her worked up like this. "I know you don't like him, Merrick. But don't you think your default hatred of him is just like how the soldiers view all of us?"

Merrick clenched his jaw, offering no response.

"It is," she continued. "I never planned on caring for an Otacian man. I didn't plan on any of this." Her voice cracked. "But he means something to me, and I promise you, I mean something to him, too."

Merrick tensed, and at the sight of Elowen's eyes welling up with tears, he pulled her into an embrace once more.

Another hour went by. It had to be past midnight now, which meant I would be creating the distraction soon. Elowen was asleep beside me, exhausted after healing me completely, and Merrick and Vi were on the other bed. My eyes were beginning to flutter shut when our door opened, and Silas emerged.

I sat up, squinting at the light peering through, then quickly stood. My friends awoke.

"Stay quiet," Silas whispered. I walked over to him, his golden eyes flickering over me, then back at my friends. "Hendry and I will be here shortly to release everyone."

They nodded, and Silas shut and locked the door behind us.

We walked down the hallway until he gripped my arms and pulled me into a dark corner.

"Hey—"

He cut me off. "If anything goes south, I want you to run, Lena."

I tried to shake out of his grip but couldn't. "I will not leave without my people. I told you that," I hissed.

"This is a dangerous plan, and I want it to work as badly as you do." He loosened his grip on my arms, his hands sliding gently down them before stopping at my forearms. My heart fluttered, and I could feel my cheeks start to burn. "But if all hell breaks loose, if we miscalculate, promise me you will run. Promise me."

"Silas—"

"I'm begging you." His voice broke.

And there he was.

Quill.

He was still in there. His amber eyes burned into mine, his expression pleading, his face mere inches away. This close, I recognized his familiar scent of pine and citrus. I wanted to lean into him.

I wanted to embrace him and kiss him. But no…regardless of his care for me, he was married. He had moved on.

But our friendship…perhaps we could have that again one day.

"I promise," I whispered, and his shoulders sagged. "But," I continued, "it would be the absolute last resort. I won't let it get to that point."

His eyes flickered to my lips for a moment before he backed away. "Let's get this done."

The plan was simple enough. I was to go to the watchtower on the west side of the fortress, which could be reached by climbing alongside the fortress exterior. I would sneak up, set a fire, then sneak down. While that distraction was occurring, I would start fires in various rooms in the Western Wing, rooms unoccupied by soldiers. Silas had told me, *"I'd rather lose materials than lose men."*

Considering the prison was beneath the Eastern Wing, most of the commotion would drive soldiers as far as possible, and at the very end, I would create a wall of fire, blocking anyone from entering as my people fled out of the closest exit.

While Silas didn't press me where specifically I wished my people to go, we both agreed that our destination was in the south.

He handed me a map, and before we went upstairs, Silas opened a cell door for me. I was to give the map to someone who could ensure my people's safety.

My mother.

"Lena," she breathed, and I couldn't stop the immediate tears as I ran and hugged her tightly. "What's going on?" Her expression went from worry to hate as she beheld Silas behind me. He quietly shut the door behind him.

"There's too much to explain and not enough time—" I shakily opened the map and pointed to an unmarked Mount Rozavar, making sure Silas did not see. "Do you know this place?"

"Yes…yes, Igon—" Her eyes went up to Silas, then to mine in fear.

"Good," I whispered. Igon had mentioned it to her as well. "When the time comes, I want you to lead our people here. Run like hell. Keep running until dawn hits. Get there as quickly as you can."

Silas went to hand her a compass but decided to separate her cuffs first.

She just stared at him in disbelief. "You still love her, don't you?"

My eyes felt like they were going to fall out of my head. Silas's lips parted, but before he could respond, I cut in.

"I will be just behind," I said, hoping not to sound as flustered as I felt. "But in case anything happens to me, I need someone to be able to lead them. Merrick, El, and Vi know, too."

Mother went to ask another question, but I held up my hand. "There isn't much time. I will tell you more after."

She simply nodded, then looked at Silas. There were so many unspoken words between them. But now wasn't the time.

I grasped her shoulder. "I will find you," I whispered. "I love you."

She nodded with tears in her eyes. "I love you, too."

We met in Edmund's room, and Hendry was already there, waiting for orders.

"About time," Hendry said dryly as we entered the room. It

took little effort to sneak up here, considering a majority of soldiers were sleeping.

"I assume everything is in order?" Silas asked.

Hendry nodded, and Edmund propped himself up as best he could.

"Silas, I insist you let me stay," he begged.

"It's already decided. I don't want to hear any more on it."

"I cannot live with myself if I get you killed."

Silas shook his head. "You will be just fine. You'll ride with Hendry on one of our horses."

"And then what?" he pressed, his green eyes tortured. "I'm useless like this. I'd only slow you down."

I exhaled loudly, and all the men turned to me.

"Where we are headed…there is a skilled blacksmith," I said carefully. "Specifically, one who works with enchantment." My eyes went to Edmund. "Igon made sure to tell me of it the day your people attacked—told me the blacksmith had made his wife an arm, as she was born without one." I couldn't help but laugh in amazement. "A fully working arm. He knew this would happen. All of it." I smiled softly. "Which means that you, Edmund, must be one of the good ones."

Edmund blinked. "I've never heard of such a thing, but," he continued, smiling, "if it means I can stay by Elowen without putting her in danger, then I am all in."

We were all startled when the door opened, Roland wearing a smirk before closing the door behind him.

I clenched my fists, and Silas unsheathed his sword.

"Relax, boss man," he crooned while holding up his hands. "You didn't think you could leave without me, did you?"

"You're joining us?" Edmund asked, quickly hiding his happy smile when Silas shot him a glare.

"You heard me," Roland replied smugly.

Silas shifted his head back to Roland. "We don't want you to come with us," he stated sternly.

His friends were clearly conflicted. Silas frowned at Hendry. "You didn't invite him, did you?"

Hendry cringed, and Silas's frown deepened.

What did Roland do to make Silas dislike him?

"You don't want an additional supporter, Your Highness?" Roland asked, crossing his arms.

"I have no issue in killing you, Roland."

I looked at Silas incredulously, and I could tell he was being serious.

"What's the problem with one more?" I asked, attempting to lighten the mood.

Silas shot me a scowl. "The problem is it's another mouth to feed, another person to worry about getting us killed. Regardless"—he pointed to Roland—"I do not trust you, Roland."

"I have given you no reason not to trust me, and you know it," he accused, then ran a hand through his brown hair. "Besides, I already know of your plan. I'm coming."

I glanced at Silas. "We don't have much time. Let's not waste it on this," I whispered.

"Are you saying I kill him?"

I gaped at him. "No!"

That earned me a smirk from Roland.

Silas groaned, sheathing his sword. "Very well," he grumbled.

We all stood by Edmund's bed, going over last-minute details. Now that Roland was involved, it was decided that he go with me, though Silas fought on it initially. It would be too much to have just one of them unlock all the cells and separate all the cuffs, and that way, Silas would be there if a diversion needed to be created.

Silas removed my cuffs and gave me a new outfit—a brown long-sleeved dress and a black cloak—before Roland and I snuck our way to the Western Wing. I wished I had a bra, but the dress was tight enough at the top they were held in. He also gave me a pair of Erabella's shoes, and I was surprised our feet were the same size despite her having a couple of inches on me. Once I was dressed, we all went to complete our tasks.

Most of the corridors were empty and silent as soldiers slept. Roland and I carefully traveled down various stone hallways, occasionally hiding behind walls when a soldier passed by.

When we got to the room with the best access to the western watchtower, Roland quietly locked the door behind us.

I slowly prowled to the large window, the one that I had been told gave an excellent view of the tower. I could see torches lit as soldiers kept watch.

I climbed out the window onto the ledge, my breathing unsteady as I looked at how far down my fall would be if I slipped.

"Can't you just shoot a fireball or something and get it done quickly? This is…dangerous."

"If they see a fireball coming, they'll know they're being attacked. We can't have that chaos just yet."

"Ah."

I took the first few steps along the outside of the fortress and nearly shrieked when I slipped, grabbing on to the edge and thankfully catching myself before falling to my death.

"Shit, be careful," Roland muttered with slight worry in his voice. "Should I follow you?"

"No, wait here. Signal to me when I am good to light it," I whispered, nodding to the two men stationed on top. "And no more talking."

He nodded. I carefully began scooting across the outer edge of the fort, being mindful of my footing and gripping any place on the wall that I could use to keep myself upright. The tower wasn't incredibly far away, fortunately.

The wind began to whirl, and I froze, holding myself as still as possible until it passed. After a couple more movements, I was just below the watchtower. My best bet was igniting the catapult, Silas had told me. Considering the whole fortress was made of stone, the only other option for ignition would be one of his men, and I'm sure he wouldn't love that.

I exhaled quietly through my nose, listening to the two men above have a conversation about returning to their families in a couple of months.

It was always strange to me, thinking of how men who could kill like it was nothing most likely went home to a spouse and children, went home like it was nothing. I suppose they had little choice, though.

I gripped the side of the tower, now looking to Roland and waiting for his signal. He kept to the side of the window, looking up at the watchtower. The wind hit again, my braid whipping around my face. A few more moments and Roland signaled to me.

Quickly, I hoisted myself up, using all my strength, and held out my fingertips, aiming for the catapult. I felt the heat, then little bursts shooting from my hand. Smoke began to crackle. Enough to cause a large fire, but not enough to give myself away.

Just as I was beginning to lower myself, the soldiers yelled, "Fire!"

I quickly scooted along the edge, my heart beating rapidly in my chest.

Please don't get caught.

Another gust of wind hit as I made it back to the window, where Roland grabbed me by the waist and hurled me inside.

"Good job. Now, let's get the hell out of here," he breathed.

We rushed out of the room, though only for a moment before Roland shoved me back inside. A swarm of guards came running, heading straight for the watchtower.

One of them stopped, and I held my palm over my mouth. I was hidden behind the door.

"Do you not hear the yelling, Aubeze? There's a fire!"

"I did—was just heading there myself."

The guard grunted, and after a few footsteps, Roland retreated into the room and turned to me. "Light this room, and let's go," he mumbled.

I turned, observing the room that contained a few tables and chairs, documents, and books lining the shelves. Without a second thought, I shot fire at it all, and Roland and I rushed out. He snuck me around on our way back to the cells, having me light up a lavatory and a broom closet.

Our last stop was a maid's room. Roland peeked in, and then we rushed inside. I noted the empty bed and raised a brow to him.

"She sneaks off every night with one of the cooks," he said, smirking, then gestured to her bed. "Light it up, Ginger Snap."

I rolled my eyes and inched forward before both our heads snapped to each other, the sound of two voices coming closer.

"Shit," Roland murmured, then grabbed me and pushed me down on the bed until he was towering over me and positioned between my legs. "Forgive me," he whispered, and I gaped at him as he pressed his lips against mine, one hand of his now on my face and the other holding him up above me on the bed.

My heart thundered in my chest. The voices that gasped as they entered the room were as if they were underwater, my whole body buzzing at the touch of Roland's lips against mine.

He pulled away, yelling back at the couple. "A little privacy, please?"

The maid nervously apologized, and I heard her scurry out of the room with someone I assumed was the cook. I wasn't sure, as Roland had them partially blocked from my view.

When the door shut, he eyed me and stood back up, holding out a hand to me.

With burning cheeks, I avoided his gaze but grasped his hand and stood.

"I'm assuming it would be unwise to light this room now?" I murmured.

"Indeed. Let us hope the fires you started were enough," Roland said as he walked to the door, quickly peeking out. "It's clear," he whispered, and without another word of our kiss, we left the room with stealth, heading to the cells.

CHAPTER FORTY-SIX

We hurried down, the sounds of yelling from the Western Wing becoming less and less audible. Just before we reached the chamber doors, Roland took extra precautions to ensure the guards were gone—and they were, thanks to Silas. We entered and ran down the stone steps. The last of my people were being led out of the back entrance just as we emerged.

"Where is Silas?" I asked.

"Outside with the others," Hendry replied.

"Merrick and El are with them," Viola added as she and Hendry helped guide our people out of the exit.

I nodded, and then my head snapped as footsteps began to come down. I turned to Roland. "You may want to watch out."

He smirked and got behind me. Tapping into my rage, I created a wall of fire just as soldiers filled the hallway. They shrieked, stumbling back before I couldn't make any out due to the flames. I could still hear their profanities.

Because the cellar was made of stone, I had to keep position until it was time for me to run.

"Get out of here! I'll hold them off as long as I can!" I called back. Hendry and Viola nodded before running, the last of my people with them. Roland didn't budge.

"What are you doing?" I shouted.

"I'm not leaving you—let's go!" Before I could protest, an arrow shot through the flames, just missing Roland.

I cursed and did the next best thing I could think of. I smothered the fire, and just as the soldiers went to charge, I made a wall of ice, trapping them on the other side. I knew it only had moments before they effectively shattered it.

"Smart girl," Roland quipped, then grasped my hand, wincing at the cold before pulling me to the fortress exit out back. When we made it through the door, I froze that entrance as well, then ran across the balcony and down the steps to where everyone was waiting. My people were already distant, running like hell, just as I had ordered.

Hendry was on a horse with Edmund holding on, Elowen and Merrick on another. Silas was standing by the same black horse he rode before, his wife sitting atop it with a scowl on her face. While Merrick, Elowen, and Viola still wore their prison clothes, they were each given cloaks.

"You made it," Silas breathed. He nervously looked up to the eastern watchtower, and I followed his gaze, seeing that the catapult had been frozen. He must have allowed Merrick to do that.

Silas mounted his horse, Erabella wrapping her arms around his waist. I then realized there was only one more horse.

"This was all we could get without getting caught, considering how many horses the Undead killed," Hendry explained.

"No worries for me." Viola smirked, then shifted into a dark stallion, her violet eyes still present.

"You should've let me know, Viola," Merrick teased. "I would've much preferred to ride you."

Despite everything, I choked on a laugh. Elowen slapped him on the arm, and Viola grunted.

I turned to Roland, who was also grinning from Merrick's stupid comment. "So, I'm supposed to share with you?"

He continued grinning, then mounted the white horse that was meant for us, I guess. "Hop on behind me, Ginger Snap."

"How come you get to be in front?" I protested but quickly got on behind him as there was no time to spare.

"I think you'll be more useful than I on the back, with your fireball-wielding abilities and whatnot." I wrapped my arms around his waist, and he sucked in sharply before tilting his head back to me. "And I really just wanted your arms around my waist," he purred.

I reached down and pinched his thigh as hard as I could, and he yelped, causing me to grin.

"Vicious thing," he muttered.

"Let's get on then, shall we?" Silas snapped. I looked over at him and couldn't ignore his grimace. "Where to, Lena?"

The last of my people were hardly visible.

"South."

When we eventually caught up with the rest of the Mages, deep into the forest, they stilled, all catching their breath and cheering. However, the cheering quickly quieted as they saw the Otacians accompanying us.

"What are they doing here?" someone snarled.

"Is this a trap?" another cried.

"KILL THEM!"

Multiple people began to charge toward us, and I urged Roland to guide our horse forward before I created a force field so large that everyone advancing came to a halt.

"No one is killing anyone!" I yelled calmly yet sternly. "The Prince set us free. He betrayed his kingdom so we may all live. If anyone tries to lay a *finger* on any one of them, you'll have me to deal with."

A few protested, but after how horrid the past few weeks had been, they decided to obey, and we continued onward.

We rode for hours, finally stopping just before dawn. Our diversions had proven successful, as no soldiers were on our tail. However, it was only a matter of time before some found us. We were to rest up for a couple of hours before continuing onward.

When we dismounted, I ran to Mother and hugged her tightly, tears of relief pouring down both of our faces. Everyone then awkwardly went to our own areas. Merrick and Viola were talking by the crackling fire I had started while Elowen looked over to Edmund, him returning her gaze. The Otacians stayed near us. With an angry group of Mages surrounding them, they had to have felt safest with me nearby to stop any attack if need be.

Silas's group had also gathered wood for a fire, and Hendry was attempting to start it himself. I sighed and walked over, the group giving me raised brows as I crouched down and conjured fire from my fingertips. The wood began to smoke as the flames ignited.

"Thank you," Edmund said kindly, Hendry nodding. Erabella just sat with her arms crossed, and Roland smiled smugly. Silas gave me an unreadable golden gaze.

What an interesting group.

I went to head back to my friends before Silas spoke. "Can I speak to you for a moment?" He stood and gestured to the privacy of the trees. Erabella frowned at him.

I nodded, and we ventured off.

It was quiet for a moment when we made it deeper into the forest, nothing but the sound of crickets audible.

"How are you feeling?" Silas asked.

I blinked. "Tired. Stressed. I will feel much better when my people are where they will be safe."

He dragged his bottom lip through his teeth. "You still won't tell me, will you?"

I tensed. He studied me with a look that didn't frighten me, but I still remembered how angry he was that first night at Fort Laith.

"You have to understand—"

"Have I not proven to you that I am with you?" he pushed.

"That isn't it, I…" I exhaled through my nose. "I've never been to this place before. I know you've risked it all…" I bit my lip. "I trusted you. Now I want you to trust me."

The muscles in Silas's jaw feathered, but he conceded, nodding while his eyes went to the ground. I grasped his hand, and he froze.

"Thank you," I murmured as my eyes bounced between his. "For everything. Once we are there, we will come up with a plan."

He looked back toward the dancing fires in the distance. "If you really don't know where the rest of your people are, we should go to the southeast territories." His gaze shifted to mine. "The sooner the better, before word gets out of my betrayal and there's a bounty on my head."

"I agree."

He nodded, and my hand slipped away as we silently made our way back to camp.

After a couple of hours and very little sleep, we continued onward, marching for a few hours at a time and then resting. Each stop a handful of Mages were released from their cuffs, and I stood by to ensure no one hurt Silas or his friends.

Silas smuggled as much food as he could carry, and my people had eaten just before we escaped. Still, with rations so short, they were growing hungry. Once we reached Mount Rozavar, Silas would give my people enough coin to feed themselves and feed them well.

By the evening of the following day, everyone was spent. "How long until we reach this place?" Roland asked as he helped me off our horse at our resting site.

"Hopefully, by tomorrow." I stretched, and he nodded. "Why don't you guys stay by us?"

Roland raised a brow, that infuriating but sexy grin forming on his face.

I punched his arm. "I'd feel better knowing you all were near in case someone decides not to follow my orders. They've done well enough so far, but still."

"You won't find me complaining about sleeping near you." He winked.

I rolled my eyes, the corners of my lips rising as I strolled to Silas. He agreed with my plan, and we all set up around the same campfire just as the sun began to set.

Merrick and Silas agreed they would take the first shift and stay awake while the rest of our group slept. I drifted to sleep watching Silas stare off into the forest, the flames giving me an intoxicating view of his beautiful, tanned face.

CHAPTER FORTY-SEVEN
SILAS

Lena was curled up in her bedroll, one of the few we were able to smuggle, resting soundly. I tried to keep my eyes off of her as Merrick continually glared at me from across the fire.

I didn't blame him for being skeptical of me, but he was pissing me off.

"Are you going to be glaring at me all night?"

"I'd be a fool to let you out of my sight." His eyes swirled dark, and I shifted in my seat. He wasn't the only one. Various Mages across the campsite were staring at me warily.

I laughed through my nose and twirled the dagger I held, admiring the sapphire in its hilt.

"Why'd you do it?" he asked in a low voice.

I raised my eyes, then continued to look down at my dagger.

That was tricky. I certainly didn't want him to think I was lying. This "gift" of his was going to be a pain in my ass.

"Do what?" I asked.

"Why did you do all of this? What is the *real* reason?"

I raised my head, frowning. "As I told Lena, I wish to take the throne."

Not a lie.

Merrick narrowed his nearly black eyes, the various piercings in his pointed ears glinting off the firelight as he tied back his white hair. "What if our people don't accept you? What if we fight back? Certainly, you would do everything in your power to end us."

Of course, the idea of Lena's people not supporting my cause crossed my mind.

"I don't know," I mumbled. "What I do know is your people are an enemy of my father. Considering he's also my enemy, I would hope we would at least put differences aside to take him down."

Merrick crossed his arms, and I resumed twirling my blade.

My traitorous eyes then went back to Lena. Her copper hair was still in a braid, loose pieces framing her face. Her cheeks were flushed, and her lips slightly parted as she slept peacefully. It was still strange seeing her with pointed ears…but I found myself not minding them. In fact…

"You're fond of her."

My eyes shot up, and I peered at him through my lashes. "Excuse me?" I nearly growled.

Merrick gave me a smile that didn't meet his eyes. "It seems you know what I'm referring to. I can tell those things too, you know."

Fuck.

I clenched my jaw and resumed my mindless twirling with my eyes on my dagger. "I don't know what you're talking about."

"Liar."

I tensed and met those charcoal eyes. I would be worried if anyone could hear, but with how exhausted everyone was, I was certain everyone else in our group was asleep.

"I haven't said anything to her, but I can feel that she feels it too." He uncrossed his arms, placing them on his knees, and leaned forward. "And there can only be one explanation, one reason why she didn't let you die in Ames…because any one of us wouldn't have batted an eye," he said just above a whisper.

My heartbeat began to pick up. I was positive Lena hadn't told any of her friends she had been with me, Silas La'Rune, but perhaps she had mentioned Quill Callon. Had Merrick figured it all out?

"The same reason Elowen is fond of Edmund."

I furrowed my brows. "I don't understand—"

"Soul-Ties."

I blinked. "What the hell are you going on about?"

Before Merrick could respond, our attention went to a crackling in the woods. I drew my sword while Merrick stood, our eyes darting around the forest.

I kept still, trying my hardest to hear over the small chit-chat occurring around the various camps. Merrick's eyes had returned to their normal light blue, and for once, I hoped those pointed ears had the ability to hear better.

"What creatures did you encounter on your way to us?" Merrick asked with deathly calm.

"Only a few—"

A roar caused us to snap our heads to the forest to witness three—no, *seven* large bears. Not regular bears. No…these had somehow been touched by a curse. Everyone was instantly alert.

Merrick shot forward an ice shard, piercing one of the bears through the throat. Black cursed blood began to ooze out of its neck as it collapsed just in front of Era, causing her to shriek. I grasped her arms and flung her behind me.

"Stay back!" I barked.

Blue sparks enveloped Lena's arms as she rushed forward, another cursed bear going to attack—and electrocuted it, its body contorting and smoking before falling limp.

"Keep your force fields up!" she called out to her people, some of them trembling but nodding. Throughout the camp, Mages held their arms in X's, creating a shield around themselves. Though the cursed bears paid them no mind. They seemed only intent on attacking *us*.

Hendry readied his bow, shooting for one at a distance, his aim striking true. Elowen shielded Edmund.

"Can't you do a wall of fire, Ginger Snap?" Roland yelled to Lena as he ran near her. I was going to snap his neck over that damn nickname.

She and Merrick shot ice at another one of the bears, but the remaining four circled us in.

"Not unless I want to alert the Otacians where we are," she breathed, all of us holding our ground as the bears growled. Their eyes were solid black, just like the Undead, and their hides were beginning to rot.

A handful of Lena's people inched forward, and one of the bears turned and snarled in their direction. They jumped back, and at that moment, Lena shot ice through its head. As she finished her move, she wasn't aware of the one whose teeth were about to snap at her. I grabbed her arm roughly and pulled her back as hard as I could, our bodies hitting the ground as she landed on top of me, those snapping teeth just missing her.

"Fuck, Lena!" I grunted. She shot out an ice shard at the same time as Merrick, and the beast went down with a thud just in front of us. At this point, several more of her people had joined in the fight, various forms of magic attacking the creatures.

"You need to be more careful," I panted as she pushed herself up, her hands still on my chest. Her eyes were wide, her cheeks stained with color, as she turned her head back to where the last of the bears were slain by her people.

She went to stand, tucking a piece of hair out of her face. "I guess we both need to be on the lookout for beasts wishing to behead us." She smirked, holding a hand out to help me up.

I blinked and knew I was blushing. I hadn't seen that expression on her in so many years, and with her messy braid and those bright green eyes, she was as beautiful as ever.

I ignored the thoughts and laughed through my nose as I grasped her hand. She winced as she tried to help lift me. Standing next to her, I was nearly a foot taller. She looked up at me for a moment before gently releasing my hand, the feel of her hand in mine instantly being missed.

Lena went to check on her people, and when I turned, Era was looking at me with furrowed brows, and Merrick was glaring at me with darkened eyes and a raised brow, silently saying, *"See? I know how you feel about her."*

I ignored him. "Are you okay?" I asked Era, my hands now on the sides of her arms.

"Yes…" she drawled. Her eyes went to Lena, then back to mine. *Surely we were not* that *obvious?*

"You saved her," Era commented, then smiled softly. "That's twice now."

I resisted the urge to cringe. Merrick looked away. Era had never had the stomach for all the killing I did, but if she knew why I'd had a change of heart, perhaps she would not be smiling. I looked to the others: Merrick, Elowen, and Viola. Would I have taken a risk saving one of them? I'm not sure. But I would for Lena. Always for Lena.

My eyes found Lena's again. She smiled gently, and then the smile faltered when she saw my hands on Era's arms. She bit her lip and looked away.

My shoulders sagged. "I did owe her, after all."

Era smiled at me, and I returned the gesture, knowing it didn't meet my eyes. It never did anymore.

Our group moved our camp over, not wanting to sleep by rotting carcasses and oozing blood. It had worked in our favor that those creatures seemed intent on attacking only us, not everyone, so we were the only ones that had to relocate.

"I had no idea animals could be affected by a necromancer," Lena breathed.

Everyone else was already asleep, and I was lying next to Era, our bedrolls being large enough to accommodate two people. I held her against my chest, and sleep evaded me as my thoughts kept wandering. I continued to listen to Lena and Roland's conversation with closed eyes.

Of course those two took the next shift together.

"We've seen it before—in wolves. But in a bear? Well, that was especially frightful," Roland said.

"How long have you been seeing these creatures? Any of the Undead?"

Roland didn't respond for a moment. "The last six months or so, I'd say."

"Gods…" she whispered. "In Ames, we all tried to stay within the town. It felt safest that way. Must be how we never encountered any ourselves." I heard her shift. "I wish Igon would have warned me of the Undead, though perhaps he didn't see them in any of his visions."

"Were you close?"

Another pause by Lena. "Yes," she murmured. "I never knew my father, never had a father figure in my life. Igon became that over the last five years." She sniffed. "He took such interest in me, in teaching me of our kind, teaching me all sorts of things."

Guilt washed over me. I had no idea he meant so much to her. I remembered Lena telling me she'd never had her father in her life, and the fact I had taken from her the closest thing to it made me sick to my stomach.

"I'm sorry," Roland said quietly.

"It's not your fault," she whispered. "Based on his reaction…he knew it was going to happen."

I hated that Roland was taking an interest in Lena, hated that she was confiding in him. It was silent for a few moments, nothing but the crackle of our fire. I was nearly asleep when Roland spoke again.

"Do you hate him for it?"

I felt my stomach drop. I wished I was asleep so I didn't have to hear this, yet I couldn't help but wait for her response.

I wouldn't blame her if she did. I hated me, too.

"Silas?"

I imagine Roland nodded.

"No. No, I don't hate him."

Even though my eyes were shut, I could swear I felt her eyes on me.

CHAPTER FORTY-EIGHT

LENA

It wasn't until the following evening that we finally reached the base of Mount Rozavar. The sun was just starting to set, so we still had some time left with light. The mountain was enormous—I recalled Igon telling me it was close to thirteen thousand feet.

"We're supposed to climb that?" Erabella asked with her mouth hanging open. My people looked at one another with widened eyes, various voices whispering in concern.

"No," I replied, hopping off my horse. "I was told there's an enchanted symbol here, only visible to a Mage's eyes." I looked around the massive mountain and let out a sigh.

Who knows what part of the mountain it's on?

"Anyway, it should teleport us up. So long as we get approval."

"Are you sure your people's clothing will be accommodating

enough?" Hendry asked. It was already quite chilly by the mountain base, and because the top wasn't visible, it was understandable to think it would be worse at the top.

"The top of the mountain is actually a warm climate, adjusted by the mountain dweller's wife—her gift is weather control," I said.

"So…does anyone see this symbol? What does it look like?" Merrick asked while squinting and glancing all around the mountain. His silver-white hair was down and moving with the wind.

I frowned as I recalled the drawing Igon had shown me. "It should be a swirl that slithers downward—little symbols along its tail."

Merrick, Elowen, Viola, and I split up, searching alongside the base of the mountain, as well as a handful of those from Ames. We stayed close enough, though—I didn't want one of us finding the symbol and the rest being far away.

After roughly twenty minutes, we found it.

"Here! I think," Elowen called. We all quickly ran over. Sure enough, the symbol from Igon's map was present, glowing a light green.

"You see something there?" Silas asked with a quirked brow.

I walked forward, running my hand along the illuminated mark the size of my hand. "Indeed. This is it."

"Who wishes to visit my mountain?" a man's voice boomed, causing all of us to stagger back. Well, all us Mages, anyway.

"What is it?" Roland hissed.

I cleared my throat. "My name is Lena Daelyra. I come with my people from Ames." I bit my lip for a moment. "Igon Natarion sent me here…more or less."

"Igon…" the voice said. "Is he with you?"

I steadied my voice. "I'm afraid not…he…he was killed." I felt a lump in my throat but pushed past it. "We were attacked in our home. My people have nowhere else to go."

There were so many moments of silence that I thought the voice might have left.

"I take it you are the Supreme now?" the voice asked quietly.

"I am."

"And it is just your people wishing to come to the top?"

I tensed. "No, sir. I have with me the Prince of Otacia and a few of his subjects. He is the one who set us free."

A moment of silence. "Who was it who attacked you?" the voice asked skeptically.

I cringed. "I know how all this must sound—but Igon gave me a message before he passed. I can trust them."

I met eyes with Silas, who looked surprised, then relief washed over when the voice said, "Very well, touch the stone again, and you may enter. Just place a hand on your horses, and they will travel too, if you wish."

I relayed that information to Silas and his group, then obeyed by touching the stone of the mountain.

In a flash, I was standing atop Mount Rozavar. I gasped at just how beautiful it was. Lush, green grass with a medley of wildflowers, multiple wooden homes with smoke floating out of the chimneys. Behind them was the largest peak of the mountain with a cave mouth. And the view of the setting sun…an orange and pink sky with light fluffy clouds.

Just as Igon said, the temperature up here was pleasant.

Elowen flashed beside me, then Viola, then Merrick. Silas, his wife, and the men were next, and all of them gaped at the stunning sight as they held the reins to the horses. After them, one by one, my people found their way up the mountain top.

An older man and woman emerged from one of the homes, strolling hand in hand. I walked toward them, an anxious smile on my face.

The first thing I noticed was how familiar the older man looked.

"Immeron," he cut in. He gestured to the woman smiling nervously beside him. "This is my wife, Ayla."

She reached out, and I shook her hand. Both Immeron and Ayla had to be around Igon's age—in their sixties.

"I must say, I was not expecting this many people," he said. The company of one probably felt strange for him, after it being just him and his family for who knew how long.

I rubbed the back of my neck. "I am so grateful for your hospitality. Igon told me of this place. He was a friend of yours?"

Immeron's eyes went to the ground. "My brother."

My eyes widened.

That's why he looks familiar.

"My Gods, I am so sorry." I could see the resemblance now—same straight nose, same full lips—though Immeron's eyes were a contrast to Igon's topaz; his were a deep blue. I wondered why Igon didn't mention it…

"Who killed him?" Immeron asked with tears in his eyes.

I froze. I wanted to lie, considering I had no idea how Immeron would react to Silas if he knew he was responsible. But if Igon was a seer, there was always a chance his brother could be one, too.

"Silas," I whispered. "But I assure you he has had a change of heart. Surprisingly, Igon even said he forgave him…with a smile on his face, of all things…" I shook my head and then cringed.

Immeron stared off at Silas, then merely nodded. "That sounds like Igon."

I looked over to Edmund, wishing to change the subject. "My… friend over here lost part of his arm and leg from an Undead," I began.

Immeron tensed, and Ayla's eyes widened. "An Undead? We… we have a necromancer in Tovagoth?" she exclaimed.

I nodded. "It seems so. One of them attacked Edmund, but thankfully, we were able to remove the limbs before the curse took his life." I paused. "I was hoping there was some way you could make something for him to walk with. A new leg, perhaps. A new arm." I looked at Ayla. "Igon told me of your prosthetic," I noted, observing the black twirling of material that made up her limb.

She nodded as she raised her arm, and I gasped when she moved her synthetic fingers, the flow as natural as real fingers.

"By the Gods," I breathed. "Incredible."

Ayla smiled softly, and Immeron stroked his beard. Frowning, he looked to Silas. "Why should I help an Otacian soldier? The Prince has a reputation even us on the mountain are aware of."

"Igon's message was cryptic. But I know his mention of your wife's arm had to be for Edmund." I looked over to Edmund, then back at Immeron.

"Perhaps him, but he didn't say anything to you about Silas?"

I bit my bottom lip, looking to the ground. He hadn't…but Igon knew what Silas was to me. I knew there was only one way I could convince them.

"What I'm about to tell you can't be told to anyone else, not even your children," I whispered, walking closer to them.

They stood straighter, exchanging looks with one another before nodding.

I exhaled through my nose. "Silas...he is my Soul-Tie."

Ayla gasped, covering her mouth. Immeron's eyes went wide. I looked over to my group, Silas looking on with a raised brow, Merrick's dark eyes swirling.

"You're sure of it?" Immeron asked in a low voice.

I nodded. "I used to live in Otacia. He and I were together before the Queen died," I said as quietly as possible. "Igon told my friend Torrin, the one who offered my mother and me safe passage to Ames, about Silas and me before we had ever met each other. He confirmed it when I met him myself."

Immeron's eyes went past me, looking to Silas, whose arm was wrapped around Erabella.

"But the Prince...he is married."

"He believed me to be dead all this time." I sighed. "It's...complicated. But if you are willing, I would be thankful if Edmund could have new limbs, if you think it possible."

His gaze stayed on Silas for a while. "I will do it," he said after a moment. "But it will take some time. My family does trades in the local kingdoms, nothing of the enchantment sort, obviously, but I will have to see what I have." He eyed my attire, then looked to his wife, who nodded before smiling at me.

"I make clothing—that's my specialty." She winked. "My boys can help with the armor and with some weapons for you. In the morning, I can measure you for some new gear."

"You would do all that?" I tried to contain my surprise.

"You will need more than limbs for your friend," Immeron noted. "Igon was an excellent seer. If he wishes for you to take this journey, I will help in any way I can. Let me know your group's preferred weapons, and I will make them for you. As Ayla mentioned, our sons can get you better armor and clothing as well. Not the best out there." He eyeballed my plain brown dress, then my friends' prisoner attire. "But better than that."

I laughed softly. "Thank you, both. We will pay, of course." I then frowned as more of Igon's words came to me. "Have you heard of Oquerene?"

Immeron nodded with a confused look. "Of course I have. It is said to be the realm where we all came from."

"Some of Igon's last words to me were 'Find Oquerene.'" I sighed. "As fantastical as it seems, something tells me that place is really out there. But I have no idea where to start."

He and Ayla looked at one another. "Well. Nereida seems like the place to go."

My eyes broadened. "Nereida? I've never heard of the place."

"It's an ancient land, once ruled by the Sea Nymphs. It rests alongside the Southern Sea. A powerful ward blocks it from the view of those they wish not to see it."

My Gods…could that be where more of my people are?

"Once ruled by Sea Nymphs?"

He nodded. "After the War of Three Pirates, the Sea Nymphs vanished, though legend claims they and other extinct species live in Oquerene." He shrugged. "Now, anyway, Nereida is said to be ruled by the Mages."

I was baffled. I had read no literature on this war. "Why wouldn't

I know of this place? Why would we stay in Ames when there was a place with better protection?"

Immeron shrugged again. "Igon was a seer. Perhaps for destiny to align the way it should, certain people need not be in Nereida." He wrapped his arm around Ayla's waist. "Plus, the journey is long and gruesome. It will be hard to survive the various obstacles, especially considering a necromancer is on the loose, let alone the trial that awaits at The Valley of Awakening."

To that, I raised my eyebrow.

He continued, "I don't know much of it, but there is a border between regular land and Nereida. It is said to show those who cross through it the truths of themselves. Not only that…" He sighed. "There have also been sightings of bloodsuckers. Bodies found drained of blood."

My stomach dropped. In all my time on the run, moving from place to place, I had never once had an encounter with a Vampire.

"There are Vampires down south, too?"

He nodded. "Some rumor of a Vampire lord lurking about. Most drained bodies have been found in the north. I suspect that's where they reside. Still, their sickness tends to spread like wildfire."

I let out a shaky exhale, and Immeron put a hand on my shoulder. "That's enough talk of dangers for tonight. Get your people situated. I'll fetch my children to help."

I gave a thankful nod, then walked over to my group.

"Well, what did he say?" Elowen asked. She and Hendry were holding Edmund up.

I smiled at him. "Looks like you will have a new arm and leg after all, Edmund."

He looked at me in disbelief, then grinned, Elowen beaming as well. Merrick kept his arms crossed.

"And," I continued, "his sons will be making weapons and armor for the journey ahead for us. His wife has agreed to supply our clothes."

Viola's eyes widened. "Enchanted weapons?"

"With the Prince's gold, of course." I smirked at Silas, who looked at me in surprise. I laughed. "I told him what Igon had told me. He's given me an idea of where we should be headed."

"And where is that?" Silas asked.

I tensed. "I am grateful for what you've done, what you've all done," I stated, gesturing at his group. "But I still cannot trust you fully. Not yet."

Erabella curled her lip. "He threw away *everything* for you, and this is how you repay him?"

Silas touched her shoulder, and she crossed her arms. She looked at Merrick, an uneasy expression on her face. I glanced at him, and his irises were swirling dark.

Merrick's ability to read people could be…unsettling.

I sighed and looked back at Silas. "I will tell you where we are heading soon. I will say it's south. Hitting the kingdoms you wish to will come first. But, for now, you will have to trust me," I repeated.

Roland let out a laugh, and I glared at him. "I'm sorry, it's just funny how you told him you can't trust him fully, but he is expected to trust you."

"Roland," Edmund said in disapproval.

He put up his hands. "Continue, Ginger Snap."

Silas shot a glare at him over my nickname, and I sighed again.

"Where we are headed is dangerous, and it will take them a while to make all of our weapons, let alone Edmund's new limbs."

"How long, exactly? And what dangers are we talking about?" Hendry asked. I looked into his mismatched eyes, his bright blue eye nearly white with the setting sun.

"A week, give or take," Immeron cut in as he walked to Edmund. "I'll need to do some measuring if you don't mind."

"Of course," Edmund said politely, and Immeron squatted down and began using a tape measure while jotting notes on a piece of parchment.

"Where are we to shower? Use the…restroom?" Era asked shyly.

I glared at her. Pretty princess has probably never had to struggle in her life.

"There is a small waterfall on the eastern side of the mountain. It will be cold, but it will do. As for the restroom…" Immeron shifted uncomfortably. "There is an outhouse over there with a bucket," he said, pointing to the outbuilding past their houses.

She looked at him in horror. "But…you have homes."

He rubbed the back of his neck. "Hard to have plumbing on top of a mountain."

"Did you not have to relieve yourself in unsavory locations when you traveled to the fort? Or anywhere else, for that matter?" Merrick asked her with an amused look.

"No, the carriages I rode in had a toilet and a bed. I thought these past two days would be the end of it," she snapped at him.

Merrick gave a taunting smile. "Well, hate to disappoint, Princess. Nothing like that around here."

She glared at him as his dark eyes swirled, and a smirk appeared on his face. She huffed and looked away.

Immeron gave an awkward nod, then headed back to his family, his adult children now walking toward my people.

After a moment of silence, I cleared my throat. "Anyway, I thought that maybe we could…train together while we are here."

Everyone looked at me like I was nuts. I crossed my arms and stood up straight. "I've taught what I know about weapon combat to my friends, but I'm sure there's still a lot we could improve on." I met Silas's eyes and then looked around the group. "And I figure we could teach you about magic. Not how to use it, obviously, but ways to avoid moves that can be deadly if struck with them."

The group remained silent, exchanging glances with one another.

"It's the only productive thing I can imagine us doing during our stay. By all means if someone can think of something better, let's hear," I said with my hands up.

"Very well," Silas agreed. "We start tomorrow."

Before Immeron and his family were to begin on our weapons, clothing, and Edmund's leg, I asked nervously about any food they had on the mountain. Because of Ayla's ability to control the weather, it was perfect up here for growing fruits and vegetables. Their sons and their wives were hard at work cooking up a large stew everyone could enjoy later while my people snacked on fresh fruit from their trees. Apples, bananas, dates—all different types spread across the mountain, with different climates accommodating them. It was truly remarkable. Silas handed a pouch of gold to Ayla, whose eyes nearly bulged out of her head at the sight of it. While this place was well equipped to self-sustain, the near hundreds of us were not anticipated. The men were to venture tomorrow to the markets in Forsmont to see what they could bring back.

I wanted to bathe, as I was sure the rest of my group did as well, but after two days on the road, all I wished to do was sleep. While the ground here was no more comfortable than the ground anywhere else, the comfort of having my people safe, my mother nearby, and even Silas here allowed me to drift into a deep sleep.

CHAPTER FORTY-NINE

"I guess I'll sit this one out," Edmund mumbled as Silas lowered him on a boulder nearby.

Once morning came, and we filled ourselves with fruit again, our little group decided to venture off to train. Erabella wasn't pleased, and while I wished to lounge around as well, training would do us some good.

The sky was light blue, the morning air slightly crisp. A handful of my people were awake when we walked off, but most on the mountain were still asleep.

"I figure each of the Mages partner up with one of…you," I said awkwardly.

"Ouch," Roland teased with a hand over his heart.

I gave him an eye roll.

"I'll take the Princess," Merrick said, and I whirled to find him smirking at Erabella.

Her eyes widened at first, and I swear she blushed, but that was quickly replaced by a grimace as she crossed her arms. Before she could respond, I spoke. "Elowen with Hendry." I glanced over to Viola.

I can either put her with Silas and risk her ripping his head off, or I could go with him and be very uncomfortable.

I glanced over to Roland.

That would also *be uncomfortable.*

I heaved a sigh. "Viola, you go with the Prince, and please, don't hurt him."

Silas frowned, and Viola scoffed, but I could tell she was holding back a smile. She would enjoy an opportunity to rough him up.

Roland gave me a sideways smile. "I should've known you would pick me, Ginger Snap."

I let out a dry laugh. "You won't have that look on your face in a few moments," I threatened.

I could feel Silas's gaze, but when I turned to him, he looked away.

"So…" Elowen drawled. "How do we go about this?"

"I figure we learn first, get better at weapon wielding and blocking."

"Uh, one problem," Erabella interrupted with a raised hand. "I don't know much about fighting."

I frowned, then looked at my white-haired friend. "Well, Merrick is good with a bow. He can show you that, I suppose."

"So, you're saying I'll be playing teacher all week?" Merrick pouted.

"We'll switch off. How about that?"

Merrick clicked his tongue, then turned back to an annoyed Erabella.

Our groups separated from one another, but we were still close enough to see each other in case we could learn from what another pair was doing.

Hendry went to show Elowen his bow, but because she was more familiar with a dagger, he opted to work with that instead.

Silas pulled out a heavy greatsword, and I caught the corner of his lip turning up as Viola struggled to grasp it at first.

Merrick pulled out his bow and began instructing Era as I turned to Roland.

"So, what do you wish to learn?"

"What are you best at?" I asked, and he answered with a devious smirk. "Don't answer that," I groaned, putting my hand to my forehead.

"I usually opt for a single-handed sword," he said casually as he unsheathed it, observing it and then looking at me. "You?"

"Weapon or magic?"

He shrugged. "Both."

I considered. "I am best with fire. Weapons, I suppose a sword or dagger, though I'm decent with a bow as well."

I glanced over at Merrick, who stood a few feet from us, hovering behind Era as she struggled to equip the bow.

"Gods, you really are an amateur," Merrick muttered.

"And you're a dick. Anyone tell you that before?" she replied, focusing again on holding the bow properly.

He smirked. "Such foul language for a princess."

She scoffed.

Roland gave me a look. "My bet is they will fuck by the end of this journey," he murmured.

I did a double-take as I wasn't sure if I heard him correctly. "Come again?"

He laughed. "Just the vibe I get." He flashed a wicked smile. "Or maybe it's because it reminds me of us." He gave me a kissy face.

"You're a—" I realized he was right about our banter, and I stopped myself as he bit his lip to prevent a smile.

I groaned. "Let's just get this over with, yeah?"

Roland was quite skilled at the sword. I actually began struggling to dodge his moves, and one almost struck me until I held out my hand and blocked it with a force field, causing Roland to stumble back.

"Cheater," he mumbled.

"Would you prefer it be impaled in me instead?" I snapped as I caught my breath.

"I'd prefer to impale you with something else entirely," he said smoothly.

I opened my eyes wide at his audacity.

"My co—"

"Yes! I got that!" I squealed, and he let out a loud laugh.

"I'm sorry, but you set yourself up for that one."

"You are…unbelievable," I muttered.

His hazel eyes twinkled with amusement, and he handed over his sword.

"Now, show me what you got, Lena."

Training went well overall. Era managed to handle the bow, at least, even if she couldn't utilize it. Viola surprisingly excelled at the greatsword, and Elowen was smiling by the end of practice with Hendry.

He seemed like a good man. So quiet and mysterious. And handsome. His one blue eye was a stark contrast to his brown skin, and I had a feeling he kept his silky, straight brown hair covering his forehead in a failed attempt to lessen his beauty. I remembered Silas telling me stories about both him and Edmund. I was happy he still had them after I was gone.

Roland actually gave me some good pointers as well, and I wondered when he and Silas had met. They both seemed to loathe each other's company. I would ask about that one day.

Once our sparring was done and we were all covered in sweat, I was ready to get clean. I certainly didn't want Ayla doing her measuring while I smelled disgusting. I decided I was going to head to the waterfall to wash up when Liette, the wife of one of Immeron's sons, was kind enough to give me a cube of soap she had made. Considering how many people were going to want to bathe, they had to be conservative when it came to how much was given.

When I reached the stunning waterfall, I dipped my toes in, wincing at the cold. I sighed, loosened my hair from its braid, and quickly undressed before submerging myself in the water. It wasn't freezing, but it wasn't warm either.

I went to work washing my hair, body, and face. I blew air out of my nose and dipped my head under, my hair sticking to my back as

I surfaced. I wiped my face and then startled and covered my breasts when I saw Roland watching me at the edge of the lake.

"W-what are you doing here?" I stuttered as Roland began to undress.

"This is where we bathe, yes?"

"Yes, *separately*."

He chuckled and threw off his shirt, revealing a perfectly toned body. I swallowed and couldn't stop my eyes from trailing over his physique.

His sides and arms were covered with intricate tattoos. I couldn't tell what the design was, and I didn't want to stare long enough to find out. They were a stark contrast to his skin despite it being a golden tan. When he began to unbutton his pants, I whirled away.

"What, don't want to see?" he asked, clearly amused.

"No. No, I do not," I lied.

Another chuckle, and I heard him hiss as he jumped in the water.

"Fuck!" he exclaimed. "It's cold in here." He shivered as he emerged from under the water, then made his way to me.

My arms were crossed, covering my breasts still, and he gave me a smirk, his brown hair looking almost black when wet. The water beaded as it dripped down his body, trailing from his pecs down his abs, and I hated that I felt a pressure between my thighs.

I flushed and winced as I lowered myself into the water, still covering my breasts.

"Don't let me interrupt your bathing," he teased and began to drift away.

I looked over and examined his back and the tattoos covering both shoulder blades. They appeared to be wings of some sort. He turned back and caught me staring.

"I-I was just finishing up," I stuttered.

"Liar," he smirked. "You just got in here." He began to rub a cut of soap over his chest, bubbles sliding down his abdomen.

"What are you doing?" I breathed.

"Bathing, what does it look like?" he murmured. The water came just before inappropriate areas began. A trail of brown hair made its way from the bottom of his belly button to an area I shouldn't be envisioning.

His smirk didn't waver. "I may not be cuffed like you were, but feel free to help me if you'd like."

I shook my head and turned away. "I still haven't forgiven you for that," I muttered.

"You enjoyed it, don't lie."

I did. But I did not enjoy that I liked it. No matter, I wasn't about to tell him that.

My thoughts trailed back to Silas, and guilt washed over me. Though, why should I feel guilty? He was married now.

I glanced over my shoulder again, Roland now rinsing himself off in the waterfall.

He was cocky. Vulgar. But also…intriguing.

He wiped the water from his eyes as he backed out of the stream and smiled at me.

The sun was high in the sky. The warm glow that was cast on him made him look like he was in a painting.

His smile faded as I studied him, and my heart began to beat quickly as he moved toward me. I wanted to run away—get as far from him as possible, but at the same time, I wanted to know how his bare body felt pressed against mine.

"It doesn't look like you're bathing, Lena." He glanced down into the water, and when I looked, I realized I had kept my little cube of soap beneath the whole time.

I cursed as I lifted my hands out. The soap cube was nearly dissolved. I realized my breasts were no longer under the water, and I flushed as I met his gaze with wide eyes. This moment was entirely too familiar.

He smiled, his hazel eyes dark with desire. "I have seen you before, remember?" he purred.

"That wasn't my choice," I breathed.

He raised a brow and tilted his head to the side. "What would be your choice now, Lena?"

I stilled. He moved in closer until he was just inches away. I stared up at him, completely frozen. I felt a desire I hadn't felt in a very, very long time.

He smiled as he leaned by my ear. "You're blushing," he whispered, and my eyes became heavy. His voice sent chills down my spine and heat throughout my body.

"Roland, Silas wants you."

I jumped, and I whirled my head back to see Hendry, who thankfully could only see my back. He shifted uncomfortably.

"Really? I didn't know he was into men," he teased, though I could sense his annoyance at the interruption.

Hendry rolled his eyes and then looked at me, his face slightly flushing.

"Apologies for interrupting," he said quietly.

"You weren't interrupting anything," I said a little too loudly, fumbling with my hair. I looked back at Roland, who just smirked at me.

"Now, Roland."

He groaned and lifted himself out of the water. I looked away toward Hendry, who was already making his way back to camp.

After a few moments, Roland spoke. "You can look now, Ginger Snap."

"Like I can trust you," I muttered, looking at him anyway. He had his pants back on and was holding his shirt.

"You can get out. Don't worry, I'll turn away."

"What, so we can walk back together so everyone thinks—"

"That we fucked?"

"Gods, you are so—ugh!"

He chuckled, and I hurled a fireball at him, his eyes widening just as he dodged the move.

He stared off to where the flame died out in the distant sky, then looked back at me.

"Now, that wasn't very nice."

"Turn around," I barked.

"As you wish."

I hopped out and wrung out my hair as Roland started to turn.

"Don't even think about it, or I will burn your balls off."

He snickered and retreated as I flung back on my outfit.

"Okay."

He turned and walked toward me, that stupid smile still on his face.

"I swear to the Gods, Roland, if you so much as—"

"Don't worry, I don't kiss and tell."

"I should've frozen your ass in that water," I muttered and found myself smiling.

He chuckled, and we started toward our camp.

I picked at a loose thread on my dress. "I never thanked you," I said quietly, and he turned to me with a raised brow. "For showing me kindness…and for being annoying as hell." I laughed through my nose. "It made everything a little less scary."

I met eyes with him, though I couldn't read his expression. He smiled softly and looked forward.

I felt an urge to grasp his hand, but I wouldn't do it.

"Why did you do it, anyway?"

He clenched his jaw. "I'm not sure…" He thought on it for a moment. "I suppose I grew to admire you, seeing how you handled everything. You're a fearless thing." He gave me a side smile, then looked forward. "And I suppose it was you saving my ass…when I did nothing to deserve it," he said quietly.

"Well, I am happy I did…mostly."

He turned to me. I winked, and he grinned at that.

When we made it back to camp, Silas was glaring at Roland and me, and I felt my cheeks heat. His eyes could burn holes with how furious he looked. He only met my eyes briefly before continuing to stare down Roland.

"Wonder what I did now," Roland muttered.

Silas stood, and the two of them walked off to talk. As they left, Ayla approached, saying she wished to measure us for clothing.

The girls went first. She led us inside their home, past the living space and kitchen, into her sewing room. I gasped at the wall of fabrics she had stacked—a large assortment of colors and materials.

"There's so many," Elowen breathed. "Where did you get it all?"

"Oh, I've collected some throughout the years, but I pick up fabrics nearly every time I bring pieces to trade in Forsmont and Faltrun." She fetched a tape measure off her desk. "Who would like to go first?"

"Me!" Elowen beamed.

Ayla smiled and began measuring Elowen's slim waist. Erabella walked along the fabric wall, eyeing the different assortments.

"Is it ever an issue traveling to those villages? I assume you all glamour yourselves?" Viola asked.

"Indeed," Ayla replied. "And no, no issues. Even though our kind isn't safe almost anywhere, I'm grateful Forsmont and Faltrun have stayed independent from Otacia—don't have to worry about the kill order and all." She continued to measure Elowen, her silver braid falling just below her shoulders as she jotted down her measurements. "What colors do you like, my dear?"

Elowen pushed her lips to the side as she thought. "That's hard to choose. Whatever you think would suit me." She smiled.

Ayla grinned and finished, then moved on to Viola. I kept my distance from Erabella—still feeling awkward around her. It was clear she didn't exactly love my presence either.

"What of you, Princess? What do you make of all this?"

I was surprised by Ayla's kindness, and it appeared Erabella was too. She flushed and tucked a piece of her short blonde hair behind her ear. "The mountain is lovely."

Ayla chuckled. "Not the mountain, dear. The journey you're embarking on."

"Oh." She clasped her hands together. "I…I am not sure. But if my husband believes it to be the right thing, I will follow him."

Husband.

I clenched my fists tightly, my nails digging into my palms. I had no right to be upset at her, but I was.

"What do *you* think the right thing is?" Ayla asked as she finished up with Vi.

Erabella let out a soft laugh. "Honestly? No one has ever asked me what I thought of anything before." She brushed her hands down her dress. "I've never loved violence. Hatred. But it is the world I grew up in. It is all I've ever known." She looked around at all of us with her brown, almond eyes. "I had never met a Mage before in my life."

"As far as you know."

"Yes, yes, as far as I know." She took a deep breath. "But I am glad that I have now. And I'm sorry for what my people have done to you. I am sorry the world has made us believe you to be monsters."

I blinked. Honestly, we all did. "What is your name again, my dear?"

"Erabella. My friends call me Era."

Ayla smiled. "Well, Era, I am glad to have met you too."

I crossed my arms and leaned against the counters in the room. I wanted to hate Erabella. I wanted to hate her for being married to the man I loved, for having the life I never could. But as it turned out, she was a decent person. I suppose I could see why Silas loved her.

I began to feel my eyes sting.

Do not cry.

"And you, Supreme, how are you holding up?" Ayla was now working on Erabella's measurements.

I clenched my jaw. "As well as anyone in my position could, I suppose."

"That's fair." She paused mid-measurement, her blue eyes sparkling as she looked at me. "How long did you live in Otacia before?"

Erabella's brows furrowed as she turned to me. "You lived in Otacia?"

I nodded, hoping to the Gods Ayla wasn't about to spill my secret right now. "Six years. The longest I've ever lived in one place." I looked at the ground.

"That's even longer than I've lived there," Erabella murmured. "Did you like it?"

I looked up at her, surprised she was initiating conversation with me. "I did. We lived in the Outer Ring. I'm not sure how it is there now, but I didn't mind it. It felt like home."

"If you liked it then, you would love it now." She cringed. "Minus the obvious."

I nodded, and she continued, Ayla finishing up her measurements. "Silas has invested a lot in the Outer Ring. Infrastructure, small businesses. Those of the Outer Ring can even come up to the Inner as they please. Hell, there's even warm water down there now."

My heart skipped a beat, and when I felt tears welling in my eyes, I looked to the ground again, unable to hide the small smile on my face.

He really did what he promised.

CHAPTER FIFTY

We were patiently waiting in the cave that I learned was Immeron's forge a week later. Today was not only the day we'd receive our weapons but also the day Edmund would acquire a new arm and leg.

The days came and went between training, helping my people get situated, and aiding the family who lived up here as best I could, considering the people in Ames would be staying here for a while.

To my surprise, Roland didn't try anything else with me, though he would occasionally catch me looking at him and would give me a smug smirk in response. The thought of actually trying anything with him was frightening and exhilarating all at the same time, but I suppose I was happy he hadn't attempted anything more.

The Otacians had kept to themselves most days, and I hardly

spoke to Silas, though our eyes met quite often. While I hadn't said Oquerene was the destination of our journey, Nereida hopefully pointing us in the correct direction, I did mention south. Silas wished to make allies, so our first target on our journey was Forsmont.

Mage lights illuminated the cave, and a large anvil caught my eye, along with various pieces Immeron was working on—swords, knives, maces, and more. A rather spacious workbench was scattered with material, and Immeron finished tinkering with something before strolling over to us.

"Well, here it is." Immeron walked with pride as he revealed Edmund's new lower leg and foot. The thin black lines that it was made of almost resembled veins. It was rugged yet sleek and elegant at the same time. There were even toes.

"That seems rather flimsy, no?" Roland questioned, Edmund slapping him in the arm and Hendry giving them both a side-eye.

Immeron smirked. "It may appear that way, but this is made up of carbonado, the strongest form of natural diamond. I expect a decent payment, Your Highness." He gave Silas a side glance, to which the Prince nodded.

Elowen and Hendry helped lower Edmund to the bench inside the cave, and Elowen lifted his pants sleeve over the stump.

"This may hurt for a moment," Immeron mumbled, and he held it in place.

The wires then twirled, seemingly coming to life, before they shot up into his healed wound. He cried out, and Elowen quickly placed her hands on his temples and relieved the pain.

After a beat, Immeron spoke. "It shouldn't hurt now. Try standing."

Elowen slowly removed her hands, and Edmund blinked and then slowly stood, shock appearing shortly after.

"It…it feels like my leg." He wiggled the toes, and I and the others gasped. Edmund and Elowen shared a grin.

"Now, here," Immeron said, walking over and bringing back a forearm and hand with the same carbonado wires. It looked nearly identical to Ayla's. Edmund bent down so El could numb his pain, and then the wires shot up again, inserting themselves inside of him. When it was over, he stood straight, rotating his new fingers.

"Part man, part machine," Immeron said with pride, crossing his arms.

Edmund's eyes teared up as he walked around. Roland cursed under his breath with a sideways smirk while Silas just stared wide-eyed. Edmund walked to Elowen, scooping her up and twirling her around as she giggled.

"It is just perfect," he said, beaming at Elowen as he placed her down. He grasped her hand with his new one and kissed the top of it.

Merrick, next to me, went to move toward him, but I gripped his arm before he could, shaking my head to say, *"Don't ruin the moment."* He glared at me before crossing his arms and looking away.

Edmund wrapped his arm around El's waist before turning to Immeron, and she blushed as she leaned into him. "This is truly the most fascinating thing I've ever seen. I never dreamed I'd walk again after the attack or have my arm back." He grinned and bowed in respect. "Thank you."

Immeron's sons Ceren and Benor then began to reveal the weapons they'd created for us.

A bow for both Merrick and Hendry, a dagger for Elowen and

Erabella, and swords for the rest of us. It was truly remarkable to see the custom-made weaponry.

I examined my blade. Its sheen was almost iridescent, and opals were in its hilt. I couldn't help but gawk at its beauty.

"Each of your weapons has special properties," Ceren said as he tucked his dark brown hair behind his pointed ear. "Your blade, Lena, can be infused with fire magic."

My head shot up. "You're kidding."

He smiled softly, his eyes the same dark blue as his father's. "Nope. You can utilize your magic to charge the weapon, making it so your strikes are even more deadly."

I gaped at my piece, and then my eyes trailed over everyone else's weapons, the most notable, other than mine, being Silas's shining golden sword. It had a hilt that was flecked with purple-red metal, shaped to appear like feathers adorned it. A large topaz was embedded in its center. I could tell he was thoroughly impressed with the craftsmanship; it blew even his royal sword out of the water.

Each person's weapon had different attributes. Because the Otacians didn't have magic, their weapons were altered to have enhanced durability.

The weapons for us Mages were made to complement our strongest forms of magic. Merrick's onyx bow was designed specifically for ice arrows, and so long as Merrick charged his weapon, regular arrows would turn to frozen ones simply by him firing it.

Viola's blade was infused with illusion magic. Just as she could shift her body, she could shift her weapon to be anything she desired.

Elowen's dagger could be charged with healing magic to take a life painlessly if need be.

We all took our time admiring our weapons, asking any questions we had, and saying our thanks for how much effort was put forth into our items.

The rest of the evening was spent packing our necessities for the trip to our first destination, Forsmont. We already had bedrolls we each would be traveling with, save for Era, who would share with Silas, so we had to pack light. We packed as much food and as many filled water skins as we could comfortably carry, and we were to change into our new clothing and armor in the morning.

I found myself alone that final evening. I sat by the cliff's edge, looking off into the distance as I contemplated the journey ahead.

The breeze was pleasant, and from this high up, I realized just how small I was.

You will be our savior, Lena Daelyra.

I wasn't much of an optimistic person, not with everything life had shown me thus far. But I had followed Igon's words, and I truly felt like we were on the right track.

"You're not going to jump, are you?" Silas said softly from behind before sitting next to me. "Being a leader can make you feel that way, sometimes."

I leaned my head toward him, laughing through my nose. After a few moments of silence, staring off at the rolling hills of Tovagoth with our feet off the cliffside, I spoke.

"Do you fear what your people think of you now?" I asked quietly.

He considered, his jaw flexing as he stared off into the distance. "Yes and no." He turned to me. "I think…I think I made the right call. I can only hope that when all is said and done, my people will understand."

"I am grateful for you, Silas, and all that you have sacrificed. Thank you," I whispered, looking to the sky.

I knew we were alone, and even if someone was secretly watching, it was so dark no one would see. I was afraid of his rejection, but I couldn't stop myself. I wrapped my hand in his, and he tensed.

For a moment, we were frozen, both so unused to each other's touch after so many years of separation. I wondered if he would pull his hand away, but then he began to drag his thumb back and forth against the back of my hand. I felt my body relax.

"Don't thank me, Lena. Remember, I have a selfish goal that drove my decision."

I looked into his amber eyes that sparkled under the moonlight as they dropped to my lips. That caused my heartbeat to quicken.

He might want to take the throne from his father. He might have had the ambition long before he knew I was alive. But I knew he still felt love for me, even if that love was but a small sliver in his heart. Even if we could never have one another again. Even though I had lied about so much.

"Here." He fished into his pocket, then extended his hand. In it was Igon's compass.

My eyes rounded. "My Gods…I completely forgot about it." I resisted the urge to slap my forehead and took the bronze compass from Silas, rotating it around and studying it. A pelican was engraved on its back.

I gave Silas an embarrassed smile. "See, not meant to be a leader."

He offered a small smile, and the sight caused my heart to skip. "I have forgotten many things. You've had plenty else on your mind," he whispered, his smile fading.

My lip trembled as I studied the man I still loved more than I wished to admit. "You kept your promise," I breathed.

His brows furrowed, and his face was just inches away as he asked, "What do you mean?"

"Erabella told me what you've done for the Outer Ring…" My throat bobbed, and my eyes began to sting. "Investing in it, giving the people heated water, lifting the damn curfew, for fuck's sake." I used my free hand to wipe the tear that had fallen, then laughed softly. "I knew you would, but still, hearing it just—" I tilted my head to him with a smile. "I'm proud of you."

His eyes widened, and he jerked his hand away, the action causing me to startle and my eyebrows to draw together.

"Lena—" He shook his head before exhaling out of his nose. "You should get some sleep. We have a long journey ahead of us," he muttered before he stood and began to walk away.

Instantly, I stood as well and grabbed his hand. He came to a stop.

"Don't go," I pleaded. He turned to me, his golden eyes flickering with anguish. "Did I…did I say something wrong?"

"I cannot bear your kindness." His honey eyes shifted back and forth between mine, a deep frown now taking over. "Do not give it to me."

He tugged his hand away again, and I stared at him in bewilderment as he walked off.

I remained standing there for a moment, mind racing, then turned to view the night sky from this high up one more time before we left tomorrow morning. I took note of the large full moon shining above.

So much had changed so quickly. But, for the first time in my life, I felt hopeful for my people. Hopeful for myself.

As I stared into the stars, a cold feeling washed over my body, causing goosebumps to spread. Immediately, I was on alert.

My heartbeat quickened.

It wasn't just a cold feeling…but a presence.

A presence that was all too familiar.

"Lena," a woman spoke in my head, and my knees buckled at the sound of Kayin's voice. *"We have work to do."*

Acknowledgments

Gosh, where to even start? This story and these characters have been in my head since 2017. I dreamed of putting them on paper, and over the years, I jotted down various scenes here and there, but I never fully sat through and wrote everything out from start to finish. It wasn't until June 2023 that I finally felt the inspiration to commit to doing so.

A huge thank-you to my husband, Lucas, for allowing me the time to write this story and truly taking an interest in my work. He was the first to read my manuscript, and his encouragement really meant the world to me. He has always believed in all my various creative endeavors, and I love him dearly.

My grandma. I wouldn't be where I am, not even close, without all she has done for me all my life. No matter what our family has been through, she has always been by my side. Words cannot express how grateful I am, not just for the support of this book but in general.

To BookTok, for all the encouragement. I am so grateful for all the wonderful people I've met on there and who have supported me wholeheartedly, even more so than some people I've known my entire life. You guys are truly the best.

To Allison Heddon, my editor, for fine-tuning my manuscript and offering so many kind words. It is terrifying putting your work out there, but she made the process so pleasant.

And the biggest of thanks to anyone who has given me and my first novel a chance. Thank you, thank you, thank you!

ABOUT THE AUTHOR

Kylie Snow is a mother and storyteller residing in Illinois. When she is not writing, she is raising two rambunctious little girls, reading fantasy and dark romance novels, drawing, gaming, or planning her next tattoo.

Socials:
Tiktok: @kyliesnowauthor
IG: @kyliesnowauthor
Website: www.kyliesnow.com